All the Paths of Shadow

Frank Tuttle

Chapter One

Meralda Ovis, Royal Thaumaturge to the kingdom of Tirlin, waved her carriage away at the palace gates and walked the twenty city blocks home.

Ordinarily, Meralda enjoyed the walk. She loved the wide clean sidewalks and the red brick shop fronts and the rattle and clop of rubber-tired carriage traffic on the cobblestone streets. She loved to stroll down Fleethorse Street, amid the florists and herb shops and tea houses. She loved the pastry shop on Ordoon, Holin's Bookstore on Kelwern, and the fruit market at the corner of Halor and Stick, where a mechanical man in a bright red suit offered pedestrians fresh apple slices with a click of a smile and a tick-tock wink.

Today, though, Meralda stalked fuming past Flayne's and Holin's without a sidelong glance. She marched, unseeing, through the fruit market, not heeding the fruit seller's cries of "Lamp River apples, fresh off the docks, half price for you, Thaumaturge!"

Meralda didn't pause until the crossing at Kemp and Weigh, and then only long enough to let the traffic master recognize her and wave traffic to a halt with quick motions of his white-gloved hands.

"Evening, Thaumaturge," he said as she passed, a gaggle of pedestrians in her wake. "Lovely day, isn't it?"

Meralda nodded, but couldn't force a smile. *Lovely day,* she thought. *Perhaps to persons not currently in my skin.*

Meralda marched down the rows of clothiers on Stringle, dodged a pair of wandering minstrels on Argen, and hit her stride on the home stretch of tall old water oaks and small, shady lawns and tidy, close-set houses between Bester and Shade.

The streets there were named for kings of old—Thinwase and Flanshot and Inlop and Gant.

Marvelous, fumed Meralda, as the names ran sing-song through her head. *Just what I need. More kings.*

Traffic on the sidewalk picked up on the king streets. Dozens of people passed Meralda, greeting her with smiles and nods. Meralda kept her pace fast and her eyes on the ground.

A few passers-by recognized Meralda. The sorceress, both the first woman and the youngest mage to ever occupy the seat of Thaumaturge in the long history of Tirlin, had briefly been the subject of notoriety in the papers. The *Post* had dubbed her "Tirlin's Lady of Mages," while the *Times* had run two full weeks of furious editorials questioning the appointment of one so young to the court. Meralda recalled how unnerving it had been, suddenly being known to strangers wherever she went.

Meralda's fame soon died, though, and she discovered that by leaving the dark blue mage's robe and black cowl in her closet she could go about as she pleased, unremarked and largely unnoticed. Her customary outfits of long skirts, soft half-knee boots, and plain, high-necked blouses made more sense, anyway. Even old Mage Fromarch, her mentor, had stripped down to pants and a shirt for serious magic. "Robes are fine for show," he'd said with a frown, the first day Meralda had shown up in her loose brown apprentice robes. "But we've got work to do."

Meralda dodged a small yapping dog and sighed at the memory. *Work to do*, she thought. *Work, indeed. That was before I learned that the office of Royal Thaumaturge was apparently instituted to provide the crown with the arcane equivalent of fancy stage lighting.*

Through a gap in the thinning boughs of the water oaks, Meralda spied the sad, pigeon spotted gargoyles that cowered gape-jawed at the corners of her apartment building. The doorman at the Oggin House doffed his hat at Meralda, and she found a smile for him, but didn't stop to speak.

Finally, Meralda clattered up the ten steps to the lobby of her building, spoke to Ernst the doorman, and took to the stairs.

Six flights of steep, narrow stairs beckoned. Meralda took a deep breath, hiked up her skirts, and sprinted for home.

From his pot on the kitchen windowsill, Mug heard the hall door open with a whoosh and slam shut with a bang. He waited for Meralda's footfalls, but instead heard two loud thumps as she kicked off her boots and flung them to the floor.

Mug swiveled twenty of his eyes toward the ceiling. *The sorceress is slamming doors and throwing boots,* he thought. *That can only mean one thing.*

Meralda's socks made quick soft pats across the floor. The kitchen door opened, and Meralda marched inside.

Mug's eyes turned and bobbed. His bottom-most leaves wilted. Meralda was pale. With anger. Mug had heard of humans changing colors, but he'd never seen Meralda do it until then.

Meralda's long hands were clenched into fists, her mouth was a thin straight line across her narrow face, and her fierce glare met Mug's quick three-eyed glance with dire, unspoken warning.

Mug turned his blue eyes quickly away from Meralda's brown ones. *What,* wondered the dandyleaf plant, *has that idiot king done now?*

Meralda shook off her jacket, threw it across the back of a chair, and was across the kitchen and in front of Mug's windowsill with four long strides. She reached past Mug, threw open the window, and squeezed her eyes tightly shut.

"Mistress," began Mug.

"A moment," said Meralda. "Just a single quiet moment."

Cool, dry air washed over her face. *Breathe in autumn,* Meralda thought. *Breathe in chilly nights and turning oak leaves and fat orange harvest moons. Breathe out thick-headed kings and snickering court toadies and long royal lists of impossible things to do.*

The scent of caramel covered candy apples, fresh made at a harvest carnival, wafted up from the park below. *A hot, fresh Lamp River carnival apple,* thought Meralda. *When was the last time I had one of those?*

"I surmise you've seen the king," said Mug, after a time. "What does Yvin want you to do this time? Lower the moon? Shorten the day? Give him back his girlish figure and his front teeth?"

Meralda sighed and opened her eyes.

The sky through the high window was cloudless and blue. A

ragged vee of geese flew by above, veering wide around a lumbering red Alon cargo dirigible dropping toward the docks behind the palace. The dirigible's long shadow raced over the tops of the towering Old Kingdom oaks that ringed the park before sliding over the park wall and disappearing.

Beyond the park and the oaks Tirlin itself rose up in a tidy profusion of red brick buildings and dark slate roofs and red-gold tree tops just touched by autumn. The towers and spires of the palace peeped through here and there, rising just barely above the banks and shops and offices that made up the heart of Tirlin.

Above it all, though, loomed the Tower, squat and black and brooding in the midst of the green and open park.

Meralda frowned, and looked away.

"Mistress," said Mug, turning all twenty-nine of his eyes toward Meralda. "Talk. What's wrong?"

"How many days remain until the Accords?" said Meralda, quietly.

"Twenty," said Mug, with a small stirring of leaf tips. "Counting today, which I suppose I shouldn't, since it's nearly gone."

Meralda sat on the edge of her battered kitchen chair. "So, in nineteen days, Tirlin will be full of Alons and Vonats and Eryans and Phendelits, all gathered here to strut and brag and eat like pigs while making long speeches explaining why they broke every promise they made at the last Accord."

Mug nodded by dipping his eye buds. "You left out carousing and spying and tavern wrecking," said Mug. "What does that have to do with you?"

Meralda slapped her hands down on the table. "Nothing," she said. "It should have nothing to do with me at all. The Accords are a political matter."

"Or so you thought."

Meralda shook her head. "So I thought." She put her elbows on the table and her chin in her hands. Just for an instant, she heard her mother's scolding voice. "Elbows off the table, young lady. We raise swine. We do not emulate their table manners."

Meralda sighed and stared at the table top. "His Highness is to give the customary commencement speech on the eve of the Accords," she said. "He plans to speak from a platform at the foot of the Tower. Carpenters are building covered stands in the park for the delegates."

Mug shrugged with a tossing of fronds. "Sounds fine. I think Kings Ortell and Listbin did the same thing, way back when." Mug lifted his three red eyes toward Meralda's face. "It's not the weather, is it? Surely even Yvin knows better than to take pokes at the climate just to make sure he has a sunny day for a speech."

"He didn't ask that," said Meralda. "Yet."

She stretched and yawned and thought again about caramel apples and fall carnivals. "Yesterday—" said Meralda, "Yesterday, the King was inspecting the stands being built in the park. He arrived at five of the clock, the same time his commencement speech is set for."

"And?"

"And," said Meralda, "it suddenly dawned on our gifted monarch that the sun sets in the west and casts shadows toward the east."

"Leaving His High Pompousness to make a speech in the shadow of the Tower," said Mug, with dawning apprehension. "Which aggravated his royal sense of badly done melodrama."

"And led him to instruct me to move the Tower's shadow," said Meralda. "Move it, or banish it, or fold it up and pack it away for an hour," said Meralda, in a mocking baritone. "Roll up a shadow? Pack away the absence of light caused by a seven hundred year old wizard's keep?" Meralda shoved back the chair and stood, hands spread before her. "What kind of an imbecile asks for a roll of packed up shadows?"

Mug cast his gaze toward the ceiling. "The kind with the scepter and the crown," he said, quietly.

Meralda stood. She walked back to her open window and leaned on the sill.

"Was it a suggestion, a request, or a royal directive?" asked Mug.

"Is there a difference?" Meralda shrugged. "The king asked. Before the full court. I stood there and nodded and made vague assurances that I'd look into the matter." Meralda sighed. "The Tower is—what? Nine hundred feet high? Almost two hundred wide? At five of the clock today, the tip of its afternoon shadow hit the park wall at the east entrance. That makes its shadow almost two thousand feet long and two hundred wide at the base."

Mug ticked off figures on his leaf tips. "How big a bag will you need, after you roll it up?" he asked.

"Mug!" snapped Meralda. "Enough."

"A thousand pardons, Oh Fiery-Eyed One," said Mug, with a mock bow. "But could it be, mistress, that you are not exclusively angry with King Yvin?" A trio of bright blue eyes peeked up through Mug's tangle of leaves. "Could it be that you are peeved at your own reluctance to describe to the king in lengthy detail just how asinine and vacuous his shadow-packing scheme truly is?"

Meralda glared. "I could get a cat," she said. "A nice quiet cat."

Mug lifted out of the bow. "Fur on the couch, a litter box to empty? I don't see you with a cat," said Mug.

"Keep talking," she said. "We may all see things we didn't expect." Meralda shook her head, ran her fingers through the strands of long red-brown hair that had worked loose from the tight bun at the back of her head.

"I was going to add that you shouldn't fault yourself for not browbeating the king before the full court," said Mug. "I was going to say that even though your hero, Tim the Horsehead, spent his career berating and insulting kings he was always careful to do so in private." Mug paused, waving his leaves. "I was going to suggest that you take a long hot bath and curl up on the couch with a cup of Vellish black tea and a book of Phendelit poetry, and that you see Yvin privately tomorrow and explain to him that you only just discovered that moving the Tower's shadow would loose a plague of biting flies on Banker Street and devalue Tirlish currency abroad and cause the collapse of the aqueducts and, incidentally, make snakes grow in his beard. He'll forget the whole shadow business and you can go back to your studies of spark wheels and lightning rods, interrupted only by occasional royal requests to shrink the royal bald spot."

Meralda laughed. Mug turned his eyes away. "And you want a cat," he said, airily. "Could a cat say that?"

"No one with lungs could say that, Mug," she said. "You're right. I should have a talk with Yvin."

"Then why aren't you making tea and drawing a bath?"

Meralda sighed. "Because I'm changing clothes and going back to the laboratory," she said. "There are things I need to look into, at least."

Mug sighed. "Mistress," he said. "Can it be done? Can the shadow be moved?"

"I don't know, Mug," she said. "Perhaps."

Mug turned a tangle of green eyes toward her. "I don't like this, mistress," he said, no humor in his tone. "The Tower isn't something to be trifled with." Mug bunched all his eyes together in an instinctive signal of grave concern. "Leave it alone, if you can," he said. "Please."

Meralda frowned. "Why, Mug? It's just an old tower."

Mug moved his eyes closer. "It was never just a tower," he said. "Not seven hundred years ago, not yesterday, not now." Mug's leaves stirred, though no wind blew. "Why do you think the old kings tried for all those years to knock it down?" Mug paused and stilled his leaves. "Leave it alone, mistress. Tell Yvin to light a few gas lamps and leave the Tower be."

Meralda stroked his topmost leaves. "Thank you, Mug."

"For what?" asked Mug.

Meralda smiled. "For not being a cat."

Mug's eyes exchanged glances. "You're welcome," he said. "I think."

"Water?" asked Meralda.

"None, thanks." The dandyleaf plant sighed. "So you're going to try this, despite my heartfelt plea."

"I have to," said Meralda. "I have to try. Not for the king, but for me."

Mug grunted. "As long as it's not a heroic effort for the glory of His Thick-headedness," said Mug. "So what's this idea of yours?"

Meralda bit her lip. She turned from Mug and began to pace slowly around the dining table.

"I see two ways to do this," she said, frowning. "First, bend the sunlight around the Tower, so it casts no shadow at all."

Mug frowned. "That would render the Tower invisible, wouldn't it?" he said. "And a working invisibility spell? Weren't you saying just a few days ago that such a thing was impossible? I believe you used the words 'penny-novel nonsense'."

"The spell would only redirect light striking the Tower from a certain angle," said Meralda. "It wouldn't be invisible. Just a bit fuzzy, from a single spot out in the park."

"I see," said Mug. "What's your other idea?"

"Leave the shadow," she said. "Just delay it a bit. An hour, perhaps. Maybe less."

"Delay it? How, mistress, does one delay the setting of the sun?"

Meralda laughed. "I'll leave the sun alone, thank you. I'd merely borrow a bit of sunlight from one day and move it to the next."

The edges of Mug's leaves all curled slightly upward. "Let's work with your original notion," he said. "Moving sunlight from one day to the next. That sounds like the sort of story that ends with the Thaumaturge being brutally suntanned and the king giving his speech from beneath the cover of perpetual night."

Meralda smiled. "Good night, Mug," she said. "I'll be late. Shall I move you to the sitting room window?"

"No, thank you," he said. "I'll stay right where I am. It's a good place in which to worry oneself sick. Lots of room to drop leaves and shrivel."

Meralda sighed. "It's only a shadow, Mug," she said. "And the Tower is just a tower. Stones and wood. Nothing more."

Mug sniffed. "Certainly," he said. "Nothing to all those old stories. Nothing at all."

Meralda snatched up her cloak and stamped out of the kitchen. Mug listened to her wash her face, brush her teeth, and change her clothes. Then the living room door closed softly, and Mug was all alone.

Meralda settled into her cab. The driver snapped the reins, and the carriage pulled onto Fairlane Street with the steady clop-clop of Phendelit carriage horse hooves.

Carriages and coaches hurried past, most bound for the shady lanes and quiet neighborhoods that lay to the west, beyond the college and the park. The sidewalks were crowded as well, as bakers and hat makers and shopkeepers closed their doors and shuttered their windows and turned eager faces toward home.

Meralda's driver, a short, bald, retired army sergeant named Angis Kert, bit back a curse as a slow moving lumber wagon pulled out of the alley by Fleet's Boots. Meralda grinned. She'd heard Angis let loose before, and was always reminded of her grandfather, who cursed at his swine with exactly the same words and tone.

"S'cuse me, milady," said Angis from his perch above. "Bloody lumber wain like to drove us into Old Pafget's pastry shop."

Meralda laughed. "No apology is necessary, Sergeant," she said. "I didn't hear a thing."

Angis laughed. "I must not be as loud as I once was, then," he said. "How late you reckon you'll be, Sorceress? Late enough for old Angis to nip into Raggot's and have a pint and a game of checkers?"

Meralda sighed. "Have three pints and ten games," she said. "In fact, don't wait. I'll catch a public cab. It'll be midnight, or worse."

Angis spoke to his ponies and the carriage surged suddenly ahead, passing the lumber wain.

"I'll wait for you," said Angis, after a moment. "You'll not find a public cab without a fight, these days, what with half of Erya camped out in the Green Wing."

Meralda frowned. "Eryans? Here already?"

Angis guffawed. "You got to stick your head out of that lab-ra-tory every now and then, milady," he said. "Eryans got here yesterday, king and queen and soldiers and all."

"I've been busy."

"You always are," said Angis. "Work all day an' work all night. It ain't my place to say, Sorceress, but if you don't slow down a mite you're gonna be stooped and grey-headed before me." Angis snapped his reins. "But I reckon I've said enough."

Meralda looked at her reflection in the carriage window glass. "You're right, Angis," she said, leaning closer to the window. "You're right."

Was he?

My hair is a fright, thought Meralda. *But that can be fixed.* She looked into her eyes, surprised by the dark circles beneath them and the weariness within them.

Angis stopped at an intersection and bellowed at the white-gloved traffic master until he waved them through. Meralda watched as a pair of shabby gas-lighter boys darted past, magefire lighters held high and leaving persistent glowing wakes drifting down the sidewalk as they rushed to light their appointed street-lamps. Meralda shook her head. She'd proposed a simple method to automate the lighting and extinguishing of the street-lamps in her first month as Mage, but the Guilds has raised such a fuss the king had refused to even consider it.

The gas-lighters vanished around a corner, leaving Meralda's reflection alone in the glass. Meralda turned away. *No wonder the papers stopped chasing me,* she thought. *I don't look eighteen anymore.*

She certainly didn't feel eighteen. Whisked off to college at thirteen, after enchanting Mug into sarcastic life. Graduating in a mere four years, when most mages take eight, if they manage it at all. A year spent as Fromarch's apprentice, before his abrupt retirement and unwavering insistence that Meralda be named royal Thaumaturge despite her youth and gender. *All that,* thought Meralda, *to wind up spending three-quarters of my time doing petty stage magics intended to impress a gaggle of bored foreign nobles?*

Meralda's stomach grumbled.

"Sergeant," she said. "I've changed my mind. The laboratory can wait until after supper. Make for the Kettle and Hearth, please, off Wizard's Way."

Angis whistled. "That I'll do, milady," he said. "A bit of Missus Pot's meatloaf would go down tasty, all right."

Angis snapped his reins, and Meralda's carriage sped westward, toward the fat towers and squat spires of the college and the darkening shadows that lay about them.

"Whoa."

Angis brought the carriage to a smooth halt at the curb, well within the pool of steady yellow light cast by the hissing gas lamp.

"Well, at least I've seen you fed," said Angis. The lights from the palace lit his face a ruddy red. "Sure you don't want to just go on back home? It's a bit late to be working, especially on a full belly."

Meralda yawned, fumbled with the door latch, and stepped out onto the sidewalk. "Thank you, Angis," she said. "But I've got work to do. I'll see you in the morning."

Angis turned and frowned at Meralda beneath his enormous cabman's hat. "Aye," he said. "Tell you what. I'll be down to Raggot's, till midnight. Send a lad down to fetch me if you get done before that."

Meralda nodded. "Oh, all right. Who do you fuss over on your days off?"

Angis grinned. "Not a soul, milady," he said. "Not a soul."

Then he doffed his hat and rolled off into the night.

The sky was filled with moving lights, as late-arriving airships sailed overhead, seeking out the docks. The palace was aglow, and the streets were crowded, even well after dark. Most of the people strolling past Meralda were Tirlish sight-seers, out for a walk and perhaps a glance of the newly arrived Eryans.

Meralda smiled, bemused. *At any given moment,* she thought, *there are probably ten thousand Eryans in Tirlin. Half the minstrels, half the fishermen, half the barge masters. All Eryan, all the time. What makes these Eryan so special that half of the North Quarter is out strolling around the palace, just hoping to get a glimpse of one?*

"Look! Look there!" said a wide-eyed Tirlish lady, who stopped suddenly beside Meralda. "It's the king! The king of Erya!"

The lady pointed, covering the wide O of her mouth with her gloved hand. Meralda stifled a laugh. The uniformed man the awestruck woman pointed out was Rogar Hebbis, coach driver to the queen of Tirlin.

Rogar nodded to Meralda, made a sweeping bow to the lady at her side, and marched into the west wing palace entrance. "He bowed to us," said the lady, to Meralda. "The king made a bow! To me!" With a squeak, the lady fluttered away down the street, purse thumping at her side like a schoolboy's lunch pail.

Meralda followed Rogar up the five wide steps that led up to the entry hall. The guards nodded. One scribbled Meralda's name and the time in a ledger.

"Evening, Sorceress," said the other. "Captain Ballen is waiting inside for you."

Meralda stepped through the open palace doors. Parts of her frown returned. Why would the captain be waiting for me here?

Meralda padded down the long hall to the stairs at the end. The hall was deserted, but filled with the muffled sounds of pots clattering and glasses clinking and waiters shouting at cooks and cooks shouting at everyone else.

A man pushing a cart of precariously stacked Phendelit dinner plates came dashing through a door just ahead of Meralda. "S'cuse me, milady," he said, leaping ahead of his cart and shoving the opposite door open with his right foot. "Coming through."

Meralda brushed quickly past. Another door opened, and out stepped the captain, a fried chicken leg in one hand and a tall glass of Eryan iced tea in the other.

Meralda smiled and halted. The captain bent his long, gaunt frame in a mocking bow, brandishing his chicken leg like a baton.

"Sorceress," he said, with a grin. "I was just looking for you."

Meralda laughed. "And naturally you thought I'd be in the kitchen pilfering the royal poultry," she said.

The captain took a gulp of tea, wiped his greying beard with his uniform sleeve, and returned Meralda's smile. "Man's got to eat," he said. Bright blue eyes glinted beneath bushy white eyebrows. "Are you calmed down yet?"

Another waiter popped out behind the captain, then darted around him, and vanished through a door behind Meralda.

"I'm better," said Meralda. "Why don't you bring your supper up to the laboratory and tell me why you've been looking for me."

"Indeed, I shall," he said, motioning Meralda forward with

his chicken leg. "After you, milady."

Meralda hurried for the stairs, mindful of the doors on either side. The captain followed, munching contentedly. "So you heard about the Tower's shadow?" said Meralda.

"I hear everything, Thaumaturge," said the captain, between bites. "By the way, you can thank that skunk Sir Ricard for bringing the Tower's shadow to the king's attention."

Meralda felt her face flush. "Oh, I'd like to thank Sir Ricard," she said, softly. "I really, really would."

The captain chuckled. "Maybe someday you will," he said. "I'd pay dear to see that." The captain bit the last bite of meat off the leg, drained his tea, dropped the chicken bone in the tea glass, and set both in the crook of the elbow of the fourth-century suit of armor that guarded the foot of the west wing back stair. "Sir Ricard aside, though, I have a surprise for you, Thaumaturge," he said, mounting the stairs beside Meralda. "You do love surprises, as I recall."

Meralda half-turned as she climbed and lifted an eyebrow at the captain. "I detest surprises," she said.

"Quite right," said the captain. "My mistake."

Meralda reached the second floor landing. The copper-bound double doors to the Royal Thaumaturgical Laboratory were just ten paces away, but in place of the mismatched suits of armor that had flanked the laboratory doors since the days of King Esperus, a pair of gangly, red-shirted palace soldiers stood at attention, right hands on sword hilts, eyes straight ahead.

Meralda stared.

The soldiers were twins. Both were blond, fair skinned, blue-eyed, and freckled. Both avoided Meralda's gaze with a terrified determination, further evidenced by the sheen of sweat on their faces and their futile attempts to remain absolutely still to the point of excluding breathing and swallowing.

"Thaumaturge," said the captain, "I present to you Tervis and Kervis Bellringer, Guardsmen of the Realm. They are to serve as your bodyguards for the duration of the Accords." The captain shook his head. "By order of the king," he said, before Meralda could protest. "All members of the court are to be assigned bodyguards. No fewer than two, no exceptions, no discussion." The captain turned away from the young soldiers and lowered his voice to a whisper. "They're good lads, Sorceress," he said. "Twins, fresh in from a horse ranch halfway to Vonath. I won't waste them on toads like Sir Ricard and I don't trust them to hooligans like Ordo or Thaft. Give them a chance. This isn't their fault."

The captain's half-smile vanished, suddenly replaced by a grimace of barely contained fury. He turned and stamped up the last few stairs. "You there!" he bellowed at the right-most lad, not halting until he was a hand's breadth from the boy's face. "Guardsman Kervis!"

"Sir," said the left-most boy. "Pardon, but I'm Kervis. He's Tervis."

"You're Kervis if I say you are!" shouted the captain. "You're Kervis, your boots are Kervis, your hat is bloody well Kervis if I say it is! Now then." The captain stalked over to the face of the boy on the left. "Do you see this woman, soldier?"

The boy glanced at Meralda, looked away, and nodded frantically.

"Do you think your brother Kervis sees her, soldier?"

The nods came faster. The captain leaned down and stepped

close to Kervis. "You and your brother are the lady's bodyguards, soldier," said the captain, his voice fallen to a whisper. "What does that mean, bodyguard?"

"Sir," said the boy, his eyes wide, "We are to protect her, um, body, from, er—"

"Enemies, sir!" croaked the other Bellringer. "Enemies, foreign or, um, domestic. Sir."

The captain glared. Kervis shook. "That's correct, soldier," he said. "So if you've got to take on the whole of Vonath single-handed with a dull butter knife then that's what you do. Because if anything happens to the sorceress it won't be the army or the crown you'll answer to. It'll be me." The captain's voice rose to a bellow. "Me!"

The captain whirled, winked at Meralda, and stamped off down the stairs.

The Bellringers, sweating and wide-eyed, watched him go.

Meralda shook her head. "Guardsman Kervis," she said, when the captain's footfalls died. "How old are you?"

The boy cleared his throat. "Eight and ten, ma'am," he said. "Soon be nine and ten."

"Me, too," said Tervis. "Ma'am."

"I surmised as much," said Meralda. "Well, gentlemen, let me make one thing clear, here and now. The king has decreed that you shall dog my steps. But it would not do for you to be too much underfoot."

"Yes, ma'am."

"Yes, ma'am."

Meralda sighed. Somewhere in the palace, a clock began striking the ninth hour, and with every bell toll Meralda felt the weight of the day settle heavy in her bones.

"Guardsman Kervis," she said, stifling a yawn. "Are you familiar with the palace?"

Guardsman Kervis leapt to attention. "Yes, ma'am," he said.

"Then you know where the basement kitchen is."

"Down the west stair, left at the Burnt Door, right and two doors down from the Anvion Room. Yes, ma'am," said Kervis.

Meralda stepped off the last stair. "Very well. Go there, at once. Tell them the sorceress wants a pot of coffee."

Kervis beamed. "Yes, ma'am," he said. "Right away."

"And get three mugs, too," said Meralda. "You gentlemen do drink coffee, I assume?"

The Bellringers nodded. Tervis' helmet threatened to fall off, despite the strap cutting into his chin.

"Good," said Meralda. "We'll all need a cup, tonight." Then she stepped to the door, fumbled in her pocket for the big black iron key, and put it in the lock.

The door crackled faintly, and the short-cropped hair on Tervis' head tried to stand up below his helmet.

Meralda whispered a word, and pushed the door gently open. "Knock, when you return," she said to Kervis. "And, gentlemen, I don't need to warn you against ever opening this door yourself, do I?"

"No, ma'am," said the Bellringers. "Not ever."

"Good," said Meralda. "Good." Then she removed the key, dropped it back in her pocket, and closed the door gently behind her.

"Nineteen days," she said, to the shadows. "Nineteen days to shrink the Tower or move the Sun."

"Ma'am?" spoke a muffled voice from beyond the door. "Were you speaking to me?"

"No, Guardsman," said Meralda. "I wasn't."

"Just checking," said Tervis. Meralda couldn't see the young man, but she was absolutely certain that he had snapped to full attention before speaking. "Ma'am."

Meralda shook her head, shrugged out of her coat, rolled up her sleeves, and went about switching on her spark lamps.

Chapter Two

Bright morning sunlight streamed through the kitchen window. "Good morning, Mistress," said Mug, as Meralda shuffled out of her bedroom, barked her shin on a chair leg, and made slowly for the cupboards. "Did you sleep well?"

"Mmmph," said Meralda, squinting in the daylight. Her bathrobe, belt trailing loose like a train, hung lopsided from her shoulders. Her slippers were mismatched, right foot blue, left foot yellow with tassels.

Mug regarded the Thaumaturge with a dozen shiny eyes. "Perhaps I should be asking if you slept at all," said Mug. "I didn't hear you come in."

Meralda shrugged and rubbed her eyes. "It was late," she said. "You were asleep." Meralda filled her coffee pot with water from the sink, rummaged in the cupboard for grounds, and sank into her chair with a sigh and a frown when the coffee urn turned up empty.

"Forgive me, mistress," said Mug. "I meant to remind you yesterday."

Meralda yawned. "I'll get a cup at Flayne's," she said. "But first, a piece of toast."

"Out of bread, too," said Mug. He tilted his eyes toward the ceiling. "I imagine the mages of legend had someone handy to do the shopping," he said. "'Fetch me a bag of flour and an onion,' they'd say, before charging off to topple the Acatean Empire or clash with the Hang." Mug shook his leaves. "Yes, that's the life. Power, magic, and all the shopping done. You really should look into conquering the world and making Yvin run all your errands."

Meralda peeped out from between her fingers. "Do you sit around at night and think of these things, Mug?"

Mug tossed his fronds in a shrug. "Last night I thought a lot about towers and thaumaturges," he said. "Specifically, I wondered what mine was doing about a certain long shadow."

Meralda groaned.

Mug's eyes clustered together. "Bad news, is it? Going to tell Yvin it can't be done?"

"Worse," said Meralda. "I'm going to tell him it can."

Mug wilted. "Oh," he said.

"Oh, indeed," said Meralda. "I think I can change the air around the Tower. Make it bend light differently."

Mug's frown deepened. "Sounds interesting, in a hopelessly implausible way."

"Water does the same thing," said Meralda.

Mug's red eyes gathered in a cluster. "Water hides shadows?" he asked, with a furtive red-eyed glance toward the half-full kitchen sink below him.

Meralda shook her head. "No, Mug," she said. "Water bends light. It's called refraction, and different materials refract light to different degrees."

"If you say so, mistress," said Mug. "Will it be difficult?"

"Extremely," said Meralda, after another yawn. "I'll have to divide the air around the Tower into hundreds of different volumes, and assign a unique refractive value to each volume." She yawned again.

"Is that before or after you buy coffee and bread?"

"After," said Meralda. She rose, rummaged in her icebox, and produced a chunk of cheese and a wax bag of Flayne's salt crackers.

A knock sounded softly at the door. Meralda grimaced. "Right on time," she said. "They've probably been standing there listening for the palace bells to sound before they knocked."

Indeed, the Brass Bell, five hundred years old and as big as a house, was sounding from the palace.

Mug divided his eyes between Meralda and the door. "They? They who?"

"My bodyguards," said Meralda, rising. "And no, it wasn't my idea, and no, I can't get rid of them."

The knock sounded again. Mug twisted all of his eyes towards Meralda, and shook his leaves in what the Thaumaturge recognized as Mug's equivalent of taking a deep breath.

"Not a word," said Meralda, her eyes flashing beneath a tangled shock of hair. "Not one."

Mug tossed his leaves and sighed.

"Thaumaturge?" spoke a voice at the door. "You asked us to report for duty at first ring."

"Thank you, Kervis," said Meralda. "I'll be out in a few moments. There's a settee just down the hall."

They won't do it, thought Meralda. *They won't sit. They'll flank my door and lock their knees and stare at my neighbors and if it takes me more than twenty minutes to bathe and dress one or both of them will fall over in a dead faint.*

"We brought you coffee," said a fainter voice. "Ma'am."

"They brought you coffee," echoed Mug. "Ma'am."

Meralda glared. "Thank you," she said.

"It's from Flayne's," said a Bellringer. *Tervis*, Meralda decided. *He's the timid twin.* What a difference a few minutes made.

Meralda smiled. A cup of Flayne's coffee was sixpence. A lavish sum, on a guardsman's pay, even split in two.

Meralda padded to her front door and opened it a hand's width. "Thank you," she said again, as a grinning Kervis thrust a steaming paper cup within. "Now, if you gentlemen will take a seat, I'll be out in a moment."

"Yes, ma'am," chorused the guards.

Meralda eased the door shut.

"Yes, ma'am," said Mug, his voice a perfect rendition of the Bellringers. "They'll both be in love with you before the Accords, you know. Ah, love," added Mug, with a tossing of leaves. "Flowers and music and moonlight and guardsmen! You'll have to get a bigger place, the three of you. What will old Missus Whitlonk think, what with the lads coming and going at all hours?"

Meralda raised the cup to her lips, kicked off her mismatched slippers, and marched wordlessly back to her bedroom.

Angis and his cab were waiting at the curb when Meralda and the Bellringers clattered down the steps and out into the hustle and bustle of Fairlane Street.

"Morning, Thaumaturge," said Angis, doffing his hat. "Who 'er these lads? Book-ends?"

Meralda laughed. "Goodman Angis Kert, meet Tervis and Kervis Bellringer. They are my guards until the Accords."

Angis guffawed. "Where you lads from?"

"Allaskar, sir," said Kervis. "Just outside Moren."

Angis took Meralda's battered black leather instrument bag and placed it carefully in the cab. "Knew a man from Allaskar, once," he said. "When I was in the army. What was his name, now?"

Meralda caught hold of the cab's side rail and climbed inside. A double-decked Steam Guild trolley chugged past, smokestacks billowing, sending pedestrians and cabs scurrying off the track lane and momentarily drowning out the clatter of the road and the conversation between the Bellringers and Angis.

Meralda settled back into the cushioned seat and closed her eyes.

"Pardon, Thaumaturge," said Tervis at the door. "Goodman Kert wants to know our destination. And Kervis wants to know if he can ride up top, to keep an eye out."

Meralda smiled. She, too, recalled a time when Tirlin was best seen from the cabman's seat.

"We go to the Tower, guardsman," she said. "And tell guardsman Kervis I shall feel most secure knowing he and Angis are scouring the sidewalks for wandering Vonat river bandits."

Meralda sensed Tervis grin, but did not open her eyes to see it. The door shut. Words were spoken. An instant later the cab door opened and Tervis climbed inside.

"We're off, ma'am," he said, his sword clattering against the cab door's frame. "We're off!"

The cab rolled smoothly into traffic. Above, Angis and Kervis were chatting away like long lost brothers. From the sound of it, Angis may well have served in the army with the Bellringers' uncle. Meralda noted with mild shock that the cabman's language never veered from strict propriety, even when a ten-horse road barge nearly forced Angis onto the sidewalk.

Wakened, Meralda kept her eyes open after that. Across from her Tervis stared through his window, occasionally biting back habitual exclamations to his twin at the sight of passing trolleys, a Builder's Guild steam shovel at work, and the distant, bobbing hulks of dirigibles moored in a field east of the docks. The guardsman went slack-jawed with awe when he spied a walking barge hauling a load of lumber up a steep hill, and again when the automaton at the fruit market singled him out for a wave and a doff of its red hat.

"Mum said we'd see wonders, ma'am," said Tervis, as the shadow of a rising airship blotted out the sun. "She was right."

"My mother said the same thing," said Meralda.

"Your mum?" said Tervis, craning his neck to follow the airship. "Weren't you born in the palace?"

Meralda laughed. Tervis stared out, lost in wonders a thousand other cab riders ignored twice a day, every day.

I wonder, mused Meralda. *Should I tell him I was born on a pig farm? Should I tell him the king is a bumbler, the court a refuge for overbred dunderheads, and the Accords are largely an opportunity for the nobles of five nations to come together and drink to excess at their peoples' expense?*

Another airship, her fans swiveling and whirling, swooped ponderously down and blotted out the sun.

"Wondrous," said Tervis.

Meralda smiled, and said nothing.

"Here we are, ladies and thaumaturges," shouted Angis. "The Tower."

Angis pulled his cab to the curb in the circle 'round that looped between Hent Street and the park's east entrance. The Bellringers stared. *No wonder so many painters set up their easels here,* thought Meralda.

The park wall, ten miles of Old Kingdom rough hewn stone ravaged and worn by the passing of centuries, rose a full thirty feet above the well-tended grass of the park. The gargoyles mad king Foon had added in the second century still danced and capered and brooded atop the wall. The age-old tradition of tying ridiculous hats to the most fearsome of the gargoyles was, Meralda saw, still observed by Tirlin's more daring youngsters. The pair of gargoyles flanking the gate-posts were sporting last year's fruit-and-feather day hats, and the right-most fellow was wearing a jaunty pink Oaftree scarf.

Well above and just inside the wall and its gargoyles, the

park's ring of Old Kingdom iron oaks rustled and swayed, like thick green mountain peaks shuffling to and fro against a pale blue sky. Meralda loved the oaks, and though she knew the stories claiming Otrinvion himself planted the seedlings were utter nonsense, she couldn't help but think those mighty old trees had watched Tirlin for a good portion of its clamorous history.

"Oh," said Kervis, and Meralda knew from his face that he wasn't seeing the wall or the Old Oaks or the line of dancing gargoyles.

"The captain says it's haunted," said Tervis, his eyes upon the Tower. Meralda put her bag in her lap and waited for the guardsman to notice that the cab had stopped.

"The thaumaturge says it isn't," said Meralda. "And she should know better, shouldn't she?"

Tervis whirled, groping for the door latch. "Yes, ma'am," he said. "Sorry, ma'am."

Angis flung open the door from outside. Tervis yelped and would have fallen, had Angis not caught hold of his red uniform collar. "Here, lad," said Angis. "First thing you've got to learn about is doors. See this here? It's what we city folks call a latch."

"Leave him be, Angis," said Meralda.

"Aye, Lady," said Angis, grinning. He reached up, caught Meralda's black bag, and held her door. "Will you be long, this morning?"

"Two hours," she said, stepping out onto the curb. "Then it's off to the palace."

"Got to greet our Eryan guests, aye?"

"Aye," said Meralda, wincing at the thought of a long afternoon at court. "But first, I've got work to do. Gentlemen?"

The Bellringers looked down, away from the Tower.

"That is the Tower," she said, as Angis tended his ponies. "It's seven hundred years old. It was built by Otrinvion the Black, himself. You've heard the name?"

The Bellringers nodded in unison.

"The Tower is central to our history," she said. "And the Tower has a long and bloody past. War and murder and madness. You've heard the stories of King Tornben the Mad? Queen Annabet the Torturer?"

The Bellringers exchanged glances, and Kervis nodded.

"The stories are true," said Meralda. "Documented fact. But I tell you this, gentlemen, and I want you to remember it." Meralda paused, shifted her bag from her left hand to her right, and waved back Kervis when he motioned to take the bag himself.

"The Tower is not haunted," she said. "It was not, is not, and shall never be. Is that clear?"

The Bellringers nodded, slowly this time.

Angis grinned at his ponies, but didn't say a word.

"Then let's go," said Meralda. "Follow me."

She turned and set foot on the cracked flagstones of Wizard's Walk, which led through the park's east gate and then wound toward the Tower. The walk was, according to local lore, another of Otrinvion's legacies.

The Bellringers, right hands on sword hilts, faces stern (except for Tervis, who kept wrinkling his forehead to push his helmet up), fell into step behind her.

"Keep a sharp eye out, lads," said Angis, after Meralda passed into the park. "Especially after dark. That's when the haunts get mean." Angis lifted his voice. "Not that I believe such, mind you."

Meralda listened to the steady tromp-tromp of newly soled guard boots and frowned. The Bellringers were marching, not walking. *Fresh out of boot camp,* she thought. *I'm sure they're not even aware they're doing it. I'll be hearing the sound of marching boots from now until the Accords. That's eighteen more days, and every one of them my own small army dress parade.*

The walk turned suddenly, leaving the shade of the old oaks for the close-cropped green grass of the park proper.

The Tower split the sky, no longer obscured by walls or oaks.

"Here it is, gentlemen," said Meralda, halting. "The Tower."

"It's taller than the palace," said Kervis.

Meralda shook her head. She knew the highest spire of the palace to be ten feet taller than the blunt tip of the Tower. Old King Horoled, a century past, had nearly bankrupted Tirlin seeing to that. But the palace was more than twenty city blocks away. One had to squint just to make out the lofty spire, which peeked above the trees. *The palace might be taller,* thought Meralda, *but here in the park, the Tower reigns.*

Reigns? No, Meralda decided. *The Tower doesn't reign. It looms. Looms above the Old Oaks. Looms above the park wall. Looms above Tirlin. Thick and tall and blunt, chipped and nicked by seven hundred years of determined attempts to pull it down, the Tower endures.*

"If a mountain had bones," said Tervis, "that's what they'd look like."

"Hush," replied Kervis. "It's just a pile of rocks."

A lumber wain rumbled up the Walk behind them. "Passing by," shouted the driver. "Make way."

Meralda stepped onto the grass and motioned the Bellringers to follow.

The lumber wain rattled past.

Tervis pointed toward the hurried band of carpenters stacking lumber and erecting scaffolds at the base of the Tower.

"What are they building?"

Meralda frowned. "Seating," she said. "For the Accords."

Meralda resumed her trek toward the Tower, which lay a goodly march ahead. "The king will give the commencement speech from there," she said, pointing toward the tall, narrow framework jutting out from the base of the Tower. "The Eryans will be there, the Alons there, the Phendelits there, and the Vonats just in front of us," she said, her hand indicating the skeletal frames arranged around and dwarfed by the Tower. "All this, for a ten minute speech no one will remember the next day."

"Kings will do what kings will do," said Kervis, with the air of one repeating a time-honored truth. "At least that's what Pop always says."

"Ma'am," he added, after a jab in the ribs from Tervis.

The Tower beckoned. Meralda fell into step with her soldiers and marched, humming, ahead.

The Tower doors, each twenty feet high and nearly as wide, were open, but blocked by a drooping length of bright yellow ribbon and a faded Danger Public Works sign bolted to a rusty iron stand.

Meralda waved to the Builder's Guild foreman, lifted the yellow ribbon, and passed over the threshold.

Three steps on stone, and the last slanting rays of the sun gave way to darkness. Meralda squinted ahead, slowing until she could make out shapes in the shadows. "Be careful," she said, as Tervis and Kervis entered. "The carpenters are stacking lumber in here."

Meralda reached out and touched the wall to her right. The stone was cold. Like the outside of the Tower, the interior hall was stone. Solid black Eryan granite, shaped and fused into a single mass by a spell or spells known only to the Tower's long-dead master. Cold and dry and as smooth as glass. Meralda knew just beyond the wall, the sun was shining, the park was green and lush, and Tirlin was bustling and busy. But here, in the windowless belly of the Tower, she felt as if it were the smallest hour of the longest, darkest night.

"It's quiet, all of a sudden," said Tervis, in a whisper. "Isn't it?"

Meralda shrugged. Oh, the hammering and pounding and shouting continued, but the Tower doors might as well have been flung shut, so faint was the noise after only a few paces. And had the daylight fled so quickly, on her other visits?

"This way," she said, when the Bellringer's footfalls fell behind. "The hall is very short, and there are no turns."

"No windows, either," muttered Tervis. "Ma'am."

"We won't need windows," said Meralda, groping in her bag. "We'll have plenty of our own light."

"Oh," said Kervis. "Should I go back and fetch a lantern?"

Meralda pulled a short brass pipe from her bag. "Light," she said, unlatching the simple magelamp spell coiled invisibly around the cylinder with the word.

The Bellringers whistled as wide beams of soft white light flared from each end of the brass tube.

"Wizard lamp," said Tervis, lifting his hand to run his fingers through the light. "Uncle Rammis saw one, once. Nobody believed him."

Meralda played the lamp around the hall. Shadows flew. Some, she thought, more slowly than others.

A shiver ran the length of Meralda's spine.

"Nonsense," she said, amazed and a bit embarrassed. "Utter nonsense."

"Pardon, ma'am?" asked Kervis.

Meralda shook her head. "Nothing," she said. "Nothing. We have a long flight of stairs to climb, gentlemen," she said, striding toward the heart of the darkness at the end of the hall. "Shall we go?"

The Bellringers followed. Ten paces further Meralda's lamplight fell across a crude table bearing half a dozen battered oil lanterns, an open box of Red Cat matches, and a half-eaten Lamp River apple.

Further down the hall, smooth-planed cedar planks were stacked neatly along each wall. Meralda thought she heard the sound of gentle snoring behind the third stack as she passed it, and her face reddened even more. *I can at least be thankful Mug isn't here,* she thought. *I'd never hear the last of this. Carpenters sleep while the sorceress trembles.*

Meralda's footfalls came faster and harder until the hall simply ended, and the shaft of light from her magelamp soared up and out, only to lose itself in the vast, cavernous maw of the Tower.

Kervis whistled softly.

"Bats," said Tervis, his face turned upward. "You'd think there would be bats."

"Not a one," said Meralda. "There isn't a crack or a gap anywhere in the Tower. It's an amazing structure." She played the lamplight out into the darkness, resting the beam finally on the far side of the Tower and the faint outline of the winding, rail-less stair that wound lazily up and away into the dark.

"We climb that?" asked Kervis.

Meralda nodded. "It's wider than it looks," she said, though she understood the badly-hidden wash of fear in the boy's voice. She recalled the first time she had ascended the stair. Darkness above, and darkness below, a magelit patch of old black stone to her left, a hungry void a step to her right.

From the idling carpenters just beyond the doors, Meralda heard the barest snatch of soft, low laughter.

There will be no more bloody shivering, she said, to herself. *I won't have it.*

"Do either of you have a fear of high places?"

In perfect unison, both Bellringers, their faces pale in the magelamp, wiped sweat from their foreheads with their right hands, set their jaws, and shook their heads.

"We're not afraid," said Kervis. "Shall I go first?"

Meralda waved him ahead. "Stay in the lamplight," she said. "Tervis, if you would be so good as to follow?"

"Right behind you, ma'am."

Meralda switched her bag to her right shoulder and set out for the foot of the stair. She knew it was her imagination, but laughter seemed to follow all the way up to the Wizard's Flat.

"At last."

The stair ended at a narrow wooden door. Kervis halted and reached out for the tarnished brass knob, but pulled his hand back before he touched it. "Ma'am," he said, panting and looking back over his shoulder at Meralda. "Is this it?"

Meralda brushed back a damp lock of red hair and nodded. "Yes," she said. "The Wizard's Flat."

Kervis flashed a crooked grin and sank into a winded slouch against the Tower wall. Boots scraped softly on stone behind her, and Meralda turned to face Tervis, who had been silent the whole of the long climb to the flat.

Both boys were streaked with sweat. Their stiff red and black palace guard uniforms looked thick enough for the dead of winter, but Tervis was pasty-faced and wild-eyed, as well as sweaty. Meralda watched as the boy inched his way, with elaborate care, up onto the last tread between them.

"Tervis?" she said, softly. "We're here. It's almost over."

Tervis met her eyes and gulped.

"He's just winded," said Kervis, quickly. "A few moments on a good solid floor and he'll be right up, ma'am," he added. "Isn't that right, little brother?"

Tervis tried to speak, but only croaked. While he licked his lips Meralda reached into her pocket and found the key that opened the flat. "We could all use a place to sit," she said. "The door is locked, Kervis." She thrust the key into the cone of light from her magelamp. "Take this and open the door, if you will."

Kervis took the key. "What about, um, spells?" he said.

Meralda shook her head. "No spells here," she replied. "It's just a key, and that's just a lock." She eyed Tervis, whose complexion was looking decidedly more greenish by the moment. "If you please?"

Kervis thrust the key into the lock and turned it.

The lock made a single loud click.

Kervis withdrew the key and handed it back to Meralda. "In we go," he said, turning the latch and pushing.

The door held fast. Kervis pushed harder.

"Open it," said Tervis, though clenched teeth.

Kervis turned the latch again, pushed. "What am I doing wrong?" he said. "It turns, but it won't open."

Meralda took two careful steps ahead, to stand beside Kervis on the stair. *Don't think about the height,* she said, in a stern internal voice. *Don't think about empty darkness, or the long, long fall.*

She turned the latch and pushed.

The door swung open and bright, warm daylight spilled onto the stair, plunged off the edge, and fell in long, slanting shafts across the dark.

Without a word, Meralda and both Bellringers charged headlong into the light.

"Well," said Kervis, from the far side of the flat. "I can't tell you how much I enjoyed that."

Meralda put her back to the wall, laughed, and squinted at the sun. Tervis joined his brother, but sank into a crouch, both hands palm-down on the floor. "We'll join the army," he said, and Meralda knew at once Tervis was mocking his older twin. "Oh, the things we'll see, the places we'll go."

Kervis shrugged and grinned. "I never said we'd ride carriages everywhere," he said, cheerily. "Still, it's not so bad. How many of old Barlo's bully boys can say they've climbed to the top of a haunted wizard's tower?" he asked.

Tervis put his head in his hands. "None," he said. "They've got better sense. And the Tower isn't haunted," he said, peeking through his fingers up at Meralda. "Is it, ma'am?"

Meralda sighed and shook her head.

"No, it isn't," she said. "It's just tall. Unusually tall." She forced herself away from the wall and stepped out into the flat.

Out into Otrinvion the Black's place of power, she thought. *All the history, all the tragedy, all the wars and magics. It all started here. Started here, and ended here, seven hundred years ago.*

The flat, like the Tower, was circular. Meralda knew the flat was exactly fifty-five feet in diameter, each of the flat's four ten-by-ten windows was set at a compass point, and the ceiling was slightly convex, so the center was exactly twenty feet high. She knew the indentations in the floor by the door were square, half a foot to a side, and one foot deep. She knew Tower lore insisted these indentations once held Otrinvion's lost twin staves, Nameless and Faceless. Meralda knew all this, but standing in the flat, she felt a touch of the same thrill she'd felt the first day she'd walked into the shadow of the palace while dirigibles swam by above.

Kervis hauled Tervis to his feet. "Look here," he said, dragging Tervis toward the north-facing window. "Bet you can see Allaskar from there!"

Tervis shook off his brother's grasp and pulled away from the window. Meralda motioned him toward her. "Hold this, if you will," she said, thrusting her instrument bag into the boy's arms.

Tervis nodded. "Yes, ma'am."

"Oh," said Kervis, his face pressed to the glass. "Oh," he said again, softly.

Meralda joined him at the window.

Tirlin lay sprawled below. The Lamp River wound shimmering from the east, passed beneath the bridge, and lost itself amid the walls and rooftops and spires of the college. The park wall and its dancing gargoyles were invisible, swallowed whole by the distance. The old oaks, tiny now, stood swaying in a ring. Meralda felt she was flying, looking down on the heads of giants.

Kervis gasped and started. A bright green passenger dirigible flew into view, fans straining, climbing steeply and bearing west. But before it turned and was lost beyond the window frame, Meralda was sure she saw the flash of a lady's white-gloved hand through a brass-worked salon porthole.

Kervis rapped the glass with his knuckles. "How thick is this, ma'am?" he asked, stepping back. "And how do they clean it?"

Meralda smiled. "The glass is nearly four feet thick," she said. "And, believe it or not, once a year a Phendelit chimney sweep named Mad Hansa hangs on a line from an airship and polishes all the glass from outside."

Kervis' jaw dropped. "Mad Hansa," he said.

Meralda nodded. "It's an all day affair," she said. "The park fills with people who come to watch." Meralda shrugged. "Especially after the year Mad Hansa hired an apprentice. Too bad about him, really."

Kervis swallowed and stepped away from the window. "Now then," said Meralda. "Work to do." She pulled back her sleeves and brushed a damp lock of hair out of her eyes. "Tervis, my bag. Please stand back and be silent."

"Yes, ma'am," said the Bellringers. Tervis came to stand before her, hefting her bag out at arm's length before him.

Meralda thanked him, reached inside, and pulled out a small black cloth bag clasped with an intricate silver catch.

Tervis' eyes bulged. Meralda released the catch, opened the bag, and pulled out a silver ball attached to a fine silver chain. A hole pierced the bottom of the ball. Meralda shook the bag until a short piece of sharpened white chalk fell into her hand. She then pushed the chalk into the hole in the ball.

Meralda grasped the far end of the chain and let the ball hang free. With her arm above her head, the ball hung just above the floor.

Meralda took a deep breath and whispered a word.

The first few windings of Meralda's spell unlatched and flailed about. Meralda let go of the chain, and before it could fall the spell caught hold, suspending chain and ball in the empty air below the ceiling.

Tervis grinned in sudden wonder, and some of the fear left his eyes. Kervis bit back a squeak of amazement.

With another word, Meralda stilled the ball's small oscillations.

"Stand back, if you will," she said, to Tervis.

Tervis made great backward-shuffling strides to the far edge of the flat. Meralda squinted, said a word and made a gesture. The ball and chain sailed to rest in the center of the flat.

Meralda followed. She kneeled before the ball and chain, fumbled in her skirt pocket, and withdrew her short, battered retaining wand. The wand was warm, and at her touch it gave off a hum like the buzzing of a single angry honeybee.

Tufts of pocket lint clung to the wand. Meralda rubbed the lint off with her skirt, took the wand in both hands, and unlatched the rest of the seeking spell with a long rhythmic word.

The spell discharged with a crackle and a flash, draining Meralda's retaining wand with a sound like frying bacon.

"Look!" said Kervis, as the ball began to dart about, swinging to and fro as if testing the air for scents.

"Hush," said Tervis.

The silver ball strained at the chain, pulling it taut until the chalk tip touched the floor. Then the ball swung to the north, pulling the chain with it at a slight angle and drawing a short straight line upon the floor.

Meralda clapped her hands, and caught the chain as it went limp and fell. "That's all," she said. "We're nearly done."

"What now?" asked Kervis, as Meralda wound the chain loosely around her left hand.

"I use a ruler," said Meralda. "I measure the length of the line on the floor. I use this to calculate the height of the flat."

Kervis tilted his head.

"A ruler?" he said.

"A ruler," replied Meralda. "Tervis?"

Tervis trotted to her, bag in hand. She reached inside, found the folding Eryan ruler in its pouch by the copper-bound Loman jars, and pulled it out.

Kervis frowned. Meralda smiled. "I need to anchor my shadow moving spell to a spot here in the flat," she said. "And to do that, I have to know exactly how high off the ground the spot is."

Tervis frowned. "Couldn't someone measure the steps, and then count them?" he said. "Ma'am?"

Meralda unfolded the ruler, kneeled, and laid the flat edge against the chalk mark. "Very good, Tervis," she said, squinting at the tiny marks on the ruler's edge. "That was, in fact, the first recorded method by which the Tower's height was surveyed. And it was a good estimate. But to move the Tower's shadow will require more than just good estimates."

Kervis stepped close, but leaped away when he saw his shadow fall over Meralda's ruler. "Pardon, ma'am," he said, scratching his head beneath his helmet, "but how does that little scratch on the floor tell you how tall the Tower is?"

Meralda put her nose nearly to the floor, decided on a figure, and used the chalk from the ball to scribble the numbers on the floor.

"Mathematics," she said, rising. "The biggest part of magic.

Not the stuff of epic legends, I know, but the stuff of magic nonetheless."

"Mathematics?" asked Tervis, wrinkling his nose. "You mean two-and-two and take away four, that sort of thing?"

"That very sort of thing," said Meralda, grinning at the thought of old Master Blimmett's sputtering, should he ever hear his High Mathematica studies dubbed a "two-and-two and take away four sort of thing".

Tervis stared down at the mark on the floor.

"The process is called trigonometry," said Meralda. "I caused the ball to be attracted to the Historical Society marker by the park gates. It pulled the chain away from the vertical by that much." She pointed to the scribbles on the floor with the tip of her boot.

"And since I know the exact distance from the center of the Tower to the Society marker, and since I know the length of the chain and the angle of deflection, I can calculate the exact height of a point just below the ceiling of the Wizard's Flat."

"As you say, ma'am," said Tervis. Then he grinned. "Magic!"

Meralda folded her ruler. "Magic," she said, putting away her gear.

The half-open door to the stair beckoned. Meralda dropped her bag and tied it shut.

"Time to go, gentlemen," she said. Tervis mopped his brow. Kervis, who had been dashing from window to window, trotted back to join Meralda and Tervis before the door.

"It's downhill, this time," Kervis said. "Shall I go first again, ma'am?"

Meralda lit her magelamp with a word and motioned Kervis toward the door.

"Last one down is a Vonat," he said, before slipping out into the dark.

Meralda followed. Tervis came after, and though his hand shook when Meralda handed him the key he managed to lock the door without fumbling.

Meralda pocketed the key, bade Kervis to wait until she set the magelamp's twin beams wider and brighter, and then brushed back her hair.

A line from a Phendelit play crept whispering into Meralda's mind. "We climb now the walls of the cold dark night," said the hero, at the base of the stair that wound down to the Pale Gate. "No sun now to warm us, no light for our feet. Just darkness and silence and down to defeat."

Meralda sighed at the memory, then realized both Bellringers were eyeing her expectantly. "Well, gentlemen," she said, forcing a smile. "It is downhill, as you said."

Kervis groaned. "If old what's-his-name had been any kind of real wizard, he'd have put in a lift."

Tervis took in his breath with a sudden hiss. "Don't say things like that," he said. "It's disrespectful to speak ill of the, um, ones that aren't here anymore."

Kervis rolled his eyes and turned away.

Meralda increased her magelamp's brightness with a whispered word and set a brisk pace for the foot of the Tower.

Between midday traffic and the extra crowds milling about the palace, Meralda was nearly late for court.

Ordinarily, she'd simply not go, since Yvin preferred absence to tardiness. And, ordinarily, her absence would have been noted, but nothing more. Thaumaturges were almost expected to ignore the routine functions of the court.

Ordinarily.

The Accords, however, were only held every five years. And of the fifth-year Accords, only one in five was hosted by any given realm, including Tirlin. So nothing, reflected a breathless Meralda, was ordinary anymore.

She'd leapt from the traffic-locked cab at the corner of Kemp and Striddle, intending to walk the five blocks to the trolley stand at Fleethorse. The Bellringers, still sweat-streaked and flushed from the morning's long climb, cleared a wide path through the busy sidewalks. Even with the twins clearing the way, though, Meralda could only watch as the Fleethorse trolley pulled away from the stand, filled to capacity and gone before Meralda could attempt to claim court preference and gain a hand-stand on the shuddering red hulk.

And as for hailing a cab, I might as well shout down the moon, she thought. Traffic was at a near standstill from Kemp to Roard. Worse, there wasn't a cab to be seen, much less hailed and ridden.

And so, another brisk walk. Meralda's calves ached. Her heels were bruised and tender. Her hair hung limp and damp. She caught a brief glimpse of herself reflected in a clockmaker's window and looked quickly away. *I'm a sight,* she thought. *A sight, and bound for court.*

A street minstrel dared the Bellringers, but Kervis sent him scampering with a growl and a pat of his sword hilt.

Eight blocks to the palace, and still the roads were clogged. Seven blocks, and Meralda's right ankle began to ache. Six blocks out, and short, sharp pains ran up her right leg each time her foot fell.

Five blocks from the palace, traffic began to flow. A dusty black army troop cab rattled past, and Kervis, to Meralda's amazement, bellowed at the driver, called him to a halt, and threw the door open for Meralda before the driver could do more than sputter and shrug.

"The palace, and before ten bells," said Kervis, before clambering into the cab and joining Tervis on the smooth wood bench seat.

The cab rolled away from the curb. Kervis put his helmet in his lap and ran his fingers through sweat-soaked hair.

"Guardsman, you are a treasure," said Meralda, rubbing her aching right ankle through her boot.

Kervis blushed. "I figured the worst he could do was laugh and drive past, ma'am," he said.

Meralda gathered loose locks of hair and pulled them to the back of her head, working them into the beret as best she could. She frowned suddenly. *I've got a bagful of sorcerous implements sufficient to fell the west wing, but I don't have a hairbrush.*

The cab rolled to a halt behind a line of carriages inching towards the palace reception hall.

"The palace, Your Majesty," said the driver to Kervis. "Mind you don't knock your crown off, on your way out."

"Thank you, Goodman," said Kervis, forcing the door open. Meralda hefted her bag, stooped, and leapt onto the curb. Tervis followed, pausing only to stick his tongue out at the departing driver's red-clad back.

Meralda ignored the pain in her ankle and trotted to the door. There she paused, fumbled in her pocket for a coin, and pressed it into Kervis' hand. "Find Orlo's," she said. "Down the street. Get a table, and hold it. We'll all have a late lunch, when this nonsense is over."

She smiled briefly at Kervis' widening eyes, whirled again, and brushed past the sentries.

A whistle blew, once and briefly. Meralda waited for the doors to close behind her, saw that the carpeted hall was momentarily empty, and broke into a dead, if limping, run.

By custom, one short trumpet blast signaled the court that the king had left his chambers and was nearing the Gold Room. Two short trumpet blasts indicated the king's descent of the east stair, and his eminent arrival at court.

The second trumpet blew as Meralda found and fell into her stiff, high-backed Old Kingdom replica chair. She shoved her bag underneath, wiped sweat from her brow, and let out her breath in a whoosh.

The Gold Room was abuzz about her. Whereas most court sessions were quiet affairs conducted by a dozen bored functionaries scattered about an echoing throne room large enough to swallow a city block whole, today's session looked like nothing short of a full coronation. Red-clad palace guards, in full parade regalia, flanked every door. Loud, long-haired Eryans, all laughing and blustering and draining King Yvin's wine cellars with typical Eryan joviality, were seated amid and mingling with the quieter Tirlish folk. Everywhere, soldiers and nobles and servitors rushed and squeezed and darted about, lending the Gold Room the quality of a flower garden in a windstorm, with shades of red and brown and yellow and blue all set twirling in a sudden rush of air.

The three legendary Tables of the King, each made of polished cherry wood and capable of seating four hundred, were ringed round on three sides with chairs and guests. The tables were arrayed in a line before the throne, which rested on a knee-high dais at the far end of the Gold Room. A trio of Red Guards stood frozen at attention before the throne. The guards would not stand down until Yvin and his queen ascended the dais and bade them depart.

The Throne of Tirlin, Meralda knew, started out as a large oak chair. Just a chair, nothing more. At first.

Then King Pollof had added cushions and a bit of carving on the arms. Then King Lertinor had decided gold-worked dragons' heads looked imposing as a headrest, and King Adoft had added the clawed silver feet, and at some point it became customary for every king to add his own personal touch to what bore less and less resemblance to a seat of any kind, ceremonial or otherwise.

Meralda had once heard Yvin threaten to haul the throne off to a museum and have a reclining Phendelit reading chair brought in. In fact, Meralda could see the corner of a threadbare red seat cushion peeking out from behind the throne's clawed feet. And was that a dog-eared Alon mystery novel, wedged down between the arm and the seat?

Above the throne and the milling court, sunlight streamed in pastel shafts through the stained glass windows set high along the Gold Room's curving cathedral ceilings. The gently moving air, an innovation of Meralda's, smelled of cinnamon and faint perfumes, all circulated by dozens of quiet spark coil fans hidden behind screens below the windows.

The north wall windows were Meralda's favorite. Each depicted Tim the Horsehead's exploits against the Vonat wizard Corrus, and Tim's narrow triumph at the Battle of Romare. *I'm surprised Yvin didn't have masks glued over them,* thought Meralda. *But then, even Yvin isn't terribly worried about offending a handful of Vonats.*

Someone shouted, and the minstrels began to pipe and strum and arrange their music. Meralda smiled at the gentle sound of Phendelit harps and Tirlish violins and settled back. *At least there'll be a bit of music,* she thought. *It's been months since I've been to the symphony.*

The third trumpet blew. Meralda groaned and rose, with the rest of the court, resigned to remain standing until Yvin arrived and was seated.

Meralda gazed about a bit, searching for familiar faces. The king's tables, reserved for visiting Eryans and highly-placed Tirls, were full of strangers. But among those seated with her in the ranks of chairs behind the tables, Meralda found a few of her former professors from the college, a handful of familiar newspaper penswifts, the conductor of the Tirlin Philharmonic, and, of course, Sir Ricard Asp, who met her gaze with a barely concealed sneer.

A sudden mad scramble for chairs began. Conversation continued, though in hushed tones, and something in the frowns and the earnest gazes and the shaking heads nearby made Meralda wonder what she'd missed.

It isn't good news, she decided, as she caught a glimpse of the captain lost in whispered debate with a pair of frowning Red Guard lieutenants. Not good news at all.

A hand fell light upon her shoulder. "Aye, lass," spoke a man, his words buried in a familiar full tilt Eryan highland brogue. "It's time you took a husband, and it's time I took a wife. What do ye say, now? Shall we hire a piper and a hall?"

Meralda's breath caught in her throat. "Alas," she said, determined to keep her voice calm and level. "I vowed not to marry beneath myself, even for pity's sake. Surely you understand."

Before the man could answer, the brass-bound doors at the end of the Gold Room were flung open and King Yvin marched inside, Queen Pellabine on his arm.

The musicians struck up "Tirlin, Tirlin," the assembled court fell silent, and Meralda turned, smiling down at the fat, grey-headed Eryan standing behind her.

"Just as well," said the older man, his eyes merry, his mouth cocked in a crooked smile. "Everyone knows Tirlish women can't cook." The Eryan bowed deeply, winking at the shocked glares of those nearby.

Meralda shoved her chair aside and caught the old man up

in a long, fierce hug.

Shingvere of Wing, Mage to the Realm of Erya, patted Meralda on the back, then gently pushed her away. "Not in front of the old folks," he said, cheerily. "That can only lead to a lot of loose talk."

Meralda squeezed his hand, and the rotund Eryan squeezed back. "Do you know who I am?" he asked the gape-jawed Tirlish noble standing to Meralda's right.

The man stared and choked back a reply.

"Good," said Shingvere. "That's a nice chair you've got. I think I'll take it. Find another, won't you?"

Then he patted the man's shoulder, winked at Meralda, and sat.

The noble scurried away, peering back over his shoulder as if memorizing Shingvere's face and clothes for the guard.

"I've missed you," said Meralda, as the last strains of "Tirlin, Tirlin" began to fade. *I truly have,* she realized, surprised at the intensity of her emotion. The old wizard had never once treated her as a child, even when she'd first arrived at college. "I'd heard you were ill, and not planning to attend."

Shingvere smiled, but the music died and he did not speak.

Yvin stepped onto the dais and escorted Queen Pellabine to her own smaller but more comfortable throne, and the two were seated.

The rest of the court sat then, with a sound like lazy thunder.

"Lots of long faces," whispered Shingvere, as Yvin began to welcome the Eryans. "And I don't wonder. Have you heard the news?"

Meralda shook her head.

Shingvere grinned. "It's the Hang," he said. "They're here, sailing up the Lamp. Twenty of those Great Sea five-mast rigs. One of them is flying the Long Dragon flag."

"Are you joking?"

"I am not," said Shingvere. "The Hang are coming, all the way from the other side of the world. Chaos and discord abound." The fat wizard fumbled in his pockets and withdrew a sticky white stick of candy wrapped in a shiny red paper wrapper.

"Penny-stick?" he said.

"Penny-stick?"

"Stop pestering her with those atrocious jaw-breakers," said Thaumaturge Fromarch. "She's here to learn history, not bad eating habits."

Meralda—then Apprentice Ovis, barely out of the college, less than a year into her apprenticeship to Thaumaturge Fromarch—kept her eyes firmly fixed on page four hundred of Trout and Windig's A History of Tirlin and Erya and Environs, With Generous Illustration Throughout. She'd read the same passage a half-dozen times, and still could make no sense of it. No wonder, when all the mages did was bluster and argue.

"Bah," said Mage Shingvere, the round little Eryan. "You're wasting her time with that revisionist Tirlish history, Fromarch, and you know it. Look at this." Shingvere spun Meralda's book around, so he could read from it. "It says here that 'the Hang first appeared in the spring of 1072, and they've visited the Realms once a century since then'."

Fromarch sighed. "Hang visits have been well documented, even from the earliest days of the Old Kingdom."

"Bah!" said Shingvere, spinning the book back around to Meralda. "The Hang have been sneaking around since well before ten hundred, and they've bloody well been back more than once a century, and you're an idiot not to see it." Shingvere shook his finger at Meralda. "You're a smart one, lass, so you listen to old Shingvere. Read what's in your books. But don't ever forget that printing a thing doesn't make it true."

Mage Fromarch groaned and rubbed his forehead. "Spare us."

"The Hang have been watching us for more than a millennium," said Shingvere, quietly. "Ask any Eryan beach comber. Ask any Phendelit fisherman. I've got a scrap of paper with Hang scribbles on it in my study. Are you going to tell me it floated from Hang to Erya?" The Eryan snorted. "They're out there, closer than you think," he said. "And one day, miss, they're going to come sailing up the Lamp to stay. Mark my words, both of you. The Vonats may rattle their swords every twenty years or so, but the Hang are the real threat, Great Sea or not."

Mage Fromarch stood. "Apprentice Ovis," he said, to Meralda. "Our Eryan associate's outlandish ideas aside, we have a history lesson to discuss. Now then. How did the advent of the airship shape New Kingdom politics in the years before the Parting?"

Meralda shook her head. The answer to Mage Fromarch's question was obvious enough. But there, on the page, was a hand-drawn picture of a Hang warship, a ship that had done what no vessel of the Realms had ever done. It had crossed the Great Sea, and would do so again.

"They're up to no good," said Shingvere, softly. "Mark my words, Apprentice Ovis. No bloody good."

Meralda closed the book, but the crude drawing of the Hang five-master haunted her dreams for days.

Chapter Three

Meralda took Shingvere's penny-stick and, just as she had countless times as an apprentice, slipped it wordlessly in her pocket.

Yvin's voice faded to a drone. Unhearing, Meralda dreamily recalled the little towns and villages strewn haphazardly along the banks of the Lamp, and wondered what sort of bedlam was occurring as the towering masts of the Great Sea ships bore down upon the fisher folk.

Meralda shivered. The Hang. Sailing up the Lamp at last. *If, of course, that Eryan rascal beside me is to be believed.*

As if he'd heard, Shingvere caught Meralda's eye and nodded gravely, every hint of humor gone from his face.

Meralda sighed. *It's true, then.* For the first time in forty-five years the Hang have crossed the Great Sea, bound for Tirlin, practically on the eve of the Accords. No coincidence, that.

"He won't say a word, today," whispered Shingvere, with a nod toward King Yvin. "We'll all pretend it's a secret, till the papers get wind of it. After that, Thaumaturge, if I were you I'd consider exercising that legendary distance mages and thaumaturges have for courts."

"Would that I could," whispered Meralda.

Shingvere grinned. "And I'd tell old windbag there to leave the Tower's shadow be."

Heads turned toward the Eryan. "Shhhh," hissed a Tirlish courtier.

Shingvere made a gesture, and the man's hair stood suddenly on end.

"Shingvere!" said Meralda, as the wide-eyed courtier lifted his hands to his head.

Shingvere glared, and the man's hair fell. "Mind your manners," grumbled the Eryan.

Applause broke out as King Yvin bade the Eryan court to rise and be made welcome.

Shingvere rolled his eyes and remained seated. "I'm meeting Fromarch this evening," he whispered, as the applause died. "You'll come too, won't you? I'm sure the doddering old skinflint will have a supper meal of some poor sort."

Meralda nodded.

Shingvere grinned. "Good. You're old enough to have a pint with us now, you know. Never drank with a Tirlish woman before. Might be fun."

Again, applause rang out. Meralda caught sight of the captain's back as he slipped through the furthest west doors. Soon, three of the captain's staff and a handful of black-clad Secret Service officers followed.

Yvin's welcome speech droned on. Within moments, Shingvere was snoring.

Meralda settled into her chair, gazed up at the stained glass murals and Tim the Horsehead's toothy equine grin, and wondered just how he would have reacted to a fleet of Long Dragon five-masters sailing up the Lamp.

"Pardon, ma'am," said Kervis, "But what's a Long Dragon five-master?"

Their waiter hovered near, fussing with napkins and forks on a recently cleared table while he eavesdropped. Meralda brought her finger to her lips, and Kervis nodded and fell silent.

Orlo's sidewalk café was bustling. Diners were being seated on the knee-high walls of Orlo's sputtering three-tiered fountain, on the backs of parked cabs, on upturned milk buckets, and, in one instance, on a wrought-iron trolley-stop bench hauled away from the curb by a bevy of brawny Builder's Guild bricklayers. Waiters ducked and bobbed, arms laden with plates and drinks, their movements more dance than stride.

A trio of skinny black-clad bankers darted like crows for the empty table beside Meralda's. The waiter bade the newcomers welcome, promised them tea, and then, with a backward glance toward Meralda, he darted away.

"Sorry, ma'am," said Kervis.

"No matter," said Meralda. "It'll all be in the papers tomorrow anyway."

Meralda swallowed the last bite of her ham on rye and washed it down with ice-cold Phendelit day tea.

"A five-master," she said, wiping her chin, "is a ship. A Great Sea ship, half as long as the Tower is tall. The Long Dragon is the flag of the Chentze, which is the Hang equivalent of the house of a king."

The Bellringers simultaneously lifted their right eyebrows.

"Big ship," said Kervis.

Meralda took another long draught of her day tea. "They cross the Great Sea," she said. "I suppose they have to be."

Tervis frowned. "No one but the Hang has ever crossed the Great Sea," he said. "Is that right?"

"It is," said Meralda. "Eryans, Phendelits, us, the Vonats. Everyone has tried. But the ships either turn back, or vanish." Meralda put down her glass. "Current thinking holds that the sea extends at least twenty thousand miles from every coast," she said.

"Fly it," said Kervis, matter-of-factly. "Why not send an airship?"

"It's been tried," said Meralda. "The ones that made it back all told the same story. No land past the Islands. Not a speck. Just sea and storms and it goes on forever," she said. "That's a quote, from the master of the airship *Yoreland*. They were aloft for more than two months."

Tervis whistled. "Two months?"

Meralda nodded. "No one has tried since," she said. "At least, no one of the Realms."

Tervis shook his head. "These Hang," he said, after a furtive look around. "What do they want?"

Meralda wiped her hands on her napkin. "People have been asking that for nine hundred years, Tervis," she said. "I wish I knew."

The palace bells struck twice. Meralda covered her plate with her napkin, and after a moment, Kervis and Tervis did the same. Meralda smiled.

"Well, gentlemen," she said, as their red-haired Phendelit waiter appeared. "Time to go." She dropped a small silver coin into the waiter's hand and grinned into his astonished face. "A Hang fleet is heading for Tirlin," she whispered, as the man blushed furiously. "Fifty ships, each longer than five Towers and each laden with forty thousand four-armed, two-headed, venom-spitting half-wolf Hang warriors. When you tell the penswifts, do try to get the numbers right."

Kervis raced around to Meralda's side of the table and pulled her chair back. "You probably shouldn't mention the war dragons or the marching ogres, ma'am," he said. "Might cause a panic."

Meralda nodded solemn agreement, turned, and bade the Bellringers to follow. The Phendelit waiter watched for a moment, shook his head, and darted off to refill another round of tea glasses.

The Thaumaturgical Library buried deep within the palace cellars held little in the way of research concerning directed refraction. Instead, Meralda found page after page of intricate, improbable spellworks intended to render mages and kings invisible.

"Nonsense," she muttered, skimming past the last ten pages of an entry listed as "Mage Mellick's Wondrous Optical Void." Frowning, she decided the only thing this Mellick ever made vanish was a monthly portion of the crown's purse.

Disgusted, she rose, closed the heavy wood-bound volume, and padded barefoot on the cool stone floor back toward the library stacks. The foxfire she'd cast followed her, maintaining its station just above her left shoulder, sending shadows darting and bobbing down the long, high ranks of books arcane.

Boot steps sounded down the corridor outside the library, causing Meralda to frown until the footfalls turned and ended with the slamming of a door. She'd practically had to threaten the Bellringers to make them stay out of the library. The last thing she wanted now was an apprentice wizard from the college pestering her with sidelong looks and first-year questions.

Meralda shoved the heavy tome back into its place and stepped back. "Oh, for an index," she muttered. "Four thousand eight hundred volumes reaching back six hundred years and not a table of contents in the lot."

The library replied with silence and darkness. Meralda sighed, closed her eyes, and plucked another name from her memory. "Mage Heldin," she said aloud. "Thaumaturge to King Roark II. Originator of Heldin's Suspended Mirror. 1740, I think." Meralda stalked down the stacks, squinting at the dates embossed on the spine of each book.

Tirlin's history fled past. Meralda wondered what was hidden there, within the brittle pages. *Oh, rubbish, for the most part,* she mused, *but no doubt a few gems as well.*

"Perhaps even a shadow moving spell," she said aloud. "Or am I the first to try?"

Heldin. Meralda slowed, urged the foxfire brighter. 1738, 1739—1740. "Here you are," she said, pulling the book gently out of the chest-high shelf and brushing away the worst of the dust and spider webs. "Let's see if you were worth looking for."

Pages crackled as they turned. Page One contained a faded but still legible *List of Works, With Page Numbers*. Meralda smiled and began to read, ticking off spells as she went. "Spinning Colored Lights" held little interest, as it was merely a simple variation of the foxfire charm that hung above her shoulder. But what was "Seeing in Circles"?

Meralda turned fragile pages and returned to her desk. Part of her mind wrestled with Mage Heldin's abysmal penmanship, but the rest was occupied with Hang five-masters.

In nineteen days Tirlin will be crowded with the royal houses of all the Five Realms. The Phendelit king, The Alon queen, the regent of Vonath, the king of Erya. All together, all vulnerable. Meralda frowned.

Tirlin had burned, once. In 1660, Meralda recalled. Parts of the palace still bore the scars. Meralda had a vision of Fleethorse Street engulfed in flames, wondered why she should think such a thing, and was suddenly chilled to the bone.

Mage Heldin's "Seeing in Circles" spell proved to be a crude method of momentarily freezing a hand-drawn image in a red-hot brass ring. Meralda sighed, stretched until her back and shoulders made popping noises, and put her chin down in her hands. Row after row of shadowed, dusty books stared back.

It appears, she said silently to herself, *that I am on my own.*

Someone knocked softly at the library door. "Ma'am," said Kervis. "Five bells. You said to fetch you, and remind you about supper with the mages."

Meralda closed Mage Heldin's book and rose. "Coming,

Guardsman," she said, her voice sudden and loud in the stillness of the library. "Coming."

She found her stockings, slipped them on, and pulled her boots on before returning the life work of one Mage Heldin, Thaumaturge to King Roark II, to its long vigil amid the dusty shelves.

Mage Fromarch, former Thaumaturge to the Kingdom of Tirlin, met Meralda on the porch of his tiny, ivy-covered red brick house.

Fromarch was gaunt. He'd been gaunt the day Meralda met him, five years before. His long, pale face with its wide-set grey eyes and hawkish nose and thin small mouth always looked tired, and perhaps a little sad. Meralda knew the last, at least, to be untrue. The real Fromarch, the one behind the long unsmiling face, always wore an impish grin.

Fromarch wore loose brown trousers and soft leather house shoes, the toes spotted with chemical burns and tiny spatters of molten metals. His white shirt bore a singe-mark in the center, the exact shape of an iron.

"Ho there, 'prentice," he said, thrusting forth a bent ladle at Meralda before she mounted the last unswept porch step. "Taste this."

Meralda took the spoon. Its bowl steamed, filled with a thick, meaty stew that smelled of onions, beef, and green bell peppers, though it was obviously far too hot to taste.

Meralda blew gently on the spoon and smiled. Fromarch didn't smile back but his scowl did soften, and his wet grey eyes neither narrowed nor blazed when they met hers.

"Mage," said Meralda. "I've missed you."

"Hmmph." snorted Fromarch. "You've got better sense than most, Mage Meralda. You taste this and tell certain upstart Eryan wand-wavers that we Tirlish folk know best how to season a bit of stew."

Fromarch jerked his thumb behind him as he spoke, and Shingvere opened Fromarch's screeching screen door far enough to poke his head outside.

"Good evening, Lady," he said to Meralda. "Since the master of the house has no better manners than to accost guests on his porch with over salted stew, allow me to invite you inside. Mind the rotting carcasses, now, and don't step into the trash pit."

Meralda brought the spoon to her lips and tasted. "Well?" boomed Fromarch.

Meralda smiled. "It's quite good," she said. Fromarch whirled and snorted in triumph.

Shingvere flung the door open wide. "Now you've done it, Apprentice," he said to Meralda, with a wink. "You've gone and agreed with him, and he'll spend hours strutting and preening." The aging wizard shook his head. "We can only hope he drinks to excess and lapses into quiet slumber before the evening is ruined."

Meralda laughed, stepped onto the porch, and gently took Fromarch by the sleeve of his plain white shirt. "Come inside, both of you," she said, handing Shingvere the stew spoon. "You know that elderly gentlemen are prone to crankiness if they miss their evening gruel."

Shingvere crowed, and Fromarch nearly smiled, and from its burnished copper stand by the door Fromarch's staff snickered audibly. "Quiet, you backscratcher," said Fromarch.

Meralda stepped inside, took both wizards by their elbows, and marched them toward Fromarch's kitchen.

After a long supper of summer stew and a thick butterscotch pudding prepared by Shingvere, Fromarch led his guests into his sitting room, opened all three windows, and bade everyone to sit and drink. An icebox of Nolbit's Dark was dragged in from the pantry, and for the first time in her life Meralda drank ice-chilled Eryan ale and swapped gossip, mage to mage.

Talk began with the story of the Vonat spy caught red-handed and nearly frozen in the mail-hold of an Alon courier airship, a sheaf of coded papers sewn into his jacket. Shingvere then recounted the troubles facing the Alon queen and the blood feud between Clan Morar and Clan Glenoch. "Look close enough and you'll see a Vonat in their midst," said Shingvere. Fromarch merely snorted, observed airily that far too many Eryans spent far too much time seeing things that weren't there, and changed the subject to talk of the near-completion of the railroad that would soon link Phendeli to Kendle.

"But here we are, two old gaffers doddering on about roads and boats when we ought to be talking about the lovely young lady in our midst," said Shingvere, as he handed Meralda another bottle of Nolbit's. "So tell us about the Tower, Mage Meralda," he said. "Seen the haunt, have you?"

Meralda groaned. "Please," she said. "Not that. Anything but that."

Fromarch, from his shadowed repose in his enormous Phendelit reclining chair, guffawed. "Oh, he's always believed in haunts and the like," he said. "Can't blame him, really, given the standards of education in dear old Erya."

Shingvere ignored the jibe. "'Tis true I spent a whole summer chasing the Tower shade," he said. "Back in—oh, 1967, it was. Did you know that?"

Meralda blinked. "I didn't," she said. No more Nolbit's, she decided. Her legs and arms were getting heavy, while her head seemed light and wobbly.

She sank back into Fromarch's couch, pulled a small copper funnel from behind the small of her back, and relaxed again.

"Nobody does," said Fromarch, after a sip of beer and a sigh. "Too bloody embarrassing. If the Exchequer found out we'd spent from the crown's purse on a spook hunt, we'd have been put out on our heads, and rightly so."

Meralda frowned. "Were you a part of this, Mage?" she asked.

"Reluctantly," Fromarch growled. "I was to make sure our Eryan friend didn't mistake flying squirrels for long-dead wizards." Fromarch leaned forward, so that his short ring of thin white hair and pale cheekbones shone faintly in the dim, slanting rays of the setting sun streaming lazily through the window.

"The ghost hunt, of course, was nonsense," he began.

"Aye, but people were seeing lights in the Wizard's Flat," said Shingvere, quickly. "Reliable people. Guardsmen. Reporters.

Even," he said, after a pause and a grin, "a noted Tirlish Thaumaturge."

Meralda shook her head to clear it. "You?" she asked Fromarch, incredulous. "You saw something?"

Fromarch snorted. "I saw lights in the Wizard's Flat," he said. "Once. Just lights, nothing more. Could have been kids with a lantern."

Meralda thought about the long, long climb to the Wizard's Flat, and the locked door at the top.

"These were clever, determined children," said Shingvere. "Aye, one might even say brilliant, since the Tower, that evening, was locked, sealed with wards, and under heavy guard by no fewer than two dozen watchmen." Shingvere assumed a pose of mock concentration. "In fact, I recall someone, I'm not sure who, making a grand proclamation early that very evening that no human being could possibly enter the Tower, that night. Who was that, I wonder?"

Fromarch emptied his bottle and put it down with a thump. "Lights at a window do not prove the existence of haunts," he said. "Neither did you, I recall, despite a whole three months of fussing about with magnetometers and radial thaumeters and that bloody heavy wide-band scrying mirror," he added. "My back still aches, some days, from carrying that thing up and down those stairs while you pretended to fiddle with the holdstones."

Shingvere held up his hand. "Aye. You're correct," he said. "I found nothing." The little wizard fixed his eyes on Meralda's. "Perhaps, though, I just wasn't looking with the right pair of eyes."

"Bah," snorted Fromarch. He waved a finger at the Eryan. "We both know that the lights, if they weren't reflections off the window glass, were nothing but a residual discharge from some old structural spell."

Shingvere shrugged. Meralda remembered the laughter on the stair and shivered and took another cold draught of Fromarch's beer.

"Bah," said Fromarch again. "So how are you going to go about moving the Tower shadow, Thaumaturge?" he asked.

Meralda wiped her lips. "Directed refraction," she said. Shingvere slapped his knee.

"Told you!" he crowed. Fromarch scowled.

"He thought you'd hang those spark lights of yours from scaffolds and aim them at the ground," said Shingvere. "I told him they weren't bright enough, and if they were they'd be too hot."

Meralda nodded. "I'm working on cooler, brighter lights," she said. "But that could take months. Months I won't get, with Yvin wasting my time at every turn."

"Spoken like a mage, lass!" said Shingvere. The Eryan donned a wicked smile. "Now you see why I spend so much time away from Erya and that blatherskite queen. She'd have me whiling away the hours as a magic carpet cleaner, you mark my words."

Fromarch snorted. "So instead you come to Tirlin and chase ghosts," he said, lifting his bottle. "Another college education, gone sadly to waste."

Shingvere grinned. "Will you be latching your refraction

spell to the Tower itself?" he asked.

"Of course," said Meralda. "The focal volume will be just below the ceiling of the Wizard's Flat." She tilted her head. "If, that is, your ghosts won't mind."

Shingvere nodded gravely. "Oh, I don't think they will," he said. "But I'd ask them nicely first, all the same. No harm in being polite, is there?"

"No harm in being a soft-headed old fool, either," muttered Fromarch. He leaned back into the shadows. "But do have a care latching spells to the Tower," he said. "We had a devil of a time, way back when."

"Aye," Shingvere said. "The structural spellworks left a residual charge. New spells tend to unlatch, after a short time. Even old skinny there had trouble working around it."

Fromarch began to snore. Shingvere yawned and rose from his settee, padding quickly across the dimly lit room toward Meralda. "Well," he said, smiling. "Just like old times. Seems we young folks need to put the oldsters to bed."

Shingvere offered his hand, and Meralda took it, and rose. "It's good to have you two back," she said, in a whisper. "I've been worried about him, since he retired. He used to come around, but lately..."

"He doesn't want you to feel like you're still working in his shadow," replied Shingvere. "He's really not such a bad old fellow, once you get to know him. And I'm sure he wouldn't mind a bit of company here, now and then."

Meralda nodded. *I'll make the time,* she vowed. *Yvin can deal with it in any way he pleases.*

Shingvere grinned. "That's my 'prentice," he said. Fromarch began to mumble restlessly.

"I'll see you at court, I'm sure," said Shingvere. "Tomorrow. But for now, we should all get some sleep. News of the Hang will break tomorrow, and that will make for a very long day of hand-wringing and useless conjecture."

Meralda groaned softly and rose. Shingvere took her hand, and the pair tip-toed, giggling and stumbling, through Fromarch's darkened sitting room.

Meralda gathered her light cloak from the rack on the wall and stepped outside. Angis and his coach sat in the dim red glow of a gas lamp. Angis' cabman's hat slumped over his eyes, and his chest rose and fell in perfect time with Fromarch's snores.

Shingvere laughed. "Looks like we're the only ones left awake," he said.

"Good night," said Meralda, struggling to regain her composure. "It's been a lovely evening." She shook her head to clear it, letting the cool night air wash over her face.

Shingvere bowed. "Aye, lass, that it has," he said. "Would that I were thirty years younger."

Meralda returned his bow. "You've been an old bachelor all your life," she said. "But I love you anyway, you rascal of an Eryan wand-waver."

Then she turned and darted for the cab. Shingvere laughed and bowed and watched her go. He waved once to Angis as the cabman snapped his reins. Then he turned back to the door and Fromarch's lightless sitting room.

Inside, Fromarch stirred. "She gone?" he asked.

"Gone," said Shingvere, settling into a chair and fumbling in the dark for his pipe pouch.

Fromarch muttered a word, and a light blazed, slow and gentle, from a point below the center of the ceiling.

"Thank you," said Shingvere, filling the bowl of a blackened, ancient Phendelit wood pipe. "May I?"

"Please do," said Fromarch. A flame appeared at Shingvere's fingertip, and he lit his pipe with it.

"She's in for a bad summer," said Shingvere, after a moment of sucking at the pipe stem. "The Hang. The Tower. The Vonats."

Fromarch nodded. "Vonats are sending that new wizard of theirs. Humindorus Nam. Mean piece of work."

"So I hear," said Shingvere. "Think the stories are true?"

Fromarch snorted. "Every other word, if that," he said. Then he frowned. "Still. Met him once, years ago, outside Volot. Don't ask what I was doing there."

"I won't," said Shingvere. "Mainly because I've known for years, but go ahead."

"Met him then," said Fromarch, squinting back as if across the years. "Called himself just Dorous, then. Mad, he was. Twisted up inside. Didn't figure he'd last long enough to be a danger to anybody but himself."

Shingvere pulled his pipe from between his lips. "He's still a danger to himself, I'll wager," he said. "Pity is, he might be a danger to Mage Ovis, too. We can always hope a manure cart runs over him first, but I don't think that's likely."

Fromarch grunted. "She's smarter than both of us put together," he said, gruffly. "She can take care of herself. And Nam too, if need be."

Shingvere nodded. "Of course, of course," he said. "After all, it's bad form for one wizard to interfere in the matters of another. She'd be furious, and rightly so."

"Simply isn't done," said Fromarch, shaking his finger. "Breech of professional etiquette. Runs counter to everything we taught her."

Shingvere wedged his pipe in the corner of his mouth and settled deeper into his chair. "Glad that's settled, then," he said. "So, which lot do you want to interfere with? The Vonat or the Hang?"

Fromarch dimmed the foxfire, conjured up a fresh-rolled Alon cigar, and broke into a sudden, awful grin.

Chapter Four

Morning broke for Meralda as it always did, with the sound of the five-twenty trolley gasping and groaning its way past while that devil of a trolley master banged madly away at his brass bell at each and every deserted, windswept corner.

Meralda gritted her teeth and strangled her pillow until the trolley rattled away. Then, within an instant, the paperboys began to sing.

"Hang fleet on the Lamp!" one cried. "Two pence for the *Post*! Two pence for the Hang!"

Mug awoke, demanding news. Meralda drowsily recounted Shingvere's revelation of the Hang, bade Mug ruminate in silence, and threw back her covers.

The morning sun was bright, and it set her head to pounding. Still, she rose, rummaged for fresh clothes, and bathed. Her coffee urn was still empty, but the Bellringers, when they arrived, bore coffee and a bag of warm donuts, fresh from Flayne's. At her cab, Angis provided Meralda with a sheaf of just read, but neatly folded, early edition papers.

Meralda settled into her seat and unfolded the morning papers. Tervis, seated across from her, had the rare good sense to be silent while she read.

"Hang Fleet–Arrival or Invasion?" screamed the *Times*. The *Post* was calmer. Meralda noted with approval at no point in the article did the word invasion appear, but the sidebar detailing the dates and summaries of past Hang visits did hint that this latest incursion was the culmination of five centuries of stealthy surveillance.

Angis bellowed at a trolley and lurched to a halt at Weigh. A pair of hotel bellhops ran past, hats in hand, shouting at each other as they darted ahead of Angis and the trolley.

Meralda finished her coffee. The morning air was crisp, and, since the wind was from the north, it lacked the stench of the stockyards south of the college. Tervis caught her eye and grinned, and Meralda found herself smiling back.

"I know there's Hang afoot, ma'am, but it is a lovely day, isn't it?" he said.

The cab charged ahead. Meralda nodded, and Tervis turned away, his eyes on Tirlin. Meralda shuffled papers and continued to read.

The back pages of the papers held news only slightly less alarming than the Hang. The Phendelit delegation had sent word to the palace that they would be arriving two days early. Possibly even later that same day, Meralda realized with a shock.

Not to be outdone, the Alons had also sent word ahead. Hang or no Hang, they were determined to make Tirlin on schedule. "We welcome our friends from across the Great Sea," the Alon queen was quoted as saying. "We only hope to arrive in time to compose ourselves before we meet."

Meralda frowned at the latest statement by the Vonats. They ignored the arrival of the Hang, stating instead that due to the deplorable condition of the Eryan roadways in southern Fonth they would be delayed, placing their arrival three days hence. The unnamed Vonat spokesman also offered to give the Eryans lessons in modern road building as an expedient to further cultural exchanges.

Meralda folded the *Post* and imagined the turmoil that must be transpiring in the Gold Room. Any one of the calamities could be handled. Indeed, any one disaster was, aside from the Hang arrival, expected. But all taken together?

As the cab rolled to a halt by the palace gates, Meralda almost felt sorry for Yvin.

The palace was abuzz. The wide, carpeted halls were thick with guardsmen and nobles and Eryans and penswifts, all marching determinedly to and fro. Except, Meralda noted, for the penswifts, who tended to lurk in corners before leaping out at distracted court members.

Meralda had to wait for admittance at the doors, and once inside she had to practically shoulder her way through the hall to the foot of the west stair.

A penswift, not one she recognized, charged up the west stair behind her, calling out "Thaumaturge! A moment, please!"

Meralda didn't slow, nor did she look back, but the Bellringer's treads halted, and the penswift's cries came no closer.

Meralda smiled and climbed serenely up the stair. At the top, she found her key, opened the laboratory doors, and stepped quickly inside. She dropped the papers in a heap by the door.

The *Times* fell face-up, displaying the words "Hang Invasion" in tall black letters.

A single flickering gas lamp lit the laboratory. Tiny hints of movement played about the shadows, and though Meralda knew they were merely reflections of the gas lamp on various reflective surfaces she couldn't help but be reminded of tiny hands waving.

Meralda kicked the paper flat and unlatched the ward spell with a word and a pat on the polished copper globe that sat atop her biggest spark coil apparatus.

The ward spell collapsed. Papers rustled throughout the laboratory, fluttering and waving in the still air as if blown by a sudden gust of wind. The big old scrying mirror bolted to the middle of the east wall flashed, bright and brief, behind the blanket Meralda kept hung over the glass.

"Lights," said Meralda, when the ward spell static discharge faded.

A pair of head-high spark coils surrounded by a cage of shiny copper bars whined and crackled in the corner. On the high stone ceiling two dozen glass rings flickered, brightened, and filled the windowless laboratory with soft white light.

"Music," she said, and from the clutter of bisected brass globes and wire-wound glass tubes heaped on a work bench just beside the door came the soft strains of an Alon violin.

"Miracles," she muttered. The big old scrying mirror pulsed blue behind its blanket, and a few of her more intelligent instruments make querulous chirps, but nothing else occurred.

Meralda sighed, and gazed around. She stood in the midst of what was arguably the best equipped, and certainly the oldest, magical research facility in the Realms. She could take two steps and put her hands on old Phillitrep's Mathematical Calculating Engine, which was still working, gears and rods awhirl, three hundred years after commencing calculations for Phillitrep's last "little" problem. She could walk to the rear of the room and, along the way, stand beneath the tall, gleaming bulk of Arkot's Walking Barge, touch the carefully folded fabric of the very first gas-filled airship, or watch the prototype of Lafrint's Steam Motor hiss and turn its heavy steel axles.

Eyes, some of steel and glass, others of stone and iron, turned and fixed themselves upon Meralda. Imeck's Pondering Noggin winked at her, and she waved idly back at it. Tarmore's Watcher blinked at her, and a moment later Meralda heard the steady scratching of a mechanical pen drawing her likeness on the same scrap of parchment she'd fed the machine months ago. All about the shelves and alcoves of the laboratory, lightning danced, caught in the glass of this or the coils of that. Some of the devices were only half finished, some so old their names and purposes were long forgotten. Still, Meralda could not look upon them without thinking that the least of them held wonders, or the keys to wonders.

Meralda turned her eyes from the ranks of intricate devices. She stalked to her desk, snatched up a fresh sheet of architect's paper, and began to draw the Tower.

Meralda heard voices beyond the door. One was Tervis. One was not. When she heard her name called Meralda put down her pencil and stretched. *Time for a break anyway,* she thought. She counted rings on the face of Opp's Rotary Timekeeper. Ten of the clock, and high time for a snack.

Meralda rose as Tervis began to knock. "Pardon, Thaumaturge," he said. "Urgent summons from the crown. May we have a word?"

Meralda winced. *Urgent summons from the crown,* she thought. *Those have to be my least favorite words.*

Meralda threw the door open, stepping back as she did. A trio of grim-faced, black-clad palace guards stood between Kervis and Tervis.

"Pardon, Thaumaturge," said the tallest of the guards. "You are required upstairs. Immediately. The king is waiting."

The guard, a stony-faced sergeant perhaps ten years older than Meralda, lowered his voice.

"I don't know what's happening, Thaumaturge," he said, before Meralda could speak. "But the captain told me to tell you to bring whatever you'll need to seek out foreign sorcery."

"Foreign sorcery?" asked Meralda.

The guard nodded.

A door slammed down the hall, and the sound of booted feet in a hurry followed.

Meralda lifted a finger. "One moment," she said, and spun.

Foreign sorcery. She darted past her desk, snatched her light staff from its hooks on the wall, found her black bag and put a fresh glass and copper holdstone in the pouch sewn into the side.

"Confound, dissuade, confuse," she mumbled, latching the ward spell with words since her hands were full.

The spark coils flared, the glow tubes died, and the doors closed softly behind her.

"Let's go," she said. The palace guards headed for the stair.

Meralda followed, the Bellringers close behind.

"What's happened?" asked Tervis, as a trio of regular red-clad army troopers charged up the west stair, causing Meralda and her party to squeeze to one side.

The palace guards exchanged glances. "Don't know," said the sergeant. "The captain just said to fetch the thaumaturge."

Another trio of army troopers charged past at the base of the stair. At the Burnt Door, five troopers stood fast, confusion evident on their faces and their hands near their sword hilts.

Beyond the Burnt Door, the hall was empty. Meralda counted doors as she sped past—eight, nine, and ten. The palace guards halted, one knocked, and after a low exchange of words the door opened.

The captain emerged. "Thaumaturge," he said. Then he turned to the palace guardsmen. "Lieutenant Heathers is patrolling the north wing apartments," he said. "Join him there."

The guards trotted away, and the captain motioned Meralda and the Bellringers inside.

Meralda had seen the door before. Two doors past the kitchen, four before the entrance to the Gold Room. *It's a storage room,* she thought. For the chairs and folding tables sometimes used at banquets, when the King's Tables weren't sufficient.

Frowning, she crossed the threshold. The room was dark, until the door shut behind Kervis.

Light flared, revealing a small, narrow room perhaps twice the length of Meralda's apartment. Another door stood in the center of the far wall; other than that, the room was bare.

Bare, yet not empty. His Highness, Yvin II, son of Histel, Lord of the House of Yvin, stood glowering at Meralda from perhaps five long steps away. Beside the king stood his queen, her eyes narrowed. *Yvin might be glowering,* thought Meralda, *but the queen is quite ready for an old-fashioned round of murder.*

Five Red Guards stood close by, short swords drawn. Another was stationed by the door Meralda had just entered.

The captain moved to stand before the king.

"We've had a visitor, Thaumaturge," said the captain.

Meralda frowned. Details of the room's construction were becoming obvious in the dim light. The doors were made of iron. Solid iron, with wood over the outer face. Those bumps on the walls weren't nail heads, but rivets.

"This is a siege retreat?"

"Aye," growled Yvin. He balled his hands into fists, and glared at the captain. "An iron-plated rat-hole, where frightened monarchs might hide. Siege retreat!" His voice rose to a bellow. "He was only one man!"

The captain bowed. "Indeed, Majesty," he said, with a glance toward Meralda. "One man. One man who walked through the palace gates and past twenty-seven guard stations without being stopped, signed, or even, as far as I can tell, seen."

Meralda put her bag down.

"He walked into the Gold Room," said the captain. "Walked up to the king's brunch table, introduced himself as envoy to the House of Chentze, and asked permission to enter Tirlin."

More mindful of the queen's glare than anything else, Meralda permitted herself no more reaction than to lift an eyebrow. "I see," she said, after a moment of what she hoped seemed careful reflection. "What, pray tell, were this person's exact words, as Your Highnesses recall them?"

The queen spoke. "'Greetings,'" she said, her voice icy. "'I am envoy to the House of Chentze, sent before my House to beg right of entry and stay from the House of Yvin.'"

Meralda fought to hide her bewilderment. *Never before has a Hang asked for such a thing,* she thought. The Hang's words had the ring of ritual to them. What ritual, though, Meralda could not say.

"And what did Your Highness reply?" asked Meralda.

Before Yvin could speak, the queen took hold of his arm and squeezed. "The king bade him welcome," she said, pride in her voice. "He finished his tea and put his cup down and bade him welcome, and enter, and stay, just as if Hang wizards interrupted our brunch every other Furlday." The queen smiled, and Meralda realized that Yvin was actually blushing.

The captain shook his head. "There were probably two hundred people in the Gold Room, Thaumaturge," he said. "Fifty of them soldiers. Ten of them my men. One of them me. And no one but the Highnesses saw the Hang until he turned and began to walk away."

Yvin snorted. "He's a wizard, Captain," he said. "Don't fault yourself for not seeing through a foreign caster's spells." The king looked through bushy eyebrows at Meralda. "That's where the thaumaturge here comes in."

Meralda kept her face impassive. "You want me to find this Hang," she said. *How,* she thought, *does one look for an invisible man?*

"We want you to find his trail," said the captain. "He must have used sorcery to conceal his movements, until he reached the king. He must have used sorcery to leave. If, indeed, he is gone."

"He's gone," said Yvin, softly. "He said what he came to say, and he left. I'm sure of it."

"I am not," said the queen, still gripping Yvin's arm. "He found his way into the Gold Room. Why not our chambers? What is to stop him?"

"I am," said the captain. He turned toward Meralda. "If he used sorcery, can you find it?"

Meralda took a breath.

"Of course she can," said Yvin, before Meralda could speak. "But she can't do it locked away in this iron-plated hidey-hole. You, there," barked the king, at a round-eyed Red Guard. "Bring us some chairs. And you," added the king to Meralda. "You go find this Hang wand-waver's trail."

Meralda picked up her bag. "Yes," she said aloud, while inside she seethed. *Oh, yes,* she thought. *I'll just find the foreign magics, I will. After all, Hang spells are only the products of an arcane science probably older and certainly much different from our own. How bloody hard could it be to find traces of a thing you've never seen before, especially if the spellcaster took pains to conceal his passage?*

A pair of guards pulled the doors to the hallway open. The captain motioned Kervis and Tervis out.

"Go with the thaumaturge, Captain," said the king.

"Sire—"

"Go with the thaumaturge," repeated the king. "We'll be fine. Go."

The door closed.

Kervis and Tervis, their matched eyes wild, looked to each other and then to Meralda. The captain, his grizzled face ruddy, looked toward her, too.

"What do you need?" asked the captain.

Meralda bit back a word Angis seemed fond of, when the traffic masters failed to suit him.

"I need to follow our visitor's route," she said, instead. "Show me where he went. From the first time this Hang was seen, to the time I presume he vanished in a puff of fog. Show me all of it. Quickly." She put her bag on the floor. "Tervis," she said.

Tervis jumped. "Yes, ma'am," he said, straightening.

"Take my bag, if you will," she said. "I need both hands for my staff."

"Yes, ma'am."

"That way," growled the captain, pointing down the hall, toward the west door entrance to the Gold Room. "No one saw him, of course, but I suspect he walked right through the west doors, regal as a lord."

Meralda nodded. "We'll need to check all doors, Captain, but we'll start with this one." She motioned him forward. "If you please?"

The captain turned and stamped off down the hall, his boots making dull thumps in the thick Rist Hill carpet. Meralda followed, the Bellringers close behind.

Her fingers traced a small pattern on the staff's center, and when the black wood grew cold Meralda whispered the first three syllables of a word. The spell unlatched, but not completely. It tugged at the wood, leaving Meralda with the impression that she was forcing the staff through a vat of molasses.

The staff's movements were random and unfocused. If a spell had been released nearby, the staff would be repelled by even the faintest leavings, thus allowing Meralda to at least guess the spellcaster's position and perhaps his skill.

Instead, she found nothing. *Not that I expected anything different,* thought Meralda. *I can think of half a dozen ways to confound such a search. So, I'm sure, can others.*

The captain stopped at the door and lifted his eyebrows at the sight of Meralda's lazily swooping staff. "Anything?" he asked.

"Nothing yet," she replied. The captain threw open the west doors, bellowed at the guards on the other side, and stepped into the throne room.

Meralda followed, holding the staff gingerly at its center as she passed over the threshold, feeling for even the slightest hint of steady pressure.

"Nothing," she muttered. The Gold Room was empty. Tables and chairs were strewn about, some overturned, some in stacks, as though workmen had been called away in a panicked rush. A crystal pitcher of water sat on a table nearby, and the water still rose and fell slightly, lapping at the top as if recently disturbed. "Nothing at all."

The captain grunted. Meralda halted. "Where was the king seated?" she asked.

"Over there," said the captain, pointing across the Gold Room to one of the small, plain tables scattered about the northeast corner of the room. "The Highnesses had missed breakfast, what with all the goings-on, and Yvin had the porters set up a brunch here." The captain frowned and raised his hands. "This wasn't planned, Thaumaturge. No one knew where the king was going to be at nine of the clock today. And yet he walked right up—"

Meralda shrugged. "Even so," she said. "But if one were looking for a king, the throne room seems to be a likely place to begin one's search, does it not?"

"He may have wandered about for hours, if he was invisible," said Tervis. The captain's neck went crimson, and the color began to creep up his face.

"He was never invisible," said Meralda, quickly.

"Then how did he just walk into the Gold Room?" said the captain.

Meralda wheeled her staff back and forth before her. "How many people were in this room, Captain?" she asked.

"Two hundred and eighty-six," said the captain. "Not counting myself, the Highnesses, the Eryan ambassador who was seated with them, and forty-four of my lads, spread all about the place. They're all being held in the big conference room on the second floor while we take their statements."

Meralda slowly started for the table the captain had pointed out. The staff continued to wobble and float, though it detected no hint of sorcery, foreign or otherwise.

Meralda bit her lip. *This isn't going to work,* she thought. "Captain," she said, and then the staff swung about, as though struck. When it halted, the ends were level with the floor, the shaft lay in a straight line between the west doors and the king's brunch table, and the wood was growing cold to Meralda's touch.

The captain halted. "Thaumaturge?" he said.

"Hush a moment," said Meralda. She took a deep breath, closed her eyes, and forced her perceptions out along the faint traceries of the faded spell she'd found.

The spell was faint. "Faint as smoke from yesterday's fire," Mage Fromarch had once said. Meralda found the phrase doubly fitting, as she tried to make sense of the twisting debris.

There, she thought. *And there.* Anchor points, and common enough. But what were those structures out along the periphery? Meralda frowned. The more she searched for the terminal ends of the operative functions, the more it seemed they looped back to the latching point.

Meralda pushed again, and her staff grew so cold the air about it steamed. The smoke-like remains of the spell vanished in a flash that Meralda saw clearly through her tightly shut eyes.

"Thaumaturge!" bellowed the captain, and at least one of the Bellringers. Boots thudded on the Gold Room tiles.

Meralda opened her eyes, blinked at the dots that swam before her, and dropped her staff before it froze tight to her hands.

"I'm not harmed," she said, at the blurs that approached. "Don't touch my staff."

"What happened?" asked the captain. "Were you attacked?"

"I thought I saw a twinkling in the air," said Tervis.

"Me, too," said Kervis. "Ma'am."

Meralda struggled to make out faces. "My bag, please," she said, at what she hoped was Tervis. "Open it, if you will."

Tervis fumbled with the latches. "Here," he said. "What happened? Did you find something?"

"I did," said Meralda. She fumbled in the bag's recesses for a pair of heavy copper-lined gloves, blinking furiously while she decided which was left and which was right. "Someone cast a spell here, recently," she said. "A very strange spell."

The captain frowned. "Can you tell what it did?"

Meralda shook her head. "Someone didn't want me to know," she said. "They even left a surprise for anyone who looked." She held up her right hand, anticipating the captain's next words. "No, the caster is not still here. No, I can't tell you if it was a Hang spell. Yes, it might have been a charm of concealment. And no, I'm not hurt."

The dancing blobs of light were fading. She could see clearly enough now. The Bellringers stood close by, watching her intently, concern mirrored on their faces. The captain, too, watched Meralda as if expecting her to fall into a swoon at any moment.

Meralda pulled on the gloves and snatched up her staff. It still trailed steam, and its shaft was rimed with a thin layer of dull ice.

"Come, gentlemen," she said. "It's a big palace."

Chapter Five

Meralda sat heavily at her kitchen table, a steaming mug of fresh coffee in her hand. Cool air breezed past, drawn in at the open kitchen window and leaving through the sitting room. A clock ticked softly in Meralda's bedroom, and in the distance traffic hooted and clattered, but for midday in Tirlin, Fairlane Street was quiet. "It's good to be home," said Meralda.

From his perch in the kitchen windowsill, Mug spread his fronds to the sun. "Indeed, it is," he said, his words slow and hushed. Ten of Mug's eyes, the smaller brown ones, studied the thaumaturge intently from behind a screen of leaves.

Mug decided the thaumaturge looked tired, but not particularly angry. Her long red hair stuff was windblown, but not tangled into what Meralda called a fright, and the skin on her forehead wasn't shiny with sweat. Her eyes were clear and bright, lacking the dark bands beneath them that so often appeared after a day at court.

The dandyleaf plant relaxed, his upmost leaves drooping in relief. *At least that blockheaded king hasn't insulted her today.*

"Now that you've done your shopping and made yourself comfortable," said Mug, "you can tell your poor neglected familiar what you've been up to, and why I see so many soldiers in the streets."

Meralda relayed her day at the palace to Mug, who gradually turned all of his eyes upon the thaumaturge. "You found how many hidden spells?" said Mug.

"Eight," said Meralda. "One in the Gold Room, two in the west wing, three in the fourth floor guest hall, one in the High Garden, and one just outside the Old Stair fifth floor landing." Meralda swirled her coffee and watched the steam rise up. "Eight recently unlatched spellworks," she said. "All of them set to discharge if discovered, all remnants of extremely powerful spells." She took another sip of coffee. "All laid within the last two weeks."

Mug bunched his eyes together in a frown. "Two weeks?" he said. "But the Hang only just arrived."

Meralda shrugged. "Nevertheless, the traces were fresh, but not new. Also, each spell was laid days apart. Even if you laid one every other day, that's two weeks."

All of Mug's green eyes looked into all of his brown ones. "The spells," he said. "What were they? What did they do?"

Meralda sighed. "I don't know," she said. "I simply couldn't tell." She put down her cup and ran her fingers through her hair. "They may have been unlatched, but still awaiting a trigger," she said. "Or they may have already fulfilled their purpose, and were merely debris. I can't be sure."

"Debris? And it froze your staff solid?" Mug's fronds tossed as if in a wind. "Mistress, if that's debris, I'm an oak. Someone meant to hurt you."

Meralda recalled the blinding flash of the first spell. She'd blocked it, the next seven times. But had her focus been closer in the Gold Room, she might have been blinded, first sight and second.

"What I don't understand," said Meralda, "is how anyone managed to unlatch such potent spells in the palace at all. You couldn't hand cast them, and you certainly couldn't just latch such spells to a wand, or anything small enough to get past the guards. There isn't enough latching mass."

Mug snorted. "Well, it follows that an invisible wizard would have an invisible staff, doesn't it?" he said.

"Nonsense," said Meralda. "Even a staff wouldn't latch any one of the spells I found. You'd need two staves and an oil-insulated Cooping Tall holdstone, at least." Meralda frowned. "And please, no comments suggesting the presence of invisible pack-mules."

"Mules," said Mug. "Ridiculous. A mule wouldn't do at all. Invisible wizards prefer mad-eyed stallions, which make for more dramatic exits."

Meralda sighed.

"And what did the king say when you told him his palace was littered with dire Hang sorceries?" said Mug.

"I never said they were Hang," said Meralda. Then she frowned. "He asked me if they had been dispelled, and I said they had. Then he asked me to set wards at the gates to detect latched spellworks," she said. "I got the impression that he was neither surprised nor terribly worried."

"Not worried?" said Mug. "We have a lone Hang, a full day ahead of his fleet. A fleet that is, I assume, under the careful scrutiny of the army, which has agents behind every outhouse and tangle-weed along the Lamp River. Our lone Hang leaves his fleet, strolls unseen cross-country and into the palace, has a brief conversation with the king, and then vanishes like a stage puppet from our midst." The dandyleaf plant rolled a leaf into a tube, and waved it at Meralda. "Then, the clever Tirlish thaumaturge, hot on the trail of the elusive Hang visitor, discovers eight powerful, mysterious spells cast at various points in the palace." Mug rolled his eyes toward the ceiling. "Not worried?" he asked. "Why, toss in a Vonat spy or two and we'll have the makings of those penny-novel dreadfuls you pretend you never read."

Meralda stared down into her coffee cup. "Leave the Vonats out of this," she said. "They arrive soon, and I'll have to greet their mage."

Mug snorted. "Who is the Vonat mage, nowadays?" he asked. "Let me guess. He'll have a name like Dreadvault of the Black Hand or Wrackruin of Doom, and he'll be tall, lean, and possessed of a piercing, malignant gaze."

Meralda laughed. "I hear his name is Nam," she said.

Mug frowned. "Isn't Nam the Vonat word for lifetaker?"

Meralda rolled her eyes. "I never taught you Vonat," she said.

"I know lots of things you never taught me," said Mug, airily.

"That, I do not doubt," said Meralda. She looked down at her cup and sighed.

"Oh, finish your coffee," said Mug. "And talk. I'm lonely, you know. Some of us don't get to dash about all day having adventures with soldiers and kings."

Meralda walked to stand before the sink, put her cup down, and stroked Mug's top leaves. "I'm sorry," she said. "But you understand I have work to do. And you know how you hate the laboratory."

"No windows," said Mug. "No sun, no air." The dandyleaf plant shivered. "Forgive me, mistress. I know it's quite cozy by human standards, but it's just a mushroom cave to me."

A thin vine-like frond wound loosely about Meralda's wrist. "Oh, go on," said Mug. "But before you go, tell me one odd feature all your mystery spells share."

Meralda smiled. "Aside from the first one," she said, "all of them were laid in places the king was never likely to go."

Mug nodded with a bobbing of eyes. "Exactly," he said. "West wing hallways, fifth-floor stair landings, eighth-floor wash rooms. Yvin's never seen those places. Probably never will." Mug gave Meralda's hand a squeeze and unreeled his tendril. "It might mean nothing, mistress, but keep it in mind."

A knock sounded at the door. Meralda emptied her cup into the sink, rinsed the cup out with a spray of hot water, and placed it in the drying rack with a dozen of its brothers.

"Pardon, ma'am," said Tervis, from the hall. "Letter for you. From the palace."

"Of course it is," said Meralda. "He said letter, but what he meant was urgent summons."

Mug sighed. "Seventeen more days, mistress," he said. "Seventeen more days, and you can skip court sessions for weeks at a time and ignore Yvin's summons and surround yourself with spark coils and magelamps from sunrise to sunset."

Meralda took a deep breath and marched toward her front door.

"There you are, lass," said Shingvere, who leaned against the wall by the Royal Laboratory doors.

Meralda halted at the top of the west stair. The Bellringers, behind her, halted as well. Meralda noted with mild amusement that Tervis remained facing the top of the stair, while Kervis turned and faced the foot.

Shingvere saw, and chuckled. "I've been waiting for you, Thaumaturge," he said, capping a small silver flask and slipping it into a pocket within his overlarge Eryan robe. He looked toward the Bellringers and waved. "Hello, lads."

Tervis nodded to the Eryan. "Sir," he said.

Shingvere chuckled and winked at Meralda. "Got manners, anyway," he said. "Ought to have been born Phendelits."

Meralda left the stair. "Mage," she said, smiling. "Have you been waiting long? I've been with the king."

"Aye, I know all about that," said Shingvere. "His Majesty made a big show out of your shadow moving project with Ambassador Elkins and my queen after you left this morning. 'Moving out of the shadow of the past,' he called it. I haven't heard such drivel since I retired."

Meralda winced. Yvin had used the same words with her, when she arrived back at court. "Tell me what you need, Thaumaturge," he'd said. "I want you to make moving the Tower's shadow a priority. Whatever you need, you shall have."

Time, Meralda had wanted to shout. *Time is what I need.* But with his next breath Yvin had casually swatted away a handful of days by reminding Meralda that as Thaumaturge she would need to officially greet and tour the visiting mages. And then the audience had been over. Meralda remembered walking dumbfounded through the Gallery, nearly in tears. Not since Last Readings at college had she felt so stretched, so overwhelmed. And at that moment she'd looked up to see a thousand painted kings staring down upon her, and she'd nearly fled the gallery at a run.

Shingvere levered himself away from the wall and moved to stand beside Meralda. "Might I step inside for a wee bit?" he asked, gesturing with a nod at the laboratory doors. "We've got things to discuss, and it wouldn't do for any invisible wizards who might be passing by to hear."

"You're as bad as Mug," muttered Meralda, as she found her key and walked to the doors.

Shingvere followed. "How is the animated salad, these days?" he asked.

"Fine," said Meralda, turning the lock. "He'll want to see you, when you can."

The doors opened, and while the Bellringers took up their stations Meralda calmed the wards with a word. Shingvere peeped inside, casting his gaze about appreciatively. "You've done a bit of tidying up, you have," he said, as the wards collapsed with rustlings and a high-pitched whine.

Meralda stepped inside. "Lights," she said.

Her glass lamps flared to life. Shingvere whistled and followed her inside. "Amazing," he said. "Bloody amazing." He moved to stand beneath the nearest ring of fat glass and bent his head back, squinting. "And you say those aren't magelamps?"

Meralda found a smile. "Merely hollow tubes, filled with a peculiar gas," she said. She pointed to a spark coil, humming in the corner. "The coils excite the gasses, even at a distance. That's what creates the light. There isn't a spell involved, except within the spark coils."

Shingvere smiled. "Lass, you're smarter than Fromarch and I put together, and that's not Eryan flattery."

Meralda flushed. The big old scrying mirror flashed red behind its blanket. Shingvere ambled toward it, gazing about and touching things as he went. "Go on about your business, lass." said Shingvere, over his shoulder. "I'll talk. You can listen."

"I always do," said Meralda. She walked past Phillitrep's Engine, patted its brass gear case, and straightened the drawings on her desk before pulling out her chair and sitting.

The Eryan's voice rose up from behind the ranks of glittering mageworks. "I've met the other mages," he said. "You've got Red Mawb, Mage of the Isles, and Dorn Mukirk, Mage of Clan Mukirk coming to see you today. Mawb hates Clan Mukirk in general and Dorn Mukirk specifically and Mukirk feels much the same about his counterpart from the Isles. Both claim the other is an upstart conjurer with no right to take the title Mage to Alonya, and that's about the nicest thing they've said so far." Something flashed and popped, and the Eryan yelped, but before Meralda could rise he was speaking again.

"The Phendelits are sending–oh, what is his name?"

"Erdrath Yonk," said Meralda. "I met him at college." She put down her pencil and smiled. "He turned his hair green in First Year, and it was nearly Third before he turned it back again," she said.

Shingvere snorted. "Aye, he's Mage to Phendeli now." Another flash cast brief shadows against the walls, and Shingvere made a pair of sprinting steps before speaking again.

"'Tis the Vonat I want to speak to you about, Thaumaturge," said Shingvere. "Humindorus Nam."

Meralda frowned. "I've heard the stories," she said. "They're the same tired old tales told about every Vonat mage, and we both know they can't all be true."

"You're right," said Shingvere. "Most of what you've heard about the other Vonat mages wasn't true. But everything you've heard about this one is." Shingvere paused. "And believe me, Thaumaturge, you haven't heard the worst."

Meralda looked up from her page of Tower calculations and sought out Shingvere.

"You'll be wanting to be careful around him, Thaumaturge," said Shingvere, from well behind the silvery ball of ice-cold water that hung suspended above Allabat's Flying Plates. "Especially when he's smiling. Aye. Especially then."

The water blurred, and Shingvere's form appeared within it. Small and upside down at first, but growing quickly larger until his distorted face filled the barrel-sized sphere. "Boo," he said, with a grin.

Meralda shook her head. "Shingvere," she began.

The Eryan raised a hand and darted from behind the Flying Plates. "No, no," he said, shaking his head. "I've wasted quite enough of your time, lass. Just wanted to pass on a bit of friendly advice, and poke about the old place a bit before court." He ambled back to Meralda's desk, hands in his pockets.

"I'll be careful," said Meralda, when Shingvere was near. "I know enough about this Nam to leave him be," she said. "Not that I can't knock him flat, if the need arises."

Shingvere nodded gravely, and laid his hand lightly on Meralda's shoulder. "Oh, it will," he said, no hint of humor in his tone. "And when the time comes, Meralda, my dear, remember this. Right after you knock Nam flat you'll need to kill him. Quickly."

Meralda blinked. "Shingvere?"

"You heard me, lass. It's a hard thing to say, and a hard thing to hear, but hear it you must, and heed it you must. Kill him. Mercy would be wasted. Hesitation will be fatal. Kill him quick. You won't get two chances." And then the fat Eryan turned and was through the doors and gone. Meralda barely had time to utter the word of leaving, and then the doors were shut.

Meralda stared after him, and it was a long time before she was able to pick up her pencil and resume work on her shadow moving spell.

Shingvere sauntered past the Bellringers with a quick word and the offer of a penny-stick to each. Both declined, and both kept their eyes alert and on the Hall, which meant neither saw the bulge under the front of the Eryan wizard's robe or noticed the odd gait he took down the stairs.

At the foot of the west stair, Shingvere stopped, looked furtively about, and hitched at his robes when the Red Guards at the Burnt Door looked away. "That's better," he muttered. Then he found a grin and managed to walk without hopping all the way through the west wing, out the west doors, and half a block down Palace Way to Fromarch's plain black carriage.

The curbside carriage door opened, and Shingvere darted inside.

Fromarch scowled at him through a thick fog of purple pipe smoke. "Well," he said, knocking twice on the carriage with his knuckles. "Did you get it?"

Shingvere grinned. "You know I did," he said, unfastening the front of his robe and reaching inside. "Walked right up to it and stuck it in my britches. Walked right out, too. No wonder you Tirls have got Hang in your palace. You wouldn't amble out so easily at Cloudcrown."

Fromarch grunted. The carriage wheeled into the street just as Shingvere pulled a solid brass cylinder out of his robe and held it up with a flourish.

"Mage Prolep's Infinite Latch," he said. Then he lifted an eyebrow. "Isn't it?"

Fromarch spoke a word. The cylinder, which was nearly long enough to stretch from fingertip to elbow and about as thick as a big man's wrist, made three sharp clicking noises

On the third click it doubled its length. Shingvere yelped, but kept his grip.

"That's it, all right," said Fromarch. He whispered another word, and the cylinder noiselessly and instantly resumed its original size. Fromarch nodded approvingly. "That's old, dark Tirlish magic," he said, wistfully. "Mage Ovis has no use for it. But perhaps you and I do."

Shingvere shut his mouth. "This Prolep," he said. "Knew his

business, did he?"

Fromarch shrugged. "He knew latches," he said. "Otherwise, he was quite mad." Fromarch tapped the latch with the bowl of his pipe. "It's a bit unpredictable, but we can latch spells to it all day and never run out of latching mass." The lean mage laughed without smiling. "Certain ugly Vonats might find this surprising in a brief, unpleasant way."

"'Ere, hold on," said Shingvere. "You just used the word unpredictable. Odd that you didn't mention it earlier, when you talked me into pilfering a foreign king's palace. So, unpredictable to what extent?" The Eryan frowned. "And why have I never heard of this Prolep?"

Fromarch shrugged. "Sometimes it unlatches all its spells at once," he said. "And that's why you've never heard of Prolep."

Shingvere gently laid the latch across Fromarch's knees and snatched his hand away. "This is your secret weapon?" he asked. "'An ancient instrument of great power'," he said, mocking Fromarch's baritone. "'Forgotten, by all but me'." The Eryan shook his head. "Simply marvelous. When the trouble starts, you can explode with the latch, and I'll set fire to my robes, and perhaps the Vonats will be so embarrassed they'll call in all their spies and go home to take up apple ranching."

Fromarch rubbed the latch's dull case with the hem of his robe. "You talk too much," he said. "Always have."

Shingvere sighed. "Aye. You're probably right," he said. Then he lifted the carriage curtain a bit and squinted into the sun. "We've engaged in skullduggery, and we have our eldritch magics," he said, as traffic rattled past. "What do we do now?"

Fromarch withdrew his pipe from his mouth. "We buy some Nolbit's," he said. "And we go back to my basement, and we spread out our tools, and we latch every spell we know to this," he said, shaking the latch, "and then we just wait for that—"

"Language," warned the Eryan, with a grin. "Profanity is the footstool of lazy intellect."

"—for that unwashed hedge conjurer to lift a paw toward the thaumaturge," said Fromarch. "At that moment, I'll start unlatching, and I'll stop when there's a pair of empty Vonat boots on the floor and a sooty spot on the ceiling."

"And if the latch fails before that?" said Shingvere, quietly.

Fromarch stuck his pipe in the right corner of his mouth and made a small shrug.

Shingvere grinned. "A hero's death, right out of a Phendelit poem book," he said. "Fromarch, as Meralda is fond of saying, you're a treasure. An idiot, but a treasure nonetheless." The Eryan saluted, laying his right hand over his heart. "Naturally, I vow to stand with you, and share your noble, if messy, doom."

Fromarch sucked his pipe, toyed with the latch, and said nothing else all the way home.

The Gold Room was, if Meralda was any judge, in a full-blown tizzy.

Meralda's grandmother had used the phrase to denote any sudden onset of frantic and ultimately futile activity. "Oh, they're in quite the tizzy," Grandma Ovis had proclaimed, that day so long ago when Meralda's older sister had wed. "You'd think the world a-turnin' depended on the roses."

Looking about at court, Meralda mouthed the phrase herself.

The Phendelits and the Alons had all arrived in the night, and were to be formally welcomed at a tenth-hour ceremony. Meralda had been summoned at eight, apparently, under the assumption that thaumaturges had nothing better to do than sit and watch the day staff set up chairs, cover tables with tablecloths, and argue over placemats and placards.

And argue they did. A bevy of retired army officers, the king's new Protocol Corps, was engaged in a round of bellowing and finger pointing with the tall, ancient palace butler known simply as Carter.

"You can't seat an Alon clan chief next to a Phendelit Silver Circle Guardsman," bellowed the tallest of the Protocol Corps officers. "The Silver will call the Alon a copperhead and the Alon will cut off the Silver's nose and we'll be at war before brunch, you imbecile!"

Carter lifted an eyebrow in mild disdain, straightened the gilt-edged placard bearing an ornate Alon clan sigil, and moved on to the next seat.

Meralda laughed behind her hand. Elsewhere, carts of chairs were being hauled in and unloaded, a small army of florists was filling the room with fresh-cut Phendelit greenrose, and scowling floorsweeps followed everyone about in a vain attempt to keep the wide, worn flagstones free of trash and debris.

A few other minor court figures were scattered about, waiting as Meralda was. There was Martin Flea, official chronicler to the court, who had plopped into his chair, waved at Meralda, and promptly gone to sleep. Cheslin Frempt, the People's

Advocate, sat a few seats away, looking bored and humming to himself. White-haired Elton Flynnedge, heir to the Flynnedge cobblestone empire, was scribbling away in a notebook by the north door.

Meralda looked up at the square-faced old clock above the portrait of King Ponnyamp IV. Eight and half-past?

"Oh, no," she said, softly. An hour and a half of this?

The west doors flew open with a bang. Meralda whirled, her hand on her staff, but the open doors revealed only a battered chair-moving cart and a pair of red-faced roustabouts.

Behind them, though, came the captain. "Thaumaturge," he said, hurrying past the cart. "What are you doing here so early?"

Meralda stood and shrugged. "Urgent summons," she said. "Be in the Gold Room at eight of the clock. Bring your staff."

The captain dodged chairs. "Ah, well," he said. "Someone probably got a bit free with the summonses up on the second floor. Yvin just wanted you to check the wards, and I'll bet you've already done that."

"I have," said Meralda. "All quiet."

The captain smiled. "Good," he said. "But as long as you're here, Thaumaturge, might I have a word?"

Meralda shrugged again. "Only if it's over coffee," she said.

The captain grinned. "That, I can do. You there!" he bellowed.

A dozen servitors froze. "Bring a pot of coffee and a pair of mugs," said the captain, fixing his gaze on a skinny youth struggling with a stack of chairs taller than himself. "Go to the kitchen. Tell them the captain wants coffee, mugs, and a plate of biscuits, and he wants them now. Go."

The boy scuttled off.

The captain pulled back a chair and sat. Meralda did the same, leaning close when she saw the captain glance furtively about and motion her near.

"The Hang dock tonight," he said, in a whisper. "They'll be escorted to the docks by a pilot boat and then brought to the palace. Yvin's cleared out half the north wing upper floors."

Meralda nodded. "Has the army had any contact with them?" she asked.

The captain glanced about again. "We have," he said. "Had to send a boat in close and ask what kind of draft their ships drew. Didn't want them to run aground in the shallows outside Defton." The captain chuckled. "The college sent over a pair of linguists and a professor who claimed he could write some Hang. They spent two hours jabbering at the Hang fleet master until the Hang broke down and asked the professors, in New Kingdom, if they needed directions to Tirlin."

Meralda's eyes widened.

"Oh, they speak New Kingdom quite well," said the captain. "Like natives, one of the linguists said. Natives." The captain sighed. "But that's a matter for another time," he said, as the serving boy trotted up with a tray of coffee and biscuits. "Have you moved the Tower's shadow yet?"

Meralda scowled and took up a cup of coffee. "Why, certainly," she said. "I had nearly twenty uninterrupted minutes just yesterday to work on it."

The captain, his face blank, swallowed, took up a coffee mug, and waved the lad away. "Really," he said. "Have you seen any papers today, Thaumaturge?"

Meralda froze in mid-sip. "Papers," she said.

"The *Times*, in particular," said the captain. "I thought the likeness of you was quite good. Most flattering, in fact. Though I did wonder if you really called the Tower 'the lair of dread Otrinvion'."

"I never said any such thing."

"Of course not," said the captain. He frowned. "But you'll want to look at the story, anyway. Your shadow moving assignment is there, along with a lot of nonsense about lights seen again in the Wizard's Flat."

Meralda shook her head. "Oh, no."

"Oh, yes," said the captain. He glared at Martin Flea, who had stopped snoring, and then he lowered his face and whispered. "I've ordered the Tower sealed for the duration of the Accords, but you and I both know that won't stop the foolishness."

Oh, no, thought Meralda. *That'll only make it worse. Before the Accords are done the Tower will be mobbed each night, as the entire populace makes a hobby of mistaking crows for dead wizards and reflections in the window glass as portents of doom, and I'll have to shoulder my way past each and every one of them.*

"Marvelous," she said.

"I've told the guards to keep the tourists at bay while you're working," said the captain. "Is there anything else I can do?"

Meralda shook her head.

"Then go," said the captain. "You've checked the wards.

Why don't I tell Yvin you had to leave to cast certain spells before the sun reached its zenith?"

Meralda stood. "That's absurd," she said. "Do keep a straight face, won't you?"

"Always," said the captain, from above his cup. "Mind the haunts, Thaumaturge."

Meralda put her back to the throne and left the Gold Room to the captain and the chairs.

Chapter Six

"Here we go again," whispered Kervis.

Meralda urged her magelamp brighter and mounted the first of the Tower's winding stairs.

Behind her, the Bellringers followed, boots scraping on the stone with measured, careful steps. Meralda thought about all the novels she'd read, in which princes, queens, or spies, who invariably bore a single guttering candle, charged up the Tower stair, or leaped fearlessly from tread to tread. *Leapt, indeed,* mused Meralda. *No one, no matter the provocation, would dare take these stairs at a brisk walk, much less a headlong dash.*

And candles? Impossible. Her own magelamp, bright though it was, cast a cone of light just wide enough at its base to illuminate three pairs of feet. Above, the magelamp lit only a tall, narrow swatch of the Tower wall.

The rest of the Tower remained cloaked in darkness. Darkness, and the faint sensation of constant movement at the edge of the light, as if Meralda's magelamp alone kept something darker than the shadows barely at bay.

Tervis halted long enough to shift Meralda's bag from one hand to the other. "I'm coming," he said, at Kervis' unspoken question. "Don't stop."

The trio resumed their climb. Meralda strained her ears for any hint of sound from the park. But again, not even a hundred paces up the stair, all the sounds of the world beyond were gone, shut away behind walls thicker than Meralda was tall.

"What was that game the Alons were playing?" asked Tervis, his voice echoing faintly. "It looked like fun."

"They call it football," said Meralda. "They played it during the last Accords, too."

"It's tearing up the grass," said Kervis. "You ought to have heard the groundskeepers curse."

Meralda grimaced. She had heard the groundskeepers bellowing, of course. Their language was such that after a moment even Angis blanched and turned away.

Kervis laughed softly. Meralda tilted the magelamp and looked down. Already, their ascent, though it had covered less than half a revolution around the Tower, had reached sufficient height that the glow of the magelamp no longer touched the floor below.

Shadows flew as she looked up. Kervis drew in his breath in a short quick gasp, and Meralda saw, from the corner of her eye, a flash of motion as the guardsman brought his monstrous Oldmark crossbow to bear on the dark beyond the stair.

"Kervis," said Meralda, turning and sending light over the Bellringers and the void beyond them. "What are you doing?"

Kervis' face was pale. "I saw something," he said, his voice low and flat. "Out there."

Behind him, Tervis shook his head and shrugged.

Meralda sighed and played the light about the Tower. "There is no one here but us," she said. "What you probably saw was the outline of the stair on the far wall. See, you can just make it out, now and then, and it can look like something moving."

Tervis whispered something, and Kervis lowered the crossbow. "Forgive me, Thaumaturge," he said, his eyes still on the dark. "I was mistaken."

Meralda smiled. "It's all right," she said. "Let's catch our breath for a moment. It's a wonder we aren't all seeing things, with all the nonsense being talked about the Tower these days." She sat, and motioned for the Bellringers to do the same. "There's no hurry."

Kervis looked toward Meralda and cocked his head. "I thought the captain said the other mages were coming by to meet you this afternoon," he said. "Weren't we supposed to be back by four bells?"

Meralda smiled. *Every minute I sit here,* she thought, *is another minute I won't be forced to endure king and court.* "Do you think they'll climb these stairs?" she asked.

Tervis shook his head and grinned. "I think not," he said.

Kervis nudged his twin with his elbow. "You're learning, little brother," he said. Then he mopped sweat from his brow and polished his crossbow stock with the sleeve of his jacket. "Anyway, we've got nothing to fear with this along, do we?"

"Just you," said Tervis. "Tell the Thaumaturge how you did at targets, this morning."

Kervis ignored his twin. "So what are you doing today, Thaumaturge?" he asked. "If it's not a secret."

Meralda wiped back a wild lock of hair and smiled. "I don't work in secret, Guardsman," she said. "I'm here to set a few wards, and test the Tower structure for its latching properties," she said.

Tervis' brow furrowed.

"You know what wards are," said Meralda. "Guard spells. The court's idea, not mine, and most probably a waste of time." Meralda shrugged. "My real reason for climbing all these stairs, though, is to test the Tower's resistance to new spells," she said. "Soon, I'll need to latch my shadow moving spell to something solid," explained Meralda. "The Tower, in this case. And before I latch such a complicated spellwork to a structure as old and unusual as the Tower, I need to determine how resistant it is to new spells."

Tervis nodded slowly. "I'll bet it's as slippery as mud," he said. "Ma'am."

Meralda's magelamp flickered. She drew the fingers of her right hand quickly down the traceries on the tube, and whispered a word, and the light steadied. But Meralda frowned, for the tube had grown momentarily cold, as though the unlatched coils of the light spell had begun to unravel.

"Is anything the matter, Thaumaturge?" asked Kervis.

"Nothing," said Meralda. She rose, and the magelamp shone steady and bright. "Are you gentlemen ready?"

"We are," chorused the Bellringers. Both stood.

Meralda nodded and turned. She shone the magelamp up, where it barely illuminated the second story ceiling, and the gaping, doorless portal that led through it.

Shadows danced. Meralda's free hand groped in her pocket, and before she realized what she was doing Meralda had her short retaining wand in her grasp. The minor ward spell latched there warmed the wand, and made it quiver like a trapped bumblebee.

"Nonsense," said Meralda, so softly neither Bellringer heard. She pulled her hand from her pocket, and set about reviewing her latch testing spell.

I'm surprised, thought Meralda, *that no one has done it before.* Simply latch a spellwork of a known capacity to the Tower, and then load the spell until it unlatches. The time elapsed between latching and unlatching, once compared to a standard, will give me a ratio. And the same ratio should hold for the shadow moving spell.

Should. That word pops up frequently when the Tower is involved, she decided. As if the Tower were a world apart, a world where the normal rules might hold sway, or might not, all at the whim of a legendary wraith.

Wraith. Haunt. Spirit. Meralda had seen the Tower's supposed inhabitant called many things, in the old books. "We laide no Spells there, for feare of the Spirit and its Terrible Wrath," quoth Mage Elvis, some two hundred years ago. More recently, she read that king Tomin III had ordered workmen to board up the windows of the Wizard's Flat, from the inside, so that the "Cursed Lights and Leering Phantoms" that looked down upon park-goers might be hidden. The king found the planks broken and scattered about the Tower the next day, and the workmen fled. Lights danced in the flat every night for a month.

Step after step, stair after stair. The second story entrance came and went, and the third, and still the Tower soared up and away out of sight. The Bellringers fell silent, aside from panting and huffing. Kervis' crossbow, Meralda knew, must be an awful burden by now.

Meralda tried to count steps, but lost her place in the four hundreds. The sight of her own hunched shadow turned her thoughts to Otrinvion. *How many times*, she wondered, *did he climb these same stairs?* Was the Tower so dark, then? So silent, so empty?

Unbidden, a nursery rhyme sang out in Meralda's memory.

The old, old wizard goes round and round the stair,

The old, old wizard goes sneaking everywhere,

The old, old wizard goes where you cannot see,

The old, old wizard is sneaking...up...on...me!

Meralda felt eyes on her back, and a chill like the stroke of an icicle raced down her spine.

Kervis began to hum. There was no mistaking the tune, or the words behind it.

"I see the door," said Tervis, his voice suffused with relief. "We're almost there."

Meralda took a deep breath. *I am a thaumaturge,* she said, to herself. *A mage. I do not quake and shiver at nursery rhymes.*

"I'll need you gentlemen to stand in the doorway while I set the ward," she said. "Can you hold the lamp while Tervis handles my bag?"

"Yes, ma'am!" said Kervis. His grin was bright in the magelamp's glow.

Meralda played the lamp upwards. There, not fifty steps away, was the notch in the ceiling that held the door to the Wizard's Flat.

"I do believe it gets taller each time," she said.

"Don't say that," said Tervis. "Ma'am," he added, quickly. "Meaning no disrespect–"

"I know," Meralda said. Twenty paces. "You've done well, this climb."

Tervis sighed. "I practiced," he said, matter-of-factly.

Ten paces. "How," asked Meralda, "did you practice?"

"Well," said Tervis. "There's a big old iron oak, just outside the barracks–"

Meralda looked over her shoulder. "Guardsman," she said. "You are not about to tell me you have taken to climbing iron oaks as practice at ascending the Tower, are you?"

Tervis' gaze fell to his boots.

"Don't do that," said Meralda, with a glare at Kervis, whose wide-eyed look of innocence was not entirely convincing. "Ever again. That's an order, from a member in full of the court of Tirlin. Is that clear?"

Tervis looked up and nodded, relief plain on his face.

Meralda turned, and was at the door.

Men, she thought. She shoved the key into the lock and prepared to push against the door, but it opened easily, gentle as a whisper.

Daylight streamed through. Meralda squinted and stepped into the flat before turning to face the Bellringers.

Both stood leaning into the sunlight, smiles on their face behind their upheld hands.

"Bright," said Tervis.

"Lovely and bright," said Kervis. He squinted at Meralda, laid his crossbow carefully down on the floor just inside the flat, and held out his hand. "I can take the lamp now, if you'd like," he said.

Meralda smiled and put it into his hand.

He took it gently, like the dented brass cylinder was made of flower petals and spider webs. "Oooh," he said, playing the light slowly about. "Magic."

Tervis stepped past, Meralda's bag held forth. "Here you are, Mage," he said. "What do I do now?"

"Just open the bag, and hold it off the floor, if you will," said Meralda. "This will only take a moment, I'll set the ward, and then we can go."

Tervis nodded, and unfastened the bag's three leather straps. "Here you are," he said.

Meralda wiped the sweat from her palms on her skirts and reached inside. She withdrew a fist-sized glass sphere, which rolled on its axis in a burnished copper cage, and a neatly folded bath towel.

Tervis lifted an eyebrow at the towel.

Meralda stifled a laugh, and took the globe and towel to the far wall of the flat. She laid the towel at the edge of the floor, took the globe in her right hand, spoke a word, and touched the copper cage gently to the Tower wall.

The spell enveloping the globe latched to the Tower.

"Watch," said Meralda. She took her hand away.

The globe stuck to the wall, spinning like a top, waist-high above the folded towel.

Tervis stared. Kervis glanced at the globe, shrugged and went back to playing the magelamp about the darkened stairs.

Meralda counted. The spell remained latched for a full count of twenty before it lost hold of the Tower and the globe fell onto the towel.

Meralda scooped up both gently. Faint wisps of fog rose from the glass, and ice coated its surface.

"Did it, um, work?" asked Tervis.

"Oh, it worked," said Meralda. "Now I take the globe back to the laboratory, and say the other half of the word. It will spin again, backwards this time, for the exact amount of time we just saw. I'll measure the interval precisely and then I'll know the Tower's latching coefficient."

Meralda folded the towel over the globe as she walked, and Tervis took a single step to meet her. She stowed the latching ball, bade Tervis to seal her bag, and then warned the Bellringers to stand at the door.

"It's only a minor ward spell," she said, as she moved to stand at the center of the flat. "It will allow me to enter the flat and dispel it. Once cast, no one else will be able to pass that door without breaking the ward."

"What happens if they try?" asked Kervis.

Meralda smiled. "Wrack and blast," she said, though she doubted either Bellringer would know a verse from Ovid. "Fury and flame and fie, fools, fie."

Meralda drew the ward wand from her pocket, raised it, and spoke the word.

The wand went cold. Meralda put it back in her pocket, and

walked toward the door, already dreading the long, dark descent. Behind her, the unlatched ward began its lazy orbit of the room.

Then, with only the faintest and briefest of hissings, the ward spell massed, leaped, and exploded, two short paces from Meralda's back.

The flat rang with a thunder-clap that echoed up and down the Tower. Meralda fell, arms outstretched, half-blinded by the reflection of the flash off the rounded walls. She saw Kervis thrown backward toward the stair, saw the magelamp spin out of his grasp. Tervis whirled, one hand on the door frame, the other straining to reach his twin's pant leg. Meralda could see that Tervis was shouting, but his cry was lost amid the echoing roar.

And then the doorway was empty. Empty and dark, though the light from Meralda's magelamp, which spun as it fell, flashed twice across the dark before fading and dying.

"No!" shouted Meralda, though she could barely hear her voice above the ringing in her ears. She sprang to her feet and raced for the door, blinking past the bright haze that obscured her vision and the spots that danced before her eyes.

"Tervis!" she shouted. "Kervis!"

Meralda's right foot struck her bag, and she stumbled, and in that instant Tervis came diving through the doorway, dragging Kervis by his uniform collar.

"Behind you, Mage!" cried a Bellringer, and with horror Meralda realized Kervis had snatched up the Oldmark and dropped to one knee. "He's behind you!"

Meralda whirled, praying that Kervis had better sense than to actually loose a crossbow bolt in a space as small as the flat.

Meralda's eyes watered, and ghostly afterimages of the door and Tervis' mad lunge wavered and spun across her vision, but the flat before her was empty.

Except, just for an instant, a bunched, small shadow did seem to dart past the east-facing window, on the far side of the flat. Meralda blinked, and it was gone, leaving her with the vague impression that a bird might have flown past outside.

The last echoes died.

"No one is behind me," said Meralda, quickly. "We're alone. Put away the crossbow, Kervis. The only thing you'll shoot here are mages and guardsmen."

"There was a man behind you," said Kervis. Meralda noted with relief that Tervis forced the crossbow down with the palm of his hand. "I saw him!"

"I saw something too, ma'am," said Tervis. His voice shook, and his eyes darted about the flat. "Not sure it was a man, but it was there." His hand went to his sword hilt, and he drew it swiftly, as though he had only just remembered he was armed. "It can't have gotten out."

Meralda lifted her hand. "Listen to me," she said. The skin on the back of her neck began to tingle and itch, as though sunburnt, and the faint odor of singed hair began to waft through the room. "Something broke the ward, yes. But it could have been an old Tower spellwork, or a fault within the ward itself. What you saw was probably the ward uncoiling."

"If a ward spell uncoiling looks like a robe on a wall hook, then that's what I saw, ma'am." said Tervis. "Tall black robe with nothing in it." The boy's eyes met hers, and after a moment Meralda shook her head.

"We can talk about it at the bottom," she said. She motioned for the Bellringers to move toward the door. "It may not be safe here, and I don't have the tools to deal with a ward gone bad. So we leave, right now."

The Bellringers nodded once, in unison.

"I lost the magelamp," said Kervis. "I'm sorry, ma'am. It flew out of my hand."

"I have another," said Meralda. "And you are not to be blamed." Meralda swallowed, banishing from her mind the image of the two boys falling through the dark. "I thought you'd both fallen."

"Nearly did," said Kervis. The boy shivered. "Tervis caught my boot." The lad forced a small smile. "Glad it's a good fit."

Meralda bit her lip and motioned for her bag.

Tervis snatched it up and loosened the straps. "Here you are," he said, holding it forth.

Meralda reached inside. She found her spare magelamp, smaller than the one Kervis dropped, but only slightly less bright.

"Light," she said, and the magelamp flared to life.

Meralda urged it brighter. Kervis moved to stand beside the door. "I'll go last," he said. "If Ugly wants to follow, he'll do it with holes in his chest."

Meralda gazed round, one last time. The flat was empty, and though her ears still rang Meralda knew it was quiet again. Sunlight streamed through the windows, though it looked cold and thin on the worn stone floor. Nothing passed by beyond, and there was simply no place to hide in the open expanse of the Wizard's Flat.

Emptiness. And yet Meralda shivered at the sudden sensation of a watchful gaze turned full upon her.

Meralda swallowed. "Be quiet a moment, gentlemen," she said. "I'm going to close my eyes. Don't be alarmed, and don't move about."

The Bellringers croaked out an affirmative.

"I'll put an end to this nonsense here and now," she muttered. Then she closed her eyes, counted backwards from ten, and extended her second sight into the flat.

Something, like the lightest caress of a spring thistle's bloom, stroked the back of Meralda's flash-burned neck. With it, fainter than a whisper, came words:

"The old, old wizard goes round and round the stair—"

Meralda wrenched her sight shut, and the Tower floor spun, and when she opened her eyes Kervis had taken a step toward her.

"What is it?" asked Kervis. "Ma'am, you're white as a sheet!"

"We're leaving," said Meralda, aloud. The flat seemed smaller, now. Smaller and darker. The open doorway to the Tower proper gaped. "Stay close. We're all half blind and a bit deaf. Keep your eyes on your feet and listen for trouble."

The muscles in Tervis' jaw quivered. "Yes, ma'am," he said.

"Kervis. Don't linger." Tervis stepped through the open door, prodding at the dark with his short, plain guardsman's sword. Meralda followed, careful to keep the light at Tervis' feet. Kervis backed onto the stair, his crossbow still trained on the empty flat.

Meralda reached past him and closed the door. The Tower, bereft of the daylight, was plunged into darkness. Meralda's spare magelamp glittered and shone, and Meralda felt, for an instant, as if she walked alone high up in the night sky, bearing a single tiny star to light her way.

"I really, really don't like this place," muttered Tervis, miserably.

Meralda waved the pool of light a few treads down. "Then let's leave it," she said, pocketing the key. "Can you gentlemen see?"

"Well enough," said Kervis. "I can close my eyes and still see you in front of the light," he added.

"Me too," said Tervis, as he began to descend. "Will it go away?"

"It will," said Meralda, with what she hoped was total confidence. "Before we reach the park, I imagine."

Tervis squinted into the dark. "Look down there," he said, pointing at an hourglass-shaped splash of light far down in the distance. "Is that your lamp?"

Meralda peeped over the edge of the stair. "That's it," she said. "We shall soon have two to light our way."

The light winked out.

"Sorry, Thaumaturge," said Kervis. "I dropped it, and now it's broken."

"Think nothing of it, Guardsman," said Meralda, quickly. "It's just a brass cylinder. I'll latch a new spell to it, and it will shine again."

They wound down the stair in silence for a time, and Meralda was glad for the darkness, for it hid her worried frown.

One could cut the magelamp in half, and then crush it, and grind it to a powder. Even after all that, though light would shine from the fragments, until the spell unlatched. A fall, even from the top of the Tower, would not be sufficient to douse the light.

"I still don't like this place," said Tervis, to no one in particular.

Meralda nodded in silent agreement as Tervis set a brisk pace to the bottom.

The king put his head in his hands and sighed through his fingers.

"Thaumaturge," he said, his face still covered. "Is there or isn't there a haunt in the Tower?"

Meralda forced herself to relax her grip on the arms of her stiff old chair. She'd been dreading this moment, ever since reaching the bottom of the Tower and discovering a ring of soldiers holding back a crowd. The flash had been seen as far away as the upper ramparts of the palace, and the roar, according to Angis, rolled like nearby thunder all through the sunlit park.

"There are no haunts, Majesty," she said, slowly and evenly. "Not in the Tower, not in the palace, not in the most ancient and blood-stained Phendelit fortress." Meralda took a breath. "Haunts are things of legend and folklore, not fact or history."

Yvin lowered his hands. Meralda was surprised to see how tired he looked, surprised to see the dark bands under the bleary grey eyes, and surprised at all the wrinkles that seemed to have crept across his wide, round face in just the last few days.

"No haunt in the Tower," he said, softly.

"No haunt," replied Meralda.

Yvin's gaze bored into hers. "You don't sound entirely convinced," he said.

Meralda looked away. A sheaf of paper on the desk caught her eye; scrawled at one corner of the top page were the words *"Who do we blame?"*

"Something happened, in the flat," she said, after a moment. "I used second sight to look around a bit."

Yvin raised an eyebrow. "Madam, I've known five mages, and you are the first to dare second sight in Otrinvion's stronghold," he said. He leaned closer. "What did you see?"

Meralda frowned. "Nothing, Majesty," she said. "Nothing. I felt what might have been a draft, and a verse from a child's play poem about the Tower presented itself to me. Nothing else."

Yvin drew himself back in his chair. "So. The ward spell failed, the blast left you and your guards justifiably shaken, and you left without further incident," he said. "Still. What burst your ward?"

Meralda shrugged. "Residual spell energies, I suspect," she said. "The Tower's construction involved structural sorceries, and some certainly linger. The sheer weight of the Tower would cause it to collapse, otherwise."

"Seven hundred years is a long time to linger," said Yvin.

Meralda nodded. "It is, Majesty," she replied. "But linger it does. Even Fromarch admits he had trouble latching spells to the Tower. And Shingvere–" Meralda halted, spread her hands. "Well, you know what Mage Shingvere thinks."

Yvin grunted. "Residual spell energies. Structural sorceries."

"Yes, Majesty."

Yvin shrugged. "Then that's what we'll tell the papers," he said. "We'll tell them, and they'll run headlines proclaiming the return of dread Otrinvion anyway. A free press." The king sighed. "What was King Latiron thinking?"

Meralda shut her mouth just as she realized Yvin was chuckling.

"Got you," he said, with a weary grin. Then he rose and sidled around the big, plain oak desk that occupied the center of his book-lined private study. "Go home, Thaumaturge," he said.

Meralda rose and went for the door. Yvin opened it for her, and smiled.

"Go home and stay home," he said. "The Hang dock tonight, and the Vonats will be here soon, and then neither you nor I will see a moment's peace till First Snow."

Yvin closed the door. Tervis and Kervis, waiting on the settee in the oak-paneled anteroom, sprang to their feet.

"Where to, ma'am?" asked Kervis.

"Home," said Meralda. From the door to the west hall, Meralda heard the captain tell a penswift that the thaumaturge was in the laboratory, and would be working late.

He knows quite well where I am, thought Meralda. She smiled at the west door, took a step away from it, and motioned for the Bellringers to follow.

Meralda took the long route out of the palace, left by the Soldier's Gate, and found Angis waiting at the curb. "Thought you'd slip out this way," he said, as Meralda and the Bellringers clambered in his cab. "Penswifts out chasing ghosts, aye?"

Meralda sighed. She opened her mouth to tell Angis what she'd told Yvin, that there are no haunts, no ghosts, no wraiths.

This time, though, the words caught in her throat. *I know the flat was empty,* she thought. *Empty and open, no place to hide. But someone was there, watching me.*

Seven hundred years of careful scientific inquiry. Seven centuries of serious, dedicated ghost-hunting, all of it fruitless. Just last year, the famed Night Walker of Dolleth Manor in Phendeli proved to be a child's enchanted toy soldier, marching sporadically to and fro inside a walled-up corridor. The Piper of Morat's Elt was just that. A wily piper who spent thirty years tormenting his neighbors because, as he said on his deathbed, "they were a right lot o' fruit thievin' rascals."

The list of hauntings turned mundane events went on and on. As a student, now and then, of Shingvere's, Meralda had been exposed to a plethora of grisly tales and paranormal goings-on. Even Shingvere admitted, despite his firm belief in what he called "the realm of the higher natures," that thaumaturgical inquiries turned up far more flying squirrels and old kitchen magics than potential ghosts. How, then, could the Tower, which had been scrutinized and analyzed by scores of mages since the birth of Tirlin, conceal anything truly out of the ordinary?

Meralda thought back to a day when she'd asked Shingvere the very same question.

"You're making the same mistake Fromarch makes, Apprentice," Shingvere had said. "You claim you're open-minded. But here you are, arguing against a haunted Tower without really examining the evidence."

"What evidence is that?" Fromarch had said. "And what beer bottle did it come out of?"

"Look to your books," Shingvere had replied. "Book after book, mage after mage, the details differ, but the facts remain unchanged. When you look hard at the Tower, Apprentice, you'll likely see something looking back."

Fromarch had snorted and left the room in disdain. Shingvere had shrugged, then grinned and waggled a finger at Meralda's poorly-concealed expression of polite disbelief.

"One day you'll see," he'd said. "Maybe not at the Tower, maybe not tomorrow. But someday, someone is going to come face-to-face with a genuine ghost, and prove it, and then you'll owe old Shingvere an apology, young lady."

Meralda closed her eyes and settled back into her seat and wondered, for the first time, if Shingvere might just possibly be right.

Meralda settled into her favorite high-backed, well-cushioned red reading chair and put her bare feet down slowly into a tub of steaming water. "Ahh," she said. "That feels nice."

The Bellringers perched uneasily on Meralda's overstuffed Phendelit couch and watched Mug watch the thaumaturge.

"You look like you've put down roots," said the dandyleaf plant. "Next you'll be sprouting flowers and asking for a bit of mulch."

Kervis and Tervis exchanged glances. Mug turned a dozen eyes upon them. "So, lads," said Mug. "Which one of you is

Kervis?"

Kervis looked toward the thaumaturge, but her eyes were closed, and she was silent. "I am, sir," said Kervis. "I am."

Mug brought more eyes to bear upon the Bellringer. "Tell me again what you saw."

"I, um, saw a shape, sir," said Kervis. "Behind the thaumaturge, after the flash."

Mug tossed his leaves. "A shape, you say. What kind of shape? A man? A dog? A milk cart? What?"

"A man-shape," he said, after a moment. "Not a man, exactly. I didn't see any hair or hands or eyes. Just a man-shape. Tall. Skinny." Kervis shivered visibly at the memory. "I think he was reaching for her."

Mug turned a pair of red eyes upon Meralda. "I see," he said. "How did you explain it, Thaumaturge? A flash-induced visual anomaly, possibly an artifact of the ward spell's faulty axial orientation?"

Mug turned his eyes back to the Bellringers. "You two see what I'm up against," he said. "She's got ward spells exploding, and ghosts reaching out to grab her, and here she sits with her feet in a bath going blithely on about axial faults and visual artifacts." The dandyleaf plant's leaves whirled, as if in a wind. "Old Otrinvion could come lurching out of the ground at her feet and she'd swear he was a reflection off the queen's left ear-ring."

"Mug."

Mug rolled his eyes. "You boys know better," he whispered. "Keep a good watch on her. And for all your sakes, next time shoot the blighter where he stands."

Meralda opened her eyes. "As Guardsman Kervis knows, discharging a crossbow in the Wizard's Flat is an excellent way to be remembered as the Tower's newest ghost. And tell me this, Mug. If indeed dead Otrinvion does come strolling down the stair, what good will it do to shoot him? Do not all of your precious ghost stories stress that spirits cannot be harmed by mundane means?"

Mug glanced sidelong at the Bellringers. "See what I mean?"

Meralda shook her head. "Pay him no attention, gentlemen," she said. "Logic fails. Reason surrenders. Silence is your only defense."

"Silence, and a whopping big crossbow," muttered Mug. Kervis grinned, and Mug winked. "That's a lad," he whispered. "There's hope for you yet."

Meralda closed her eyes again, and said nothing. Instead, she listened.

Through the four open windows of her sitting room, she could hear Tirlin quite clearly. The last downtown trolley thundered past, right on time, at six-ten. Soon after, traffic halved, and halved again, and the Brass Bell clanged out the seven of the clock. The cries of the paperboys, strident and clear during the closing time bustle, were reduced to a single lad's weary, hoarse cry of "Hang dock tonight! Two pence for the *Post*!"

Finally, even the clomp-clomp of straggling pedestrians and early evening revelers died. Meralda pictured Fairlane Street. It sounded empty, a thing she had never before seen, and yet the effort to rise and look out a window was just too much to bear.

"Everyone must be down at the docks," said Mug. "I hear the Hang lit their ships with lanterns on the rigging. Looks like a city gone to sea, they say."

"I'm sure it's beautiful," said Meralda. She looked up at the Bellringers. "If you two would like to go and see, go ahead. I'm home, for the evening."

"We'll all see the Hang soon enough," said Tervis. Kervis nodded assent. "We thought we'd better stay here, until they are docked and we know they're peaceful."

Mug chuckled. "Good idea," he said. "That way, if the Hang attack, you two can ambush them in front of old Mrs. Whitlonk's room. Kervis can use his crossbow, Tervis can wield both swords, and Mrs. Whitlonk can grab a hundred or so Hang at a time and complain to them about the noise." he said.

Meralda sighed. "Shut up, Mug," she said.

The sun set, and soon after, a trumpet blew in the distance. Meralda sat bolt upright, and the Bellringers leaped to their feet, and Mug even turned all his eyes toward the north, where the docks lay hidden behind the sprawling, twinkling heart of northwest Tirlin.

The first trumpet was joined by another, and then both began to play "Tirlin, Tirlin." The faint sounds of cheering and the thump-thump of a Royal Guard kettle drum joined the song of welcome.

Meralda sat. The Bellringers moved to stand at the window.

"That's a welcome to our shores, not a call to battle bloody," said Mug. "Looks like the Hang are guests after all."

"For tonight," said Meralda. *Hang and ghosts and Vonats tomorrow,* she thought, *but at least tonight we can sleep in peace.*

"That's the sound of history being made, lads," said Mug. "Something I hoped never to hear."

The Bellringers nodded, as one, and watched late at the window while the faint music played.

Chapter Seven

Meralda was up and dressed before the summons to the palace arrived, via a breathless Kervis. "I saw the Hang!" he exclaimed, thrusting a thick brown envelope at Meralda before she fully opened her door. "They're all lined up in the west garden, dancing."

Meralda took the envelope and bade Kervis and Tervis to enter. The guardsman went on to describe the Hang's odd morning dance, noting with awe that every one of them stood and moved together, all led by a spry little man in baggy short-legged pants who never spoke a word.

"Like birds, ma'am," said Kervis, as Tervis rolled his eyes. "Like this!"

Kervis stood on his right foot, attempted to straighten his left leg and extend it away from his body, level with his waist, and fell over on Meralda's couch when he lifted his arms over his head.

From the kitchen came the sound of applause. "Bravo!" shouted Mug, adding the faint roar of a tiny crowd behind him. "Bravo!"

Kervis reddened and stood. "Well, they didn't fall," he said.

Meralda shushed Mug and hid her own smile behind the sheaf of papers stuffed into the envelope. At the top, printed in a hurried court scribe's neat hand, were the words "A Brief Summary of Our Hang Guests, and a Schedule for Today."

Meralda sat. "There's coffee in the kitchen, Tervis," she said. "Have some, and don't mind Mug."

Tervis nodded, and headed for the kitchen.

Meralda flipped through the papers, searching for the schedule. The last page was a list of places and times. Meralda winced and read on.

Eight of the clock. Informal breakfast with the Eryans, the Phendelits, the Alons, and the Hang.

Ten of the clock. Court meeting, closed session.

Noon. Lunch, informal. Not mandatory.

Two of the clock. Tour of the palace. Informal.

The captain had added, in a hasty scrawl, *The Hang will be at breakfast, and may join the tour. Forget the court session. Lot of arguing about room assignments and troop postings.*

Meralda shrugged. *Very well,* she thought. *Breakfast, skip the lunch, and then the rest of the day is free.*

And at last, I'll see a Hang.

Tervis came out of the kitchen, coffee in hand. "Thank you, ma'am," he said.

Meralda looked up from the papers. "Well, sit down," she said. "You're not on a parade ground, you know."

Tervis backed up to the reading chair and sat. "Yes ma'am," he said.

"Docile, too," said Mug, from the kitchen. Meralda glared, and flipped back to the first page of the captain's report, and began to read.

The Hang, wrote the scribe, *have sent, as we thought, representatives from the house of Chentze. Chentze, we believe, means "long dragon," or perhaps "long-lived dragon".*

Chief among these visitors is Que-long. We are as yet unsure whether this is a name or a title, or indeed something of both. Suffice it say that Que-long is the ranking member of the delegation, if not of Chentze itself. We are asked not to address Que-long directly, or to offer directly to him any gifts, documents, or objects of any kind. All interaction with Que-long is to be performed with Chezin. Direct all statements to Chezin. Give all gifts to Chezin. You will know Chezin by his red robes, and the fact that he alone of the Hang bears a weapon.

Note that the king has relaxed the customary ban on weapons in the Gold Room for Chezin. Chezin is to bear his sword wherever he will, and no one shall challenge or attempt to disarm him on pain of the most direct and severe royal displeasure.

The other ranking members of the Hang delegation are:

Donchen - Rank unknown. Introduced himself merely as "Donchen." Probably an ambassador, or the Hang equivalent thereof.

Loman - Court Mage? Bears a short plain staff, cast a magelight from his hands during last night's procession to the palace.

Sopan - Wife of Que-long. Attended by three black-clad females introduced as "Sopan's shings." The shings may be bodyguards, though they bear no weapons and are slight of build.

Tolong - Captain of Long Dragon flagship. Statesman, perhaps, as well. Chezin defers to him with nearly as much respect as to Que-long.

The captain had added one final note:

Meralda. Que-long has expressed a desire to see firsthand the wondrous magics of this fair and happy land. That means you, so whip up something wondrous, won't you? We'll pop around in a day or so.

He'd signed it with a scrawl.

"You scheming old chicken thief," muttered Meralda.

The Brass Bell rang seven times. Tervis finished his coffee by the sixth peal, and he and Kervis and Meralda were out the door by the seventh.

Alone in the kitchen, Mug spread his leaves to the rising sun and watched the Tower's shadow swing wide around the park.

Carter, himself, escorted Meralda to her place at the middle King's Table. "Enjoy your breakfast, milady," he said, as he pulled back Meralda's chair and waited for her to take her place.

"Thank you, Carter," she said, sitting.

Meralda's tablemates were entirely Tirlish. At her sides sat bankers and scholars. Across from her, Yugo Austin toyed with his fork while to his right, iron magnate Cobblestone sat in barely concealed slumber.

Meralda twisted round in her seat, hoping for a glance of the Hang, and noticed many others were doing the same thing. Meralda even thought opera star Lydia Grace looked a bit annoyed as people looked past her in search of more exotic sights.

The Alon delegation was seated at the north end of the table to Meralda's right, though the Good Mother's place at the head of the table was empty. Meralda did recognize the Alon ambassador to Tirlin, who was engaged in a whispered, but agitated conversation with a red-bearded, red-kilted man who wore the diamond-braided shoulder sash of an Alon mage.

Red Mawb, said Meralda, to herself. *If so, this Red Mawb looks more like a Spree Isles pirate than a mage.* Meralda could see the man was missing an upper incisor, and a thin red scar ran the length of his face, vanishing under hair at his forehead and beard at his jaw.

And if that's Mawb, Meralda decided, *then the fat little bald man glaring at him from across the table must be Dorn Mukirk.* The fat man shifted in his seat, and Meralda caught a glimpse of a diamond-worked sash on his shoulder, as well.

Then the north doors opened, and three iron-helmed Alon guards marched in, and every Alon in the Gold Room, mages included, leaped noisily to their feet.

Meralda rose as well, remaining standing until the slight, grey-haired queen of Alonya was seated, and the rumble of conversation began anew.

The king and queen of Erya walked in a few moments later, to no fanfare, even from the Eryans present. Soon after a small army of waiters appeared, pushing silver-worked wheeled serving carts which steamed and sizzled and smelled of scrambled eggs and Westfield sausage and pancakes. But Yvin was absent, and the left-most King's Table, which was covered in white linens and marked off by red velvet ropes in obvious reserve for the Hang, was empty.

The first trumpet blew, and the waiters busied themselves with coffee urns and serving spoons. Soon after the north door opened again, and a small, black haired man darted through it.

At first, Meralda mistook him for a server. His shirt was plain, long-sleeved, off-white, with a button front and a plain circle collar, not unlike what the waiters wore. But then he turned to speak to someone behind him, and in that instant Meralda saw clearly his tawny skin and the upturned corners of his wide grey eyes.

Conversation in the Gold Room died in that same instant. The Hang in the doorway heard, and turned back to face the crowd while he held the door open.

"I present the House of Chentze," he said, in perfect, unaccented New Kingdom. "Good is the guesting in the House of Yvin."

Then he stepped forward, opened wide the north door, and held it open.

An even smaller, much older man stepped into the Gold Room, bright eyes peering around, small mouth growing into a smile. The older man wore a loose white robe belted at the waist with a thin golden braid. Soft black shoes peeked out from under his robes.

The Alon queen rose to her feet. "Let us rise in honor of our guests, who have come so far to grace us with their presence," she said, in a voice that rang throughout the Gold Room. "Rise, and show them honor."

People rose. Meralda lost sight of the Hang after that. *They are a small people,* she thought, amazed. Her last sight of the old man was of him smiling and reaching out to stroke the corner of a battered, time-worn King's Table.

Three trumpet blasts rang out, and the west doors opened, and Yvin and Pellabine charged through. Yvin took a few hurried steps, saw that the Hang were en route to their seats, and halted, Pellabine at his side. They stood until the last of the Hang were seated.

Yvin motioned the court to sit, and he and Pellabine resumed their own march for their places at the head of the center King's Table. Yvin seated his queen, and lifted his hands, turning toward the Hang.

"We bid you welcome, honored guests," he said. "Will you do us the honor of breaking fast with us?"

Now that the court was seated, Meralda could see most of the Hang delegation. There were perhaps two dozen of them, all peering back at the court with smiles and nods.

The slight, almost frail man seated at the head of his table was certainly Que-long. Meralda stared until she realized what she was doing, and turned her gaze away. But, try as she might, she could find no hint of menace in the small man's merry smile. His hair was close-cropped and white, his face round and smooth, his eyes large and dark, belying his age. When he smiled, his teeth were white, and perfect. Just before Meralda looked away, he poked his fork into a pancake and laughed.

Seated on Que-long's right was a grim-faced man, clad in a plain red robe, who sat, hands at his side, eyes moving slowly about the room. *Chezin,* thought Meralda, surprised by the man's size. *He's no bigger than Kervis.*

Que-long's wife sat to his left, primly regarding her sausages as though they might be something other than food. Her hair, too, was white, though long, and pulled back into a tight bun. Her robes were white and worked with gold fluting at the hems. She laughed at something her husband said, and laid her hand upon his shoulder, and then looked shyly up and about the room.

The Chezin rose. "It is you who do us honor, King of Tirlin," he said, his voice even and surprisingly deep. "Let the meal begin."

He sat. Que-long raised his fork high, stabbed a sausage, and brought it to his lips.

The court was suddenly full of clattering silverware and clinking glasses. Meralda ate, all the while stealing looks at the Hang, who seemed both amused and mildly embarrassed by all the attention.

Meralda tried to match faces at the table to names in the captain's report. Que-long, his Chezin, Sopan, and her shings were easy enough to single out. But what of Tolong the Long Dragon ship captain, and Donchen, the may-be ambassador?

Meralda cut up her sausages and watched. She decided Captain Tolong was seated four places to the left of Que-long. Beardless and small, he was a shade darker and quite a bit more muscular than any of his fellows.

Meralda swallowed, and cast her gaze to the other end of the Hang table.

The man who had been first through the north door met her gaze, and smiled. He was Hang, but while the other Hang sat upright or stood straight or marched with purpose toward their seats, this man lounged with an air of easy grace. *That must be Donchen*, Meralda thought, mentally checking off all the other names on the list against other members of the Hang party.

Meralda looked away, and when she glanced back he was still regarding her from across the room, his fork loaded with scrambled eggs and halted halfway from his plate to his mouth.

He smiled, and mouthed the words "good morning."

A waiter pushed a serving cart passed between them, and Meralda turned her gaze away, horrified that she might blush. *Gawking like a farm girl,* she chided herself. *I do hope he's not really an ambassador.*

When Meralda next dared a glance, the man was talking merrily with his fellows, his plate nearly empty. He did not look her way again.

Soon, the serving carts were replaced with clearing carts, and the tables began to empty. Meralda waited until Yvin wasn't looking, rose, and departed, hoping to reach the laboratory before the king or the captain could waste half of her day.

At the door, she turned for one last look at the Hang, who were being served coffee.

"They don't look like monsters, do they?" said the captain.

Meralda started. The captain stood beside her, grinning, a cup of coffee in either hand. "Thought you might need this," he said, handing her a cup. "You did seem to be in a bit of a hurry."

Meralda glared, but took the cup.

"You'll not be bothered until late today," said the captain. "If then."

Meralda let out her breath in a sigh. "Wonderful," she said. The captain sipped his coffee and motioned toward the door. "Please, let's walk," he said. "Don't want to slow you down."

Meralda walked. The captain fell into step beside her. When they were well out of earshot of the guards and halfway down the empty hall, he spoke again, in a whisper.

"There were lights in the flat, last night," he said, lifting a hand against Meralda's protests. "I saw them myself, Thaumaturge," he added, quickly. "Bright flashes. Hundreds of them. Some white, some red. Started at midnight. Exactly at midnight, with the last tolling of the Big Bell. Ended an hour later, to the minute." The captain fell silent, as a harried trio of waiters bearing sugar bowls and a platter of sausages rushed past. "Any theories, aside from mischievous ghosts?"

Meralda slowed and studied the captain's face. "Bright flashes," she said.

"Bright flashes," agreed the captain. He frowned and waggled a finger at Meralda. "You're not about to suggest I saw reflections of airship running lights, are you?" he asked. "Because that's what I told the papers, and a right lot of nonsense it was. Reflections. Bah. These were lights burning within the flat, Thaumaturge. Lights far brighter than any Alon lumber barge lamp, and certainly brighter than any reflection, of which, by the way, there weren't any." The captain lowered his hand and his voice. "You've said all along the Tower isn't haunted, Mage," he said. "Do you still hold to that? Really?"

Meralda frowned. Did she?

"I won't stand here and tell you I understand what's causing the disturbances inside the Tower, Captain," she said. "But keep in mind that we're seeing flashes of light. Nothing more, and I can think of a hundred things that might cause them, aside from restless spirits."

"Name four," said the captain. "I'm running out of things to tell the penswifts."

Meralda sighed. "You might suggest that the lights are

reactions of Tower structural spellworks to modern ward spells," she said.

"That sounds good," said the captain. "Quite reasonable."

Meralda paused at a door. "No one will believe it, of course," she said.

"No, they'll go right on blaming Otrinvion," agreed the captain. He glanced warily about. "The latest popular explanation is that our famous dead wizard is warning us that the Hang are up to no good," he whispered.

Meralda rolled her eyes. "Oh," she said. "I see. Otrinvion the Black, champion of the public good." She shook her head. "Well-known for his selfless altruism."

The captain shrugged and opened the door, looking back at Meralda with a grin. "Just so," he said, motioning Meralda through. "I've got things to attend," he said. "The Vonats are due in tonight, and we'll want to fluff their pillows beforehand."

Meralda laughed and waved, and the door shut, and she was alone in the brightly lit hall.

She made for the west stair. The palace was oddly deserted, while everyone, even the serving staff and the guards, gathered near the Gold Room for a glimpse of the Hang. Meralda's footfalls were loud and fast, and she thought of the Tower and the long, winding stair.

Flashes, she thought. *Red and white. Bright enough to be seen from the flat. A possible interaction between my failed ward spell and what?*

"Structural spellworks," she whispered, with a small frown. Six centuries of mages had poked and pried at the Tower for traces of just such spells, hoping to glean from them some hint as to how the monstrous structure was erected.

Not one single spell had ever been detected, much less isolated or studied.

Meralda reached the west stair landing, and heard the Bellringers speaking and laughing from their post above.

Meralda banished her frown and mounted the stair. "Good morning, Thaumaturge," said Kervis, as she clambered up. "What will we be doing today?"

Meralda brushed back a stray lock of hair.

"Chasing shadows," she said. "What else?"

Meralda put down her pen.

About her, the laboratory whirred and clicked and sparkled. Meralda rubbed her eyes and twisted in her chair, finally lifting her arms high over her head and stretching until her back popped and some of the stiffness fled.

Her desk was covered with architect's papers, and they were covered with sketches of the Tower and calculations for the latching spell. Meralda sighed and shuffled papers, searching through them for errors or omissions. Finding none, she opened a desk drawer, pulled a fresh page from within it, and set about her final set of calculations.

Done, she stared at the numbers.

"Two hundred and forty-two," she said aloud. "Two hundred and forty-two unique refractive spellworks. Minimum."

Let's see, she thought. *Sixteen days remain, which means that even if I started today, I'd need to shape, cast, and latch fifteen refractive volumes each day until the Accords.*

Meralda took in a slow, deep breath. She wasn't sure if it was panic or rage or a mixture of both that welled up in her chest. Fifteen spells a day? More, if either the Tower latch or the refractive spells needed refinement?

A knock sounded at the laboratory door.

"Thaumaturge," said the king. "Open the doors."

Meralda sprang to her feet and marched for the doors. She felt the blood drain away from her face. *If Yvin is here,* she thought, *he's probably got the entire Hang delegation with him, and he's idly promised them I'll levitate the palace by lunchtime.*

Meralda reached the doors. As she turned the doorknob and pulled, the king spoke again. "Open for your king!" he cried, his voice lifting to a shout. "Open, lest I halve your pay and turn your laboratory into a stable!"

Meralda barely had time to lift an eyebrow and step backward as the doors swung open.

Before her stood a red-faced, open-mouthed palace guard. In his right hand he held a large bird cage, draped over with a white bed sheet. The guard's expression was one of extreme and sudden horror.

Kervis and Tervis, wide-eyed, flanked the lad, though their own twin faces were masks of barely concealed mirth.

The birdcage spoke. "Good morning, Mistress," it said, in Mug's voice. "Take me inside, won't you? All this swinging about has left me quite ill."

The guard, a young lad unknown to Meralda, thrust the birdcage out to her. "He asked to be brought here, Thaumaturge. The door guards approved it."

Meralda took the bird cage. The guard saluted, turned, and fled. Kervis, straight-faced, quietly shut the laboratory door.

"I'm impressed," said Meralda. "How did you manage this?"

A single red eye poked out beyond the bed sheet. "I sang," said Mug. "'La Volta' from *Nights in the Sun*. I did all four voices," he added, proudly. "Friend and music lover Mrs. Whitlonk called for Doorman Smith. I asked him to call for a guard, a bird cage, and a bed sheet, and here I am, ready to serve," he said. The eye turned away from surveying the laboratory and fixed itself on Meralda. "How do you stand it?" he asked. "The world, spinning and moving about like this—ugh," he said, retracting his eye.

Meralda bore him to her desk, cleared a space of papers, and set the cage gently down.

"No more spinning, at least for the moment," she said. "May I remove the sheet?"

"Please do," said Mug. Meralda lifted the bed sheet, and Mug blinked in the light.

"I see things haven't changed here," he said, peering about in all directions at once. Half his eyes fell upon the papers scattered across Meralda's long desk. "You're making progress," he added.

Meralda shrugged. "Some," she said. She frowned at the bird cage, and tilted her head. "You'll lose leaves if you sit here all day without the sun," she said. "Wait a moment."

Meralda walked quickly to the west wall, where old Goboy's scrying mirror stood, glowing faintly behind its blanket. Meralda grasped it by both sides and pulled, dragging it carefully across the floor until it rested beside her desk, leaning against a cabinet filled with second century glassworks.

Mug regarded the covered mirror with all of his eyes. "That's old Goboy's scrying glass, isn't it?" he said. "Still have to keep it covered, I see."

"It is, and I do," replied Meralda. She reached out, grasped the plain blue blanket that covered the glass, pulled it away, and let it drop to the floor.

For a moment, her reflection looked back at her. Meralda brought her hand to her lips, considering her words. The Meralda in the mirror, hands still at her sides, smiled and took a single step forward, as if she were about to step out of the frame and into the laboratory.

"Spooky," said Mug.

"Mirror, mirror," said Meralda, as her reflection winked and put forth its right hand, palm up, beckoning Meralda to take it, and follow. "Show me sky," said Meralda, forcing herself to meet her reflection's gaze. "Sky, above the palace, and none of your tricks. I'm not in the mood. Is that clear?"

Meralda's reflection drew back its hand, blew Meralda a kiss, and vanished. Sudden bright sunlight poured from the glass.

"Ahhh," said Mug, swiveling his leaves toward the light. "Better. Thank, you, Mage," he added.

Meralda kicked the blanket aside and pulled back her chair. With a sidelong glance at the mirror, which showed only blue sky and the top half of a slow-moving airship, she sat, and regarded her papers.

"I'm glad you're here, Mug," she said, with a sigh. Meralda considered Mug's aversion to travel and sought out a pair of his blue eyes. "What made you do it?"

"Well, what sort of assistant perches above the kitchen sink all day when his thaumaturge is off casting eldritch spells in the palace?" said Mug. "A poor one, that's what," he added, quickly. "So I decided a bit of traveling was in order, until this ordeal is done." He tossed his leaves dismissively. "It's not so bad, really, once one gets over the nausea, the vertigo, the feeling of one's roots falling as the earth plummets away."

Meralda shook her head. "Thank you," she said.

"You're welcome," said Mug. "Now then. It looks like you've got the spellworks roughed out, if nothing else."

"I do," said Meralda. "All two hundred and forty-two of them."

Mug was silent a moment. "One at a time, mistress," he said. "Just like in college." Mug poked forth a tendril and pointed at a diagram. "You'll start here, will you?"

Meralda leaned back, and closed her eyes. *It's only sixteen days,* she said, to herself. *Sixteen more days.*

"Yes," she said. "I'll start there." Just like college. One crisis at a time. "The latching spell will be the worst of all. Before I cast the real thing, though, I need to latch a quarter-scale version to the Tower, and hang a pair of refractors to that, and keep everything hung there a day and a night." She opened her eyes. "If I hurry, I could latch and hang all three today, before sunset." *If,* she added silently, *that idiot king will leave me alone long enough to work.*

Mug tapped the paper. "Spoken like a mage," he said. "Shall

I check over your math, just in case?"

"Please do," said Meralda. She rose and spread her papers for Mug to see. "I'll get started on the latch."

Mug's eyes poked between the wire bars of his bird cage, and he peered at papers and began to hum. By the time Meralda was at her work bench, Mug was issuing a perfect rendition of Sovett's *Music for the Night*, including the hundred-voice chorus and the flute ensemble.

Meralda smiled, spoke a word, clamped a copper cable that ran up from the floor to the metal bench top, and put forth her Sight. Her work bench was suddenly lit with dozens of small glows and hanging traceries of light. The sharp silver tines of the five hundred year old charge dissipater bolted to the far end of the bench began to hiss and spit tiny sparks toward the ceiling.

She picked up a fresh holdstone. Then twisted the top, exposing the silver and gold contacts formed in the shapes of grinning dragon faces, and placed the holdstone down carefully on a sheet of oft-scorched felt. Then she found her favorite brass retaining wand amid the clutter, thought back to her calculations, and began to shape the latch.

At noon, a courier arrived, bearing a note from Yvin. "Be excused from the noon court session," it read. Meralda smiled. It was already half-past. *I excused myself, thank you very much.* "But please send word on the status of your shadow spell. The Hang seem fascinated by the idea."

The courier shuffled nervously from foot to foot, just outside the laboratory doors. Kervis and Tervis, Meralda noted, appeared to take no notice of the flashes and crackles that shone and sounded faintly at her back.

She turned the king's paper over and pulled a pencil from behind her ear.

"Testing first spellworks today," she wrote. "Will advise if test is successful."

Good, she thought. *It's vague and worrisome, but absolutely true.*

"Thank you," she said, handing the message tray and paper back to the courier.

He turned and trotted away.

"Shall one of us fetch you some lunch, Thaumaturge?" Kervis asked.

"Do that," replied Meralda. "Get some for yourselves, and wrap something up for Angis, too," she said.

"Are we going to the Tower?" asked Tervis.

Meralda met his eyes. "To the Tower, yes," she said. "But not up it. We'll be working from the park today."

Relief eased the features of both Bellringers' faces. "Good," said Tervis. "The night watch saw lights again last night."

Meralda nodded, as if she knew. *I've got to get a paper,* she thought. *Not that a word of it can be believed.*

"That won't concern us today," she said. "If one of you will fetch us lunch, I'll be ready to go when you return."

"I'll go," said Tervis. He grinned slightly. "I'm sure the general here can't carry food and his new siege piece."

Kervis reddened. Meralda glanced down and to her right, at the crossbow propped against the wall, and realized this weapon was even larger than the monstrous Oldmark the boy had been carrying the day before.

"The armorer said it was the very latest weapon available," said Kervis, airily. "It's got twice the stopping power of an Oldmark."

Meralda lifted her hand. "I'm sure it's a formidable crossbow," she said. "And I appreciate your zeal. Both of you." She smiled. "Now then. Lunch? And then to the Tower?"

"We'll be ready," said Tervis. "Back in a bit."

Meralda nodded, stepped back, and let the doors swing shut.

"What's he got out there?" asked Mug. "A mule-drawn catapult?"

"Nearly," said Meralda, softly. She made her way back to her work bench. "The lad seems to expect a surprise attack by armored assassins," she added.

"He might do better to expect ghosts," said Mug. Meralda pretended not to hear.

"Let's see," she said aloud. "I'll need the holdstones, both retaining wands, the charger and the Riggin bottles." She pulled her instrument bag from beneath the work bench and opened it. "What else?"

Mug reeled off more instruments and implements, and Meralda began to pack them carefully in her bag. *More lights,* she mused, as she worked. *Unless news of the Hang overshadows the Tower, the papers will be full of news of the haunting.*

Or worse, thought Meralda. Thus far, the papers had been content to play up the lights. But Meralda remembered something else she'd read, more than once, in old books about the Tower. The lights in the flat were also said to precede disaster for Tirlin.

Lights, Meralda recalled, were seen in the summer of 1566. In the autumn of that year, the Red Fever had swept through the Realms, taking half of Tirlin to the grave. The lights in 1714 preceded a great shaking of the ground which toppled two of the palace spires, destroyed half a city block in the Narrows, and sent the Lamp River running backwards for three days.

Dates and calamities raced through Meralda's mind. She assured herself that many of the stories were no more than just stories, and tales of lights in the flat almost certainly sprang up well after the events.

Still, though, the lights in 1566 and the ones in 1714 were well documented, as were the calamities they were said to presage.

And yet the papers—even the *Post*—said nothing. Meralda wondered idly if Yvin had some control over the press after all.

"Mistress?" said Mug. "You're ignoring me, aren't you?"

Meralda looked up and smiled. "Constantly," she said.

Mug snorted. "I was saying," he said, in Mrs. Whitlonk's voice, "that perhaps you ought to consider rummaging through this wizard's treasure trove and picking out something small and lethal to carry. Surely some of these wondrous mighty magics have offensive uses."

Meralda stared. "Have you been talking to Shingvere?"

"Certainly," he said. "I hailed a cab and searched him out just this morning. We had coffee, and then went bowling." Mug snorted. "Really, mistress, why would you think such a thing?"

Meralda went back to her packing. "It sounds very Eryan,

this notion of walking about with military magics hidden in one's pockets. Shingvere hasn't been by to see you?"

"He has not," said Mug. "And why is the notion of protecting oneself so outlandish? You cannot deny these are unusual times."

Meralda placed a coil of copper rope in the bag, counted her glass insulating rings, and added another to the bag. "The best weapon is an alert mind."

Mug moaned. "Fine. Throw that at the Vonats when what's-his-name attacks with flaming tornadoes."

Meralda closed her bag and frowned. "You have been talking to Shingvere."

Mug sighed, long and loud. "I'm merely urging you to a bit of caution, mistress," he said. "I hardly need the advice of foreign wizards to do that, now do I?"

Meralda hefted her bag. "I suppose not," she said. "And I appreciate it. I'll take measures if the need arises. Is that satisfactory?"

Mug tossed his leaves. "It will have to do." His eyes whirled about the room. "Time to take another journey, I see."

"You can stay here. Watch the mirror. Check my math."

Mug gathered in his leaves. "No," he said. "I go, too."

Meralda walked to her desk and put down her instrument bag. "Are you sure?"

"I'm sure," said Mug. "Bed sheet, if you please. I'll leave my dignity here."

Meralda covered Mug's cage and waited for Tervis to knock at her door.

The park was, if anything, more crowded than the day before. Schools had been let out, so in addition to the sightseers and the carpenters and the court officials, children of every age were about, darting past in screaming mobs, a harried, open-mouthed nanny or parent in determined, but futile pursuit.

The Alons, shirtless and bellowing, were also present, and quite a crowd was gathered to watch their football game. Food sellers wandered among the spectators, their calls of "Sausages! Apples! Hot rolls, hot rolls here!" nearly drowned out by the rush and thud of the madly charging Alons struggling on the field.

The stands about the Tower, mere skeletons and scaffolds just a few days ago, were quickly taking shape. Meralda chose to work from Yvin's half-completed speaking platform, as it afforded a good view of the Tower and the park while keeping the press of the workers and the crowds from wandering too close. After commandeering a work table from the Builder's Guild and convincing Mug that the barely perceptible breeze was hardly capable of leveling the platform, Meralda set to work.

Before she could latch to the Tower, she first had to raise and shape the spell. Mug helped, reeling off whole sections of her notes from memory while Meralda stored the sections in her wands, but even so the shaping of the latch was no quick task.

As the afternoon wore on, the crowd in the park grew larger. *It looks like a sea of hats,* Meralda noted, as the throngs milled about beneath her. *It's a good thing Tervis and Kervis are guarding the stair, or I'd be shoulder-to-shoulder up here.*

Beyond the Tower, though, the crowds were not nearly so

thick. In fact, a stone's throw on the Tower's backside, only carriage drivers and particularly naughty children idled in the sun on either side of the Wizard's Walk. Past them, there was no one, save one lone child, and his bright yellow kite.

Meralda wiped her brow with a handkerchief, muttered a word, and held her retaining wand to a fresh holdstone. The wand crackled and spat as it charged, and as Meralda waited she watched the child.

Back and forth he ran, stout legs pumping. His yellow kite with its slanted red cat eyes and long red tail bumped off the grass behind him.

Meralda felt for any hint of a wind on her skin, but even from atop the king's platform she felt none. *It's a beautiful day*, she thought, *but hardly a day for kites.*

Still, the child ran on. He would start at the edge of the walk, then dash south, his right arm held high, his body leaning into his charge. He ran as far and as fast as he could, and when he began to falter, he would stop, pant for a moment, then gather his kite, wrap the tail carefully around his arm, and walk slowly back toward the walk. Then he would charge toward the west wall, all over again.

The holdstone emptied with a hiss and a brief blue flash. Inside the glass bottle, the silver and gold elements of the holdstone whirled, moving away from each other in a complex spiral as the spell energies escaped. When the coils were still, Meralda took the wand away, and Mug touched her wrist with a tendril.

"Ready for the next thread?" he asked.

Meralda smiled. It felt good, to be doing magic again. Even if it was magic for a questionable cause. "I'm ready," she said. "Shall I turn to a fresh page?"

Mug agreed, and she took the sheet of architect's paper from the top, slid it beneath the others, and replaced the emptied holdstones at the corners of the stack, in case a breeze blew past.

Mug began to read, and Meralda lifted her wand. The child began another mad dash across the grass. Meralda felt again for any hint of a breeze, but the air was still, and the kite darted and spun, but never flew.

The wand buzzed and crackled, holding the untethered spell threads to its mass as Meralda added yet another. To anyone watching with second sight, Meralda knew she would appear to be grasping a handful of glowing, windswept ropes, all writhing and tangling and knotting with their fellows. Only when she spoke the final word would the spell take shape and latch to the Tower. But to the crowds below, she appeared to be standing and muttering, a short brass wand held at eye level before her.

Another spell thread joined the rest. Meralda moved the retaining wand from her left hand to her right, and prepared for the next.

When she cast a glance toward the child and his kite, she saw that he was no longer alone. A man was waiting for him, as the boy marched wearily back to his starting place on the walk.

The man dropped to one knee, and the two spoke for a moment. Then the boy carefully unwrapped the kite's tail from his arm and presented kite, tail, and ball of string to the man, who took them all before rising to his feet.

Time to go home, thought Meralda. *It simply isn't a day for kites.*

Then, to Meralda's surprise, the man bowed, lofted the kite, and charged onto the grass, following the same path the boy had taken so many times before.

Meralda watched, as did no small number of the cabbies and idlers on the walk. Arms went up, as fingers pointed, and though Meralda heard nothing she could imagine their laughter.

The man ran. *No, that isn't right,* Meralda thought. The child ran, legs pumping, arms churning away madly at the air. This man was gliding.

Only his legs seemed to move. His chest barely rose, barely fell. He held his right arm up, playing out the string.

On and on he ran. He reached the point where the child had stopped and turned, and on he went, his gait increasing, his steps long and fast. Meralda nearly lost the latch, and when Mug snapped out "Mistress! Mind the spell!" she had to look away, and calm the wand.

When she cast her glance back toward the man, he was merely a dot against the green grass of the park. But the kite rose above him, the red cat eyes wheeling and darting, the tail coiling and snapping.

The faint sound of cheering rose up, and Meralda saw the cabbies and the idlers had risen to their feet, their laughter turned to cheers and shouts, and their hands uplifted. The boy danced and waved, his voice lifted with the rest.

The kite whirled and swooped, climbing and rising, playing in a wind Meralda still couldn't feel. Soon, it, too, was merely a dot and a faint streak of tail.

The man turned and began to walk back toward the walk and the child. Meralda watched the far-off kite for a moment, expecting it to plummet at any moment. It remained aloft, straining at the string, snapping faintly from high above.

Meralda hung another thread by the time the man reached the child, who still danced with glee. The cabbies rose to their feet and gave the small man a final round of cheers and hoots. The man halted, bowed to the cabbies, placed the string gravely in the boy's hand, and patted the child's head once before the lad darted away, kite string in hand.

After a moment, the man put his hands in his pockets, turned his back to the Tower, and ambled away, alone on the walk.

Meralda watched him go while her wand recharged. Soon he reached the Old Oaks, and vanished beneath them, swallowed up by the distance and the dark beneath the boughs.

"What are you mooning about?" said Mug.

"Nothing," said Meralda, turning back toward her makeshift work bench and Mug. "Just catching my breath."

"Hmmph," said Mug. He strained to lift a pair of green eyes over the rail.

Meralda ignored him, and hung another thread.

"That should be most of the primary latchwork," said Mug, when she was done. "Good thing, too. Six bells."

Meralda lifted an eyebrow. "Six o'clock? Already?"

"Time flies," said Mug. Meralda hadn't heard the Big Bell ring, but she realized Mug was right. The Tower's shadow had engulfed the stands, and the air had gone damp and cool. *I'll do well to latch to the Tower today*, Meralda realized, with a frown. *The refractors will have to wait.*

Her stomach growled. She walked to the head of the stair and shouted down to Kervis. "Guardsman," she said, above the din. "Bring up a biscuit, will you?"

Kervis nodded and darted up. "Here you are," he said, halting just below the top, a paper-wrapped biscuit held forth. "Nearly done, Thaumaturge?"

Meralda took the biscuit. "Nearly so," she said. Kervis nodded in relief.

A crowd had gathered at the foot of the stair, and Meralda was surprised at how closely they pressed about Tervis. "Has it been like this long?" she asked, with a nod toward the ground.

Kervis sighed. "Yes ma'am," he said. "Half of 'em are penswifts. We'd like to have knocked a few heads when they decided they could just shove on past," he said. "The other half are aldermen and civilian Street Watch volunteers," he said, lowering his voice. "They want to talk about the haint."

"The haunt," corrected Meralda, automatically.

Kervis tilted his head. "I told them they wouldn't be allowed to waste your time talking about such nonsense. I hope that was the right thing to say."

"Keep saying it. Maybe they'll listen, sooner or later."

"Yes, ma'am." Kervis glanced down. Tervis had been forced by the press of the crowd to retreat a step up the stair.

"I'd better get back," said Kervis. "Don't worry about leaving. We sent for help, to get you through the crowd."

"Thank you," said Meralda. Kervis nodded and darted down the stair, bellowing.

When Meralda turned, she found Mug's eyes upon her. "Did you hear?"

"I heard," he said. "The *Post* will just make up whatever it is they think you aren't telling them."

Meralda tore the paper wrapping from her biscuit. "Do you suppose," she asked, wearily, "that, before the Accords are done, every storied childhood boogie from every one of the Five Realms will put in an appearance?"

"Sooner or later," said Mug, cheerfully. "It's the dragon I'm looking forward to the most."

Meralda took a bite, marched back to her worktable, and set about hanging the last few threads of the latch.

Meralda lifted her hands, touched the ice-rimed ends of two fat copper wands together, and unleashed the latching spell with a long, loud word.

The spell leaped. Meralda watched it go. To her second sight, it appeared as though an enormous blob composed of tangled, luminous spider's webs wobbled and darted through the air, rising up against the Tower's bulk to seek out the Wizard's Flat.

Meralda looked up and up, craning her head as the latch ascended. Mug's eyes followed as well, and he began to count aloud.

"One, two, three, four..."

The spell reached the top of the Tower, surrounding the flat. The glowing threads lashed about, flattening into a fat circular disk centered on the top of the flat like the brim of a hat.

"...five, six..."

The hat brim spun, faster and faster, threads straightening and elongating at right angles to the Tower's axis until the spell was a flat, red-edged blur. Then, with a flash, it vanished.

"...seven."

The wands in Meralda's hand went icy cold.

"And done," said Meralda. She watched for a moment, but the spell remained latched. At last she lowered her face, and met Mug's gaze.

"Not just done, but well done," said Mug. "You do realize that you're the first mage to latch a work to the Tower in the last four hundred years."

Meralda yawned. She couldn't stop herself. Weariness fell hard upon her as the latch sailed skyward. Weariness, and a sudden urgent longing for a water closet.

Mug chuckled. "I see," he said. "I suppose you're open to my suggestion that we pack up and go home. Even if you hung a refractor tonight, you'd not know if it worked until the morning."

"Home it is," said Meralda. She leaned over the rail, cast a despairing eye upon the close-packed crowds still gathered at the foot of the Tower. *Waiting for the lights,* she thought. Waiting for the shade of dread Otrinvion.

"At least the captain can blame any lights tonight on me," she said, dreading the walk through the mob.

"I've kept a pair of eyes on the flat, but haven't seen any yet," said Mug. "But, if our spook sticks to strict ghostly custom, they won't start until midnight or after. He's a traditionalist, our

Otrinvion. None of these contemporary early evening haunting practices for him, no, ma'am."

Meralda looked up from the shadowed crowds below, and sought out the flat again. The Tower sulked against a sky gone nearly dark. No stars were out yet, but they would be, and soon.

Meralda thought about the empty space within the Tower, and the darkness on the stair, and she shivered and looked away.

"Let's go home," she said, briskly. "Reasonable people don't stand in the dark and gawk at empty rooms."

"Indeed not," said Mug, as Meralda folded papers. "They go home, and read about it the next morning."

Meralda wrapped her wands with thick cotton pads and shoved them in the bag, well away from the holdstones. "Only if one takes the *Post*," she said. The spent Riggin bottles, which still glowed faintly, went in next. "One wonders what they'll print when the lights stop and the Hang go home."

Mug tossed his leaves. "The haunted Tower ought to be good through First Snow."

Meralda grabbed and shoved and packed until the guild work table was bare. She slung the bag over her shoulder and prepared Mug's cage and sheet.

"Ready?" she asked.

"Ready," replied Mug. Meralda gently lifted him from the table and made for the stair. "Tervis," she called, at the first tread. "A hand, please."

Tervis clambered up the stair. "Coming, ma'am," he called.

"Take Mug, if you will," said Meralda.

Tervis reached the top, and carefully took the bird cage

handle from Meralda. "There's a man waiting to see you at the bottom," said Tervis, in a whisper. "He won't say who he is, but we think he's a penswift."

Meralda groaned. "I've been standing on this bloody scaffold for six hours," she said, to Tervis' back. "Unless he's prepared to follow me into a water closet, I don't have time for this."

Tervis had turned his back, but his ear lobes went suddenly red, and Meralda rolled her eyes. "Forgive me, Guardsman," she said. "We mages are a grumpy lot."

Tervis sped wordlessly down the stairs. Mug groaned softly.

"The thaumaturge has, um, pressing business elsewhere," said Tervis, to someone at the bottom of the stairs. "Go away."

Meralda smiled.

More words were spoken, but were inaudible over the din of the crowd.

Three-quarters of the way down the stair, she slowed. The crowd pressed close against the Bellringers, who had to take a step ahead every few moments to hold their ground against the press.

Meralda felt her chest tighten at the thought of forcing her way through such a press. At sight of her, the murmuring redoubled, and a tall man in a light tan overcoat, staring up at the sorceress, snatched a pencil from behind his ear.

Meralda lifted her hand and spoke a word. A magelight flared noiselessly to life, hovering above her right shoulder, bright in the darkness of the stairwell.

"I have no comments," said Meralda, in a near shout. "Other than to point out that I'm tired, and I'm going home."

"Then you wouldn't care to dispute allegations that your work here today was intended to bind the shade of Otrinvion to the Tower," shouted the man.

"Guardsman Kervis," said Meralda. "Which is more annoying, street minstrels, or penswifts?"

"Penswifts, ma'am," shouted Kervis, without turning. Meralda left the stair, and met the penswift's eyes.

"My work here today concerned moving the Tower's shadow for the King's Accord Commencement speech," she said, eyeing the crowd with growing dismay. Even with the Bellringers at the fore, they'd never make it to the walk through that.

If the help Kervis mentioned doesn't get here soon, she thought, *I swear I'll part them myself.*

"What of the lights in the flat, Thaumaturge?" said the penswift, scribbling away. Meralda realized the man was not only writing, but sketching her likeness as well. "They were seen by at least a hundred people. Are you willing to dismiss all these reports?"

"I deny the Tower is haunted," snapped Meralda. "The lights could be anything. Except ghosts." Out in the dark the crowd began to move. And were those horsemen, bobbing above the shoulders of the rest?

Hooves clopped on stone, and in the darkening distance Meralda saw riders drawing nearer. "They're here," said Kervis. "You'll be leaving now," he added, to the penswift.

"Thank you for your time, Thaumaturge," he said, closing his pad before Meralda could get a look at his notes or her sketch.

"You're welcome," said Meralda gruffly.

The crowd withdrew, and a half-dozen mounted City Guards trotted up to the base of the stand.

"Let's go home," said Meralda, stepping onto the dew damp grass.

"Mind the wobbling," said Mug.

Meralda hefted Mug's cage and hurried for Angis' cab, and home.

Chapter Eight

Meralda slept, and dreamed.

She saw Hang ships sail into Tirlin. Their masts rose up taller than the Tower, so tall the crow's nests trailed shreds of clouds and shoved the sun aside. Meralda watched the streets fill with terrified crowds, and heard the Big Bell peal out alarms, and smelled smoke from distant fires. Still the masts came nearer, riding over and grinding down the palace, sailing inexorably toward Meralda.

Thick black smoke rose and spread behind the ships, until it blotted out the sky. Unable to move away from her window, unable to close her eyes or look away or even scream, Meralda watched the smoke swirl and billow and swell until it became a monstrous, mad-eyed face, eyes full of glowing red sparks.

The mouth moved and grumbled thunder, and the eyes turned full upon Meralda, and with a wrench and a start she awoke.

The five-twenty trolley rattled past, and then Fairlane was silent. Meralda lay gasping beneath her tangled, sweat-streaked covers and waited for the pounding of her heart to slow.

"Mistress?" came Mug's sleepy voice from the kitchen. "Are you dreaming?"

"It's all right, Mug," she replied. "Go back to sleep."

"You cried out," he said.

Meralda poked her head out of the covers and took a breath of cool air. "Nightmare," she said. She remembered Hang masts in the clouds, threw back the bedclothes, and sat up wearily.

Might as well get an early start, she thought. *I certainly won't go back to sleep after that.*

She yawned, rubbed her eyes, and arose. *What was it Grandmother always said, when we children had nightmares?*

"Hot baths banish boogeymen," she muttered.

"Then take a long one," chirped Mug. Meralda heard his leaves rustle as he stretched. "It's still dark," he announced. "Where's that lazy sun?"

Meralda headed for her water closet, kicking slippers out of her way as she went. She passed her bedroom window. It was dark, and the curtains were drawn, and yet Meralda hurried past, a small part of her sure that a face in the sky was still trying to peer in at her, still trying to open its mouth and speak horrors to her in a voice as loud and harsh as thunder.

"Nonsense," she said, and she reached her bathroom, called up a light, and shut the door behind her.

"We're a sight," said Meralda, smiling into a soft, chill breeze. "A mage and her bird cage, out for a lark."

She stood alone on the sidewalk in front of her building, waiting for Angis and the Bellringers. Traffic on Fairlane hurried past, turning sleepy-eyed but questioning faces toward the thaumaturge and her drape-covered birdcage, from which a trio of blue eyes on vines protruded and looked about.

Mug chuckled. "You're being recognized, mistress. Must be the papers." he said. "Ah, fame. Better drag out the hats with the veils again."

Meralda shrugged. The bright sun beamed down, its rays slanting out of a deep blue sky. The wind that sailed past was cold, but dry. Tirlin awoke, safe and secure, bustling about her as if the Hang and the Tower and the Vonats were all on the other side of the sea.

Mug spoke. "Here comes Angis," he said, and Meralda followed the aim of his eyes up the street.

Fairlane was full. Carriages and lumber wagons and cabs and road barges thundered past, but Meralda saw no sign of Angis. "He's coming, just around the corner," said Mug. "Listen."

Clop-clop, multiplied by a hundred sets of hooves, blurred by the rattles and roll of as many tires. Meralda lifted an eyebrow, marveling at Mug's hearing as Angis wheeled around the corner at Kemp.

Before her, a black army troop cab braked with a screech, rolled to the curb, and disgorged the Bellringers.

"Good morning, Thaumaturge," said Kervis, with a small bow. "You're up early."

Meralda smiled. The troop cab rattled away. "Up before the guardsmen. I hope you gentlemen have had breakfast."

"Some of us have had it twice," said Tervis, nudging his brother.

Angis brought his cab to a halt. "Well, well," he said, to

Meralda and her guards. "Good morning, Thaumaturge. Lads," he added setting his brake and clambering down. "Good to see you all out and ready."

Meralda spied a rolled-up newspaper peeking from beneath Angis' vest.

"Oh, no," groaned Meralda. "That's for me, isn't it?"

Angis withdrew the *Post*.

"Got a good likeness of you on page two," said Angis, with no hint of a grin. "Kind of winsome-like. I think the lad was a bit sweet on you."

Meralda took the *Post*, but didn't unroll it. "Save me some time," she said to Angis as Mug sent a half-dozen eyes weaving toward the paper. "Just the high points, please."

Angis shrugged. "Well, let's see," he said. "The Hang are buying up bookstores. Not the bricks and the doors. Just the books. All of them. They pay in gold, and I gather more than one or two booksellers just got rich, because the Hang don't haggle. They just pile up gold until someone says yes."

"Tell her about the haint," said Kervis.

Angis chuckled. "Right lot of hogwash, that," he said. "A street minstrel claims something grabbed him in an alley off Newbrick," he said. "Just after dark, last night. Claimed it took three of his fellows to beat it back. Street minstrels," spat Angis. "They'd claim they climbed the Tower if there was a penny in the tale."

Kervis chimed in. "We heard some of the boys in the barracks talking, ma'am," he said. "The Watch called the guard out last night, after the attack." Kervis glanced about. "A couple of them claim they saw a gaunt. Right here in Tirlin!"

Mug lifted a corner of his bed sheet. "Do you even know what a gaunt is, lad?" he asked.

"It's somebody dead who died in a marsh, and comes back to get their vengeance," said Tervis. "It's just an old story from Phendeli. Isn't that right, ma'am?"

Meralda nodded, stuffed the rolled-up paper under her arm, and lifted Mug's cage. "That's right, Guardsman Tervis," she said. "It's just an old story. In any case, the nearest marsh is a good four hundred miles from here."

"Long walk for a dead man," said Mug. "Unless, of course, our Phendelit friends packed him in their luggage."

"Would you get my bag, Tervis?" asked Meralda.

"Yes, ma'am," said Tervis.

Angis held the door, and Meralda found her seat. Tervis clambered in behind her, smiling and smelling of a rather strong army soap.

"Why do you suppose the Hang would buy whole bookstores?" he asked, as the cab rolled into traffic.

Meralda shrugged. "I imagine they'll take the books home to study," she said.

"That's what I decided," said Tervis. "Going home, I mean. After all, if they were planning to stay, or invade, why would they bother to buy anything? They could just wait and take what they want after the war."

Meralda tilted her head. "Oh, I don't think they came to invade us," she said. "Five ships is hardly an invasion fleet, even if they are Great Sea five-masters," she added.

Tervis looked about, leaned forward, and lowered his voice.

"Ma'am," he said, in a ragged whisper. "I heard something. They said not to tell it again, but..." His brow furrowed, and he took a breath. "I hear there might be other ships on the way."

Mug whistled softly. The cab rolled into a pothole, and Meralda had to steady herself with the door latch.

"Are there?" asked Tervis. "Other ships, I mean. I know it's a secret and all, but are there?"

"Guardsman," said Meralda. "I have heard no news of any additional Hang ships, of any sort, anywhere. I say this as a member in full of the Court of Tirlin, and I spoke to the king just yesterday. Can the person who told you about this new Hang fleet say the same?"

Kervis let out his breath in a whoosh. "No, they can't," he said, with a relieved grin. "I'm pretty sure they spent yesterday cleaning latrines."

"Ah," said Mug. "That alone should tell you something about their sources," he added.

Tervis' grin vanished.

"Don't worry, lad," said Mug. "I rather like you, and your brother what's-his-name. I won't tell the captain you were discussing state secrets in a public cab."

"That's right," said Meralda, nudging the cage with her boot toe. "He won't."

Tervis sat back in his seat. "I don't mind telling you I was worried," he said.

"I'll bet most of the army is still worried," said Mug, lifting a red eye up toward Meralda. "Wonder where such a tale came from?"

Yes, thought Meralda. *I wonder*. It was, after all, just a story.

Wasn't it?

Meralda dismissed the thought with a shrug. "Well," she said, unrolling the paper and rifling through it. "Let's see what that miserable penswift did to my hair."

Meralda stared in horror at her picture. "I don't own a blouse with a neckline that low," she fumed.

Mug sneaked an eye up and snickered at the drawing.

"He fancies you a cabaret dancer, seems like."

Meralda quickly turned the page.

"More soldiers," said Mug, sweeping the park with a dozen of his eyes. From his perch on the platform's rail, he commanded a good view of the entire southern park. "And another dozen mounted guards. Something's up, mistress," he said.

Meralda nodded. In her hand she held a cold retaining wand. The holdstone it drew from was nearly depleted, and the first refractor was only half cast.

"Hold," she spoke, biting back one of Angis' words. Mug waved his eyes her way.

"Problem?" he asked.

"Blasted holdstone went warm," she said. The half-cast refractor whirled and twisted in her second sight as she groped on the work bench for a fresh holdstone.

A trumpet blew, loud and close and shrill, and Meralda started and dropped the refractor.

The spell whipped away, tangling and coiling and writhing, grounding itself in the park halfway to the Tower amid a single brief dance of shadows.

Meralda leaned glaring over the rail. Down in the crowd at the base of the half-completed speaking platform, a child hooted in glee and raised his battered trumpet to his lips in preparation for another blast.

"Shall I have him shot?" asked Mug. "Kervis is dying to shoot someone."

Meralda turned from the rail, took a deep breath, and counted to ten. Mug waited silently.

"It's early, yet," said Meralda at last. "I have plenty of time."

"Of course you do," said Mug. "Still, perhaps a minor wound?"

"Mug," said Meralda.

"Silent meditation, I understand," said Mug. His eyes resumed their sweep of the park. "Take a deep breath, won't you?"

Meralda found a fresh holdstone and a new retaining wand. "Begin," she said, and extended her second sight. "Refract."

"The Hang," said Mug. "Coming this way." He paused, then brought more eyes to bear on the Wizard's Walk. "Sorry, mistress," he said. "Looks like we'll be entertaining, this morning. Better conjure up a couch, and some drinks."

"Finish," spat Meralda. Her wand buzzed angrily, but soon fell quiet, and Meralda wrapped it in a cloth and put it down on her worktable. "I really should come early and set wards at all the bloody gates and leave them there until the Accords," she said. "It's the only way I'll ever get any work done."

She watched as a half-dozen Hang, led by six mounted palace guards and surrounded by several dozen of the Watch, ambled down the walk. Meralda recognized Que-long, his red-robed Chezin, and Loman, the elderly Hang wizard. Loman was being pushed down the walk in a plain infirmary-issue wheelchair, by a lad whose head barely peeped over the back. Fromarch and Shingvere flanked Loman's wheelchair, and all three wizards seemed lost in hand waving and animated conversation.

As the party drew near, Meralda tried to make out the faces or the names of the other Hang, but the press of the crowd and the mounted guards prevented her from seeing them more clearly.

"Marvelous," she muttered, under her breath.

Tervis came clambering up the stair, halting when his head was just above the floor. "The Hang are coming to see you, ma'am," he said. "We just got word from a runner."

"Thank you, Guardsman," said Meralda. "Allow them up. And remind Kervis to keep that crossbow of his on the ground."

"Yes, ma'am." Tervis turned and descended.

Meralda pushed back her hair. "What time is it, Mug?"

"You don't want to know," said Mug. He reached out with a long, thin tendril and patted Meralda's shoulder. "They won't stay long, mistress," he said. "There's nowhere to sit. They'll make polite noises, and you'll be polite back, and they'll go away. Nothing to it." Meralda watched Mug swing more eyes toward her. "Is something wrong, mistress?" he asked. "You seem a bit distracted, today."

"I didn't sleep well."

"It was a very bad dream, wasn't it?"

"It was," said Meralda.

Voices rose up from the stair. "They're here," said Mug. "Smile a lot."

Meralda turned to face the stair, clasped her hands before her waist, and found a smile just as Que-long's red-clad Chezin came smoothly up the stair.

"The House of Chentze bids you good morning," said Chezin. He did not smile, but his voice was level and, while lacking in warmth, his tone held no threat, either. "The House would impose but briefly on your hospitality, if you would grant us an audience."

"Your house is welcome here," said Meralda. "Please, join me."

Chezin made a small, fast nod and took the last two steps onto the platform.

Meralda watched, marveling at the way he moved. Smooth, like a cat. *No, like a tiger,* she decided. *His black eyes dart this way and that, never still, and if his ears could move they'd always be swiveling, listening for danger from every direction.* Meralda had the uncomfortable impression that when Chezin looked at her he was deciding how best to strike her down.

Next up the stair came Que-long. Meralda made a small bow as his eyes met hers, and the old man halted and returned her bow before taking his last small steps.

He looks even older up close, thought Meralda, as Que-long stepped onto the platform. *Old, but hardly frail.*

Que-long was nearly bald. Only a fringe of short white hair remained, ringing his scalp just above his ears. He had narrow brown eyes, eyebrows so light and sparse they were barely visible at all, a small straight nose, and tiny ears set close to his head. When he smiled, his teeth were straight and whole and white.

He was attired as he had been at the breakfast two days ago. Loose white robe, black trousers woven of some sheer, shiny material, and soft, laceless black shoes.

He bowed again, still smiling.

Que-long spoke a soft, faint word, which Meralda didn't understand. Chezin nodded, and spoke.

"The dragon apologizes for interrupting your work," he said. "He hopes you will overlook an old man's eagerness to see wondrous foreign magics wrought by the hand of a master."

Mug emitted a barely audible snort of derision, and Meralda felt the blood drain from her face.

"The House of Chentze is an honored guest here," she said, quickly. "I am delighted that Chentze finds my work interesting, but I fear that the task at hand is rather, um, mundane. Still, I shall—"

A new head popped up from the stair. "Terribly sorry," he said, halting. "A thousand contrite apologies for my intolerably rude intrusion. May I approach?"

Meralda nodded, and swallowed. The newcomer was the Hang man who'd bidden her good morning at court two days ago. Meralda had never learned his name.

The man came swiftly up the last few steps, his soft shoes silent on the treads. He leaped past the last step and landed just beyond the stair, his hands suddenly clasped behind his back, his slight frame relaxed and still.

I've already been caught staring once, thought Meralda. Still, she allowed herself a good look before she looked away and made a small bow of her own.

In that brief moment, she saw he had grey eyes. Light, bright grey, the exact color of fresh-poured lead. Like all the Hang, his eyes were more almond-shaped than round, from a downturned fold of skin at the inner corners. His nose was small, his hair was straight and black, and his frame was angular and compact.

The newcomer wore a plain white shirt, with the sleeves rolled up to his elbows. Meralda could see that his arms were smooth and hairless. She tried and failed to guess his age, deciding he might be twenty or twenty-five or neither.

Meralda bowed. From the corner of her eye, she saw Chezin grimace slightly, and she couldn't tell if he was troubled by her response or the newcomer's sudden easy smile.

"Hello," said the man. "I'm Donchen." He glanced about, crooked his finger at Meralda, and leaned slightly forward before speaking in a conspiratorial whisper. "I think that I might be a foreigner."

Mug laughed out loud. Meralda blinked. Que-long stared in wonder at Mug, who shrugged and lifted more eyes toward Que-long.

Chezin's jaw muscles tightened, and he stared for a moment at Mug, but then his eyes resumed their patrol of the platform and the stair.

Donchen regarded Mug and then Meralda with a hint of wonder. "I have heard the Tirlish thaumaturge enjoyed the company of a most uncommon helpmate," he said. "I see the tales were understated."

Que-long whispered something. Chezin nodded, then stepped toward Meralda.

"The Mighty Dragon wishes to better know your familiar," he said. "We were told it has the power of speech."

Meralda felt herself nodding. "Of course," she said. What better way to start war than with Mug's candid social observations?

Mug moved his leaves, and bunched his eyes together in clumps, according to color. "Hello," he said, as Que-long and a reluctant Chezin approached. "I have twenty-nine eyes."

Meralda frowned. Mug's voice had changed. He was bright and cheery, all traces of his usual mocking tone gone.

"Marvelous," said Donchen, who watched with Meralda as Que-long put his face close to Mug. "And you created him as a child?"

Meralda nodded. Donchen had somehow come within a single pace of her.

"It was, um, unintentional," she said. "It's a fairly common occurrence among young mages. Mage Fromarch, for instance, has a staff he crafted from his father's walking stick."

"No one knew I had any talent until this stick started singing, one day on the trolley," gruffed Fromarch.

Donchen laughed. "I'm sorry," he said to Meralda, after a moment. "I was rude to you the other morning, at breakfast." He shrugged. "Chezin once said I have the spirit of a lotash trapped inside me."

Meralda fought away a blush. "If anyone owes anyone an apology, it is I," she said. "I was gawking. Forgive me." She took a quick breath. "What, may I ask, is a lotash?"

"A mischievous supernatural being, which of course does not exist," said Donchen. "And you weren't gawking. It is only natural to be curious about new things. We, for instance, are curious about you." His smile widened. "I do hope the dragon isn't upsetting your familiar."

Meralda glanced toward Que-long, and saw that he was moving his finger back and forth in front of Mug, who was following the fingertip with clumps of moving eyes. Chezin stood by, motionless.

"On the contrary," she said. "Mug loves attention, more than water or mulch."

Donchen watched Mug for a moment, and then he looked away, turning his gaze upon the Tower. Meralda watched him follow it all the way up, until his head was tilted back and he squinted at the sunlight.

"So this is the Tower," he said. "Immortal, eternal, legacy of an age, enduring remnant of a mighty sorcerer's grim reign." He glanced sideways at Meralda and grinned. "So says the marker in the park."

"It tends toward hyperbole," she said. "Otrinvion was a monster, and if the kings of old could have brought the Tower down it would have been rubble a hundred times over."

Donchen nodded, his eyes still on the Tower. "That, I think, would have been a shame."

More footsteps sounded on the stair, and Meralda heard Shingvere's voice, raised in laughter. Donchen turned back to face her.

"Your Eryan friend tells us the Tower is haunted. He suggested I ask you for the details."

"My Eryan friend," said Meralda, struggling to keep her smile, "also tends toward hyperbole. The Tower is no more haunted than this platform. But there are those who see ghosts in every patch of shadow." She cast a nod toward the stair. "Eryans, you will find, are particularly susceptible."

Donchen nodded. "In my country, it is assumed that any structure larger and older than last year's bird nest is infested with the most bewildering variety of phantoms," he said. "A regrettable superstition, but one to which people cling." He gazed again upon the Tower, and lifted his hands as he spoke. "We should have to invent whole new classes of specters, were we to find such a tower in the midst of our land."

Shingvere stepped onto the platform just as Donchen spoke. "Morning, Thaumaturge," he said. "I see you've met our friends."

Meralda nodded, and Shingvere stepped aside, and another Hang sidled past him.

"May I present Loman?" said Chezin. "Wielder of the Word, Bearer of the Staff."

"The approximate equivalent of your own title," whispered Donchen, to Meralda. "He makes magic for the king, at least when the court isn't badgering him with trivia."

The platform, built for a king and four guards, not a thaumaturge, a work bench, three Hang, and a Shingvere, was suddenly crowded. Loman shuffled his way past Shingvere and Donchen to stand before Meralda, who marveled when she saw Que-long motion Chezin back and squeeze himself in the corner between the rail and Meralda's table so the aging Hang wizard had room to walk.

Of all the Hang, only the wizard Loman showed signs of age

in his walk. He was stooped and slow, shuffling one foot forward at a time, his face turned toward the floor planks, his knuckles white upon his staff, so tight was his grip. His hair was shoulder-length, grey like dirty snow. His downturned face was wrinkled, though Meralda could see little of it aside from bushy white eyebrows and the tip of his blunt nose.

He wore a loose white robe, black pants underneath, and his shoes were plain black slippers. Phendelit slippers, Meralda realized.

Fromarch's Phendelit slippers, in fact. *I gave those to him First Snow, two years ago.*

Now I know where the mages have been.

Loman halted, and looked up. His face was ancient, all wrinkles and sagging skin. His eyes, though, were brown, bright, and clear.

He spoke. "Greetings, Mage." His voice was as thin and frail as his frame.

Meralda bowed. "Greetings, Wielder and Bearer." She saw Donchen nod approval at the edge of her vision. "You honor me with your presence."

The old man smiled. "It is good that we are met, Mage of Tirlin. Perhaps one day we will stand side by side and cast our magics together."

He bowed again. And then, before Meralda could speak, he lifted both arms, hands open and even with his shoulders, spoke a short phrase in Hang, and brought his hands together with a single loud clap.

Then he turned, and shuffled back toward the stair.

Meralda made a hasty bow.

Donchen stepped to her side. "He just said hello, in an official sense," said Donchen softly.

Meralda nodded. "I'll ask later what he said," she whispered.

Donchen nodded, clasped his hands behind him, and fell silent. Meralda noted the Hang, even Que-long, stood still and watched Loman go.

Meralda watched as well, though she did exchange a brief look with Mug's red eyes, which Mug held in the upright line that signaled bemusement or mild surprise.

Shingvere, waiting upon the stair, nodded to Meralda, took Loman's hand in his, and helped him down the first tread.

The Big Bell pealed out, striking eleven times from the palace, faint above the traffic and the crowds. Meralda felt her stomach tighten, partly from hunger, partly from realization of just how much of the day was gone, and how much remained to be done.

Chezin nodded, as if she had spoken aloud. "The mage has much work to do," he said. "We should leave her to it."

Que-long nodded. "Goodbye," he said, to Mug. Mug bowed, sweeping all is leaves and eyes down and forward. "I hope we meet again, Mighty Dragon," said Mug, his voice still high and cheery.

Chezin frowned, but Que-long clapped and beamed. "This is a wondrous land," he said, and Meralda smiled despite herself.

"Thank you," she said, only barely remembering to turn and address Chezin. "We are glad you think so, and glad you came."

Que-long made a small bow, and turned, and departed.

Chezin came close behind, halting long enough before

Meralda to repeat Que-long's bow before following his dragon down the stair.

Donchen watched them go. "Goodbye, Mage," he said. He bowed, and turned to go, and then turned back toward Meralda again. "Will you join me at my table, tomorrow night? I believe we are to join your court for a 'feast of traditional Alon cuisine, with sherberts'." Donchen hesitated, and his features took on the appearance of sudden concern. "These 'sherberts,'" he said. "They would not be the finely-chopped snout of an oxen, would they?"

Meralda laughed. "Sherbert is a frozen dessert," she said. "Ice and milk and...sugar, I suppose," she said. "Not a scrap of ox snout."

Donchen lifted his hand to his forehead in mock relief. "Thank heavens," he said. "One must be careful, so far from home."

And then he turned and glided down the stair.

Mug bunched his leaves. Meralda glared, and he fell silent.

"Tervis," shouted Meralda.

After a few moments, Tervis came thump-thumping up the stair.

"Yes, ma'am?" he asked.

"Send word to the Watch and the Builder's Guild foreman," she said. "I'm going to test the spell during lunch. It is a harmless spell. They may see a darkening in the air about the Tower, nothing more. Tell them there is no cause for alarm."

"No cause, yes, ma'am."

"Thank you," said Meralda. Tervis turned and sped down the treads.

"Can you be ready by lunch?" asked Mug. "That's only an hour away, you know."

Meralda watched as the Hang and their entourage made for the Tower. Shingvere, from his post at the right of Loman's wheelchair, gestured and pointed toward the Tower, while Fromarch waved his hands and shook his head in angry negation.

Meralda looked away, and picked up her wand. "Begin," she said. "Refract."

Her wand buzzed and grew cold in her hand.

Meralda sagged, put both hands on the workbench, and leaned over it while the Big Bell clanged out noon.

"You all right, mistress?" asked Mug.

"I'm fine." Meralda looked up. In her second sight, Mug was ablaze, lit within by tongues of fire.

Tervis clambered up the stair. "I warned the watchmen and the guilds," he said. "Is it time?"

Meralda straightened. "It is time."

"Good luck, ma'am," said Tervis. "Yell out, if you need us." He turned, and hurried down the stair.

Meralda turned her sight upon the Tower. "Well," she said. "Have I forgotten anything?"

"Aside from refusing to attempt the thing, no, you've made all the necessary preparations," said Mug. He pushed eyes closer to Meralda.

"Do be careful, Meralda," he said. "I swear it's watching you back."

Meralda frowned, but said nothing. She looked up and up, seeing the flat with her eyes, and the latch with her Sight, and she took a breath and found the first retaining wand with her right hand and lifted it.

People in the park below saw, and the din of conversation muted. "Look!" cried a man. "Here she goes!"

Meralda spoke the word that released the first refractor. The wand went hot, and then cold, and it twitched in her grasp as the spell leaped away toward the latch.

A ragged hush moved over the crowd. Meralda felt hundreds of eyes upon her. Sweat broke out on her forehead, and she resisted the urge to step back away from the rail and out of sight.

The first spell reached the latch, and stopped. Meralda spoke and released the second, and the third, and the fourth, and then she dropped the frost-rimed wand in a bucket of water and watched and waited.

Without Sight, Meralda knew, the Tower appeared unchanged. But seen through trained eyes, the latch was a murky sphere impaled by a quarter of the Tower's upper length, and the refractors were shreds of playful rainbows racing and darting just within the sphere's smooth skin.

Meralda groped for her staff, her eyes still upon the spells. "To your right," said Mug, and it was.

"A bit of flourish, now," said Mug. "The taxpayers are watching."

Meralda lifted her staff, and though shouting the final word was hardly necessary she did speak it in a loud, commanding voice.

"Disperse!"

Her staff made a cracking noise, like the breaking of dry timber, and the darting shreds of rainbows vanished as they fell into place. The dark sphere about the Tower grew fainter, and fainter, and though the Tower's shadow was small and fat in the midday sun, the shadow shrank, inching back over the grass toward the foot of the Tower.

"So far so good," said Mug. Half his eyes were on the Tower. The other half were on the brass-faced stopwatch clicking madly away on Meralda's workbench. "Fifteen seconds since unlatching."

Meralda turned her gaze from the flat and watched the shadow shrink. Spectators drew hastily back into the sun, though one child followed the line of darkness, stamping it with his foot as it moved, until he reached a stern-faced guard and was marched away from the Tower.

"Forty seconds," said Mug.

Meralda wiped her brow with her hand. Elation rose within her. *I've done it,* she thought. *It's going to work.*

She turned her Sight back to the latch. Faint as distant smoke against the blue of the sky and the black of the Tower, Meralda struggled to see it.

"Eighty seconds," said Mug. "Shadow nearly gone."

Inside the latch, something moved.

Meralda pushed. Sight can be intensified, its resolution limited only by the skill of the seer and the arcane qualities of the objects being seen. Meralda frowned and held her breath and extended her Sight so intently that her normal vision began to fade.

The latch and the refractors were a spherical haze about the flat. Within the haze, though, things moved. Meralda saw barrel-sized masses, dark bulks against the Tower, circling the flat like falcons tethered to a pole. She counted as they flew. Six, eight, ten, a dozen.

Meralda pushed her Sight further, hoping to distinguish details of the masses. Instead, she saw clearly the wakes each dark mass left in the latch as it flew. Wakes that represented wide, encircling rips in the structure of the latch.

Rips that had, over the course of the night, torn the heart of the latch neatly in half.

Meralda gasped and lifted her staff.

"Thaumaturge?" said Mug. "Is there a problem?"

Before Meralda could speak, the weakened latch darkened, swelled like a street minstrel's balloon, and lost its grip on the Tower.

The refractors within spun and tangled like rags in a whirlwind. The sky about the Tower flashed dark, then light, then dark again, blurring as the broken latch fell. Shouts and a few inebriated cheers rose up from the crowd as the latch and the refractors fell away from the flat and drifted toward the ground.

The latch swelled again.

Every bird in the park took sudden, noisy flight.

Meralda spoke a word, and her staff went ice cold, but the latch still fell, unchecked. Five heartbeats and halfway down the Tower, the refractors began to flail about outside the wobbling orb of the latch. Shadows flew, and shafts of sunlight, and the cheers became shouts and a few onlookers took flight.

Nearly at the Tower's foot, the latch rolled away from the Tower entirely and proceeded down Wizard's Walk. The walk cleared as people dashed aside, leaving Meralda and her platform directly in the latch's wide path.

"It's a harmless collection of refractors, correct?" asked Mug, half his eyes still on the clock.

Meralda nodded. *That's all it is,* she said silently. But as she looked with her Sight within the rapidly approaching spellwork, the refractors came together in a writhing bunch, spun, and then grew still.

Meralda blinked, and when she looked again, the shadows in the latch were gathered in the shape of an angry, open-mouthed face.

Meralda shivered. The eyes in the face opened, and they burned like the eyes in her dream.

"*Otrinvion,*" she heard, and Meralda knew the voice was not her own. "*Vonashon, empalos, endera.*"

Meralda's sight broke. The latch loomed up and engulfed her, and shadows wheeled like birds, and then it was past and gone.

Meralda squeezed her eyes shut. When she opened them again, all she could see were moving bands of dark and light.

"Mistress!" said Mug. "Are you all right?"

Tervis came charging up the stair, heard Mug's words, and leaped onto the platform.

Meralda rubbed her eyes. "I'm fine," she said. She squinted

back toward the park wall, her normal vision still blurred from her long use of Sight. "Is it gone?"

"Earthed itself here, I think," said Mug. "Probably on your staff."

Meralda blinked and stepped to the rail.

The spectators, calmed now, were milling about, pointing and talking and laughing at the temerity of their fellows. "Good show!" came a shout from below. "Now that's good magic!" bellowed another.

Meralda waved and smiled, unable to make out much more than blobs of color and hints of movement.

"Was it supposed to do that?" asked Tervis. "Come down and roll about, I mean."

"No, it wasn't," said Meralda. She turned back toward the Tower. "Guardsman. Quickly. Tell the mob of penswifts no doubt gathering at the foot of the stair that the test did what it was meant to do. Nothing more."

"Yes, ma'am."

"Then get Kervis to go to the guards at the Tower door. Tell him to tell them that no one goes in or out. No one, for any reason, until I arrive. Is that clear?"

Tervis nodded. "Yes, ma'am."

"Go." Tervis sped away.

Mug turned eyes on Meralda. "'Until you arrive?'" he asked. "Why would you arrive at all? The latch failed. Did you see something I didn't?"

"I did," she said, sorting through her instruments until her fingers found the cloth-wrapped wand that held her single ward work.

Meralda felt it, and it was warm. *It's a killing spell,* she thought. *I never thought I'd cast a killing spell.*

Mug imitated the sound of fingers drumming in impatience, and Meralda drew her hand away. "Well?" said Mug. "You can't go around claiming you saw strange things in the Tower and not provide details. It's rude." He pushed eyes toward Meralda. "You saw the face from your dream, didn't you?"

Meralda lifted her face to meet Mug's eyes. "How did you know?"

"Because that's exactly how ghosts do things," said Mug. "They have rules to follow, you know."

Meralda frowned. "I'll have no more of this ghost nonsense." She glanced back at the stair, wary of penswifts. "What I saw was something else. There are spellworks about the Tower. They ruined the latch."

Mug frowned. "Spellworks? Whose?"

Meralda closed her bag. She remembered the words the latch had brought, but she did not speak them.

"I don't know," she said. Her vision clearing, she dared a look at the Tower, and though the brightness of the sky made her squint she saw nothing unusual in the air.

"What kind of spellworks? Could you tell?"

Meralda looked away, and shook her head. "No," she said. "Aside from knowing something is up there, and part of it, at least, extends beyond the Tower walls around the flat, I don't know a thing."

Mug pretended to lift a small leaf and turn it to and fro in deep consideration. "Some might say that such a statement alone would justify sealing the Tower for the next hundred years and then going home," he said. "Not that you'd ever agree with such a person."

Too late for that, thought Meralda. *What if my spell damaged an old structural spell, just as the old spell tore apart the latch?*

And what if persons unknown were preparing the Tower as a place from which to attack Tirlin?

Meralda hefted her bag. "I'll have a guard stay below to keep the tourists away," she said. "We shouldn't be more than a few minutes."

Mug sighed. "You shouldn't," he agreed. "Of course, there shouldn't be faces in the sky, or spells on the Tower, should there?"

Meralda marched down the stairs. The Bellringers looked up at her, confusion mirrored in their features.

"You," said Meralda, to one of the half-dozen strange guards gathered behind the Bellringers. "Stay here. No one but me goes back up those stairs. Is that clear?"

"Yes, ma'am," said the guard. Meralda reached the last tread, and the grass of the park and the press of the crowd.

"We're in a hurry," she said. "Make way, will you?"

Guards bellowed, and the crowd melted away. The Bellringers fell into place on either side of Meralda.

She set a quick pace. The Tower loomed up ahead, doors ringed by guards, guards ringed by penswifts. Meralda saw them, and felt her chest tighten.

"Thaumaturge!" came shouts all about her as she reached the Tower. "Thaumaturge!"

Meralda steeled herself. *I do not hear, I do not see.*

"Sergeant," she said, over the din. Kervis and Tervis kept the most insistent of the penswifts at arm's length.

"Yes, ma'am?"

"Has anyone been in or out of the Tower?"

"No, ma'am," said the sergeant. "They hauled the last of the lumber out yesterday. Sealed ever since."

Meralda nodded. "Open the doors, please."

As the penswifts shouted, a pair of guards swung the Tower doors open and the Bellringers darted ahead. The penswifts leaped aside, still shouting questions, but before they could follow the Tower guards converged and the doors swung shut.

Darkness fell. Meralda and the Bellringers came to a sudden halt. Meralda found her magelamp, took a breath, and spoke the word.

Light flared.

"Pardon, ma'am," said Kervis, his eyes on the darkness. "What are we looking for?"

"Evidence," she said. She put her bag on the floor, bent, and opened the catch.

Tervis cleared his throat. "Will we be climbing to the flat?"

Meralda bit her lip. *The spellwork I saw radiated from the flat,* she thought. *The only way to see it again is to climb those stairs, up into the dark.*

But she'd be foolish to do so with nothing but a pair of magelamps and a single charged ward wand. "No, we won't be seeing the flat just now," she said aloud. The Bellringers, as one, let out their breath in a rush. "This is as far as we go."

Meralda pointed the lamp into her bag, and withdrew the cloth-wrapped retaining wand.

It buzzed at her touch.

"I'm going to release another ward spell," she said. "It's far more powerful than the one I loosed in the flat."

She heard the Bellringers each take a short step backwards.

"Don't worry," said Meralda. "This is a new spell. It won't trigger until we're all gone." She raised her voice so that it echoed throughout the Tower. "Of course, it will target anyone hiding in the Tower the instant we leave. That would be a pity, since this new spell is easily capable of melting rock. At a distance. Still, if no one comes forward now..."

Silence. Meralda counted to ten, removed the cloth, and spoke a word.

The wand howled like a thousand angry hornets. The ward spell, when it leaped from the copper wand, burned bright as a gas lamp, and big as a fat pumpkin.

It expanded until it was a whirling, ragged ball of fire, and then it shot up into the heart of the Tower, touching the walls in every direction with an angry ring-shaped crimson glow that flashed wide and round against the first story ceiling before vanishing abruptly. The howling continued, muted, but furious.

"Can it really melt rock?" asked Tervis.

"Oh, yes," said Meralda. "Rock, metal, hidden intruders. I suspect they'll all leave behind the same mass of ashes."

Kervis whistled. "That ought to give Old Ugly something to chew on."

Meralda grinned. Then she sought her bag again, and withdrew a small cloth bag of Old Maid flour.

Tervis cocked his head. "Aha!" he said. "Going to sprinkle that on the stair, are you?"

Meralda untied the bag. "We'll go up high enough that no one could jump down to avoid it," she said. "And we'll cover twenty treads or so, to keep clever persons from leaping across it."

Kervis frowned. "Is that magic powder?"

Meralda smiled. "I doubt it," she said. "But it does make good biscuits." She played the light on the stair, on the far side of the Tower. "If you gentlemen will accompany me?"

The Bellringers tramped with her toward the stair.

Meralda was still squinting in the sun, halfway down Wizard's Walk and halfway to her carriage, when Kervis looked up, frowned, and fell out of step with Tervis.

"Uh oh," he said.

Meralda followed his gaze to the head of the walk. She still couldn't make out faces, but the uniforms were plain enough. Palace guards, with the captain himself at the fore.

Meralda groaned. "Tell me that isn't the captain, looking for me."

"It isn't, ma'am," said Kervis. "But it is. Must be half a dozen with him, too." Kervis shifted his crossbow and sighed. "Whatever it is, it isn't good."

Meralda quickened her pace. Traffic on the walk cleared as the captain and his men bore down it. Two hundred paces, one hundred, fifty. As the distance between them closed, Meralda tried and failed to read the captain's face, and guess what calamity had brought him all the way to the park.

Meralda heard a rush of booted feet behind her, and though she didn't turn to look she could imagine a mob of penswifts racing to catch up with her.

The captain saw, and his face went crimson, and Meralda could see the muscles of his neck tighten and bunch.

"How nice of you to drop by, Captain," said Meralda, through a forced smile. "My days are full of surprises."

The captain muttered to his men, and they flanked him and hurried past. Meralda grinned at the thought of the penswifts arguing with the captain's grim-faced lieutenants.

The captain came puffing to a halt. Meralda stopped as well, noting with satisfaction that the penswifts had been shouted to a dead halt some distance behind.

Meralda blinked away a row of dancing bright spots, and saw at last the troubled set of the captain's face.

"What has happened?" she asked, in a whisper.

"Alons," said the captain. "Robbed."

Meralda went wide-eyed.

"Robbed?" she said. "Of what?"

"Their bloody crown jewels, of course," said the captain. "The Mountain Tears. Right out of the east wing safe room. The locked and guarded east room safe room." The captain took a deep breath, and glanced about before continuing. "The Alon queen was talking about leaving the Accords when I left," he said. "We've got to find the Tears, Thaumaturge," he said. "Got to find them soon."

Meralda stared. We?

"Yvin thinks the thieves used sorcery," replied the captain. "He told me to find you and fetch you," he said. "Shall we go?"

"Oh, why not?" said Meralda. "I've got latches falling off the Tower, rumors of haunts, fifteen days until Commencement. Certainly, let's go chase down jewel thieves." She whirled. "We've been found and fetched, gentlemen," she said, to Kervis and Tervis. "We're done here, for today."

She whirled again, and the captain shook his head. "I'm sorry about this, Thaumaturge," he said. "But when you see how the Tears were guarded and stored, I think you'll agree sorcery may well have been involved."

Meralda sighed. "I'm sorry, Captain. I know you didn't run all the way here to ruin my afternoon." She put her hand on his shoulder. "When this is all over, let's both retire, shall we?"

The captain barked a short laugh. "Soldiers and mages don't retire, Thaumaturge," he said. "We just die quietly of over work."

He turned, and stamped back toward the wall. Meralda motioned the Bellringers to follow, and fell wearily into step behind him.

Chapter Nine

The palace was quiet. Guards hurried to and fro, staff darted and dodged among them, somber-faced court officials popped in and out of doors. Everywhere, voices were muted, doors were closed softly, and orders were given in near-whispers. And no one, no one at all, was smiling.

Meralda hurried through the palace at the captain's side. He chose a route intended to avoid the more public areas. Meralda knew the Alons were housed in the east wing guest halls, and the safe room was on the third floor, but she'd never seen many of the hushed corridors and dim, narrow passages she passed through with the captain.

Meralda's Sight lingered, and she had to look away from a gas lamp lest she see afterimages of the face from the park dancing in the flame. "*Vonashon, empalos, endera,*" came the words, over and over. Meralda remembered just enough from her year of Old Kingdom to translate them.

Walk warily, walk swiftly, walk away.

A storybook warning, mused Meralda. *How quaint.*

The captain halted, banged three times on a door so old its face was blacked with coal soot, and motioned Meralda through as it was opened from the other side. "Nearly there," he said, as

Meralda passed. "But don't expect a warm welcome from our Alon brethren."

Meralda nodded. "I won't," she said, and she saw mad eyes wink in a gas lamp's flame and put her gaze quickly back to the plain oak floor.

Tervis and Kervis tromped behind, exchanging short bursts of whispers at each portrait or Historical Society placard. "The Moon Room," she heard Tervis whisper, as the party passed a barred and bolted door. "That's where Mad King Foon thought he saw the vampire!"

She heard Kervis pause at the door. "Been barred up ever since," he said, and Meralda could almost see his sudden grin. "What if I knocked, little brother?"

"What if I yanked up your boots and boxed your ears?" asked the captain, casually. The Bellringers fell back into step.

The floors went from threadbare rugs to polished hardwood and then to newly-laid carpet. After a dozen corridors and three sets of stairs, Meralda rounded a corner to find a foursome of Alon copperheads—wearing their namesake blunt-topped copper helmets, no less—facing her. The copperheads flanked a wide set of black oak double doors.

"We're back," gruffed the captain.

"You may pass," said one of the copperheads, as the others drew back the doors.

Meralda, the captain, and the Bellringers stepped through, and Meralda realized that, by law, she was now on Alon soil.

Angry Alon soil, at that.

A short march down a straight corridor, and a turn, and the

party faced a dead-end hall and yet another door. The door stood open, dimly lit from within by flickering candlelight, and flanked by another pair of glaring copperheads.

"The safe room?" asked Meralda.

"The safe room," said the captain. He stopped. "Would it be best if you went in alone?"

"It would," said Meralda. *Not that it really matters,* she thought. She had no spells prepared, no wands charged, her second sight was all but useless, and her staff just earthed an errant major spellwork. She couldn't see a barrel-full of ward spells if it was lit with torches and marked with a placard.

But here I am. Meralda remembered something Shingvere had said, years ago. "Sometimes a piercing glare and a few nonsense words are all the magic you really need."

Good, she thought. *Because that's really all I have.*

"I'll call you in a moment, Captain," she said. "Tervis, I may need my bag later."

"Yes, ma'am," said Tervis, who set it down on the floor.

Meralda nodded to the Alon guards and marched into the safe room.

It reminded her instantly of her dorm room at the college. It had bare walls, a bare floor, a low, bare ceiling. It was about the same size, as well. Just large enough for five paces from one wall to the next.

Meralda stood in the middle of the safe room and turned in a slow circle. The only door was open behind her. To her left, the wall was fronted by a plain wood table, on which burned a five-tiered candelabrum. Otherwise, the table, which took up nearly the length of the wall, was empty.

Before the table sat a chair. It too was plain and none too new. One of the legs had been replaced with lighter wood than the rest.

Centered on the far wall, directly across from the door, was a painting. The frame was on hidden hinges and had been left open, so Meralda could only see the back of the canvas and frame. Behind the painting was a steel wall safe, its door perhaps two feet high and just as wide.

The safe door was open. The safe, itself, was empty.

And that was all. A table, a chair, an open safe, a missing crown jewel, a black eye for Tirlin.

What did they want her to do?

Meralda bit her lip. *All right,* she thought. *What can I do that the guards and the Watch cannot?*

"Captain," she said.

"Thaumaturge?" replied the captain, poking his head in the door.

"You said the jewel box was found smashed on the floor," she replied. "Where is it?"

The captain spoke to the copperheads, then came inside, shaking his head. "The Alon wizards took it," he said. "Right after I came for you. Claimed they were going to use it to, and I quote, 'track down the Tirlish conjurer who dared steal from our queen'."

Meralda bit back an Angis-word.

"It's their country, in here," whispered the captain. "We're being allowed inside only as a courtesy, and that isn't going to last much longer, judging by the shouting and the fist waving I saw before I left." He paused. "Meralda, do you see anything? Anything at all?"

"Nothing. An empty room. Guarded, you said, at all times."

The captain nodded. "Our Alon friends tell us the safe was undisturbed at the room check this morning," he said. "When four of them opened the door for the afternoon check, though, they found the safe open, the box smashed, and the Tears gone. No one had been in or out."

"Do you believe that, Captain?" asked Meralda.

The captain sighed. "I do," he said. "Copperheads aren't my favorite people, but the way they've got their guard rotations arranged you'd need to have twenty-two people in cahoots, just to get these doors open. You might find one Alon willing to betray clan and queen, but twenty-two? From different clans?" He snorted. "Impossible."

Meralda stared at the empty safe. It was perhaps two feet deep. She could see all the way to the back, though it was in shadow.

"Nevertheless," she said, stepping toward the safe. "It is empty."

Voices rose up, outside the safe room, Alon, by the accent. Meralda heard Kervis tell someone, "The thaumaturge is working now, you'll need to wait a moment."

Working. Meralda touched the cold metal of the safe door, swung it nearly shut so she could see its face.

Centered on the safe door was a knurled round dial. Old Kingdom numerals were etched along the edge of the dial, counting clockwise from zero to ninety-nine. A down-pointing arrow engraved in the face of the safe pointed to the dial, which now read fifty-six. Meralda recognized that as the last number of the safe's combination, and wondered who had been so careless as to leave the dial set there.

The safe presented no other features, save for the lion's head emblem of Oaken Lock Works stamped at the bottom.

Meralda stepped back, and swung the painting closed, and there, in the flickering candlelight, Tim the Horsehead grinned back at her.

He'd have had no trouble with this, thought Meralda. A flash of light, a muffled shout, and the thief would be dragged, kicking and screaming, all the way back to the safe room, Tears in hand, while Tim gloated and munched hay.

Meralda sighed.

"Captain," she said. "Please step outside."

"Of course." The captain grinned. "I knew you'd think of something."

He turned and walked away.

Meralda closed her eyes, and took five long deep breaths, and opened her eyes again. "Sight," she whispered, struggling to see past her ordinary vision. "Sight, Sight, Sight."

Bare white walls, a painting, bare cold floor.

"Sight," hissed Meralda. Her eyes began to water and sting.

"Sight," she whispered.

Nothing. Nothing at all. No hint of magic, no trace of subtle spells.

I must See!

Sight rose up, just for an instant, and lit the safe room with lines of fire. Tiny glows and bursts of radiance sprang up along every edge, danced on the every plane, showered cold fire from the serrations set into the safe's dial. Meralda shifted her gaze toward the shadowed rear of the empty safe, and her Sight went white, as though she had looked into the noonday sun. Then it was gone, leaving her blinking and half-blind and with no idea of what she had seen.

"Did you see anything?" asked the captain, from the door.

Meralda took in a breath, and wiped her eyes before turning.

"I assume this door will be locked, when we leave," she said.

The copperheads, who both stood just outside the door, nodded.

"You will continue to guard it?" asked Meralda.

"Until ordered otherwise, aye," said the rightmost. "Ordered by our queen," added the other, with a glare.

Meralda lifted her staff, held it horizontally out before her, and silently mouthed a very rude Angis-word.

The glaring copperhead, she noted with satisfaction, drew away from the door in a quick backward shuffle. "I'm done here, Captain," said Meralda. "Let's go back to Tirlin, shall we?"

"Gladly," said the captain, who turned on his heel. Meralda brushed past the copperheads, and the Bellringers fell in step behind her.

Meralda folded the king's summons until it was too small to fold again, and dropped it in the trash bin by her desk.

Mug, who sat basking in the late afternoon sun streaming from Goboy's scrying mirror, saw, and laughed.

"If Fromarch was here, he'd have a conniption fit," he said.

Meralda shrugged. "I saw him do the same thing, more than once. I'm tired of being summoned, today. Enough." She stretched and yawned. "All he'll do is ask me if I've found the Tears yet. Does he really think I might say 'Why yes, I found them hours ago, must have slipped my mind, isn't it amazing how daft I can be'?"

Mug chuckled. "Our king thinks a wizard stole them, so naturally he also thinks said wizard may have mentioned his motive and methods to you in the course of idle conversation," he said. "What about that, mistress? Do you think sorcery was involved?"

Meralda sighed. "It's easy enough to look at the situation, see the Tears stolen from an impenetrable safe room, and say 'Oh well, the thieves used magic'." Meralda lifted an eyebrow. "Very well, then," she said. "Tell me. What sort of magic? Used in what manner?"

Mug shrugged with a flurry of leaves. "The same kind of magic someone used to hide spells throughout the palace," he said. "One is even led to speculate that an entirely new brand of thaumaturgy is at work here. Hmm." Mug cast all his eyes toward the ceiling. "What recently arrived group of mysterious foreigners might we be led to consider?"

Meralda thought of Que-long's open, easy smile, and she shook her head. "I can't believe the Hang sent a fleet across the

Great Sea just to pilfer the odd jewel box," she said.

"Indeed," replied Mug. "Why, pray tell, did they send their fleet at all? Have they offered any reason for their visit?"

"The captain tells me they have a reason, but they are waiting for the Accords to begin before announcing it," said Meralda. She glared. "And that, Mugglewort Ovis, is a state secret. Understood?"

"Understood," said Mug. "Still, though. You must admit suspicion of the Hang is a perfectly reasonable attitude." Mug swung eyes toward Meralda. "You rather like the Hang, don't you?"

I do, thought Meralda, surprised at the realization. *All these years, thinking them faraway monsters. But they seem so genuinely nice.*

"Consider," said Mug. "Isn't muddying your judgment with fondness just as dangerous as basing it on fear?" Mug paused. "The Hang are well-spoken and polite, I'll grant. But that doesn't mean they're angels."

"You sound like Shingvere."

"That may well be because we're both right," said Mug. "Unless you know something I don't. And, given the complete lack of attention certain thaumaturges, the guard, and the watch are giving the Hang, I suspect you do."

Meralda shrugged. "It's knowledge, I suppose, but only indirectly," she said. "But according to the captain, Yvin has ordered all involved to treat any evidence that the Hang were party to the theft as evidence planted by the real thieves."

Mug blinked, with all his eyes. "Yvin said that?"

"He did," said Meralda. "He's also ordered the court to deny any theft has occurred."

"What about the Alons?" asked Mug. "Did he order them to smile and think happy thoughts, too?"

"Begged is a better term, I think," said Meralda. "They'll talk, of course, if the Tears aren't returned. Soon."

"Alons? Talk?" Mug made a snorting sound. "They'll riot, is what they'll do," he added, "just before they pull out of the Accords."

Meralda nodded. *He's right,* she thought, imagining a thousand wild-eyed, bearded Alons raging down Fleethorse with a greater fury than they displayed at any football game. For some reason, she thought of the lone traffic master at Kemp trying to hold them back with his white glove and silver whistle. "We can't let it come to that," she said, rubbing her temples. "But how do we stop it?"

The scrying mirror flickered, losing its hold on the darkening, red-streaked sky. Meralda patted the mirror's frame. The image steadied, and Meralda fought back a yawn and rose to her feet.

"Ah," said Mug. "A bit of mage-like pacing."

Meralda ignored him and began to pace, hands clasped behind her back, mouth set in a frown. She paced to Phillitrep's Calculating Engine, turned, and returned to her desk before starting again.

"Let's forget the how of the theft, for a moment," she said. "Let's talk about the why."

"Why, what?"

"Why steal the Tears? Really. What do you do with them, after you magic them out of the safe room?"

"The Tears are worth a fortune, are they not?" asked Mug, with a rustling of fronds.

"As long as they are the crown jewels of Alonya, yes, they are," said Meralda. "But steal them from the queen's person, and what do you have?"

Mug pretended to whistle. "A hundred thousand furious Alons bearing down on you with swords," he said.

"Exactly," said Meralda. "You couldn't sell the Tears to anyone who could afford them."

"So remove the jewels, and melt down the settings," replied Mug.

"And you have a few pennyweights of gold, a bit less silver, and a sack of gems known to every jeweler in the Realms," said Meralda. "As a theft, stealing the Tears just doesn't seem worth the trouble."

"But as a political maneuver, it works beautifully," said Mug. "Anger the Alons. Break up the Accords. Cast suspicion on the Hang. Sully the good name of Tirlin." His eyes all converged on Meralda. "Forget the Hang," said Mug. "Let's start blaming the Vonats."

"They aren't even here," said Meralda.

"They haven't paraded through town, no," said Mug. "But I'll bet they're here, all the same."

Meralda halted, hands on the back of her chair.

"Well," she said. "If I'm forbidden to consider the Hang, I suppose a Vonat will do," she said. "Though, of course, the who and why is not nearly so important at the moment as the where."

"Agreed," said Mug. He tossed his leaves. "Let's assume the guard and the Watch are pursuing every mundane means at the kingdom's disposal," he said. "What can we do that they can't?"

Meralda frowned. "My Sight won't be of any use for a day or two," she said. "And what I saw in the safe room told me nothing."

Mug considered this. "You saw no trace of recent spellworks," he said.

"I saw the coronal discharges from the metal of the safe," she said. "And the room showed the usual arcane buildup any old structure displays."

"Hmm." Mug brought eyes to bear on Meralda. "Doesn't that strike you as a little odd?" he asked. "After all, didn't the Alon wizards lay some sort of wards on their own crown jewels?"

"I asked," she said. "According to the captain, the Alons laid no wards. It's all that clan feuding they're so fond of. Red Mawb and Dorn Mukirk's clans have been at it for fifty years, with neither side having the courtesy to surrender or die. Because of the feud, the Alon queen forbade them to enter the safe room, for fear they'd ensorcel the place to dust in a show of inept one-upmanship. Imbeciles."

"I see." Mug imitated the sound of fingers drumming on a tabletop. "And they have the smashed jewel box, arguably the best clue left at the scene. How convenient for the thieves."

Meralda nodded and sighed. She recalled the picture of Tim the Horsehead that covered the safe, and wondered if the thief felt even a hint of fear as he swung back the portrait to reveal the locked safe.

Probably not, she decided. After all, Tim the Horsehead was long dead and long gone, and the current mage in Tirlin was Meralda Ovis. Daughter of a prominent family of swine herders and sausage makers. First in her class of bespectacled, serious young men who were more banker than mage.

She halted in her pacing, facing Mug and looking past him and the mirror into the ranks and rows of magics stored and twinkling in the shadows. Was each glittering trinket perhaps the life's work of a mage?

Mage. *I wonder,* she thought. *Has the title lost all meaning?* Since Tim's time, how many names had risen above the rest, to be remembered forever as mighty wielders of magic?

None, thought Meralda. *None, and neither shall my name be remembered, unless it is as a footnote on first year midterms.* She could almost see the question written, almost see the frowns it raised. Who was the first woman to wear the robe? And some would know and scribble "Meralda Ovis" and some would shrug and guess and that would be the end of it, the end of her, the end of Mage Meralda.

She thought back to college, remembered how many of those somber young faces were bound for the guilds, and happy to be so. "Forget that court nonsense," she'd heard one of them snicker at her back during commencement. "Let her have mage. I'll take a Master's robe from a guild, any day, and be glad of it, too."

Meralda looked away from the ranks of cabinets.

"Now just you wait a moment, Miss Ovis," said Mug. "I see those big moon-eyes getting all misty because you didn't conjure up the Tears and throw them at the copperheads," he said. "It's just like college all over again. You set impossible goals, and then act surprised when you can't achieve them."

Meralda sighed. "Mug," she said.

"Don't 'Mug' me," replied Mug. "I'm right, and you know it. I'll tell you something, mistress," he said. "I studied history right along with you. I've heard all the stories. I've read all the old books. I believe your hero Tim the Horsehead made things up as he went along, took a lot of wild chances, and had a lot of wild strokes of wholly undeserved, utterly blind, plain dumb luck. I think you are already his equal, if not his superior, in spell shaping and use of Sight, and I know you're a lot better at mathematics, because Tim's staff did all his math and his writings are full of errors after the staff was broken at Romare." Mug paused, rolled a long leaf into a finger-like tube, and shook it gently at Meralda. "So stop berating yourself for not being Tim, Mage Ovis. We don't need Tim anymore. We need Meralda."

The faint sound of applause rose up behind Mug, and he made a mocking bow toward the sound.

Meralda realized her fists were clenched at her sides. She took a breath, relaxed her hands and her jaw, and forced a smile. "Thank you," she said.

Mug blinked at her. "You're welcome," he said. His voice softened. "I meant all that, by the way."

"I know you did," said Meralda. She walked to her chair, pulled it back, and sat. "So," she said, licking her lips and pausing a bit when she realized her voice was shaking. "When our history is written, what will it claim we did next?"

Mug considered this. "Well," he said, slowly. "When

confronted by knotty dilemmas, most wizards turn to relics and whatnots," he said. He turned his eyes upon Goboy's scrying mirror, through which the last rays of the sun still streamed. "Shall I?"

Meralda sighed in exasperation. "You know full well it's a waste of time," she said, patting the mirror frame when the glass flashed at her words. "Not that our friend here isn't a wondrous and useful work," she added, hastily, "but the glass can only display images of actions taking place in the present." *And since all of those tend to be images of bedrooms or bathhouses,* she thought, *the mirror tells us more about Mage Goboy's favored entertainments than it ever has about anything else.*

"Well, then, let's ask it about the present," said Mug.

Meralda frowned. The mirror could reflect some things, well enough. Ask it for the sky, or the clouds, or Tirlin from high in the air, and one could expect several hours of reflection before the image broke apart. But ask for anything smaller than the sky, a room, for instance, or a person, and the mirror would flash an instant's reflection on the glass, and then begin its random perambulation through the more private parts of Tirlin. Meralda's early investigations of Goboy's mirror had resulted mainly in a good deal of embarrassment and ultimately the blanket.

"Mirror, mirror," said Mug, before Meralda could stop him.

The sky and the faint sun vanished, replaced by reflections of Mug and Meralda and a single glowing spark lamp on the ceiling.

Meralda looked at her reflection, and looked away when it winked back at her.

"Show me the Tears," said Mug, in the king's own voice. "Show me the Tears, wherever they are."

The mirror flashed bright white, casting brief shadows on Meralda's desk. Startled, Meralda looked up at the glass, but it was dark.

Dark, but not black. Indeed, a dim light flickered at the right edge of the glass, halfway up the frame.

"I'll be trimmed and pruned," said Mug.

The image grew lighter and clearer. The flickering light became the guttering stub of a candle, burnt down nearly to nothing. Its four fellows were gone, mere lumps that neither smoked nor glowed.

The candle stand sat on a plain wood table. A chair was pushed beneath it. And on the wall adjacent to the table, faint but visible in the failing candlelight, Tim the Horsehead grinned out of a painting.

Meralda rose, eyes wide, biting back an exclamation.

"That's the safe room, isn't it?" whispered Mug.

Meralda nodded, brought a finger to her lips. Mug nodded with a tossing of leaves and fell silent.

Meralda sought out Opp's Rotary Timekeeper and watched the rings whirl round. Ten, twenty, thirty full seconds, and still the image in the mirror held.

The safe room. Meralda let out her breath, afraid to move or speak or even look away.

"Show me the Tears, wherever they are," Mug had said.

And now we see the safe room?

Meralda rose, banged her right knee on the desk leg, shoved her chair sharply backward, and bit back a shout.

"Mistress?" said Mug, who turned half his eyes upon her, but left the other aimed motionless at the glass.

"The Tears," said Meralda. "You asked...oh, blast, the nature of your question was such that the object in question would have its whereabouts revealed," she said, wary of using words the mirror might interpret as a new command. "Think about it, Mug. Imagine you're a villain. You want to cause trouble. You put a spell on the safe, or the jewel box, and you make it look as if the Tears have been stolen."

Mug tapped the glass with a leaf. "But you hide the Tears, instead," he said. "Somehow. Hide them in the safe room."

"And then you just wait," said Meralda. She stepped closer to the glass. "You just wait, because sooner or later, the Alons will be gone," she said. "And sooner or later, Yvin will remove the guards from the safe room. Oh, he might also bar it and lock it, but given time, you can get in. And if not? Well, the damage is done."

Meralda stared into the glass. *I'm right,* she thought, smiling at the guttering candle, shifting her gaze to the ghostly equine smile of the Horsehead in the portrait. *I'm right.*

Mug blinked with fifteen eyes. "It sounds plausible," he said. He blinked again. "I can't find anything wrong with it." He paused. "Except, of course, for the mirror's sudden spate of competence."

Meralda felt her smile shrink, just a bit.

"Odd," she said. "Though not undocumented. Remember the missing princes, back in 1810?"

"I thought you said that Mage Lommis made that story up, to implicate the Vonats," said Mug.

"I may have been wrong about that," said Meralda. She reached out and touched the dark oak frame. "I may have been wrong about a lot of things."

Mug shrugged. "Glasses showing rooms, mages admitting errors. This is a night for rare occurrences," he said. He thrust an eye toward Meralda. "That aside, what now?"

Meralda turned from the glass to Mug. "It's time someone else had a very bad day," she said, and she smiled. At the sight of it Mug pulled his eye hastily back.

"Oh, my," said Mug.

In the glass, the candle guttered and went out.

Midnight. Meralda yawned and stretched. Mug muttered in his sleep, and Tervis rose from his chair and stood.

The scene in Goboy's mirror was dark, aside from the faint line of light that crept in from under the safe room door.

"Shut up, you awful hyacinth," said Mug.

"Ma'am?" said Tervis.

"He's dreaming," said Meralda. "Ignore him." She reached up and stroked the topmost of his leaves.

"Never thought about plants dreaming," said Tervis. Then he yawned. "But I reckon they get tired; too."

"Don't we all," said Meralda.

Tervis muttered assent, and sat again.

The mirror remained dark. Meralda had sent for the captain, told him of her suspicions, then asked that a contingent of guards be kept ready just beyond the Alon halls. She'd refused the captain's offer of additional guards to watch the mirror, deciding there was simply too much potential for mischief in the lab. *Or,* Meralda wondered, *is it that I, like Fromarch and all the mages before us, simply don't want strangers in my lair?*

Meralda smiled at the thought. *Next I'll be slouching around in old robes and muttering to myself in public,* she thought.

"Hedge-bush," said Mug, and Tervis chuckled.

Meralda bit back another yawn and idly shoved her now-cold cup of coffee around on her desk. She was beginning to question the wisdom of insisting that she keep her own watch on the mirror, instead of assigning Kervis and Tervis to watch it in shifts.

But here I sit, she thought, half-asleep and bone weary. *I can't just go home and lie down. Not yet.*

She lifted the coffee cup, took a sip, made a face, and put it down.

Sometime during her first hour of watching the mirror, she'd decided that one of the rival Alon wizards was probably the culprit. If so, he'd also be the one to recover the Tears. Meralda's hope was she could find them first.

And then she'd begun to think about how the Tears were hidden, and she'd decided the Alon mages were, if the captain and Shingvere were correct, simply not up to the task.

Arcane concealment of the Tears, which would mean visual and tactile suppression of form and mass, was not something she'd like to try, she decided. If Red Mawb or Dorn Mukirk cast such a spell, there was more to Alon clan wizards than the college ever taught.

Mug shook his leaves, and Meralda yawned again.

"You'll have the Tears in hand by tomorrow night, I'll wager," said Tervis.

"I wish I shared your confidence," replied Meralda. "But I hardly know where to begin looking."

Tervis nodded and smiled. "You'll know when the time comes."

"She can't know of this," mumbled Mug, in Shingvere's merry voice. Meralda smiled and patted Mug's pot. "Poor thing," she said. "You'll have to go outside tomorrow, get some real sunlight."

Tomorrow. She looked to the clock and saw that sunrise was only five hours away.

Night is fled, and with her slumber, thought Meralda. Phendelit playwrights must lose as much sleep as Tirlish thaumaturges.

"And I still have shadows to move," she said, aloud. She pushed an image of the face from the park aside and looked down at the drawings and calculations that covered her desk, and the words she'd scribbled earlier on a drawing of the Tower.

"Vonashon, empalos, endera," she'd written. "Walk warily, walk swiftly, walk away."

Spoken by a mad-eyed death's head from within a broken spell. She looked at Mug and shook her head. *I'll never hear the end of this, if I tell him,* she thought. *Though I suppose I really should.*

In case something happens to me.

Meralda rubbed her eyes. What did she see?

She picked up her pen, and shuffled her papers until the Tower sketch was before her. She thought back to that instant of Sight, just before the latch tore and fell away, and she began to draw.

"There," she said. "What, pray tell, are you?"

She'd drawn a ring about the Wizard's Flat. Riding the ring were a dozen evenly spaced, barrel-sized, round-ended masses, each circling the flat at a hawk's pace. She noted the direction of flight about the flat, and guesses as to the size and shape of each dark mass, and then she drew a question mark and put down her pen.

I never actually saw the masses, she realized. She'd only seen their shadows, shadows they cast in the latch, as they flew through it.

A shiver went through Meralda. Not at the thought that she might have actually seen a spellwork cast by the hand of Otrinvion the Black himself, but that her latch might have touched Otrinvion's spell in the same way his had touched hers.

What if I damaged Otrinvion's circling masses as badly as they damaged my latch?

"Tervis," said Meralda, jumping at the loudness of her voice in the silence of the laboratory.

"Yes, ma'am," said Tervis, leaping to his feet.

"Go to the guards in the hall," she said. "Send one to the park. I want any news of lights in the flat. Real news, mind you, from the watch or the guard." Meralda bit her lip, considering. "I'll want hourly reports, all night tonight, delivered here. Compiled and delivered each morning every day after."

"Yes, ma'am." Tervis frowned at the mirror. "Did you see anything, ma'am?" he asked.

"Nothing at all," she said. "And find me a pillow, will you?"

"Yes, ma'am," said Tervis, and then he turned and darted away.

Mug opened a sleepy red eye. "What's the matter?" he asked. "Locusts?"

"Nothing. Go to sleep," said Meralda. Mug's eye closed and drooped on its stalk.

Meralda shifted in her chair, put her chin on her hands, and watched the dark, still glass.

"Thaumaturge," said a voice.

What, thought Meralda, *is Tervis doing in my bedroom?*

"You might want to wake up, ma'am," said Tervis, from close beside her. "The captain and the other mages are heading this way."

Meralda opened her eyes, a drawing of the Tower filling her vision, and realized she was face-down on her laboratory desk.

I've a face full of ink smudges, she thought, and then she rose.

Her back popped and twinged. Her right arm, which was beneath her face, was numb and stiff. Her stocking feet were blocks of ice from resting all night on cold stone. She rubbed her eyes with her left hand and shook her right arm and Mug began to chuckle.

"It's a secret mage waking spell, lad," he said to Tervis. "In a moment, she'll stand on one leg and squawk like a bird."

"Shut up, Mug," said Meralda. She forced her eyes wide open, pushed back her hair, and sought out the mirror.

"Nothing ever changed, ma'am," said Tervis. "Kervis and I kept a good watch."

"Thank you," said Meralda. Then, in mid-yawn, she recalled Tervis' earlier warning that the captain and the mages were bound for the lab.

"What mages?" she asked. "All of them?"

"No, ma'am," said Tervis. "Just Mage Fromarch and Mage Shingvere, as far as I know."

Thank fate for that, thought Meralda. "I'll be washing my face," she said, motioning to the door of the lab's tiny, dark water closet. "If they get here before I'm done, let them in, and warn them to be careful what they say around the glass."

"Yes, ma'am," said Tervis. "By the way, ma'am, I sent for coffee and pancakes earlier, if you've a mind for breakfast."

"Thank you, Tervis," said Meralda. For the first time, she saw the smudges beneath Tervis' eyes, and the wild stand of his short blond hair. He's probably slept as little as me, even with a brother to spell his watches.

"You've done very well," she said, and Tervis smiled.

Meralda heard footfalls in the hall, perhaps upon the stair. She turned for the water closet, then stopped and turned again. "I must have missed the last few reports from the park," she said.

"Kervis took them while I slept, ma'am," replied Tervis. "Same as the others last night. No lights, no sounds, nothing. He said he didn't want to wake you to tell you that."

No lights. Meralda frowned, recalling her fear that her latch might have affected an ancient structural spell and wondering whether the sudden cessation of luminous activity was perhaps proof of this.

"Is that a bad thing, ma'am?" asked Tervis.

Meralda shook her head and forced a smile. "Not at all," she said. "Thank you." Boots sounded again, nearer this time, and Meralda raced for the water closet door. "Tell them to wait," she said, and she shut the door firmly behind her.

Chapter Ten

"Well, there she is," said Shingvere, rising to his feet and wiping biscuit crumbs from his loose brown shirt front. "Fresh as a daisy, and twice as fair."

Beside him, seated in one of the folding-chairs from which the Bellringers had kept watch, was Fromarch. He chewed, swallowed and wiped his lips. "Leave her alone," he said, gruffly. "I've slept in that chair, too, and it doesn't leave one well disposed toward chirpy early morning Eryan nonsense."

The laboratory, windowless and lit only by her spark lamps, still seemed dark, as though night hung just beyond the walls. Indeed, Meralda realized the palace was oddly quiet, still gripped in a midnight hush despite the sunrise.

Coffee, thought Meralda. *I smell coffee, and if those aging gluttons have left me the dregs I'll turn them both into toads.* She picked up her stride, boots making loud stamps on the cold stone floor.

She emerged from the ranks of shelves, and saw that Tervis was gone, as was Mug, and that the captain was nowhere in sight.

"Your guardsman took the houseplant outside for some sun," said Fromarch. "And the captain received a message on the stair, and said he'd join us in a moment."

"Aye, he has stomping to do, people to shout at," said Shingvere. "Can't have enough bellowing, you know."

Meralda stepped around the glittering, moving levers of Phillitrep's Engine, and smelled the plate of hot pancakes and sausages steaming on her desk. Beside it sat a silver pot of coffee, twin to the one resting on the floor by Shingvere's right foot. And, Meralda noted with mild chagrin, a single red rose in a fluted crystal vase.

"Good morning, gentlemen," she said, pulling back her chair, but not sitting, suddenly thankful for the absence of windows and bright morning sun. She'd done what she could with water, soap, and a tattered washing cloth, but she still felt as if she'd slept in a ditch.

The mages nodded. Shingvere sat, smiled, stabbed a sausage with his fork, and waved it toward Meralda. "Eat, before it gets cold," he said. "We'll talk after."

Meralda sat. Her stomach grumbled, and she realized she'd missed supper, in all the excitement over the Tears.

She frowned and bit her lower lip. *Missed supper, I did. Supper at the Hang's table. Supper with Donchen.*

"Lass, I thought you liked pancakes," said Shingvere, his tone injured.

"Oh, I do," said Meralda, quickly. "I just remembered something I forgot to do yesterday."

"Anyone who got old Goboy's glass to do as it was asked deserves a few omissions of memory," said Fromarch. He stared hard at the mirror, which displayed the same dark room as before, and then shook his head and looked back at Meralda. "I gave up on that thing my first year."

Meralda ate. A *fine ambassador I am,* she thought. *First I stare at the Hang, then I give insult by not coming to dinner or sending word.* She thought of Donchen seated by an empty chair, and her frown deepened. *Blast it all,* she groaned inwardly. *And I can hardly explain my absence with the truth, either.*

"You could have called us, you know," said Fromarch. "We can watch the glass as well as anyone, and we're not likely to burn down the palace trifling with the trinkets."

Meralda swallowed a forkful of pancakes and reached for the syrup flask beside the coffee. "It was quite late," she said. "But now that you've volunteered, I thank you." She lifted her coffee cup, found that it still contained half a cup of yesterday's brew, and, after an instant of hesitation, she poured it in the half-filled waste basket by her desk.

Shingvere guffawed. "You used to scold me for doing that," he said.

"You hadn't been up all night watching scrying glasses," said Meralda, as she poured a fresh cup and savored the aroma. "Now then," she said, after her first sip. "Aside from the free breakfast, what brings you gentlemen here this morning?"

The mages exchanged a brief glance Shingvere poked Fromarch in the ribs with his elbow, and Fromarch glared and hissed. "You tell her, you confounded hedge mage, even though she's already figured it out."

"Tell me what?" said Meralda, warily.

"We think we might know where the Tears are," said Shingvere, nodding at Goboy's Glass. "'Tis clear you do as well."

Meralda lifted an eyebrow, and carefully kept her face blank. "They're in the safe room, of course," she said. "Right where they've been since this small calamity began."

Fromarch smiled, if only for a moment.

"Well done, Thaumaturge," he said. "Well done."

Shingvere slapped his knee. "Rake me with a cat's claws," he said. "I knew we wouldn't surprise you, lass."

Meralda sipped her coffee, and kept her expression serene.

"We think someone wants to break up the Accords," said Fromarch. "We don't think it's the Hang."

"Neither do I," said Meralda. "Though Mug has raised some good points against such a surmise."

"It's the Vonats, of course," said Shingvere. "They've got people here, in the palace, and they've intentionally delayed their arrival to remove their entourage from suspicion," he added. "Deplorable condition of the roads in Fonth. What nonsense."

Meralda took another bite of a sausage. "The Hang," she said, after a moment. "Why don't you suspect them?"

"We've been keeping company with their wizard nearly the whole time," said Fromarch.

"He means we've been drinking," added Shingvere, with a wink.

"He's a talkative fellow, once you get to know him," said Fromarch. Then he snorted and lifted his hands. "Harmless, really. Not that he can't do a bit of magic. He can, and don't be fooled. But stealing jewelry and interrupting trade talks? Ridiculous."

"Mug reminded me that good manners don't necessarily

reflect good intentions," said Meralda. "What do we really know about these people?"

The mages, as one, took a deep breath and exchanged a sidelong glance. "Well," said Fromarch, "this is just speculation, mind you. But we think that the Hang may have opened diplomatic channels with Tirlin ten or more years ago."

Meralda swallowed, kept her face blank, and carefully put down her fork.

"We think Yvin may have even invited them to the Accords," said Shingvere. "We think the Hang may be here to join the Five Realms as a trading partner," he said. "That's what we think." He smiled, set his empty plate down on the floor, and lifted his coffee cup to rest on the arm of his chair. "We think the Great Sea is about to be crossed, Meralda. After all these years of wondering, or trying and failing and trying again, we're about to see the whole wide world, Great Sea and Hang and who knows what else. Marvelous, isn't it?"

Meralda was silent, sorting out Shingvere's words. *It does make sense,* she thought. The king's nonchalance concerning the Hang's arrival. His instructions to consider the Hang above suspicion. The Hang's flawless command of New Kingdom. She suspected Yvin knew things he wasn't sharing with the full court, but nothing like this.

Fromarch met her eyes, and nodded. "Which makes all this nonsense with the Tears more than a mere inconvenience," he said. "Say the Alons pull out. Any agreements four of the Realms make with the Hang will be forever contested by the fifth. And who knows? The Hang might leave, too, rather than have any dealings with a factious lot of simpletons who can't all sit down long enough to sign a few pieces of paper."

"That's why we're here, lass," said Shingvere. "Not that we think you can't handle it, mind you. Not at all. But you've got a heavy pack, these days. We're only here to help you bear the load, if you'll have us. And watching this mirror while you go off and save the kingdom seems like just the chore for two grumpy old wizards, now doesn't it?"

Meralda pushed back her chair and stood. *I've got to walk around a bit,* she thought. *My feet are still cold in my boots, and my joints still ache from sleeping in that torture chamber of a chair.* "What makes you think Yvin asked them here?" she said, stretching.

Fromarch shrugged. "It's simple, really. I don't think they'd have come unless they were asked."

"They certainly wouldn't have loaded their entire royal family onto a boat, not knowing what sort of reception to expect." Shingvere filled his fork with more pancake. "Which means this was all arranged well beforehand."

"Oh, Yvin wouldn't tell anyone, of course," said Fromarch. "Best to get the Hang all here and just spring it on the Realms. That way no one gets worked up into a frenzy too soon, and we don't have foreign troops hiding all along the Lamp."

"He could have told us," snapped Meralda.

"Hmmph," snorted Fromarch. "Since when have kings sought advice from their betters? Mark my words, though. If this bit of scheming goes bad, we'll be the ones who'll have to sort it all out."

Meralda glared. *He didn't tell because he doesn't trust,* she thought. *And he doesn't trust,* said a voice within her, *because I'm a woman.*

"He wouldn't have told me, either," said Fromarch, gently. "I once heard Yvin tell someone, doesn't matter who, that magic and mages were best left to the guilds, and the tradesmen. He said the age of the wizard was over, and done, and the Realms were better for it." Fromarch sighed. "He's wrong, of course," he added. "But he's the king, and that's that."

Meralda found her chair again. Her head began to pound, and her clothes, wrinkled and ill-fitting from a day and a night of constant wear, rubbed and stuck and sagged. She put her head in her hands and closed her eyes and sighed.

"Perhaps I should just send Yvin a message," she said. "Perhaps I should tell him that since the age of wizards is done, he should seek the help of the guilds and the tradesmen in recovering the Tears."

Shingvere chuckled. "I dare you," he said.

Meralda heard Fromarch set down his cup with a small sharp click and rise slowly to his feet.

"Agree or not, the world is changing," he said. "And we will have a hand in it, for good or ill. Might I suggest we all get to work? For the good of the realm, if not its shortsighted nitwit of a monarch?"

Meralda opened her eyes. "I'm for a bath," she said. "Now, and Yvin be hanged."

Shingvere crowed. "At last, our battle cry," he said. "A bath, and the king be hanged!" he shouted, brandishing his fork. "Clean clothes, then victory!"

Meralda found a brief laugh. "Vonats," she said, after Shingvere bowed and sat. "If you two are correct, they'd be the obvious choice for our scheming villains," she said. "If the Hang enter the Accords as a sixth realm, Vonath will have to mind its manners. Forever."

"Perhaps," said Fromarch. "Or perhaps this is mere coincidence. The Vonats do love to make trouble at Accords, if you'll recall."

Shingvere snorted. "But this smacks of mage-cast mischief, not some bugger sneaking around with a dagger," he said.

Boots sounded in the hall outside. "All of this is mere speculation, though," said Fromarch, hastily. "We have discussed it with no one but you, Mage. Make of it what you will."

A knock sounded at the door. Meralda started toward it, but Shingvere darted ahead and bade her to sit down.

"I'll see to this," he said, hand on the handle. "From now on, Meralda, we're the hired help. Let us do the chores. You've got better things to do."

He swung the door open. "Yes?" he inquired, managing somehow to convey through his tone and bearing that the caller was neither welcome nor, most likely, even in the right neighborhood. "Who is calling, pray tell?"

"It's me, as you bloody well know," said the captain, from the hall. "Are you going to get out of the way, or not?"

Shingvere flung the door open, and stepped aside with a bow and a flourish. "May I present Captain Ernest Ballen," he said. "Late of a kitchen, somewhere," he added.

"Eryans," muttered the captain, stamping past Shingvere without a backward glance. "Morning, Thaumaturge," he said, moving to stand beside Meralda. He squinted into the mirror and frowned. "Any luck?"

"No one has been in or out," she said. "Have the mages explained our suspicions to you yet?"

The captain turned and glared. "All they've done is puff and moon like a pair of hoot owls," he said. He looked back to Meralda. "I knew I'd have to ask you before I'd get an answer."

"We believe the Tears are still in the safe room," she said. She explained her theory to him, from her doubts concerning the Tear's post-theft value to Mug's joking query of the mirror and its sudden display of the safe room, and the implications she had drawn.

Halfway through it, the captain asked for a chair, and Shingvere scooted his over to him. The captain sat, and Meralda watched him sag and go nearly limp.

"You haven't slept a wink, have you?" she asked, at last.

Shingvere stuck a fresh cup of coffee in the captain's hand. "He's not likely to, for a while, either," he said.

"That's the truth," muttered the captain. "Interviewing doormen. Interviewing night watchmen. Listening to the Watch interview jewelers and fences and petty thieves. Bah." He looked up at Meralda with bloodshot eyes, and smiled a crooked smile. "I came here hoping you'd have some news for me, Thaumaturge," he said. "Thank you."

Meralda felt her cheeks redden, and she looked away. "You're welcome," she said. "But until I can get back in the safe room, I haven't done a thing," she said.

The captain sipped coffee and frowned. "Won't be easy," he said. "The Alon wizards are making a big fuss. They've all but accused each and every mage in Tirlin," he said. "Even the Hang." He hesitated. "Even you, Thaumaturge."

Meralda whirled back to face the captain. "They've done what?"

"They've bawled to Yvin that only a mage could have done such a thing," he said. "Around sunrise, they demanded that all the mages be hauled in before the Alon queen and put to the question," he said. "You and Loman included."

Meralda felt her heart begin to race, and the red of her cheeks spread. "How dare those posturing wand-wavers accuse me of theft," she said. "If any mage stole the Tears, it's likely one of them."

"I know, I know," said the captain, lifting his hand. "And Yvin told them to go soak their heads. Said he'd not be delivering anyone to Alon law before Tirlish law was done with them," he said. "He also suggested that accusing real mages of petty theft was just the sort of thing that left scorch marks on the carpets and bad smells in the halls," he added. "You should have seen their faces when they worked out the implications of the real mages' comment," he said. "Priceless, really."

Meralda returned the captain's grin. "All right," she said, after a deep breath. "We won't know if I'm right until I can return to the safe room, Captain. From what you've just said, I might not be welcome."

"You won't be." The captain frowned. "But if that's what you need, I'll see it done." He drained his cup, set it down, and stood. "I'll see it done," he repeated. "When do you want to go?"

Meralda brushed back a lock of hair. Her body still ached. Her head hurt, a dull pain that throbbed in time with her heartbeat. She was bone tired, though barely awakened. Tired from a day of spellwork, followed by a night of scant and fitful sleep. *If my Sight returns at all today,* she thought, *I'll be fortunate indeed.*

"Late this evening, at the earliest," she said. "Though perhaps tomorrow morning would be best."

"I'll get you in, Mage," said the captain. "Somehow. Is there anything else you need?"

"Hourly reports from the Tower," said Meralda. "Were you told I requested them last night?"

"No," said the captain. "But you'll get what you asked for, or I'll have their heads on a string."

Meralda smiled. "That won't be necessary."

"Oh, you never know," said the captain. "It feels like that kind of day."

And then he turned, and was at the door, and gone.

Shingvere closed the door behind him.

"Tell you what," he said. "We'll watch the mirror, and send a lad if anything happens. Why don't you go home, have that bath of yours, and then come back here and find the Tears?"

Meralda stood. "I'll do that," she said. "How," she added, "I don't know. Yet. But I will."

Age of wizards is done, is it?

She marched for the door. "Tell the Bellringers and Mug to wait for me here," she said. "I won't be long."

"We will," said Fromarch. He refilled his coffee cup, and as Meralda passed him he spoke. "Tradesmen," he snorted. "I should have turned all his teeth backwards and filled his ears with hair."

Meralda laughed, squeezed the old man's shoulder, and made for the street and the sun.

Tomorrow morning, nine of the clock, said the captain's note. *And the Alon mages insist on being there. I told them your spell would require them to stand at the door. So put a bit of flash it in, if you will. Can't have these hedge wizards getting in your way, now can we?*

Meralda folded the note. Tervis stood by her desk and looked expectantly down at her. "Was it good news, ma'am?" he asked.

"Of a sort," said Meralda. She shoved the note in a stack of papers held down by a molten blob of blue-green glass and sighed. "We'll be visiting the safe room again, tomorrow morning," she said. "Looking for the Tears."

"Oh," said Tervis, and his half-smile vanished. "In the Alon wing."

"Yes," said Meralda. "Has there been trouble?"

"A bit," said Tervis. "Some of the lads got into a scuffle on the second floor. Something about a copperhead shoving a floorsweep. The guard broke it up."

"They weren't playing football in the park today, either," added Kervis, from his post at the door. "People are beginning to wonder."

Meralda nodded. "I imagine they are."

Tervis joined Kervis at the door. "We'd best get back to our posts," he said. "Yell if you need us," added Tervis.

Meralda nodded, and the lab doors shut, and aside from the

soft clicking and whirring from the shelves, the laboratory was silent.

Silent, as it had been all afternoon. The mages watched the mirror, exchanging whispers at times, but never once breaking into spates of name calling or joke telling or, as Meralda had feared, advice giving. They'd watched the glass and kept Meralda in tea and fresh paper and that was that.

Even Mug had barely spoken, though Meralda noted his blue eyes were always upon her. Silent Mug, silent mages. *Heavens,* mused Meralda, *perhaps the world is changing, after all.*

Meralda stretched, rubbed her eyes, and counted rings on Opp's timepiece. Seven of the clock? Already?

The Brass Bell began to peal out, and Meralda went back to work.

She'd been at home, soaking in a hot bath, her headache gone, but her mind awhirl from the events in the park and the daunting task that lay ahead. *How will I find the Tears,* she had wondered, *as she sank into the hot bathtub. How will I?*

And then she'd remembered the park. Remembered the latch breaking and falling, recalled discovering the outlines of a spell that had been flying above Tirlin, unseen for perhaps a millennia. She had leaped from the tub so fast she'd sent water sloshing across her water closet, soaking her towels and her bathrobe in the process.

"That's how," she'd said, her voice a near shout. "That's how!"

And then, of course, Mrs. Whitlonk had banged on the wall, and Meralda had laughed and clapped her hands and slipped smiling back into the bath.

That, and a day's work at the lab since, and she was nearly done.

A few more pen strokes, another set of twisting Foumai folded space calculations, and then Meralda put down her pen, and took a breath.

"There," she said. "There!"

Mug swung more eyes toward her.

"Mistress?"

"It's done," she said. "If the Tears are there—"

"They are," chimed Shingvere.

"—this will find them," she said. "It must."

Mug swung a pair of eyes down upon her papers. "Hmmm," he said. Meralda heard Shingvere's chair creak, and Fromarch mutter something, then Shingvere sighed and settled back into his chair.

"Oh, come and have a look, both of you," she said. "If you see a flaw, I want to know it now, not after the Alons start snickering."

The wizards rose and hurried to Meralda's desk. "Well, if you insist," said Shingvere.

"Hah! I see it!" said Mug. "You're not looking for the Tears," he said. "You're looking for...what? A weak spell interaction?"

"Exactly," said Fromarch. "This bit here," he said, pointing. "This bit here. It's a repeating latch, isn't it?"

Meralda smiled. "You're correct," she said. "I'll go over every inch of the safe room. Latch the spell, spin the latch, watch the illuminators. Any spell interaction will cause polarized hue shifts."

Fromarch, who had been leaning close to the drawings, rose. "How small an interaction can this detect, Meralda?" he asked.

"Ten to the minus eight," she said. "Ten to the minus ten, if I have time to halve the spinner diameter."

"You're a genius, Meralda Ovis," he said. "I never said that before, but I should have, and I'm sorry."

Meralda turned to face Fromarch, but he turned quickly away. Shingvere shook his head when she reached for Fromarch's sleeve.

"It's a brilliant design," said the Eryan, quickly. "It won't matter how well concealed the Tears are, if you're looking for the concealment spell itself."

"Unless the Alons took the Tears away with the broken jewel box," said Meralda.

Fromarch snorted, and turned once again to face Meralda. "I know them both," he said. "They aren't that clever. And anyone clever enough to hide the Tears wouldn't just hide them in the jewel box, knowing that pair of buffoons will spend all their time aiming who-knows-what spells at it," he said.

"I hope you're right," said Meralda.

"I am," said Fromarch. He nodded toward the drawings. "You'll have the Tears in hand by lunchtime," he said. "A hero of the realm."

"Not unless she gets this built and cast," said Shingvere. He frowned. "What are you going to call it, anyway, lass?" he asked. "Meralda's Marvelous Locator? The All-Seeing Lamp of Mage Ovis the Great?"

"Mage Meralda's Optical Alon Embarassor?" said Mug.

"It's a weak charge interaction detection device," said Meralda. "Or it will be, by midnight."

Mug sighed. "Weak Charge Interaction Detection Device," he said. "Rolls lyrically off the tongue, doesn't it?"

"Quiet, you two," said Fromarch. "The thaumaturge has work to do." He glared at Shingvere, who shrugged and ambled back to his chair.

"You're right, of course," Shingvere said. "It's going to be another long night." He sat, and fumbled in his pockets. "Penny-stick?"

Fromarch followed, waved away the candy, and sat. Meralda gathered her papers, eager to move from the desk and her pens and Foumai calculations and onto the workbench and its copper ropes and charged banks of holdstones.

"Will you need me, mistress?" asked Mug. "I can help with the latch, if nothing else. Save your Sight for the morning."

"I'd rather you watch the glass, just now," said Meralda. "This isn't a terribly complicated spellwork, and your eyes are better than any of ours."

"Aye, Captain," said Mug. "As you wish."

Meralda caught up her papers and hurried away. Mug sighed, turned all but a pair of his green eyes back to the dark, still image in the mirror, and softly began to play Meralda's favorite Eryan bagpipe piece. Shingvere hummed along, his voice soft and mournful, long into the night.

Yvin himself met Meralda and Mug on the west stair. "Good

morning, Thaumaturge," he said. "I understand you're going to pay the Alons a visit."

Meralda nodded. She'd finished the detector around midnight, had been home by one, had slept until six. Now she had but an hour to check the detector's latch, charge the illuminator, try her Sight, and gather her wits.

What I don't have time for is this, she thought.

"I am," she said. "But first, I have certain preparations to make."

The king, who stood with his six-man guard blocking the stair, nodded but didn't move. "The captain tells me you think you can produce the Tears today," he said. He glanced around, lowered his voice. "Can you, Thaumaturge?"

Oh, now you need a wizard, do you? Meralda bit back the words, and merely nodded.

"I hope so," she said. Mug stirred in his bird cage, and Meralda gave it the tiniest of swings.

Yvin's face reddened, and he sighed. "I suppose that's all you're willing to say, isn't it?" he said.

"It is," replied Meralda, amazed at her temerity. *Must come with the title,* she thought. "For the moment, Your Highness."

"Then I'll wish you good luck," said Yvin. "We'll get out of your way. Oh, and Thaumaturge? We'll be just outside the Alon wing, with two hundred house guards and a door ram. If we must make war with Alonya I'm willing to start it here and now, so if they lay a finger on you call out."

Meralda nodded. "I will," she said. The king looked her in the eye, and his scowl softened, and he held out his hand. "Thank you, Thaumaturge," he said. "Come what may, we thank you."

Meralda took his hand, and shook it, and then Yvin stamped off down the Hall, his guardsmen on his heels.

"Well, you certainly told him," said Mug, when they were gone. "He won't soon forget that fire and lightning comeuppance."

Meralda mounted the stair, scowling. "Oh, shut up," she said. "What was I supposed to do? Call down thunder claps, here on the stair?"

"Oh, no," said Mug. "Shaking his hand was much more effective."

Meralda stamped up the stair, reached the landing, and nodded at the Bellringers, who stood bleary eyed and yawning by the laboratory doors. Before either could speak, though, Fromarch flung open the doors and burst into the hall.

"Blow that whistle, lad," he said. "We've got people in the safe room."

Kervis fumbled with the silver guard's whistle at his neck, brought it to his lips, and blew a single short blast.

Down the hall and through the palace, the whistle was repeated, fainter and fainter each time until it was gone.

Meralda leaped from the stair. Fromarch saw her, and beckoned her in. "Those Alon bumblers are inside," he said. "Better have a look." He turned and hurried away.

Tervis rushed to Meralda's side and wordlessly took Mug's sheet-draped bird cage. Meralda let go, and sprinted for the doors.

"Go on, follow her!" said Mug. "I can take a bit of swinging. Run, blast you, run!"

Tervis hurried after, bird cage held high, as eyes poked and thrust their way through folds in the bed sheet.

Meralda ran. The mirror stood by her desk, in what should have been plain sight from the doors. But Shingvere stood before the glass, and his rotund form blocked any view.

"Stand aside!" shouted Fromarch, slowing to a halt. "We can't see through your thick Eryan bottom!"

Meralda followed. One whistle meant stand alert, Meralda recalled. She wondered if the captain had actually given orders that Tirlish guards were to enter the Alon wing on the traditional three-whistle "fire, foes, fie" signal.

If so, Tirlin was only two whistle blows from war.

Meralda gently moved Shingvere away from the mirror.

There, in the glass, was the safe room, dark no more. In the room, Red Mawb and Dorn Mukirk stood before Tim's portrait, locked in a silent round of red-faced hand waving and finger pointing.

"Off to a good start," muttered Mug, as Tervis placed his pot on the edge of Meralda's desk.

Meralda's jaw dropped. In one hand, Mawb held a human skull, from which the lower jaw and most of the upper teeth were missing. The skull twitched and spun in Mawb's hand, as though moving erratically on its own. Indeed, after one particularly violent sideways jerk Mawb slapped the boney face with his free hand.

A ruddy, smoking flame rode the air a hand's breadth above Mawb's bald head. Mawb's robe, like Mukirk's, was festooned with a variety of symbols, some of which Meralda recognized as numbers and Old Kingdom astrological markings.

"Give 'em a wagon and a tent and we'll have a bloody circus," muttered Mug.

Dorn Mukirk, who had appeared at first to be empty-handed, reached within his robe and withdrew a bone. *It's a leg bone,* decided Meralda, with a disgusted frown. *A yellowed human leg bone.*

"Now there's a use for pockets," muttered Fromarch.

Dorn Mukirk struck a stiff pose, arms and leg bone uplifted, and mouthed a long word. The leg bone took on a glowing golden aura that left a trail in the air when the wizard swung it down level with his waist.

The Alon mages glared at each other, and began to warily circle the room, each brandishing his respective bone and muttering to it. Red Mawb's skull twitched and jerked. Dorn Mukirk's leg bone emitted brief tongues of pale, cold flame. Both wizards circled and chanted and, at one point, bumped into each other and broke into a fresh fit of shouting and fist-waving.

Meralda looked away, and bit back a laugh. "I can hardly believe this," she said. "Bones?"

"The Alons have always been a bit fond of necromancy," said Shingvere. "Though I thought they'd grown out of it, of late." He shook his head. "Seems I was wrong."

Bones, thought Meralda. *Here, in the twentieth century.*

"Will you gentlemen keep an eye on our Alons and their

body parts? As amusing as this is, I need to prepare the detector."
And test my Sight, Meralda thought, with a tightening of her chest. *I hope I don't have to do this blind.*

Shingvere dragged his chair close to the glass. "Aye, we'll watch the circus, lass. And if they find the Tears I'll eat my robes."

Meralda hurried to her workbench, shedding her long coat as she went. The first real bite of autumn had been in the air this morning, reminding her of just how close the Accords were, and just how little she'd done to move the Tower's shadow.

"First things first," she muttered, as she draped her coat over a glassware rack and pulled back her chair. "Won't be any Accords unless you work, my friend."

She regarded the detector. She'd had no time to do more than assemble a crude framework from cast off bits of this and remainders from that. Finished, the detector was simply a half globe of copper bands, perhaps a foot across, that held a pair of glass discs mounted midway through the half globe's shell. The glass discs were a finger's breadth apart, and a faint bluish haze rode the air between the glasses.

Meralda had mounted a plain wooden broom handle to the edge of the half-globe, and had wrapped the gripping end of the handle with thick copper wire. *All in all,* Meralda decided, *it bears an unfortunate resemblance to a plumber's toilet plunger.*

Meralda took a third glass disc from its stand on her bench, slipped it carefully between the two already mounted to the apparatus, and smiled when she heard a tiny click and felt the binding spell lock the disc in place.

"Skulls and leg bones," she said, softly. "And me without a single bubbling cauldron."

Mug laughed, and Meralda reached for her notes. *First, charge the repeater, and prime the latch,* she'd written, just before she'd left for the night. *Then set the illuminator and the polarizing bands.*

Simple enough. But her nagging worries about her Sight arose again, and Meralda knew she'd have to try now, before she could concentrate on anything else. *I can see the colors in the glass change without any Sight,* she thought. *But who knows what else I might need to see?*

"All right," she said, taking a deep breath, and closing her eyes. "Sight."

She reached out, willing into being that peculiar sense of things unseen that always preceded the advent of Sight. She felt it blossom, willed it from within to without, and opened her eyes.

"Sight."

Her workbench was alight with traceries of fire. The five-tined charge dissipater was bathed in a ragged nimbus of shifting blue. The grounding cable was barely visible through its aura of midnight black. The detector, charged and shaped with only the most subtle of spells, sparkled and shone like a jeweler's display case lit with a noonday sun.

Meralda smiled, and closed her eyes, and willed back a portion of her Sight. *I'll keep what I need to finish the detector,* she decided, but save what is left for the safe room.

"Everything all right, Meralda?" asked Fromarch, from his place before the mirror.

"Everything is fine. I'm ready."

And then she opened her eyes, rubbed her palms together, and caught up a wisp of cold, taut fire.

"Here we are," said the captain, as he and Meralda and the Bellringers reached the four Alons flanking the doors to the east wing. "Friendly, picturesque Alonya."

The copperheads glared. One rapped sharply on the door with his knuckles, and a moment later the doors opened and half a dozen Alons spilled out.

Meralda immediately recognized Hermish Draunt, the Alon ambassador to Tirlin. He'd been the Alon ambassador for twelve years, and Meralda knew he was regarded in the court as a reasonable, level-headed man who held the Alon queen's favor despite being brother to the chief of Clan Fuam, which had dared a blood feud with the queen's clan a mere two centuries past. Hermish smiled at Meralda and even bowed slightly. As Meralda returned his greeting she saw the other Alons glare.

The others were unknown to her. Each wore the plaid kilt and shoulder sash of his Clan, but to Meralda, every complicated red-and-green plaid looked very much like any other, and the sigils on their buttons were too small to make out at arm's length. She counted five bearded, scarred, unsmiling faces, and decided introductions by name were neither advisable nor forthcoming.

"Welcome to Alonya, my friends," said Ambassador Draunt. "The thaumaturge and her attendants may enter freely."

Beside Meralda, the captain glared. "The thaumaturge, her attendants, and myself, thank you," he said.

Ambassador Draunt reddened. "Regrettably, Captain, the invitation specified only the Thaumaturge to Tirlin, and her two attendants," he said. His gaze fell. "No one else."

"That isn't what we were told," said the captain.

"It's what you're being told now," said a gravel voiced Alon, who stepped from behind the ambassador to face the captain. "It is not to be questioned or negotiated. Your thaumaturge, her honor guard, and that's all. Or nothing."

Meralda put her hand on the captain's shoulder.

"The thaumaturge accepts," she said, and she squeezed when she felt the captain inhale. "How could one refuse such a gracious, gentle-spoken invitation?"

The Alon reddened, and Meralda smiled. "I'll be back soon," she said, before anyone could speak. "This really shouldn't take long."

And then she steeled her jaw, lifted her chin, and marched straight into the gathered Alons.

At the last possible instant, they stepped aside, though Meralda was certain Ambassador Draunt pulled at least one Alon out of her way.

"Come, gentlemen," she called out, to the Bellringers. "Let's not dawdle, and impose too long upon the obvious good nature of our hosts."

Behind her, she heard the hurry of booted feet and let out a shaky breath.

I'm here in Alonya, she thought. *Now all I've got to do is find the Tears.*

As the Alons trotted up behind her, finally sidling past her and splitting up so that three went ahead and three followed behind, Meralda began to sweat and her heart began to pound. The Alons turned, and Meralda followed, and behind her she heard Kervis whisper. "Wish I had the Oldmark," he said. "What am I going to do with this?"

Meralda knew he referred to the ornamental swords the captain had insisted both Bellringers take. *I should perhaps have left the Bellringers behind with the captain,* she thought. *After all, I'm not likely to be mugged here, even by the Alons.*

As the Alons led her through their halls, though, Meralda began to wonder. Her six Alon guides quickly became nine, then a dozen, then sixteen. Every hall they passed or crossed was guarded by or full of soldiers, in full armor.

The Alons about her fell into a thudding marching step, and Meralda had to fight to keep from falling in, herself. The Bellringers, she noted, refused to join in as well. Kervis began whistling a Tirlish marching song which, she recalled, mentioned the Alons in less than flattering terms.

They aren't afraid, Meralda realized, *because they are with me.*

I wish I was half so confident.

The party halted at a door, voices rose up, and then the door was opened, and Meralda saw past it and realized she was nearly to the safe room. She breathed a sigh of relief, but it caught in her throat as she heard Tervis say, "Now she'll show you lot a thing or two."

Before her, the Alons made a path. Standing at the end of it, just beyond the door, were Red Mawb and Dorn Mukirk.

"Good morning," she said, when it became apparent neither Alon intended to speak. "We haven't met, formally."

"I am named Red Mawb, Mage to the Alon Queen," spat Mawb. Beside him, Dorn Mukirk grimaced.

"As am I," he said, his round face darkening. "As am I."

"Oh?" said Meralda. "Your name is Red Mawb, too?"

The rotund wizard spat a curse word, and stepped forward, and as Ambassador Draunt leaped into the space between Meralda and the Alon wizards Meralda struggled to keep her smile intact.

"Please, please," said the ambassador. "We're all tired, and perhaps overwrought," he said. "Let the thaumaturge be about our queen's business, and perhaps we can lay this...unfortunate matter to rest, at last," he said, turning and lifting his hands to the mages." By the order of the queen, as I said."

Dorn Mukirk mouthed a curse word, but stepped back and away from the door. Mawb followed.

Here I go, thought Meralda. *Into history. Or into infamy.* Her earlier convictions that the Tears lay within the safe room began to waver. What if it isn't here? What if all I find is a table and a chair?

Meralda turned. The Alons gathered close at her back.

"Let's go," she said. Her voice shook, and she heard it, and she clenched her jaw and stepped forward. The Bellringers followed, and an Alon threw open the safe room door and stepped aside.

The room was dark, and Meralda halted at the threshold. "Guardsman Tervis," she said, softly. "My bag."

"Yes, ma'am," said Tervis, rushing to her side and opening the bag.

Meralda reached inside. She nearly reached for her magelamp, but decided the detector and it glowing discs would be easier to see in the darkened room.

A shuffling of feet broke out behind her, and she turned to see Kervis shoving Red Mawb back with his shoulder.

"Make way," snarled the wizard, to Kervis. "Make way, or I'll–"

"Or you'll what?" snapped Meralda, surprised at the steadiness in her voice. She turned to face the Alon wizard. "Are you making threats upon the person of a Tirlish guard in the palace of the king of Tirlin?"

Hushed voices rose, and hands grasped the wizard's shoulder, and dragged him back.

"I thought not," said Meralda. "Only myself and my attendants are to enter this room while I work," she said. "That was the agreement. It is subject to neither discussion nor negotiation." The Alons glared, hands on hilts, mouths set in mid-curse.

"I've had enough of this," she said. "Anyone who wishes to argue may do so with a ward spell. You are familiar with ward spells, are you not?"

Then she lifted her arms, muttered a nonsense word, and brought her hands together with a clap.

The Alons surged back, away from the door. Even Kervis gritted his teeth and flinched at the sound, though he winked an instant later.

Meralda grinned and turned her back to the Alons.

Now find the Tears, she thought. *If they're here at all.* She wiped sweat from her forehead, reached into her bag, and found the detector's wire-wrapped handle. She drew it carefully forth, raised the copper basket to the level of her eyes, and spoke the last half of the long word that would mesh and engage the two dozen spells tied to the glass and copper.

The glass disks flickered and began to glow. Within a moment a light shone from the glass, bright as a magelamp and a soft, deep blue.

Hushed exclamations rose up from the hall. "Bah," she heard Dorn Mukirk spit. "Why are we wasting our time with this foreigner's party lamp?"

Meralda closed her eyes. "Sight," she intoned, in a whisper. "Sight, Sight, Sight."

And she opened her eyes, and the room was aglow.

Relief washed through her, and she let out her breath in a sigh. *To work,* she thought, resisting an impish urge to turn and wave at the corner. *Goboy's mirror seems to look in from there,* she decided, *and Fromarch, Shingvere and Mug are surely watching this very moment.*

Not until I find the Tears, she thought. *Not until then.*

"I'll start with this wall," she said, to Tervis. "I'll need you to move the table back, if you will."

The Bellringers nodded, and sprang for the table.

Meralda lifted the detector and followed. Once there, she put the detector's flat side to the wall, let it latch, and watched the blue light shine as she moved along the stones.

"It'll be there, ma'am," said Tervis. "I know it will."

Meralda nodded and swallowed. Sweat ran down her face,

plastered her hair to her temples and the back of her neck. She wondered if Fromarch was pacing now, or if Mug was holding all his eyes in a bunch.

She'd covered three of the room's four walls, and the floor, without so much as the faintest flicker. Now she was halfway done with the ceiling, and she knew, deep in her heart, that the light wasn't going to darken no matter how slowly or carefully she moved it across the polished ironwood beams.

"Careful, ma'am," whispered Tervis, who stood below her and held the chair. Meralda had been forced to use the chair, as the ceiling in the safe room was higher than she recalled, and her handle had proved too short. "You nearly stepped off, that time."

Meralda nodded, and moved the detector until she could reach no further. "Let's move the chair," she said. "One more time ought to do it for the ceiling, and then we'll check the safe."

"Good idea," said Tervis. Meralda put her hand on his shoulder as she stepped down from the chair, and felt that his uniform jacket was wet with sweat. "I was surprised when you didn't start there," he said, nodding toward the portrait of Tim and the safe behind it.

"Oh, I know I'll find traces there," she said. *Or, at least, I bloody well hope so.* "But if the spell passed through the walls before latching, I want to know where it came from, and I decided I'd need fresh Sight for that." *And the spell must have passed through a wall,* she thought. *A wall or the ceiling or the floor, unless our scheming friend hid it months ago.*

Tervis nodded, and a fat drop of sweat rolled down his nose.

It's hotter than a furnace in here, Meralda thought, wiping her own brow with her sleeve. The Alons must have every fireplace and cook stove in the east wing going full blast. Coincidence, or more Alon hospitality?

Meralda took another long breath of hot, still air. She heard a distant clock strike ten, and Red Mawb laughed to his fellows.

Tervis scooted the chair toward the wall. *Nothing,* Meralda thought, and frowned. *I've found nothing at all.*

She pushed the thought aside. *Well, of course you haven't,* she reasoned. *Even if the spell passed through the walls, it never latched to them. The safe will likely hold the only traces of the spell. The walls and the floor needed to be checked, of course, but only out of thoroughness. No, if the Tears do remain, they are in the one place we haven't looked yet.*

Meralda bit her lip, stepped into the chair again, and quickly finished checking the ceiling. The steady blue glow never wavered.

"Well," said Meralda, forcing a smile and climbing down to the floor. "That's done."

Tervis frowned. "Nothing?"

"No traces of projected spellworks," replied Meralda. Her chest tightened. *What if I'm wrong? What if the Tears aren't here at all?*

From beyond the doorway, a bevy of close-packed Alons watched, the wizard Red Mawb at the fore. Meralda met his eyes, saw in them a bemused, haughty sort of boredom.

"Is that bad?" asked Tervis.

Meralda looked away from Mawb. "It changes nothing," she said, to Tervis. "The Tears are here, and we shall have them."

And then she turned on her heel, walked to the portrait of Tim the Horsehead, and set her Sight upon it.

Nothing. Oh, she saw the usual eddies and swirls of radiance that hung about any surface, if one's Sight were sensitive enough. But that was all. There was no trace, not the faintest, of the ordered patterns an old spellwork might leave behind. Meralda hadn't brought her staff, simply because any spell too subtle to be Seen or found out by the Alon wizards wasn't going to be found by her staff, either. But now she wished she had it, if only to hold something familiar.

"Here we go," she whispered. Then she placed the detector firmly against the wall, just to the right of the portrait.

Right or wrong, thought Meralda. *Now, we see.*

After the slightest of hesitations the lighted disks went dark.

Tervis whooped and stamped his foot. "Well done!" cried Kervis.

"And not a head bone in the room," added Tervis, under his breath but not so faintly that the wizards outside couldn't hear. "Ma'am."

Meralda smiled a wide, sweaty smile and propped herself against the wall with her free hand and imagined she could hear, faint but clear, the sound of cheering and clapping from her mages and from Mug, half a palace away.

She stepped back, mopped her brow, and moved the detector, letting the latch take hold once more. The blue light returned, but faint and flickering steadily.

"Good old Tirlish magic," remarked Tervis, airily, and Meralda grinned.

Move, latch, test, move. In a few moments, Meralda saw that a spellwork had, indeed, been attached to the safe, and the wall about it. The spellwork's footprint was circular, about four feet in diameter, with a pronounced notch running vertically above the safe.

And utterly invisible to Sight. Strain as she might, without the detector Meralda could see nothing at all, even though she knew what to look for, and where to look. *I'd have never found this with my staff,* she thought. *Not with my staff, not with two dozen staves and every mage in the Realms.*

Her elation dimmed at the realization. This is not the work of a guild master or a rogue wizard or a renegade Alon necromancer. *No,* Meralda decided, *this is the work of a mage. A mage with skills I've never seen.*

Mumbling and jostling sounded from the hall.

Meralda bit her lower lip, reached up, and swung Tim's portrait away from the safe. When she lifted the detector to the back of the canvas, the light flickered and went out, and Meralda smiled. *Yes,* she thought, following the faint traceries of light that billowed and swam in the shimmering blue glass. *This lot here. One end bound to the back of Tim's portrait, the other end coiled like a spring. It pushed the portrait out before the safe door opened, and pulled it shut when the work was done.*

She waved the detector toward the safe, which was still ajar, and the blue glasses went momentarily dark. Meralda latched to the safe door, and the glow returned, this time as a faint, rotating pattern of tiny criss-crossed lines.

Meralda frowned. Ordered, mobile traces? Of an old spell?

She reached out, opened the safe, and slowly pushed the detector inside.

The glow grew brighter, spun faster.

Meralda pushed farther.

The blue light began to beat, pulsing and ebbing like blows from a hammer, or a heart.

It's still active, thought Meralda. *An active spell, so subtle it's too faint for Sight.*

Meralda pulled in a breath, and willed her Sight deeper, farther, clearer. Memories of the exploding spellworks in the Gold Room rose, but after a moment's observation in the glass Meralda decided this spell wasn't preparing to strike, and she proceeded.

She fixed her mind upon the spell latched to the detector, saw it as a bright blue sphere cupped in a copper bowl. She pushed again, and her normal vision faded, and then she saw, just for an instant, a tangled skein of blue-lit spell traces, all spilling out of the wall safe like an explosion of Phendelit pasta noodles. There, at the back of the safe, she saw that the metal was lit by worm tracks of fire, and that at the center of the glow the metal was hollow.

She held her breath. *Sight,* she begged, and there, in the void, a glittering thing took shape. *Fat raindrops caught in a spider's web,* thought Meralda, and her heart raced, and then her Sight went close and clear and the raindrops became pale diamonds and the web a delicate lattice of finely worked gold.

"The Tears," said Meralda. *I was right,* she thought, elation rushing through her. *They're here.*

Now to get them free.

Meralda opened her eyes, and though she let her Sight recede a bit she could still see the tangled outlines of the foreign spell riding across the disks.

Meralda tried to follow the patterns, make sense of the turnings and the whirls and coils, but it was like trying to count raindrops as they fell. *What is this structure? And why would anyone cast a spell which linked large portions of the framework to itself?*

"Ma'am," said Tervis, from her side. "Ma'am, are you well?"

Meralda blinked. The blue glow from the detector pulsed faster now, as though the spell suspected it was under scrutiny and was growing troubled.

"Too late," said Meralda, triumph in her voice. "I fooled you. Now I'll beat you."

"Ma'am?" said Tervis.

Meralda withdrew the detector. "The Tears are here," she said, stepping back. She handed the detector to Tervis, mopped her face with her sleeve, and turned to Kervis. "Guardsman," she said. "In my bag you'll find a hammer, and a long chisel. Will you be so good as to take them up, and break out the back end of this safe?" She smiled and winked toward the corner. *Let the Alons,* she thought, *make of it what they will.* "I believe you'll find a handful of trinkets, at yonder end."

Kervis grinned, threw his helmet to the floor, and charged to her side. "Glad to," he said. "I knew you'd have us home by supper."

Meralda returned his smile and sought out the chair at the other end of the room.

Mawb and Dorn Mukirk now stood shoulder-to-shoulder in the doorway, glaring ferociously at Meralda when they weren't muttering behind their palms or jabbing each other in the ribs with their elbows. Meralda ignored them, and sat.

"Careful, now," she said, as Kervis placed the long steel spike on the back of the safe, and hefted the blunt-faced hammer in his right hand. "The metal is thin, and the cavity that holds the Tears is small. It wouldn't do to hand our hosts their crown jewels in pieces," she said.

Kervis nodded, set the chisel, and gave it a blow.

It rang, but nothing happened. "A bit harder, this time," he said, and he struck, and Meralda heard from across the room a faint crunch and then a sharp ping as the tip of the chisel broke through one layer of oddly brittle steel, traveled a short distance, and then struck another.

Kervis withdrew the chisel, stuck his arm in the safe, and felt about. "You're right, ma'am," he said. "The back of the safe is all brittle. I think I can break it with my hand."

Kervis set his face in a scowl, strained, and grunted. There came a faint snapping noise from within and Kervis' eyes went wide. He smiled and pulled his arm out of the safe.

Meralda resisted the urge to stand. Tervis rushed to his brother's side. A hush fell over the Alons, and Tervis stepped aside just in time for Meralda to see Kervis hold up the Tears in sweaty, grinning triumph.

Meralda stood, and returned his smile. *We've done it,* she thought. *I was right.*

She looked upon the Tears, watched the diamonds sparkle in the dark safe room, marveled at the delicate skeleton of gold and silver that held the jewels in place. Then, in the hall, the gathered Alons erupted in a roar of shouts and bellows.

Dorn Mukirk produced his leg bone. "Thief!" he cried, brandishing it like a staff. "You brought them with you! Thief! Thief!"

The Alons roared. Meralda saw Ambassador Draunt lift his hands and shout, but his words were lost, and he stumbled back toward the doorway as a soldier shoved him hard in the chest.

"Liar!" bellowed Red Mawb. Kervis' face went crimson. He took the Tears in his left hand, and drew his sword with his right.

Kervis looked toward Meralda, terror in his eyes. "Ma'am?" he asked.

Dorn Mukirk lifted his leg bone, and it began to glow. "Witch!" he shouted, spittle spraying from his lips. "Witch!"

The shouts from the crowded Alons muted, and there was a general shuffling away from the doorway. Dorn Mukirk, though, stood firm.

"Witch!" he bellowed.

Witch, thought Meralda. She knew what the word meant to an Alon. It meant warty old crones, gathered about a cauldron, stirring the remains of babies into a thick gruel as part of some evil spell.

Witch.

The anger which had been welling up inside Meralda evaporated. She heard the shouts, but they went distant. She saw the shaking fists and the half-drawn swords, but they might as well have been on a stage, in a play, for all the threat they presented.

Even the two whistle blows, which rang out faint from the hall, brought with them no panic.

I'm smiling, thought Meralda, amazed at the realization.

Smiling and calm and I'm walking steadily toward the door.

"Witch?" she said, to the Alon wizard, and her voice carried over the remaining shouts. "You wave a femur in my face and dare call me witch?"

She didn't actually recall taking all the six or eight steps across the safe room. Suddenly, though, she was there, at the threshold, at arm's length from Dorn Mukirk's sweaty red face.

"Witch!" he spat.

She slapped him. She brought her open right hand hard and fast across his sweat-soaked, bearded cheek. The hall went deathly silent, and Mukirk's close-set eyes bulged in fury.

Meralda stepped back. The Bellringers flew to her sides, their swords drawn, held low and straight.

Meralda locked stares with Dorn Mukirk. "If witch I am, step across this threshold," she said to him. Her voice rang out clear in the hall. "If thief I am, come forward and take the Tears from my hand. Dare my ward. Your talisman can dispel it, can it not? Surely your mighty relic can break the ward of a lowly Tirlish witch?"

Mukirk waved the bone frantically about. It glowed and sparked and made mutterings Meralda couldn't understand, but the wizard did not step beyond the threshold.

Meralda watched the bone trail fire, its mutterings growing louder and angrier as it sought out a ward that wasn't there.

"Enough," said Meralda. She put a hand on each of the Bellringer's shoulders. "Sheath your blades, gentlemen," she said. She pushed each gently back, hoping they would step once again into the mirror's view, and perhaps prevent the captain from blowing three whistles. "And step back. We will make no war today."

The Bellringers reluctantly left Meralda alone at the door.

"I found your Tears," she said, lifting her voice above the grumblings and her gaze above Dorn Mukirk's furious glare. "I came in good faith, at the invitation of your queen." She put her hands on her hips, and let her gaze wander amid the crowd. "We have endured insult and threat," she said. "I tell you now we shall endure no more."

Ambassador Draunt shoved a soldier aside, put his elbow in Dorn Mukirk's ribs, and pushed him yelping out of the doorway.

"Thaumaturge!" hissed Tervis. "In the corner, to your right."

Meralda half-turned and saw a shimmer ride the air, hanging like a cloud in the corner from which Goboy's mirror gazed.

The shimmer spun and shrank. *Red Mawb,* Meralda thought, and she turned her gaze back upon the hall. *Where is Mawb?*

She searched the close-packed hall, but Mawb was not to be seen. When she again risked a glance aside, the shimmering in the corner was gone.

Could have been Shingvere and Fromarch, thought Meralda. *Though I can hardly believe they'd risk a sending through a scrying glass.*

The mob in the hall jostled and shoved. More soldiers joined the fray, forcing their way toward the ambassador with curses and shoves.

"Thaumaturge Ovis," panted Ambassador Draunt, with a small bow. "Forgive the unthinking ardor of my countrymen," he said. He paused to take a breath and brush back his hair, which had fallen in damp white locks across his forehead. "Alonya gives you thanks, for your service to Alonya and our queen."

Dorn Mukirk growled something, but his words were muffled when, at a nod from Draunt, a copperhead clasped his hand firmly over the fat wizard's mouth and dragged him away, bone flailing, boots kicking.

More boots sounded down the hall, and with them a whistle blow. Meralda's heart raced until she realized only one whistle sounded, not three. *Stand down,* she thought. *The captain is calling Tirlin to stand down.*

Ambassador Draunt found a smile, and beckoned to the soldiers at his back. Those soldiers all wore the same colors on their sashes, Meralda noted. Clan Fuam, no doubt. Another man, this one tall, bald, and sad-eyed, squeezed through the crowd to stand beside the ambassador.

"Thaumaturge," said the ambassador, putting his hand on the shoulder of the tall man. "May I introduce Goodman Russet, jeweler to the queen? With your permission, he will accompany me, and inspect the Tears for authenticity." The ambassador took a breath, and spoke his next words in a near shout. "After Goodman Russet sees the jewels you found, we shall have no lingering doubt that we have recovered the Tears."

"Of course," said Meralda. She briefly considered pronouncing her ward spell defunct, but the thought of sharing the room with three dozen sweaty Alon bodies was too much to bear. Just a few more moments...

Meralda lifted her right hand and let her fingers dance. *Let Dorn Mukirk wonder what that meant,* she thought, and then she silently mouthed her grandmother's maiden name.

"You and Goodman Russet may pass," she said.

The Alon ambassador put a toe gingerly over the threshold, hesitated for only an instant, and then dashed into the room. Jeweler Russet followed close behind, jeweler's loupe in hand.

Meralda nodded, and Kervis held out the Tears. Ambassador Draunt waved them away, indicating his companion. The jeweler moved to stand before Kervis, solemnly regarding the Tears for a moment, then pulled a black cloth from his jacket pocket, and used it to gingerly take up the Tears.

"Tervis," said Meralda. "My magelamp."

"Yes, ma'am," said Tervis. He found the bag and reached inside, his eyes still on the Alons. When he withdrew the lamp, Meralda spoke a word and from across the room her lamp flared to life.

"Give the lamp to the ambassador, Guardsman," she said. "I want him to be sure."

More boots sounded in the hall, outside. But where the other footfalls had been furtive scuffles or pounding runs, these boots marched.

In an instant, the crowd in the hall melted away, except for the Alons bearing the sashes of the ambassador's own clan. Even these saluted and stepped aside. Then, from out of the crowd, the Alon queen stepped up to the open door.

Red Mawb was at her side, panting. He met Meralda's gaze, surprised her by winking, and turned to his queen.

"May I present to you the Mage of Tirlin?" he said, bowing. "Who has, it appears, solved our little problem."

The tiny Alon queen met Meralda's gaze and tilted her head forward the merest fraction. Her grey eyes shone below her brow, and the powder on her face did little to hide the blotches of fury beneath it. "I gave orders you were to work in private, Thaumaturge," she said. "It seems my orders were ignored."

Meralda bowed in return. "No matter," she said. "The work went well, despite my audience."

"I am told you may have been insulted," continued the queen. "If so, you may claim retribution." The queen turned to the towering copper-helmed soldier at her right. "Fetch Headsman Gaudling," she said. "And an axe. A bucket, perhaps, as well."

Meralda cleared her throat. "I claim no retribution," she said, quickly. "Let there be peace among our folk."

The Alon queen grinned. It was a small grin, quickly hidden, but Meralda saw it and smiled. "Very well," she said, to her guards. "Still, fetch the Headsman. And bring him and Dorn Mukirk to my chambers."

"The axe and the bucket?" asked her guard.

"Those as well," said the queen. "Make sure Mukirk sees them, won't you?"

"As you wish, my Queen," said the soldier, his face utterly blank. "Shall I have a lad sharpen the axe, while he waits?"

The Alon queen smiled and beckoned to Meralda. "What a wonderful idea," she said. Then she looked toward Ambassador Draught, who, like Goodman Russet, had snapped to full attention at the sight of his queen. "Pray, proceed, gentlemen," said the queen.

Tervis crossed the room and gave Ambassador Draunt the short copper tube. The ambassador bowed, played the light on the Tears, and watched as Goodman Russet set his eye upon the thumb-sized diamond central to the Tears.

Silence and scowling, but only for a moment. Then Goodman Russet lowered his glass, looked up at the ambassador, and nodded.

"These are the true Tears," he said, first to the queen, then again to Meralda. "These are the Tears, and no doubt. Heavens, Thaumaturge, you've done it!"

Goodman Russet wrapped the Tears in his cloth, bowed to Meralda, and said, his words barely audible over the rising cheers outside, "I'll never get the scratches out, but thank you all the same."

Meralda collapsed into her desk chair as the Bellringers closed the laboratory doors and took up their posts outside in the hall.

The laboratory was cool. And, aside from the muted sound of voices in the hall and the gentle busy clacking of Phillitrep's Calculating Engine, it was quiet. Meralda was surprised to find that her ears weren't ringing, after all the shouting in the halls.

Goboy's Scrying Mirror still stood in its place by her desk, though now the glass showed only a cloud-tufted sky. Mug basked in the sun, silent and still after so long with only spark lamps for light.

"Busy day," said Shingvere. He disappeared among the ranks of shelves, and was back in a moment, dragging a bucket heaped with crushed ice and the tall, narrow necks of Nolbit's dark. "I imagine we're all a bit thirsty."

Fromarch rose from his chair, took two of the bottles from

Shingvere's hand, and brought one to Meralda.

"Thank you," said Meralda, and she drank. As the icy ale poured down her throat the weight of the day settled over her like a coat of lead.

Her trip from the Alon safe room to the Tirlish end of the east wing halls had taken four hours. The Alon ambassador had spoken. Half a dozen clan lords had spoken, and then half a dozen more. Meralda was convinced she had either grasped hands with, or exchanged bows with, every single soul in Alonya, some of them twice. She'd found no respite back in Tirlish halls, either. The king himself had led a cheering procession back to the Gold Room, where, after a brief private meeting with Meralda and the captain, he had declared an impromptu feast, which even the Alon queen had joined.

The queen had been gracious and appreciative without ever actually mentioning the disappearance of the Tears. She referred instead to Meralda's 'great service to Alonya,' and her 'lasting place in the annals of Alon heroes'. She quickly realized that the queen couldn't truly acknowledge the specifics of the event. Meralda recalled something the captain once said. The clan version of forgive and forget translates roughly as "we'll not kill all the grandchildren." *That's why the Alon queen didn't arrive until after I'd found the Tears,* Meralda decided. She couldn't have arrived earlier without breaking the peace.

And a fragile peace it was, too, thought Meralda. She took another draught of Nolbit's. *One quick footstep, early on, is all it would have taken.* A rush of Alon guards, three whistle blasts, the flash of swords. Meralda shook her head and shivered.

And those Alon bone wavers. Meralda would never forget the glare Dorn Mukirk turned upon her when the Alon queen named her a hero. Pure hatred, it was. *I've never been truly hated before,* mused Meralda. *Certainly not by a man I barely even know.*

Red Mawb, though, had surprised Meralda. Not only had he run to fetch the queen, as Mukirk tried to provoke a fight, but as his rival fumed and glared, Mawb had, in the presence of the queen and the Alon court, bowed to Meralda, and congratulated her openly upon her "mastery of a rare fine magic".

A rare, fine magic. Meralda sipped her Nolbit's and let the phrase echo in her mind. *If either Alon wizard had known how frightened I was, in that instant before the glass went dark by the safe, or when I heard that single whistle blow and steeled myself to hear two more...*

Fromarch dragged his chair closer to Shingvere, and the ice bucket.

"That was a nice bit of flummery, with the ward spell," he said.

"Had five hundred copperheads and two frothing bone wavers terrified of an open door," said Shingvere. "Took guts to even try it."

Fromarch snorted. "Took brains," he said.

"I was angry," said Meralda. She shrugged, shoving aside the growing realization of exactly what she had dared. "I'm just glad no one tested it."

The late afternoon sun, which streamed from Goboy's mirror, flickered as the glass momentarily lost its place in the wide blue sky. Another flicker, and the sky reappeared, this time dotted with far-off birds, a wisp of high, thin clouds, and a lone red lumber dirigible, outbound and shrinking by the minute.

Meralda frowned at the image. The glass had held a steady image of the safe room for nearly two full days, and now it could barely remain locked on the sky.

"Show me the Tears," Mug had said, and it had. According to the mages, the image had collapsed the instant the Tears left the room.

Meralda remembered the brief shimmer she'd seen in the corner of the safe room, and she turned to face the mages.

"Tell me," she said. "Did either of you attempt to send a spell through the mirror while I argued with the Alons?"

Fromarch and Shingvere looked up from their beers.

"Hardly," said Shingvere. "As I recall, skinny here used foul language. Something about dogs and swine and parentage, I believe. And the houseplant called for the king to make war."

"While certain Eryans vowed to visit a variety of embarrassing afflictions on all of Alonya," muttered Fromarch. "Just before he went into a fit of shoe throwing. But sendings? No."

Mug stirred, waving his leaves in the sunlight from the mirror. "He's got holes in his socks," he said, his voice sleepy.

Fromarch shook his head. "You know we've got better sense than to try and pass spellworks through a scrying glass, Thaumaturge," he said. "We aren't daft."

Meralda nodded and sipped her Nolbit's. "Of course, of course."

They seem to be telling the truth, she thought. *But if not the mages, who?*

"You saw spell traces in the safe room?" asked Fromarch, joining Meralda in frowning at the glass. "From the spot where the mirror was watching?"

"I saw something," said Meralda. "It could have been the initial formation of a projected spellwork."

"Wasn't us," said Fromarch. He lifted an eyebrow. "Could it have been the scrying glass itself?"

Meralda nodded. *It could have been,* she thought. *Old Goboy left no notes, and we know so little about his glass. Why, though, did I only see it briefly, and only once?*

Mug's leaves quivered in a long vegetable yawn. Meralda yawned, too, unable to resist. "I'm exhausted," she said aloud. Exhausted, and seeing ghosts in all the shadows.

"I thank you for your help, gentlemen," she said. "Even the shoe throwing and cursing."

Shingvere finished his bottle, searched the ice bucket for another, and frowned when he discovered it empty.

"We'll call the day done, then," he said. "The Tears are found, war is averted, and we're all out of Nolbit's." He rose, took the bucket by the handle, and lifted an eyebrow at Fromarch. "You coming?"

Fromarch rose and gathered empty bottles. Meralda watched, bemused, as the aging wizard collected a full dozen and dropped them in the wastebasket.

"I'm coming," Fromarch said. He wiped his hands on his pants and paused at Meralda's side. "You ought to get some sleep," he said. Then he hesitated, shoved his hands in his pockets and rocked on his heels.

"Oh, tell her you're proud of her and let the woman be," said Shingvere as he stamped toward the doors. "Bloody ice will be all melted before a pair of Tirls can work up the courage for a heartfelt goodbye."

Fromarch laughed, squeezed Meralda's shoulder, and stamped out after Shingvere.

The mirror wavered again, and when it steadied the sky was full of blackbirds. They cast brief darting shadows across Meralda's desk, and then they were gone, and the glass was bright and still.

"Ah," said Mug. He opened a dozen eyes, swung them close to Meralda.

"Hello, Thaumaturge," he said, dreamily. "Here's a riddle for you."

Meralda groaned. "Not now, Mug."

Mug ignored her. "What goes round and round the Wizard's Flat," he said, "and says 'Vonashon, empalos, endera,' to meddling Tirlish thaumaturges?"

Meralda stared. "How do you know—?"

"You sketched the flying things on one of your Tower drawings." Mug opened another dozen eyes. "And you wrote the words below it. In quotes, no less. I saw the drawing, mistress," he said, his tone injured. "When were you going to tell me?"

Meralda sighed.

"It's been a very long day," she said. "I found the Tears, nearly started a war, pretended I was safe behind a ward spell that wasn't there, and slapped an Alon necromancer. And I still don't know what I saw flying about the Tower, or what spoke those words to me in the park." She raised her hand as Mug bunched his eyes. "All right," she said, closing her eyes. "I won't deny this might be related to Otrinvion. I won't deny the Tower might be, for all practical purposes, haunted by his shade. I won't deny there are forces at work here I do not understand." She opened her eyes. "There. Are you satisfied? I've said it. The bloody Tower might bloody well be haunted, and now I've got to go back inside it and find out by what, or who."

Mug's leaves went utterly still.

"You've got to go back?" Mug asked, incredulous. "Inside the Tower?"

Meralda nodded. "Yvin wants me to proceed. I talked to him this afternoon, just before we dined," she said. "I am to move the Tower's shadow, and use my efforts to do so as a means to investigate the masses about the flat."

Mug brought all his eyes upon her.

"Mistress. That's insane."

"No," said Meralda, rising. "That's my job. I'm the thaumaturge. I've seen evidence that the Tower or something within it is casting or directing spellworks." Meralda bit her lip, considering. *Might as well say it out loud*, she thought. "And consider this, Mug. What if my latch damaged the Tower spell as much as the Tower damaged my latch?"

Mug's eyes all opened at once.

"Exactly," said Meralda. "What if I've unknowingly meddled with a hidden Tower maintenance spell?"

Mug shook his leaves. "Hold on a moment, mistress. How do you know some passing Vonat didn't cast a spell on the Tower last week?"

Meralda shook her head. "If the Vonats could cast spells on the Tower, Mug," she said, "we'd all be speaking Vonat and hauling rocks right now, and you know it."

"Have you told Yvin?"

"I told him I saw what might be an original Tower spellwork, about the flat," she said. "I told him my latch might have interfered with its function."

Mug whistled. "Now that must have taken the steam out of the we-found-the-Tears victory feast."

"He didn't even curse." Meralda yawned. "He just looked tired. Told me to deal with it as a threat to Tirlin, and use the shadow moving project as an excuse to study the Tower."

"Meddling with the likes of Otrinvion represents a threat to Tirlin," said Mug. "Not to mention the threat to the meddler, who certainly isn't that fat-headed king."

Meralda stretched, and her eyes sought out Mug's bed sheet, which lay wadded on the floor a few steps away from her desk.

"Enough," she said. "Let's go home."

Mug fell silent, and turned most of his eyes away. "You really don't have a choice, do you?" he said.

"Not in this," she said. "It's take off the robe, or go back to the Tower."

"I don't suppose a career with the guilds holds any appeal, does it?"

Meralda pushed back her chair, covered Mug's cage, and made wearily for home.

Chapter Eleven

Meralda's next four days passed in a blur. The Vonats arrived, to little fanfare, and were stationed in the vacant north wing. The Hang held a feast of their own, complete with Hang delicacies prepared aboard the Hang flagship, served with Hang eating utensils consisting of a pair of plain wooden sticks. Meralda was told that Yvin made a great show of using the chopsticks, until Que-long relented and handed Yvin a fork.

Were it not for the papers, the Bellringers, and Mug, Meralda would have heard nothing. She saw no Vonats, dined on cold sandwiches, went nowhere save the laboratory and, twice, the park.

She sent Donchen a letter, begging pardon for her absence at his table, and other court functions since. She had given as explanation only "pressing business for the king," and she hoped that was sufficient.

Well, it's absolutely true, thought Meralda, with a frown. Even so, she had very nearly dropped her work and gone to the feast aboard the flagship. Only the thought of losing yet more sleep, and the sight of her bloodshot eyes and wild hair in the mirror, had kept Meralda in the lab and working.

And work she did. Dreading a return to the flat, but deeply

troubled by the sight of the flying masses about the top of the Tower, Meralda fetched her weak spell detector, gathered her notes, gritted her teeth, and took it apart.

New spells replaced the old, a fourth glass disk was added, and, much to Mug's delight, the worn broom handle was replaced with a straight length of polished cherry wood.

"Now it looks like a wizard's gadget," said Mug, as Meralda wrapped fine silver wire around the handle. "Got nice heft, too. Just the thing for bopping heads, if need be."

Meralda sighed, put the detector aside, and called for the Bellringers. By then, night had fallen, but there were no lights in the flat. Nor had there been, since Meralda's latch had failed and fallen.

Meralda ordered coffee and began to design a new latch for the Tower. This latch, Meralda decided, would extend no higher than the halfway point of the Tower's bulk. "That will put Yvin's platform in the light," she told Mug, as she began to sketch. "Though the back rows of the seating stands may catch a bit of shade."

Building the new latch for the Tower's lower half took all of two days. Meralda struggled to cast fifteen refractors a day. With the Accords and Yvin's commencement speech only nine days away, Meralda didn't bother with a scaled down latch. This one was, if it worked, intended to be a full-scale version of the Commencement Day spell.

As such, it required more refractors than the first latch. Meralda cast thirty-five in one grueling day, working from well before sunrise until late into the night.

Through it all, Mug remained at her side, basking in the uncertain light of Goboy's scrying mirror, which had quickly returned to its former habit of spying out bathhouses and dress shop dressing rooms. "Mirror, mirror," Mug would mutter, when the sunlight failed. "Sun and sky, looking-glass, or I'll have the Bellringers clean you with a hammer."

And the sun would return, for a time.

The king sent word, at odd intervals, inquiring as to Meralda's progress. She would scrawl hasty replies in return, often suppressing the impulse to add notes such as "Abandoning spellwork to continue this fascinating correspondence," or "Slept late, long breakfast, taking the day off for a stroll in the park."

"As if I have nothing better to do," grumbled Meralda, late in the evening of a long day of refractor calculations. She planned to cast the new latch early the next day, which left her to finalize refractor spacing, charge all the holdstones, and load her staff with the framework of the latch.

Cast the latch, and dare the Tower. She thought of the long climb in the dark, of the echoes and the way her magelamp shone bright, but was soon swallowed whole by the wide and hungry dark. And she saw the face in the park again, heard the words, saw Tervis and Kervis cast back, spilling down the stair...

There came a knock, loud at the door, and Meralda started and dropped her pen.

"A missive from His Highness, no doubt," said Mug. And indeed here was yet another nervous young guardsman at the door, with yet another note. She took it from his hand, exchanged an exasperated roll of the eyes with Kervis, and stomped back into the lab as the Bellringers shut the doors.

"You would think the man's hand would get all cramped, badgering you with letters every quarter hour," said Mug.

Meralda halted at her desk and unfolded the thick royal paper.

Thaumaturge, it read, in an unfamiliar hand. *I do hope you're hungry.*

Meralda creased her brow.

"What is it?" asked Mug.

There came a knock at the door.

"Oh, no," said Meralda. "It can't be."

"Can't be who?" asked Mug. He brought twenty eyes to bear upon Meralda. "Mistress?"

From beyond the door, Kervis spoke. "Thaumaturge?" he said. "There's a gentleman here to see you."

"A gentleman?" piped Mug. "Oh, a gentleman!"

"Quiet," said Meralda. She pushed back a lock of hair and made for the door, note still in her hand.

I could beg off again, she thought. *I could explain I'm in the midst of a complicated spellwork, one that requires more time, one dangerous to onlookers. I'd even be telling a good portion of the truth.*

Meralda frowned. *Why should I do that? He's only a man, Hang or not. I've not been made Thaumaturge by hiding behind doors and hoping men who made me uncomfortable would just go away.*

Meralda took a breath, straightened her blouse, and opened the doors.

There, in the hall, stood a smiling Donchen, flanked by a confused pair of Bellringers. Donchen stood behind a silver-trimmed kitchen serving cart, which smoked and made a faint sizzling sound. The aromatic steam that wafted from beneath the closed lid crept into the laboratory and immediately set Meralda's stomach to grumbling.

Donchen wore an apron. A palace-issue, heavily starched white kitchen staff apron, complete with a palace sigil over the heart and an oversized key pocket sewn onto the right bottom hem. Under the apron he wore plain black pants and a white round-collared Phendelit button-front shirt. Crumpled in a ball on the lid of the serving tray was a soft, shapeless Eryan beret, which half the serving staff wore to fight off the chill of the palace halls.

Just the thing, Meralda realized, *to go sneaking about the palace in.*

Donchen stepped back from the cart and executed a perfect Phendelit bow, keeping his hands clasped at his back, his heels together, and bending his body smoothly at the waist. "Good evening, Thaumaturge," he said. "My, doesn't this smell good?"

"It does," said Meralda. Behind Donchen, Kervis met Meralda's eyes and made a frantic 'what do we do?' shrug.

Donchen couldn't have seen, but his smile widened all the same. "I see you received my note," he said, looking at the paper Meralda still held.

"I did," said Meralda. She took a breath and found a smile. "And I am."

She flung the doors open wide, and stepped aside, motioning Donchen within. "Won't you come in?"

Donchen cocked his head. "I brought picnic gear, as well as dining utensils," he said. "I realize the Royal Laboratory to Tirlin might not be an appropriate place to host a foreigner."

"The Royal Laboratory of Tirlin is, at the moment, mine," said Meralda. "I keep no secrets here. So if you promise not to make off with state treasures I'll vow not to ask you pointed questions about your nation's foreign policy. Fair enough?"

Donchen bowed again. "Fair enough." Donchen broke from his bow, lifted the cart's lid, and withdrew two bulging white paper bags from within the steaming depths.

"Here you are, gentlemen," he said, turning and thrusting a bag at each Bellringer. "Dinner, compliments of the Mighty Dragon, long may he reign, so forth and so on."

The Bellringers went wide-eyed, but took the bags.

"Sir, thank you, sir," said Tervis, hefting the bag as if to see if it might move in his grasp.

"Egg rolls and fried rice," said Donchen. "And forks. I do hope you like it."

Then he turned back to Meralda, and put his hands on the cart handle. "Are you sure, Thaumaturge?" he said, before he started to push. "I won't be in the least offended..."

"Nonsense," said Meralda. *You're not the only one who can be bold and thumb your nose at propriety,* she thought. "Let's eat."

Donchen smiled, and pushed, and crossed the threshold.

The meal, Meralda decided, was fabulous.

What the meal consisted of was still largely a mystery to her. There was a tiny yellow grain that Donchen called rice, which formed a bed for most of the other entrees. And there was pork in a thick, sweet red sauce, and chicken with garlic and almonds, and a fried roll that crunched when Meralda bit into it, and was full of, among other things, chopped shrimp bits.

Donchen brought only forks. "No, we'll not struggle with chopsticks," he'd said, when Meralda asked how the king and court were faring with the Hang utensils. "To be honest with you, I myself may adopt your fork as my dining tool of choice," he added, with a grin. "Chezin will have a conniption fit."

Meralda laughed, and eyed the silver bowl that held the almond chicken.

"Oh, do have more," said Donchen, beaming. "Nothing flatters a chef more than a healthy appetite."

Meralda reached for the lid. "You cooked this?"

"I did," said Donchen, wiping his chin with an embroidered palace napkin. "Cooking relaxes me. I should have been a cook, really."

Meralda lifted the lid. "A cook, as opposed to what?" she asked.

Donchen laughed. "Well put, Thaumaturge," he said. He pushed his empty plate aside and leaned back in his chair. "But what I am is not an easy question to answer."

Meralda heaped three serving spoons of almond chicken on her plate.

"And yet you want me to ask," said Meralda. She noticed Mug, who had feigned sleep as soon as the doors opened, slowly swivel another half-dozen barely open eyes her way. "That's why you came here, isn't it?"

Donchen stretched, and met her gaze.

"Just so," he said. His smile softened. "I wish we had more time, Thaumaturge," he said. "We have a proverb. Trust, it is said, must be built over time, lest it fall away as quickly as it was born." Donchen shook his head. "It's a bit of a cliché, really, but there is an element of truth there. I can hardly expect an intelligent person such as yourself to suddenly trust a mysterious Hang visitor, even if he does cook an excellent almond chicken."

Meralda swallowed a mouthful of rice and chicken and put down her fork.

"And what am I to trust you with?" she said.

Donchen sighed. "That, Thaumaturge, is for you to decide," he said. "But here. I've done nothing but speak in riddles and proverbs. A failing of my schooling, I'm afraid." He pushed back his chair and stood. "Enough of that," he said. "All that blathering about trust. Well, I've made up my mind, Thaumaturge. I've decided to trust you. You. Not your king, not your captain, not your House of Lords. You. So ask me anything. I'll tell you, plain and true."

Meralda saw Mug blink all his open eyes at once. She wiped her lips with her napkin and stood to face Donchen.

"All right," she said, after a moment. "Why are you doing this?"

Donchen bowed. "I need an ally here," he said. "Someone with the king's ear, someone he trusts. I hope this person is you."

"Why not the king?" asked Meralda. "Why bother with thaumaturges at all?"

Donchen smiled. "The king will act with caution, at all times," he said. "And caution would tell him that I am not to be trusted. Not yet. Listened to, perhaps. Observed, of course. But trusted?" Donchen shook his head. "He'd be a fool to trust me. A fool to trust any of us. And your king, Thaumaturge, is no fool."

Meralda stiffened. "And I am?"

"No," said Donchen. "You may believe what I tell you. You may not. But your office will allow you to make the choice. Is it not true that Tirlish thaumaturges often work well apart from both court and king?"

Well spoken, thought Meralda. *Well spoken, or perhaps just well rehearsed.*

She motioned Donchen away from the remains of their meal. "We can walk about a bit, if you like," she said. "The laboratory is a favorite spot for touring among our guests."

Donchen nodded. "Of course," he said, moving to Meralda's side.

"And we can talk about the purpose of your visit to Tirlin," said Meralda. "Or is that question best left for later?"

Donchen shook his head. "Trust knows no bounds," he said. "And if it does, it is not trust."

"Why, then?"

"We believe it is time for our cultures to meet," said Donchen. "We wish to establish regular trade, and diplomatic relations. Your Accords presented the perfect opportunity to introduce ourselves. What, pray tell, is this?"

Donchen had halted before Phillitrep's Calculating Engine.

"It's a calculating device," said Meralda.

Donchen stepped close, put his face as near the whirling gears as he dared. "What is it calculating?" he asked.

"No one knows," replied Meralda. "Phillitrep never wrote

down the question, and he died suddenly in office about three hundred years ago."

Donchen watched the tiny rods shuttle and click. "Amazing," he said. Then he straightened and once again turned his grey eyes upon Meralda.

"Aren't you going to ask me why we've come now, after all those years of waiting and watching from afar?"

"All right," said Meralda, and she recalled the time, long ago, when she'd first seen a drawing of a Hang five-master while Shingvere waggled his finger in her face. "*Mark my words,*" she heard the Eryan say, again. "*They're up to no bloody good.*"

"Tell me why you came," said Meralda. "Tell me how long you've been watching us. And then tell me why."

Donchen nodded. "As you wish," he said. "First, a bit of history, if you don't mind."

Meralda nodded, struggling to keep her face impassive.

"Oh, not at all," she said. "Go on."

Donchen clasped his hands behind his back. *Just like a schoolmaster,* thought Meralda as Donchen began, once again, to walk.

"The date was 640, as you number years," he said. "My land was at peace, but the Emperor? Well, the Emperor went mad, one day."

Meralda indicated a row of shelves to her right, and Donchen proceeded down it, his eyes darting from this to that as he spoke.

"He looked upon our land, and saw that it was his, as far as his eye could see," said Donchen. "But it occurred to him that there was plenty he could not see, and that made him think. And we all know how dangerous it is when monarchs begin to think, do we not?"

Meralda laughed. "We do," she said. The glass and silver eyes of Movan's Talking Head swiveled slowly around to fix on Donchen, and he leaned close for a better look.

"It occurred to this mad emperor, whose name was Sosang, that his mastery of the world was incomplete," said Donchen. "Sosang called together his ministers and bade them tell him how he might bring the farthest shores closer, that he might rule all, as was his right."

Movan's Head lifted a silver eyebrow, and Donchen's eyes went wide.

"One of Sosang's advisors whispered to another. 'Does he think he can cast a rope about the world, and draw it to him?' asked this man." Donchen smiled at Movan's Head, and it smiled back, and Donchen laughed. "Sosang, of course, heard this whisper. And, being mad, he took it not as a criticism, but as a rare fine idea."

Meralda tilted her head. "Stretch a rope around the world?" she asked. "Why?"

"So you can hold either end and pull, of course," replied Donchen.

Meralda frowned. *I'm surprised Yvin hasn't asked for that,* she thought. *It might well be true.*

"Emperor Sosang was mad, but not forgetful," said Donchen, moving away from Movan's Head and continuing his stroll down the ranks of mageworks. "From that moment on, the resources of my land and my people were turned to one goal. We worked to stretch a rope around the world, so that a mad-eyed king might pull the horizons closer." Donchen shrugged and shook his head. "What an awful waste."

Meralda cast a warning frown at an unnamed glass cylinder that held a writhing bolt of bright white lightning. It tended to nip at passers-by. *And now is not the time,* intoned Meralda silently.

The lightning dimmed, and its writhing grew less frantic.

"Nineteen years passed," said Donchen. "Two vessels were built. Monstrous vessels, far larger than anything built before, or since. The very first of the Great Sea ships. Each was large enough to carry one of the five-masters docked by your wharfs as a lifeboat." Donchen sidled past the jar of lightning with a wry smile. "Of course, they built them inland, another of mad emperor Sosang's suggestions, and it took another eight years to get either one of them to a coast," he said. "But this at least gave the rope-makers a head start."

Meralda tilted her head. "You mean they actually tried to make a rope long enough to cross the Great Sea?"

Donchen met Meralda's eyes. "They had no choice, Thaumaturge. None at all. Whole provinces were planted with hemp. Two enormous cities sprang up, one on each coast, at the places from which Sosang decreed the ships should set sail. Day and night, they wove ropes, ready to pay out the line on turning wheels so large each was visible from nearly a mile away."

"Your kings have considerable power," she said, thinking the most a mad Tirlish king was ever able to accomplish was the line of dancing gargoyles atop the park wall.

Donchen smiled. "We are an obedient people," he said. "To a fault, at times, as you would say."

Meralda shook her head. "And these ships?" she asked. "What became of them?"

Donchen shrugged. "Oh, they were crewed with the sons of noble houses," he said. "Again, at the whim of the Emperor, who bestowed it as an honor. The crews, being sane, if overly obedient, considered themselves doomed and bade their families farewell."

"The day came for departure," said Donchen. "And so they set sail, vanishing from sight as they dragged their ropes behind. One went west, the other east, and soon the only evidence of their leaving was the slow, steady turning of the monstrous wheels on the shore."

Donchen had begun to walk again, and the pair quickly reached the end of the row of shelves. Ahead of them now lay the shadowed rear of the laboratory, where larger mageworks were stored. There, tarps stretched across hulking frames of wood or dark iron, and all was silent and shadowed and still.

Meralda halted at the end of the shelf, and motioned Donchen toward the right.

"And did one of these vessels reach the Realms?" she asked.

Donchen entered the next rank of shelves and nodded. "Indeed," he said. "But only after three years of sailing. Three years of drifting, actually. Mad kings make poor sailors, as the saying goes. The ship couldn't tack, dragging such an enormous weight. After a time, both ship and rope were simply dragged along on the current, and the captain struck his sails and gave up."

Meralda walked and nodded. *Wait until Shingvere hears this,* she thought.

"There was a storm, and the rope was torn away, and lost,"

said Donchen. "The captain sailed and searched for the rope, determined to fulfill his charge, fearful that if the rope wheels stopped, his family would suffer Sosang's mad wrath. But the captain never found the rope, and soon another storm cast the vessel upon a reef, and tore it apart," said Donchen. "One sailor clung to a floating door, and I imagine you can guess the rest."

"He was cast up on an Eryan beach?" asked Meralda.

"A bit farther south, but correct in essence," said Donchen. He leaned down and peered into the eyepiece of Delby's Far-Seeing Glass, and laughed when he was presented with a bird's eye view of his own backside. "Our castaway sailor awoke to find himself in the bed of a Kiltish fisherman."

Meralda went wide-eyed. "Kilt is only forty miles south of here," she said.

Donchen nodded, and continued his stroll. "I know," he said. "Charming place."

"Is it," said Meralda, blithely.

"The sailor was afraid, at first," continued Donchen. "As he recovered, he realized he was in a foreign land. This was a new concept, for him. How would he be treated? Would he be held prisoner, or cast into the wilderness?" Donchen shrugged. "He didn't know. Time passed. He healed, learned a bit of Kingdom, rose from his bed. And found that, after a time, he was welcome among the fisher folk."

Meralda slowed. "How do you know this?" she said. "If the ship was lost but for him, how did word get back to your people?"

Donchen shrugged. "Our sailor settled down," he said. "Married, even. Had children."

Meralda halted.

"Yes, that's right," said Donchen. "All those black-haired, small-framed fishermen? My cousins, many times removed." Donchen chuckled. "The Hang have always been closer than anyone thought."

Meralda heard Mug whistle softly. She suspected Donchen heard as well, but if so he pretended not to notice.

I'd whistle myself, if it weren't impolite, she thought. Centuries of watching the distant horizon, while the fisher folk laughed and went about their business.

"Children aside, though, the tale is not yet done," said Donchen. "You see, while the ships were at sea, mad Sosang died. Messily, I'm afraid, by means of a sack of serpents and a bottle of poison, proving that he was King of Death as well as life."

Meralda lifted an eyebrow, but was silent.

"The mad king dead, the families of the nobles aboard the two doomed vessels set forth to rescue their fathers and their sons," said Donchen. "They built ships, crewed them with wizards, and set sail from the rope-weaver cities, just as the big ships had. And they searched. Searched for years. Forty years, in fact."

"Forty years?" said Meralda, unable to hide the disbelief in her voice.

"Oh, they weren't continually at sea for forty years," said Donchen. "Five years was the longest single voyage." He saw the confusion on Meralda's face, and smiled in sudden comprehension. "Ah," he said. "All our vessels can make fresh water from salt. And the original Great Sea rope haulers could grow their own food, as well. So it was feared that the great ships might lie, becalmed, with the crew helpless, but very much alive."

said Donchen. "Also, the rescue ships did not merely search at random. Each of the original sailors wore a *chosong*. A *chosong* is a small medallion, which houses a finding charm specifically designed and secretly crafted against the day the mad king might reign no more."

"Fresh water from salt?" asked Meralda. "How?"

"The process is very similar to that by which your guilds extract lifting gas from ordinary air," explained Donchen. "We carry a number of spare devices. I'll have one sent round for your inspection, if you like."

Meralda nodded. Hang magic, at last. *And one that might extend the cruising range of our own airships tenfold, if I can work out how it functions.*

Donchen halted before Finnick's Second Lifting Plate and watched the pair of spectacles suspended in the air above it bob and turn. "One by one, these new ships searched out the rope-hauler *chosongs*," he said. "And, one by one, they found them, all lying on the bottom of the sea. All save one, and the wizards pointed west, and one ship sailed after," he said. "On and on they sailed, until one day in late summer of your year 714, a Great Sea five-master dropped anchor off a beach near Kilt," he said. "The awestruck wizards claimed the very last *chosong* was near. And it was. Still around the neck of their long lost countryman, who sat mending a net in the shade while his grandchildren played at his feet."

"I imagine he was shocked," said Meralda.

Donchen laughed. "He set his dogs upon his rescuers," he said. "And would have taken a stick to them, as well, had his sons not rushed from their boats and stayed his hand." Donchen shook his head. "Everything the old sailor said was dutifully recorded by the ship's scribe," he said. "He used a variety of colorful terms, but basically he'd had enough of mad kings and doomed quests and, most especially, he'd had quite enough of the Great Sea. 'I am home,' he said. 'This is the happy land, and I am home.'"

"The captain of the five-master explained to this man that his house was minor no more, and that as the eldest of his house he was, by rights, the rough equivalent of a duke. This caused the old man to throw his stick at the captain, and once again call for his dogs. 'Hear this, then,' he said, as his sons held him back. 'I tell you to go. I tell you to pass the rule of my house on to the eldest of my nephews and give him my blessing and leave me, my sons, and these people alone'."

"And they did?" asked Meralda.

"They did indeed," said Donchen. "Are we not, after all, an obedient people?"

"And your ships stayed away until last week."

"Well, not entirely," said Donchen, his lips turning upward in the faintest of smiles. "Subsequent voyages mapped the entire Great Sea, and, of course, all your coasts. And I'm sure you've read accounts of the dozen or so brief diplomatic landings, which were meant only to establish that the Hang mean no harm." Donchen lifted an eyebrow, and put his finger to his chin as though in deep contemplation. "And we may have made a few other landings, as well. All to satisfy the curiosity of various naturalists, I assure you. Always in uninhabited areas, and only in the pursuit of science."

Meralda lifted an eyebrow. "And yet you've learned our

language and our customs," she said. "How very perceptive of your naturalists."

Donchen laughed. "Of late, I confess, our landings have grown more direct," he said. "But out of necessity, not a desire for mischief."

Meralda started walking again. "What sort of necessity, Donchen?" she asked. "Since we're trading state secrets," she added.

"Two reasons," said Donchen. "First, because contact is now inevitable. The Great Sea is no longer wide enough to prevent your airships from completing the journey."

Meralda frowned. "We've tried," she said. "The *Yoreland*—"

"Was within a few days of sighting land," said Donchen, gently. "Had they not turned back, they would have seen the coast. Had they come down for one last look at the sea, they'd have seen driftwood. Had they been paying attention to the sky, they'd have seen gulls." Donchen shrugged. "Had they not been so weary, Thaumaturge, you would not be the only Tirlish woman in the world to know what you know." He smiled. "But I would have missed telling you," he said.

Meralda bit her lip. "The king doesn't know all this?"

"He knows the important parts," said Donchen. "But he doesn't know that I grew up reading the *Post* and the *Times*, or that I'm about to give you this."

He reached inside his shirt, and withdrew a piece of paper. "Even your king has not seen it."

Meralda made herself look away from the paper, and straight into Donchen's grey eyes. "What is it?"

"The world, of course," said Donchen. "All of it."

Meralda took the paper.

"I should go now," said Donchen. "I'm sure you have things to think about."

The paper in her hands was strange. It was brilliant white, thin, yet stiff and smooth to the touch. Faintly, Meralda could see the outlines of what might be part of a map, and her heart began to race.

The world. All of it. At last.

"All the notations and measures are in New Kingdom," said Donchen. "And I'll be happy to supply you with a whole book of maps, later, if you wish." He made a small bow. "But for tonight, I hope this will suffice."

"It will," said Meralda, and her voice nearly caught in her throat.

Donchen turned, casting his gaze down the aisle of glittering mageworks. "Is the door that way?" he asked.

Meralda nodded. "One last question," she asked.

Donchen turned back to her.

"Anything, Thaumaturge," he said.

"Were you the man who appeared in the palace and asked Yvin for permission to bring your ships into the harbor?"

Donchen's half-smile vanished. "I was not," he said. "Nor is that man among our party."

Meralda began to speak, but Donchen held up his hand. "He was probably Hang, yes," he said. "And the formal request for passage and lodging is an ancient tradition among our Houses. But I assure you that no one of the House of Que-long would have dared such an act, in the palace of your king." He bowed. "That is another reason we have come," he said. "For now that contact is inevitable, it seems there are those from both our shores who would see our peoples spend the next hundred years glaring suspiciously at each other from across the Great Sea."

From both our shores? Meralda lowered the map.

"The Vonats," she said.

"I believe so," said Donchen. "And a certain small number of my people."

Meralda gaped. "The Accords," she said, biting back mention of the strange spells in the palace and the disappearance of the Tears.

"Precisely," said Donchen. "Destroy the Accords. Sow discord and mistrust. Provoke hostility and suspicion." His half-smile vanished. "We stand at a crossing of ways, Thaumaturge," he said. "Willing or not, we will write our own history, in these next few weeks. It is my wish to avoid including the terms warfare and bloodshed."

Meralda nodded absently in agreement, and looked again at the folded paper in her hands. "And so you've decided to trust me," she said. "Knowing that I might go immediately to the king, or the papers, or both."

Donchen shrugged. "That is for you to decide, Thaumaturge. If you choose such a thing, I am undone, but that is your choice." He bowed, and when he rose his smile was back, and his eyes were merry. "But I must go, before friend Cook misses his serving cart. Do give my regards to the *Post*."

"I shall do no such thing, and you know it," said Meralda, unable to frown at Donchen's smiling face. Meralda shook her head and sighed in exasperation. "Though it's lucky for you Mage Fromarch isn't still the thaumaturge in Tirlin."

"Indeed," said Donchen, as he backed the last few steps out of the aisle. "I am most fortunate. Good evening, Thaumaturge, and thank you for your company."

And then he turned, and walked away. After a moment, the serving cart wheels squeaked, and Meralda heard the laboratory doors open, Donchen spoke to the Bellringers, and then footsteps came into the laboratory.

"Thaumaturge?" said Tervis. "Thaumaturge, where are you?"

"I'm here," said Meralda, striding forward, out of the aisle. "I'm all right, Guardsman," she said.

Tervis was just inside the laboratory, one hand still on the door.

"You can come in," said Meralda. "I've set no wards or guard spells."

Tervis let the door shut. "Just, um, checking, ma'am," he said. "Mr. Donchen just left, and we didn't see you."

Meralda sought out her desk, shoved aside her refracting spell papers, and pulled back her chair.

"Is that what I think it is?" said Mug, all his eyes open and straining.

"It is," said Meralda. She sat, then turned to face Tervis.

"Coffee, please," she said. "A pot."

"Yes, ma'am," said Tervis. He wiped his chin with his sleeve. "Not bad grub, whatever it was."

Meralda smiled. "No," she said. "It wasn't."

And then she unfolded the map, and Mug wordlessly swung all his eyes to bear on it, and they looked in awe upon the world.

Chapter Twelve

Meralda didn't take to her bed until two of the clock, and even then she tossed and turned and wrestled with the sheets. Her wonder at seeing the world on Donchen's map was giving way to a niggling whisper of fear. The Realms were so tiny. Small and alone on the wide Great Sea, and the land of the Hang, once so far away, was nearer now, and so much bigger.

Indeed, Donchen's homeland dwarfed the Realms. Hours after putting the map away, Meralda could still see it in her mind's eye. Especially the set of drawings which represented the world as a globe, as if they had taken a child's kick ball and drew all the lands upon it. The Realms were a fingertip-sized dot on one half of the ball, alone in the Great Sea. But turn the ball around to the other side, and the land of the Hang occupied half of the hemisphere, with a spray of islands running nearly to each pole from both the north and the south.

Half a dozen of these islands were at least equal in size to the Realms.

Down on the street, a cab rattled past, and a man who must have been perched atop it was bellowing out a rude tavern song. Meralda leaped from her bed with an Angis-word, stamped over to the half-open window, and was about to shout down at the hoarse-voiced reveler when Mrs. Whitlonk's window slammed open and without a word or a warning the elderly lady hurled a flowerpot down toward the cab.

The pot smashed on the cobblestones just behind the open carriage, the driver snapped his reins, and the singer fell over backwards into the carriage bed to gales of laughter from his fellows. The carriage sped away, and in a moment the street was quiet.

Mrs. Whitlonk's window closed with a gentle click, and Meralda laughed, and suddenly weariness swept over her.

And then, at last, she slept.

Even in her dreams, Hang place names ran sing-song through her mind. Shang-lo. Ping-loc. The great river Yang, the plains of Hi, the vast inland sea Phong May. But, perhaps strangest of all, Donchen's map labeled the Realms as "The Happy Land".

The Happy Land? Here?

But despite the dreams, she slept until the five-twenty trolley rattled past, bell clanging. And after that, she slept again until the sun rose, and even then she buried her face in her pillow and slept until Mug woke her with the blasting sound of off-key trumpets and the shouting voice of the king.

Meralda rose, found a pair of slippers and her robe, and stumbled into the kitchen.

"Keeping wizard's hours, I see," said Mug. "The lads will be here at any moment."

Meralda glared. "Is that your way of telling me I'm a fright?"

"Merely passing the time with idle pleasantries, mistress," said Mug, casting all his eyes toward the ceiling in mock disdain. "I thought to refrain from discussions of maps and mysterious foreigners until you've had your coffee, a good frown, and a brisk round of pacing about the table."

Meralda bit back a response and fumbled with the lid of her coffee urn.

"Do we return to the Tower today, mistress?" asked Mug.

Meralda nodded, filled her coffee pot, set it to boil on the stove, and sat. "Back to the flat," she said, through a yawn. "With the new detector. I'll hang the shadow latch afterward."

"Unless the spooks protest," said Mug. Meralda glared through tangled hair, and Mug looked away.

"I'll go with you, of course," he said. "One of the lads can take me."

Meralda frowned, but said nothing. *Not even the Bellringers can go this time,* she thought, *but I'm too groggy to argue about it right now.*

Instead, she cradled her face in her hands and listened to the coffee pot gurgle and pop.

"Have you decided to tell Yvin about your map?" asked Mug, after a moment.

"No. Not yet," said Meralda, as the smell of fresh coffee wafted through the chilly kitchen. "Though later today I think I'll track down Fromarch and Shingvere."

"Ah," said Mug, sagely. "A conspiracy of mages. Amusing, but historically linked with–what is the word?" Mug rolled his eyes, as if pondering. "Oh, yes," he said. "Disaster."

Meralda closed her eyes. For a moment, the sun was warm and bright.

But then a shadow passed, and the light in the kitchen dimmed, and Meralda imagined she was high and alone on the winding, silent stair.

Thunder smashed and rolled, muted, yet not silenced by the Tower's thick walls. Meralda took off her high-necked black raincoat at the foot of the stair and wished in vain for a coat rack.

"Oh, bother," she muttered, putting her magelamp on a chest-high stair tread before shaking her rain soaked coat out on the Tower floor. *Half a dozen raincoats in my closet,* she thought, *and today of all days I grab the Farley and Hent.*

As she spread out her coat on the floor, another peal of thunder rang out, so loud and lingering Meralda wondered if it had struck the Tower. Park lore claimed such a thing had never happened, and immediately Meralda wondered if this, too, was another indication that her shadow latch had damaged some ancient Tower spellwork.

"Nonsense," she said aloud, as the echoes of the thunder clap died. "I can't be blamed for everything."

She picked up her magelamp and played it up and around the winding stair. The white flour she'd strewn about the first dozen steps was undisturbed. *As if anyone could get past the guards,* she thought. *Still, it's good to know I am truly alone, here in the dark.* She imagined someone hiding in the shadows, high on the stair, and she pushed the thought quickly away.

Now is not the time, she chided herself, *to start filling the dark with penny-novel villains. Especially when a large, ferocious ward spell is waiting to pounce on anyone but the Bellringers or myself.*

"I'd best make sure it's still waiting," she said. And then she sang out a single word of the ward's unlatching spell, heard an answering buzz from high above, and smiled, satisfied that the ward still roamed the dark, invisible, but vigilant.

"Well," said Meralda. "Time to go." Her echo died quickly, and she hefted her instrument bag with a groan. *I'll miss having Tervis carry this,* she thought. *But I can hardly trot back down the stair if I decide I need a fresh holdstone or a piece of one-way glass. And I certainly can't have the Bellringers underfoot if yonder ward spell goes bad.*

She slipped the bag strap over her shoulder and regarded the damp, cloth-wrapped bundle still dripping rainwater several feet away. Inside the cloth, the new weak spell detector sizzled faintly, sending tiny blue flashes of light twirling about like gnats.

Meralda groaned. "You should not be doing that," she said. Her words echoed through the empty Tower. What could it possibly be detecting, this far from the flat? Or am I only now seeing the flashes because the Tower is so dark?

It occurred to her that the blanket she'd used to shield the detector from the rain was the same blanket that usually covered Goboy's scrying mirror. The detector might be reacting to traces of spell energies latched to the blanket, faint though they must be. And if that were so, the tiny bursts of fire would cease when the blanket was removed.

Meralda grasped the damp blanket with her left hand and unwound it until the detector was freed.

The darting flashes stopped.

Meralda sighed in relief. "Marvelous," she said, taking the detector up by its handle. "Ten to the minus twelfth, or I'm a cabaret dancer."

Meralda spoke a word, and the dark half-globe of the detector began to glow, spilling a candle's worth of soft blue light at her feet.

Meralda spoke the second word, and the light began to brighten. By the time she reached the flat, Meralda fully expected to be engulfed in a globe of light fully twenty feet in radius. But for now, she played the magelamp on the treads, shifted her bag on her shoulder, and set foot on the stair.

Her wet boots squeaked until the soles touched the flour, and then they went slick. Meralda climbed the first dozen steps carefully, then turned, scraped her toes and heels off on the edge of a tread, and listened to the thunder boom and crackle far above.

If Mug were there, he'd be saying things like "Nice day to meet ghosts," or "good weather for spook hunting,". *And I'd sigh and tell him to shut up,* thought Meralda. *But in truth, isn't that what I'm doing?*

Meralda took a few careful steps upward. Satisfied that her boots were clean–*it would be a shame to face the shade of Otrinvion, but then slip off the stair because of flour on my boots,* she thought–she continued her trek toward the flat.

The detector's globe of radiance slowly expanded, spitting tell-tale sparks and flashes as the sharply defined sphere of light brushed the treads of the stair, or the wall, or the corner of Meralda's instrument bag. Meralda watched and smiled, heartened by the detector's seeming eagerness to reach the flat. She knew until the spells were latched to the Tower the glows and sparks were nothing more than random trace events. Still, though, she was glad for any sign the spells were still active.

Scritch, scrape, scritch, scrape. Even the thunder wasn't enough to mask the lonely sounds of Meralda's slow progress up the winding stair. Determined to reach the halfway point to the first floor landing before changing her bag strap to the other shoulder, Meralda set her jaw and kept a steady pace.

The darkness grew about her, made even darker and much larger when the Tower floor vanished, and Meralda once again had the sensation of walking up the walls of the night. Shadows danced on the wall beside her, causing Meralda to force her eyes strictly upon the stairs ahead. "I will not be spooked," she said aloud, her voice quickly lost to the grumbling thunder.

Still, shadows flew, and the whirls and flashes from the detector's slowly expanding sphere of influence only added to their brief dances. *Just like in the stories,* thought Meralda. No wonder the mages of old preferred to leave the Tower alone.

A few had dared the dark, though. Meralda pulled down every musty old tome in the laboratory the night before, while her new illuminator spells were building, and for the first time she'd read through the books with an eye for tales of the darker shadow said to lurk in the heart of the Tower.

"*We saw a Flitting shape,*" wrote one mage, the ink of his scribbled words faded and flaking. "*And Heard sudden cruel Laughter, and then our Spelles of Warding were broken, and Fire rolled Down the staire, and we fled, and None of the Guard will go back, not even for their Swords.*"

Meralda guessed she was halfway to the first floor landing, and she halted long enough to shift the bag strap to her right shoulder. This put the bag on her right, and forced her to walk a step closer to the dark than before.

"We saw a Flitting shape," she'd read, and the words now danced in her mind. "*Flitting Shape, wrathful Spectre, gruesome hollow Man.*" Tale after tale, mage after mage. They'd all used different words to describe the Tower shade, but their stories were always the same.

The shade appears, ward spells go awry, guards and mages take to their heels. Meralda had found eight such encounters, spread out over four centuries, in less than an hour of reading. Immediately, she had seen a pattern of ghostly encounters emerge.

Mages with spells enter the Tower. What mages, with what spells, for what purpose—none of these things seemed to matter. Meralda suspected the mere act of hauling major unlatched spellworks into the Tower was enough to stir the shade.

And the shade, once stirred, soon appears. It allows itself to be seen, or be heard, or both. And then it attacks ward spells or spellworks, and in doing so it frightens the intruders away, generally for decades to come.

Meralda had wondered why Fromarch and Shingvere never saw the shade, until she realized that Fromarch had insisted they convey no unlatched spells within the Tower. The scrying mirrors, the lookabout staves, the sixteen pieces of Ovaro's Image Capture Box, all were passive spellworks, firmly latched to mechanisms carried in from the laboratory. True, Fromarch had latched a few see-you spells to the Tower proper, which would have alerted them to any sneaky mortal intruders. But they had been tiny spells, hand cast, on the last days of their search. *Perhaps,* thought Meralda, *hand cast spells simply aren't worthy of the shade's horrific attention.*

The detector weighed heavy in Meralda's hand. *And here I go alone,* she thought, *to latch a major spellwork to the heart of the Tower itself.*

"Vonashon, empalos, endera." Meralda recalled the words, and that awful face. *Walk away. Good advice, it seems,* she thought. *I only wish I could.* "Perhaps the guilds are hiring," she muttered to the dark.

The detector flashed suddenly, and Meralda started and gasped. But the light settled back to its normal steady cast, and Meralda took a deep breath and continued her climb.

The sphere of light cast by the detector had expanded to engulf all of the handle and Meralda's hand and half her forearm. Grateful for the extra light, Meralda held the half-globe close to the stair, and wondered if the shade was curious about what she carried.

The shade, thought Meralda. *Well, there, I've said it, even if only to myself. But I can hardly deny it any longer. Something here, in the dark, is watching me. Has been watching me since the day I first set foot in the hall.*

The light from her magelamp caught the seamless black ceiling of the first floor, not fifty hands above. Meralda quickened her pace, well aware that she was no closer to daylight, but eager to quit the darkness below and see a floor under her feet, if only for a moment.

First floor, second floor, third floor at last. Meralda stopped, mopped sweat from her forehead, and let her bag drop to the stair.

Both shoulders ached, bruised by the bag strap. Her arms were weary from the weight of the detector, which now glowed bright as a magelamp and sent worms of cold blue fire wriggling and crawling across those parts of the Tower it touched.

"Not much farther," she said aloud, swapping the bag strap from left to right and wincing as she hefted the bag again. "Good thing, too."

She resumed her climb. Shadows still darted about her, but not so near, now that the detector's glow had engulfed her. She could sense the ward spell passing occasionally, but it never ventured close or lingered too long.

Still, Meralda was wary. *It's just about this point,* she thought, *that most of the mages of old ran into the shade.* High on the stair, nowhere to hide, nothing to do but make a mad dash downward for the hall and the park. She shuddered at the thought of running any distance down the narrow winding stair.

Soon, though, the magelamp's light washed over the final ceiling, and then caught the tarnished brass door knob of the plain wooden door set in the upright notch at the top of the stair. Meralda found herself, if not exactly dashing, at least walking briskly the last hundred treads to the flat. As if by hurrying she could somehow miss the sudden awful appearance of the shade of dread Otrinvion.

At the door, she dropped her bag and the detector on the tread behind her and fumbled in her pockets for the key.

It wasn't there.

At her back, she felt the darkness gather.

She put the magelamp under her chin, bent her head forward, and held the cold lamp tight against her neck while she used both hands to search her pockets. *I put it in my right skirt pocket before I left for the park,* she thought. *I know I did.*

Thunder broke, and rolled in echoes through the dark, and Meralda was overwhelmed by the sensation that if she were to turn, if she were to face the stair, something would be standing there, just past the glow of the detector. *Wrathful Spectre,* she thought, and shivered. A gruesome hollow man, waiting for her to turn so it could open its awful mad eyes and split its rotted face with a wide and hungry smile.

Handkerchiefs, ward wands, an old pair of theatre tickets, fused into a smooth mass of paper pulp by the wash. Then her right hand closed on cold, smooth iron, and she pulled the flat key from her blouse pocket, thrust it hard in the door, gave the key a savage twist, and shoved.

The door flew open, and daylight spilled out of the flat and onto the stair.

Meralda took her magelamp in her hand, drew in a ragged breath, and turned around to face the dark.

The stair was empty. But empty in a manner that suggested to Meralda it was only very recently emptied. Vacated, perhaps, in the brief moment immediately before she worked up the nerve to turn and look.

"No more of this," she said. "Sight!"

Meralda closed her eyes, and for the first time since entering the Tower she willed forth her Sight.

The detector's sphere of influence blazed like a tame globe of fire. Her bag, within the detector's sphere, cast whirling loops and probing red and blue and green-hued tangles writhing about the stair. Meralda pushed her Sight out, into the dark, past the light that shone weakly through the open door.

Nothing. Darkness and darkness and no hint of anything else.

Meralda opened her eyes and let her Sight abate, though she did not let it fall. Normal vision and glittering Sight left the flat glowing and indistinct, but revealed only smooth stone and those things Meralda had brought. She picked up her bag, took the detector in her hand, closed the door with her heel, and walked to the center of the flat.

She dropped her bag to the floor beside her.

This is it, she thought. *If the Tower is haunted, I am about to come face-to-face with the shade of Otrinvion the Black.*

Or, more likely, make a complete fool of myself.

Meralda cleared her throat.

"Greetings," she said, aloud. "I am Mage Ovis, Thaumaturge to the Kingdom of Tirlin." She licked her lips, which had gone dry as she spoke.

"It was I who latched the shadow moving spell to this place," she said, her voice loud and ringing in the round, empty flat. "I meant no harm, but harm I may have done, to a spellwork I did not know existed until my own spells broke apart. For this," she said, "I am sorry."

Shingvere, she thought silently, *must never ever hear of this.*

"Furthermore," she added, "I plan to loose another spell here today. It is a passive spell, one I shall latch to the space in this room, rather than to the Tower itself. This spell is meant to reveal any older spellworks active here, so I might determine their function and assess any damage I might have unknowingly done." She paused, considering her next words. "It is not my intent to usurp, remove, or modify any part or portion of the Tower, or its works," she said. "Nor do I intend upon proving or disproving the existence of any, um, unseen residents to this place. I only want to know what, if any, harm I may have done. I also need to know if there is a safe way to latch a shadow moving spell to the lower half of the Tower."

The only sound was thunder, the only shadow Meralda's, cast briefly by distant lightning.

"That is who I am," she said. "And that is why I am here. I ask for your forbearance, that I might do my work, and then leave you in peace. May I do so?"

Meralda kept her eyes open, and let her Sight move out into the flat.

Nothing stirred. Aside from the sounds of muted thunder and her own rapid breaths, the Tower was utterly silent, utterly still.

Utterly empty.

Foolishness, said the part of Meralda that had never believed Shingvere's tales, never credited the old mages with anything but a fondness for strong drink and a desire to tell scary stories to a breathless court. And that face in the park? Fatigue. Fatigue and an imagination fed by a lifetime of ghost stories and Shingvere's sincere nonsense.

"Very well," said Meralda. She lifted the detector so the copper half-globe was level with her shoulders, took a deep breath, and spoke the long word that activated two dozen eager spells.

The flat was filled with a blue haze, as if it was suddenly flooded with still, sunlit water. Whips and bubbles of light, like shining ropes chasing fireflies, spread out from Meralda's bag until she spoke another word and the detector removed the bag spells from view, one by one, until none were visible.

The flat was empty now. Meralda turned in a circle, but found nothing, not even at the notches in the floor where once Otrinvion's twin staves were said to stand.

Meralda spoke another word, and the glow from the detector intensified.

She swept the flat again, spoke another word, turned and looked. And though the glow from the detector shone bright now, no hint or sign of disturbance marred its face.

The detector's handle grew warm in her hands. Meralda urged her Sight further, finer, knowing the spells couldn't be maintained much longer.

"Three more words," she said aloud. *No need to become discouraged yet, either,* she thought. *If the spells are there, I'll find them.*

She said another word, and the detector buzzed faintly in response as copper bands began to shake and blur. The mist became a fog, so thick now that Meralda could barely see the door. But still, no trace of hidden spellworks appeared.

Meralda spoke the next word, and the handle grew hot, but Meralda held on. The fog went thick and bright, and the outline of the door vanished, then the walls, until only the faint squares of the windows remained.

"I'm only trying to help," said Meralda, through gritted teeth. The buzzing became a sizzle, and acrid wisps of smoke began to curl toward Meralda's face. "Do you understand that? I only want to help."

The blue fog blazed suddenly, and the detector spat a stinging glob of molten copper on Meralda's right boot toe. Meralda shouted her final word.

The flat exploded. There was no noise, no felling blow, but the rush of light was so sudden and intense Meralda dropped the detector and fell to her knees, her hands flying to cover her eyes, her Sight all but obliterated by the ferocity of the blast.

But in that instant, before the detector fell, she saw the flat ablaze with the glow of a massive spellwork. Like a monstrous tree, it rose through the floor of the flat, engulfed Meralda whole within its fiery trunk, and sent branches thrusting horizontally outward to meet the Tower walls on every side. The branches were not still, though. Even in the brief Sight presented to Meralda, she saw they rose and turned in unison, spiraling upward and around the central trunk in a dizzying whirl.

Meralda's head reeled. She'd reached out with her Sight, tried to look closer, tried to follow the shuttling and turning of a single line of power around and through the trunk. But the effort had been too much, and she knew, had the flash not blinded her Sight, she might have lost it forever in the tangled midst of the Tower.

Meralda forced her hands from her eyes and rose from her knees. Her normal vision was blurred, criss-crossed and overlaid with fading images of the spellwork she knew still engulfed her.

Now I know the Tower's secret, she thought. *The Tower isn't haunted.*

The Tower is alive.

The spellwork flared. Even with the tiniest vestige of her Sight remaining, Meralda saw the shimmering air and took a step backwards.

It heard me, she thought. *It knows I know.*

The flat went dark, and the floor seemed to tilt and fall a finger's breadth away. Meralda stumbled, nearly went to her knees again, and groped for her magelamp. She took a single step forward in the dark, determined to remove her body from the midst of the hidden spell that filled the flat, and then she brought forth her magelamp and stroked the brass tube.

Light shone, and Meralda gasped. Her Farley and Hent raincoat lay two steps from her feet, still spread wet upon the floor. The foot of the stair stood dim at the edge of the light, and on the first dozen treads Meralda saw plain her own damp boot prints, leading up into the dark.

Meralda turned in a circle. She was alone, but she was no longer in the flat, and the stair and her coat were no tricks of her still blurred sight.

She recalled the brief sensation of falling, and shivered, realizing that she had fallen from the flat to the floor in the blink of an eye.

Her bag was gone, and the detector, though wisps of smoke from the hot copper bands still hung in the air about her.

A heavy blow fell upon the Tower doors, and echoed through the empty Tower. Heart pounding, Meralda turned her lamp upon the empty hall.

"Thaumaturge!" shouted Kervis, faintly from beyond the door. "Thaumaturge!"

A new fusillade of blows fell upon the door, and just as Meralda began to wonder why the Bellringers didn't just open the unlocked door she heard the furious droning buzz of her ward spell from above.

And then, in the dark, hands touched her back, at her shoulders. They touched her back, and gave her a gentle shove toward the hall and the door.

Meralda stumbled, caught herself. The sensation was gone.

"Vonashon," boomed a voice that echoed throughout the Tower. Walk swiftly, it meant, in Old Kingdom.

Meralda whirled, but the shaft of light from her magelamp illuminated only emptiness.

"Empalos," said the voice, so loud Meralda winced. Again, invisible hands touched her, this time from the front, still on each shoulder, pushing her back toward the door. Gentle, but forcing her back a step.

"Walk away!" The voice shouted, loud as thunder, more fearful than commanding. "Walk away!"

Meralda played her magelamp before her, but nothing caught the light. She swatted the air with her left hand, and though she felt the touch of a man's hand upon her she swatted empty air.

She tried to raise Sight, and saw nothing but after images of the column of fire from the flat. "I came to help you," she said, fighting a rising urge to bolt for the door. "Do you understand?"

The droning of her killing ward drew nearer, and a ruddy

orange glow filled the second story opening in the ceiling, and the voice in the Tower screamed. Not a word, this time. Just an unceasing, ear-splitting howl that rose in both pitch and intensity until Meralda turned and ran for the door, her eyes watering, her hands held over her ears.

Halfway down the hall, Meralda's teeth began to quiver, and her head felt as if it were about to burst. She could hear nothing but the scream. Not her own footfalls, not the thunder, not the pounding on the doors. Just a howl of agony far louder than any one man, or any hundred men, could ever make.

Meralda jammed her hands tighter against her ears, careened into a wall, forced the wildly bobbing magelamp beam to face the hall before her. The Tower doors appeared, twenty paces away, and Meralda blinked back tears and ran toward them.

The doors flew open. Dim grey sunlight and the splash and smell of rain rushed into the hall. The Bellringers dashed inside.

Kervis and Tervis charged to meet her. Kervis dropped his crossbow and drew his sword. Tervis sheathed his own blade and rushed to Meralda's side.

"Go," said Meralda. She groped in her pocket for a wand and turned back toward the stair, searching the dark for any sign of the killing ward.

Tervis spoke, but Meralda couldn't make out the words over the ringing in her ears. "The ward may be bad," she said, interrupting him. "We've got to get out."

He shut his mouth and nodded. Meralda held the wand at ready, prepared to speak the three words that would cause the ward spell to latch itself harmlessly to the glass.

The hall, though, was dark.

Meralda motioned the Bellringers back, toward the door. The ringing in her ears abated to the point that she began to hear footsteps. Footsteps, but no tell-tale droning of a ward on the hunt.

Beside her, Tervis looked warily about, then bent and picked up the shadowy bulk at his feet. *That looks like my bag,* thought Meralda, and she stepped closer and stared.

It is my bag, chalk marks and mended handles and all. My bag, which I left in the flat, here and in Tervis' left hand.

Meralda blinked, and found her black Farley and Hent raincoat folded neatly atop her instrument bag. Folded, and laid through the bag handles, just as she'd have done it.

Meralda reached down, put her hand on the coat, found it dry. Dry, and as free of wrinkles as if she'd just had it pressed at Minton's.

"Ma'am?" said Tervis, confusion on his face. "Is something wrong?"

"Nothing," said Meralda. *I don't dare tell him here that the Tower put bag and coat at his feet, an instant ago.* "Kervis?"

Kervis passed her, facing the dimly lit hall with his sword still drawn.

"I don't hear the ward," he said. "Is it still there, ma'am?"

Meralda pulled her hand away from her coat and joined Kervis in facing the dark. No glow shown forth, no buzzing rode the air. She took a breath and spoke the ward word.

Silence and darkness were her only replies. *My mighty killing ward, puffed out like a candle,* thought Meralda. She spoke the word again, heard nothing, and then motioned the Bellringers toward the door.

"The ward is gone," she said. "And we're leaving, too."

Tervis nodded. "Are you all right, ma'am?" he asked as he began to walk. "We heard an awful racket."

"I'm fine," said Meralda.

"Did you see it?" began Kervis.

Tervis interrupted. "Not in here," he said. "None of that until we're outside and the doors are shut and the thaumaturge has a breath of fresh air."

Kervis shrugged, but fell silent. Ten more paces brought them to the doors, where they met a dozen anxious red-coated guards all peering into the hall from the park.

"We're all right," said Kervis, before any spoke. "Make way."

The guards melted away, and the Bellringers halted, and Meralda took a breath and stepped out into wan grey sunlight and the damp, chilly park.

"Beetles and droughts," muttered Mug, when Meralda was done describing her encounter in the Tower. "It touched you? It spoke?"

Meralda nodded, and Mug's leaves shook.

Meralda hugged her chest with her arms and wished for a blanket. She'd gotten wet in the park before regaining the presence of mind to don her raincoat, and now the laboratory's windowless, dark space felt like an ice box. *But the mirror blanket is still in the Tower,* she thought, *wet on the floor by the stair, and I'm certainly not going back there to fetch it.*

"And you haven't left anything out?" asked Mug, turning all his eyes upon the Thaumaturge. "Nothing at all?"

"Nothing," said Meralda. "The Tower spoke, it moved me from the flat to the floor, it showed me a massive spellwork, and it touched me. All before it snuffed out a killing ward like a half-penny candle."

"Amazing," said Mug, "and all the while it was cleaning, drying, and folding your Farley and Hent raincoat." Mug leaned forward, dropped his voice to a whisper. "Mistress, I think the Tower likes you."

Meralda shrugged, dumbfounded. Her raincoat hung on the rack by the door. It had indeed been cleaned and pressed, as Mug had said, and even smelled faintly of a subtle perfume Meralda had never encountered and certainly did not own.

"Well, it's a first among the annals of thaumaturges," said Mug. "Next trip, take a whole load of laundry, and see what happens."

"Mug!"

"Sorry," he said. His blue eyes came forward in a bunch. "Why did it mess about with the ward spell? As a warning?"

"I thought so, at the time," said Meralda.

"Seems a bit odd that it felt the need to simultaneously threaten your life and press your raincoat," said Mug. "And it returned your instrument bag, but kept the detector. I wonder why?"

Meralda shrugged, and at that moment there came a knock at the door.

"Oh, no," groaned Meralda. "Not now."

Mug swiveled his eyes toward the sound of the captain's voice. "It's me, Thaumaturge," he said, his voice faint through the heavy door. "Hurry!"

Meralda rose, trotted wearily for the door, and threw the bolt open. "Come in," she began, biting back her words as the captain darted past her and inside.

"Remember what I told you, soldiers," he said gruffly to the Bellringers, and then he slammed the door.

Meralda backed away, one eyebrow lifted. The captain mopped sweat from his forehead and fell heavily back against the door.

"I don't suppose you keep anything to drink hidden away in here, do you?" he said.

Meralda shook her head. "I can send the lads..."

"No," said the captain, with a sigh. "The lads need to stay put." He pushed himself upright, took in a breath, and shook his head, his expression rueful. "I hear you roused the Tower shade today," he said with a grin. "Flashes and thunders, all through the park."

Meralda nodded, mute, and motioned toward her desk and the chairs that flanked it. Goboy's mirror flashed as she did so, and a blurry image of a brick sidewalk and a bright white store front formed suddenly in the glass.

The captain nodded, and made for the chairs.

"What did you tell the penswifts?" he asked as he walked. "The palace has been full of them, all day. You may thank me for closing the west stair to them, by the way, or they'd be camped outside your door."

Meralda grimaced. She had no more than set foot outside the Tower before finding herself beset by a mob of shouting penswifts. Deafened, breathless, and still in mild shock at her meeting with the Tower's hidden presence, she'd said a very rude word before ordering Kervis to clear her a path.

"Such language," said the captain, looking back with a grin. "And did you really call them witless, mewling, rumor mongers, who spew out mindless drivel for a small, but exceedingly ignorant, readership?"

I did say that, didn't I? thought Meralda. *To a mob of penswifts, who took down every word.*

"I've wanted to say that hundreds of times, over the years," he said, settling into a chair. "Good evening, houseplant," he added, to Mug.

"Your Grace," replied Mug, with a sweeping dip of his eye buds.

"Bah," snapped the captain. Meralda pulled her desk chair away from the desk, and set it so she faced Mug and the captain.

Voices sounded from outside the door. The captain smiled.

"That will be Sir Envid and the Vonats," he said, cheerily. "The Vonats insisted on a tour. I instructed your lads that you weren't here, and that I hadn't been around in days, and that if Envid asks them why they're here and you're not they are to shrug and say they were told to guard the laboratory and Tirlish soldiers follow orders whether diplomats like it or not."

"Thank you," said Meralda. "The last thing I need now is a herd of Vonats wandering about, trying to slip things in their pockets."

The captain lost his smile. "The last thing you need now is Humindorus Nam," he said.

"The Vonat mage," said Mug. "We've heard so many pleasant things about him."

"He's the one insisting on a tour," said the captain. "He's insane. Not climb the walls and run about naked insane, but mad in worse ways. They're up to something, Meralda, and I'm afraid you're a part of it."

The voices faded, and footsteps fell away.

Meralda waited until they were gone. *I have the oddest impression,* she thought, *that someone is crouched just beyond the door, listening.*

She fought back a shiver, looking to see if the captain noticed. But his eyes were upon Goboy's mirror, which had begun to flash again, and present brief scenes of rainy Tirlish streets.

"Captain," said Mug, after a moment. "If you know something definite, why not share it with the thaumaturge? She doesn't keep secrets from you, now does she?"

Meralda glared, but the captain nodded and turned away from the mirror. "That's why I'm here," he said. "I've got things to tell." He sighed, and put his hands on his knees, and met Meralda's eyes.

"It all started a year ago," he said. "And naturally, it all started in Vonath."

Chapter Thirteen

The captain stomped out.

Mug regarded Meralda with all of his eyes. "Well. Vonat spies, trained in sorcery. This day gets better and better by the moment, doesn't it?"

Meralda nodded. In her hand was a pencil. She resisted a sudden urge to chew on it.

"Why doesn't Yvin just arrest every last Vonat and toss them in the dungeon until after the Accords?" sputtered Mug.

"You know why," said Meralda. "They have to sign the treaty too, or the Hang will sail away and never come back."

"Oh? And that's a disaster, is it? Why?"

Meralda sighed and put down her pencil. "Because the world isn't as big as it once was, Mug. And we're a part of it now, like it or not."

"Well, I don't like it." The dandyleaf plant tossed his leaves. "I just want that understood."

"I'll make a note of it." Meralda rose, stretched, yawned.

"If that Vonat wizard is in with the meddlers, as the captain suspects, he'll likely try and meddle with you, mistress. Probably with something shiny and sharp. Please tell me you're going to take steps to protect yourself."

"I am." Meralda gazed back across the ranks of shelves and stacks of crates. The captain's warning had been clear.

I can expect a magical assault by a skilled Vonat wizard, she thought. *What would best protect me from such a thing?*

"Migle's Mighty Armor," said Mug, guessing her thoughts. "Turns arrows and knives, too, as I recall."

Meralda imagined herself stumbling about in eighty pounds of iron and frowned. "Made for a man, and one two feet taller than I," she said. She paced toward the first row of shelves, finger to her lips. "No. I need something subtle. Something he can't see. Something no one can see."

Items on the shelves were stored, in Shingvere's words, "according to malevolent whim and infernal caprice." Before Meralda were half a dozen intricate devices designed to make ice. Beneath them was a line of six silver gloves, all snapping their fingers in perfect time.

"Naigree's Vanishing Amulet?"

Meralda walked past a jar containing the skeleton of a rat, which put its bony face to the glass and wiggled dry whickers at her as she passed.

"Won't work in direct sunlight."

The faint strains of music rose up from a music-box before her. Meralda smiled, and the box scuttled away, leaving tiny footprints in the dust.

"Carvile's Temporary Displacer?"

A crystal snake, its gold spine bending and twisting within it, coiled suddenly at Meralda, flicking its metallic tongue at her until she lifted her eyebrow and frowned.

"You have to constantly sing to it."

Mug sighed. "Surely there's a bloody enchanted sword somewhere in this clutter, mistress!"

"There are at least eight. Five had to be wrapped in chains and sealed inside lead boxes. Two are broken."

"That leaves one," said Mug.

"It grows an inch a year," said Meralda. "It was twelve feet long, last time I checked." Meralda found herself halfway down the first rank of shelves. Magical implements glittered and moved and spun, illuminating her one moment with strange glows, and the next with flashes of harsh white light.

"Here you are," she said.

She reached up and took down a small, dusty oak box. The top was worked with sigils and runes. A tiny key protruded from the delicate brass lock.

Lavey's Here-now Gone-now Charm of Hiding. Meralda cleared a space on the shelf before her and put the box carefully down.

"Mistress?" called Mug. "Have you found something?"

Meralda bit her lower lip. The charm was reputed to be quite powerful, allowing its wearer to somehow go about their business, but remain hidden to those seeking them out. Not invisible, either. Just...gone. Absent. Away. All without ever actually hiding.

Which is just the thing to be, when Vonat wizards mean to do you ill, thought Meralda.

But first, of course, there was the charm's famous here-now gone-now nature to contend with. "Mistress?" called Mug, louder now.

Meralda took a deep breath, held it, and turned the tiny key in the dusty brass lock.

There was a click.

Meralda lifted the lid, and peered inside.

The velvet lined case was empty.

"Bother," said Meralda.

"What?"

"I opened Lavey's little oak box," said Meralda. "It's empty."

Mug groaned. "When can you try again?"

"After the next new moon. It doesn't matter how many times I open the box from now until then, it'll be empty. The spell doesn't reset until the new moon." Meralda closed the box and shook it. She could hear and feel the charm rattling about inside, but when she opened the box, it was empty, as it would be until the spell reset. Then there would be a fifty out of fifty chance the charm would appear.

"Bugger. Good idea though. What next?"

What next, indeed?

Meralda replaced Lavey's box on its shelf. Mattip's Sideways Positioner? Calit's Bracelets of Furious Wind?

Neither is very reliable, she thought. *The Bracelets of Wind are as likely to injure me as the Vonat.*

Meralda walked, her mind racing, her eyes fixed on the objects before her. Etter's Phantasmal Twin?

No. Anyone with Sight could easily tell twin from original.

She stubbed her right toe on something on the floor.

The spark lamps cast more shadows than light, between the ranks of shelves, so Meralda didn't recognize the object with which she had collided at first. But she suspected how it came to be out of place.

"Shingvere, no doubt," she muttered, straining to see in the dark. "Probably looking for a bottle of brandy he hid in here twenty years ago."

She reached down and lifted the object from the floor.

It looked like a staff, at first. An old one, by the wear on the rough hewn ironwood. But it bore no markings, no sigils, no runes. It had neither iron shod foot nor copper plated head.

Meralda frowned at it. *Probably not even a staff,* she decided. *Probably just a chunk of cast off lumber stuck beneath the shelves to level them. I just hope removing it doesn't bring one of these shelves down on my head.*

Meralda leaned the length of wood against the shelf behind her and continued her prowl amid the works of the mages of old.

"Any luck?" said Mug, from the shadows.

"I could make ice or raise a sudden fog or cause empty shoes to dance," said Meralda.

"Marvelous. We're saved. Mistress, surely there's something nasty back there!"

Oh, there's plenty of nasty, thought Meralda. Kingen's Bell causes massive internal bleeding in anyone who hears it. Stovall's Blighted Candle melts the eyes of anyone who gazes into the flame. Both were locked away in sturdy chests, but neither offered much in the way of protection from stealthy Vonat mages.

Meralda reached the end of the shelf row, and sidled around the end of it, ready to begin searching the other side.

She walked into something hidden in a shadow and it fell with a bang and a clatter.

Meralda jumped, careened into the laboratory's back wall, and bit back a curse word.

"Mistress? You all right back there?"

"I'm fine." Meralda forced a smile. "Too much clutter."

There, on the floor, was the twin to the ironwood staff she'd encountered moments before.

Meralda nudged it with the toe of her boot. It scooted with a rasping sound.

Your nerves are getting the better of you, she thought. Then she reached down, snatched the ironwood up, and leaned it carefully against the wall.

"What about Gilbert's Cloak of Grounding?" asked Mug. "Didn't half a dozen mages wear that when they were working with unstable wards?"

Meralda nodded. "That they did," she said. She tried to recall where the cloak had been stored. Wasn't it wrapped in canvas, in that yellow chest by the south wall?

She made for the far end of the row, where the lights shone bright and there was open space and room to move. The cloak wasn't a bad idea. Particularly if one enhanced the original spells.

She took half a dozen steps. Just half a dozen steps, and then, though she heard nothing, saw nothing, sensed nothing, Meralda turned and looked back at the wall where she'd leaned the troublesome scrap of ironwood.

The wall was empty.

As was the floor.

"Mistress," called Mug, his voice filled with rising panic. "Mistress, I think you'd better grab something right now, because we have company."

A shadow flew over her, and with it came the sound of wings.

"Mistress, *run!*"

Meralda ran. Again, the whoosh and dart of shadow. She reached out, caught the first thing she grasped, and threw it toward the sound.

"Missed," cried Mug. Something metallic landed with a clatter. "Mistress, there are two of them!"

Meralda forced her Sight up and out.

The laboratory was suddenly ablaze with moving, spinning, flashing lights. Thousands of spells shone and moved like noon in a field of wind-blown mirrors.

But above the crowded ranks of magical items about her, two blurs of purest, darkest black sailed and spun and flew.

Meralda's Sight collapsed, and she sank to her knees, suddenly blind, suddenly exhausted. She reached out again, fumbling with the items on the shelf before her, and gasped as she found Mahop's Portable Inferno.

I may burn down half the shelves, she thought, *but let's see how quickly these staves ignite.*

"That will not be necessary, Mage Ovis."

The voice was not Mug's. It was far too loud to be any of

Mug's mimicry, either.

It spoke perfect New Kingdom, with no trace of a Vonat accent.

"Nameless. Faceless. Desist. Return."

Above came the sound of troubled air, but it faded quickly, and was gone.

Meralda rose. Her hands found the two small indentations that, if covered, would cause the open end of the Inferno to spew gouts of fire reputed to be so hot they melted glass and stone alike.

"My apologies, Mage. They were intent on childish mischief, but I do not believe they meant you harm."

"Mistress," hissed Mug. "You are not going to believe this."

"Oh, but she must," replied the booming voice, to Mug. "All your fates depend upon her belief. Without it, Tirlin is doomed."

Meralda held the Inferno in front of her, ready to bring it to life.

"Who are you?" she said, her eyes straining to penetrate the shadows about her.

"I have no name," replied the voice. "Please. Come forward. I mean you no harm."

"Mug?"

"No one else is here, mistress," he replied. "It seems to be speaking from inside Goboy's mirror."

"The construct is correct. I am using the glass as a portal. Please approach. We have urgent matters to discuss."

Meralda warily emerged from between the shelves, the Inferno at the ready.

Mug swiveled half his eyes toward her, keeping the rest fixed on Goboy's mirror. From her vantage point, Meralda could not see into the glass, so she moved cautiously toward Mug and her desk.

"Those things, whatever they were, flew inside the mirror," said Mug. "Hit it and vanished inside."

They couldn't possibly have done that, thought Meralda. *The mirror is just glass.* But she nodded and made her way to a spot behind her desk.

Goboy's mirror showed a scene from inside the Wizard's Flat. Late afternoon sunlight streamed in through the windows. The two plain ironwood staves stood upright, their ends inside the holes carved into the floor.

Dust motes danced and twirled in the sun.

"Master often referred to me as Tower," said the voice. "In the interest of ready communication, you may do the same."

"Pardon me," said Mug, "But when you say 'Master,' are you perhaps referring to Otrinvion the Black?"

"Master had many names," replied the voice. "That was one of them."

Mug's wilt intensified.

Meralda's mind raced, and her heart began to pound. *I'm talking to the Tower,* she thought. *Otrinvion's Tower. What am I supposed to say?*

The Tower let the silence linger.

"I am... honored by your wish to converse," said Meralda, after a moment. "I hope my visit earlier today has not caused you any distress."

"My actions were born of caution, not distress," replied the Tower. "I feared your brief inspection of my form had caused you injury, so I used the transport word to place you close to your friends. Your sudden displacement caused your ward work to erroneously identify you as an intruder, forcing me to both expedite your departure and disable your ward."

Meralda exchanged a glance with Mug, whose leaves still drooped in a terrified wilt.

"I thank you for your concern," said Meralda. She bit her lip, hesitant to say more.

How many mages spent how many lives trying to pry even a single hidden spell out of the Tower? And what would they say, if told the Tower itself were alive?

What would Shingvere ask, if he were here?

"Very well, Tower," she said. "Do you mind if I ask a few questions of you?"

"It is vital that you do so," replied the Tower. "Else I would not have revealed myself."

Mug's leaves shook. "I knew it," he said, in a whisper to Meralda. "I knew it. All this meddling with shadows and wards. Something's wrong. So badly wrong it's breaking a thousand years of silence and using your mirror to do it."

"Hush," said Meralda, with a glare.

"The construct is correct," said the Tower. "Master forbade me to reveal myself, and I have obeyed. Until now."

"Why?" asked Meralda. "And why to me?"

"Because Tirlin is doomed," said the Tower. "Doomed, by Master's hand. I can no longer stay his wrath. It is my hope that perhaps you can."

Meralda put down the Inferno. *Steady,* she said to herself. *Perhaps it is merely engaging in melodrama.*

"Doomed, in what way?"

"See this."

The image in the glass rippled, twisted, and became an exterior view of the Tower.

From the flat, a series of spokes shot out, parallel to the ground. At the end of each spoke, a dark mass formed, and then the spokes began to turn.

Mug turned eyes upon Meralda. "You've seen this before, haven't you?"

"Briefly," she answered. "In the park, when my first latch collapsed."

"Yes," said the Tower. In the glass, Meralda saw her latch and refractors form, watched as the latch was chewed in half by the turning spokes, saw it fall away and vanish.

"I allowed your shadow moving spell to latch," said the Tower. "I thought it harmless. I was wrong."

The spokes began to wobble as they turned, and the steady flight of the dark masses took on a bobbing quality. "The instability is growing," it said. "Soon, the binding will fail."

In the glass, the spokes jerked and flailed. Some lost speed, some began to turn faster. Then they collided and tangled and tore each other apart.

The dark masses broke free, one by one, and were hurtled

out and away, vanishing from the glass.

Meralda shivered. *Like falcons tethered to a pole*, she'd thought, upon glimpsing them in the park.

"Curseworks," she said, aloud. "Aren't they?"

"They are," replied the Tower. "Fire. Pestilence. Decay. Madness." The Tower paused. "And others, more subtle, yet no less destructive. There are twelve. Master was vengeful, at the end."

The image in the glass flashed, and the spokes and the masses were gone, replaced by the flat and the staves.

"How long?" asked Meralda.

"I may be able to maintain the binding for another two hundred and forty hours," replied the Tower. "Perhaps less. But certainly no more. After that, Master's curses will fall, and Tirlin will be consumed."

Even Phillitrep's Engine seemed to halt, as if listening.

"Two hundred and forty hours is ten days," said Mug.

"Consumed," said Meralda. "Are you speaking figuratively, perhaps?"

"Burned, razed, broken, ground to dust," replied the Tower. "Employ what euphemism you will. Master designed the destruction to be complete. 'Utter and thorough,' he said. 'Let us visit upon them what they have brought to me'."

Meralda met Mug's wide and staring eyes. *He's dying to ask the Tower why it isn't just keeping quiet and letting the curseworks fall,* she thought. *And that isn't a bad question.*

"If that was your master's plan," she said, slowly, "why aren't you just letting it happen?"

The Tower image flickered. "At the end, Master seemed confused," it replied. "He was dying. His works were lost. His lands were aflame. But he looked upon the curseworks, and he was saddened, and I believe he tried to dispel them."

Meralda nodded. Nothing was known about Otrinvion's final hours. Perhaps he wasn't the heartless villain of legend, after all.

"Did your master perhaps leave records concerning these curseworks behind?"

"He did not. They were crafted in a place beyond my senses. I know almost nothing of their basic natures."

"And yet you believe I can render them harmless."

The Tower hesitated.

"My knowledge of the kingdoms and the mages they employ is extensive," it said. Meralda thought of Goboy's glass, hanging in the laboratory for the last four hundred years. Had the Tower been watching and listening, all that time? Before that time, even? "You are the most skilled mage in all the Realms. If you do not try, then doom will befall Tirlin. I believe Master would find this event undesirable. Thus, I am bound to make every effort to forestall it."

Mug swapped eyes between Meralda and the mirror.

"Are those your master's staves?"

"They are."

"Mistress," said Mug. "If that's true, and friend Tower is telling the truth—"

"I am."

"—they would certainly be able to handle a Vonat or two,

wouldn't they? What about it, Tower? We help you with your little doom problem, you let the mage here borrow Nameless and Faceless?"

"Mug!"

"The staves are not under my control," said the Tower. "They obey me when it suits them, but only then. I have already directed them to assist the mage in her efforts. If the mage is in danger, then I believe they will act to protect her."

"You believe?" Mug tossed his leaves. "How about it, kindling wood? Do we have a deal?"

Meralda nearly shoved Mug in a drawer.

The staves stood still.

"Is that a yes or a no?"

"Mug, be silent." Meralda pulled back her chair and sat.

It could be lying, she thought. Or it could be a Vonat trick. Or a trap left by Otrinvion. Or any number of other nefarious schemes brought to life by who knows who. It could be the Hang, the Vonats, or rogue members of Tirlin's own court.

Or it could be exactly what it says it is, and it could be telling a terrible, terrible truth.

"Tower. You said you knew nearly nothing of the curseworks and their natures."

"Correct."

Meralda shoved aside a heap of papers, found a fresh sheet and her pencil. "So tell me everything you do know. In as much detail as you can provide, please."

Mug shook his leaves and brought all his eyes together in a multi-colored blinking clump.

The Tower began to speak, filling the glass with diagrams and symbols, and Meralda wrote long into the night.

Chapter Fourteen

Even exhausted, Meralda could not bring herself to sleep in the laboratory. Not with Goboy's mirror and whatever lay within looking out at her all night.

So she put Mug in his birdcage and roused the Bellringers and headed for home. She was sure she heard something very much like the flutter of wings overhead, but she did not lift her gaze.

After all, she mused as the cab rolled homeward, *there is precious little I could do against them, if they are indeed the Nameless and the Faceless of legend.*

Mug didn't speak at all. His eyes remained upturned, staring at the cloudy, starless sky.

It was two of the clock by the time Meralda tip-toed over her threshold. Mug kept all but two of his eyes shut against the swaying of the cage, and didn't stop shaking until he was once again safe on the kitchen table.

"I don't suppose you'd tell me all that was just a bad dream, mistress," he whispered.

Meralda shook off her boots on the rug. "I'm afraid not, Mug."

"Do you think they're here? The you-know-whats?"

"I don't know. Probably. But if they are, I expect them to behave. This is my home, and they are guests within it."

"And if they wake Mrs. Whitlonk she'll shave them down to toothpicks," added Mug.

Meralda gazed about her kitchen. If the staves were present, they were quiet and remaining out of sight.

I don't suppose I can hope for more than that, thought Meralda.

"You should get some sleep," said Mug. "I'll keep watch, if you like."

Meralda smiled. "No need. We're as safe as we can possibly be, I suppose."

Mug tossed his leaves wearily. "At least move me into the bedroom." He clenched his eyes shut. "Quickly, please."

Meralda rose and caught Mug up, before he could change his mind.

The five-twenty trolley roused Meralda from a troubled, restless sleep. She moaned and fought her way out of her tangled bedclothes and stumbled toward her bathroom.

Mug tossed as she passed, but none of his eyes opened. Meralda paused to draw back her curtains, so the dandyleaf plant would have the first rays of the sunrise, and then set about bathing and dressing.

That done, she sought out breakfast, remembering too late that her cupboards were bare. So she sat and combed her hair while Mug spread his leaves to the bright morning sun.

The Bellringers came trundling to her door precisely on

time, bearing coffee and pastries. Meralda seated them at her tiny kitchen table and ate while they traded 'how many Vonat' jokes with Mug.

Meralda wiped pastry crumbs off her chin and drained the last sip of coffee from her cup. "Thank you, gentlemen," she said, rising. The Bellringers leaped to their feet. "We should be on our way."

"I'm going too," said Mug, mournfully. "Pray prepare my carriage."

"At once, Your Highness." Kervis fetched Mug's cage, while Meralda pulled a folded sheet from her linen closet.

"Cheeky little devils, aren't they?"

"Hush, Mug," said Meralda. She gently put Mug in his cage and draped the sheet over it before handing it to Kervis.

"To the Tower, court, or the laboratory, ma'am?"

"The lab," replied Meralda. She forced herself to smile. "I have a lot to do."

Angis deftly maneuvered the carriage through the press of morning traffic. Meralda had called for him to stop at Flayne's for one more cup of coffee, which she held carefully aloft as the carriage bumped and wobbled. The coffee steamed, fresh out of the pot and blazing hot.

Meralda was glad Tervis sat with her, because his presence certainly kept Mug from questioning her choice of destination. *I'm sure he's wondering why I'm not immediately going to the king with news of the Tower, and the curseworks.*

And I'm not sure I have a good answer for him, just yet.

On one hand, if doom truly is about to befall Tirlin, the king should be the first to be told. There might be time to abandon the city.

Outside the carriage, traffic flowed past. Voices were raised in greetings and laughter. Shopkeeps struggled to remove their window shutters as they opened for another day of business. Dirigibles soared past overhead, casting long fast shadows over storefronts and crowded sidewalks.

Abandon Tirlin?

How?

She shook her head. *No. That we cannot do.*

Even if I somehow convinced the king of Tirlin to flee the crown city and drag the entire populace with him at sword point, where would we all go? Cappas is a third the size of Tirlin. Romin not even that.

I refuse to live in a tent, vowed Meralda. *There must be another way.*

If I tell Yvin before I'm sure, she decided, *he would only complicate matters by involving the army or the guilds. He might even decide to mount another attempt to knock the Tower down.*

Meralda shivered at the thought.

"Something wrong, Mage?"

"Nothing. Just a chill."

Mug snorted from beneath his bed sheet.

Also, thought Meralda, *if what the captain said yesterday was correct, the Vonats started bribing court functionaries a year or more ago, all with the aim of wreaking havoc at the Accords. They may have even installed Hang eavesdropping spells in the Gold Room itself, and if so, discussing the Tower's story of the doom bound for Tirlin would be nothing short of disastrous.*

So no. Not the king. At least not today.

"Penny for your thoughts," quipped Mug.

Meralda closed her eyes and tried to blow her coffee cool.

The castle was awash in uniformed soldiers, court members arrayed in all their finery, and a roving mob of penswifts which swept from place to place shouting questions and trying with little success to elbow their way past a dozen bemused guardsmen armed with short, stout lengths of oak.

Meralda was halfway to the doors when the penswifts spotted her and charged with two dozen strident cries of "Mage Ovis! Mage Ovis!"

The Bellringers stepped ahead of her, hands raised. "Don't crowd, don't crowd," cried Kervis, above the din. "Back off, I say! Back off or else!"

Meralda frowned and marched ahead. *If I let them stop me,* she thought, *I'll be half an hour elbowing my way through them.*

Penswifts and court functionaries and Bellringers all met in a mob. Mug shouted something, but Meralda couldn't make out his words.

"Mage Ovis," bellowed the closest penswift. His words were instantly repeated by a dozen of his fellows, and Meralda was quickly surrounded by a press of arms and chests and faces.

The Bellringers shoved and shouted. Penswifts yelled back. A paperboy caught in the press squealed and managed to slip past a sea of legs.

A splash of red and green moving through the crowd caught Meralda's eye, as she shoved and sidled her way through the penswifts. *Looks a bit like an Alon kilt.*

"Mistress!" cried Mug. "Something isn't right!"

The crowd shifted, just for an instant, and in that instant Meralda caught of glimpse of a tall, bearded, red-haired Alon, clad in kilt and sash, shoving his way through the mob toward her.

Mug shouted again. The only word Meralda made out was 'knife'.

The Alon marched steadily forward, shoving penswifts to the pavement, pushing court staff roughly aside.

Meralda looked for his hands, and saw a brief glimmer of steel.

She tried to run. She tried to force her way past the ring of penswifts who shouted questions at her face, at her back. She didn't dare put Mug's cage down for fear he'd be trampled and her other hand still gripped the oversized paper mug of hot coffee and though she shouted for the Bellringers she could see neither of them.

The Alon charged. Penswifts went flying. Meralda tried to hurl herself backwards, but the tightly packed bodies at her back kept her pinned to the spot, and the bearded Alon shoved his way to her, knife uplifted.

Meralda hurled her hot coffee square in his face. The Alon howled and stabbed, missing Meralda's chest by a hand's breadth and allowing her to land a single solid kick somewhere in the region of his ornate clan belt buckle. The man folded at the waist, cursing and spitting.

Meralda tried to dash away, but again the crowd held her fast. As the Alon straightened and lifted his knife again, Meralda snatched Mug's sheet away and hurled it at his face.

He batted it away.

Blurs rushed past Meralda on both sides. The Bellringers flung themselves at the Alon, both striking him at his knees. Alon and Bellringers and half a dozen bystanders went down in a tangle, grappling and punching, rolling and shouting.

Whistles blew. A column of guardsmen charged into the fray, swords drawn, and the crowd evaporated as quickly as it had formed.

Three burly guards in full plate encircled Meralda. The rest grabbed combatants and fallen penswifts and Bellringers alike, hauling each to their feet and warning them to stillness and silence with gruff shakes and glares.

The Alon was gone.

"There was an Alon!" said Kervis, wiping blood from his lip. "I tackled him!"

Meralda whirled, but the people hurrying away from the guards were Tirlish or Phendelits or Eryans. Not a scrap of Alon plaid could be seen anywhere on the street.

The captain, himself, came charging out of the castle, sword drawn, eyes ablaze. He saw Meralda and ran for her. More boots sounded from just beyond the doors.

"Thaumaturge!" he shouted. "What happened here?"

"Nothing at all happened here, Captain," she said, forcing a smile. "Nothing at all. Why don't you see us inside?"

The captain frowned. His men exchanged confused glances. Kervis kicked Tervis in the shins when the younger Bellringer made as if to protest.

"Someone get my bloody sheet," muttered Mug. "It's going to be that kind of day."

Meralda nodded a quick thanks to her trio of perplexed guards, gently hefted Mug's cage, and bade the Bellringers follow her into the dubious safety of the castle.

"He tried to kill you, mistress," said Mug, quivering with fury. "How can you be so calm about it?"

"She's using her head, houseplant," said the captain. "Something you should try, now and then."

"Demanding an arrest, threatening the Alons? That's just what they want me to do, Mug. Calm down and you'll see that."

"All I saw was a bloody big knife, mistress. And a man determined to stab you with it." Mug tossed his leaves and bunched his eyes. "Tervis? Kervis? Either of you care to chime in?"

The Bellringers withered under the captain's sudden glare.

"Perhaps we saw an Alon, and perhaps we didn't, Mug." Meralda shivered at the memory of the bearded man bearing down on her. "He came from nowhere. He vanished without a trace, despite being a foot taller than everyone else and wearing more bright red plaid than anyone in the crowd. Doesn't that strike you as suspicious?"

Mug snorted. "So he's sneaky and a fast runner. Mistress. Dorn Mukirk was ready to kill you himself, just a few days ago. What makes you believe this Alon wasn't some kin of his?"

"Because Alon blood feuds follow certain rules, houseplant. One of them is the formal declaration of feud by the offended party. Has Dorn Mukirk sent you a letter, Thaumaturge? A letter which mentions a fight to the death, honor of the clan, that sort of thing?"

"Of course not."

The captain nodded. "There you are, then. This wasn't a blood feud. Someone just wanted to make it look that way."

"A murder committed in a crowd of penswifts would be just the thing to wreck the Accords."

Mug deflated. "You won't even talk to the Alon queen, mistress? She liked you. You could at least be sure."

"I am sure, Mug. That man was no more Alon than you or I." She looked to the captain. "But he looked the part. The penswifts will certainly claim this was an act of hot-headed Alon mischief."

"The penswifts can write whatever they want. I sent a runner to the king before the fight broke up. The papers won't print a word of it."

Meralda lifted her right eyebrow. "Even the king can't deny them the right to publish."

The captain chuckled. "No. But he can appeal to their patriotism and beg them for silence."

"He might as well whistle them a dancing tune," snapped Mug. "Murder sells papers."

"Bribes seal lips," mused the captain. "Especially very large royal bribes, which are usually accompanied by subtle hints of royal mayhem."

"So the papers won't print a story of an assassination attempt on the steps of the castle."

"Not this time." The captain turned to face the Bellringers. "You two. Charging that fiend, knocking him down. Rare good sense, that. I don't have access to the royal purse, but will put in a word for both of you. End of summer might see you lads promoted."

The Bellringers exchanged grins. "Thank you, sir," said Kervis.

The captain rose, groaned, and turned toward the door.

"Got to get back out there," he said. "I'll be back around later. You two see that the thaumaturge doesn't run into any more vanishing Alons."

The Bellringers nodded.

Mug tossed his leaves in disgust. "So that's it? The king bribes the papers, and you just go about your day as though nothing happened?"

"Kervis. Tervis. Take your posts, please. We won't be leaving for a while."

The Bellringers leaped to their feet.

"And thank you. You were both very brave out there."

The brothers blushed in identical shades of crimson and bolted for the door.

Meralda waited for the door to slam before rising and pulling the scrap of tarp off Goboy's glass.

The Wizard's Flat was there, lit by horizontal shafts of early morning sun. Nameless and Faceless were gone.

"Good morning," said Meralda.

"I assume your remark is rhetorical in nature." The image in the glass wavered a bit, then stabilized. "Yes. An informal greeting. Forgive me. I have not carried on a conversation in nearly a millennia."

"The mage was attacked not an hour ago, Tower," snapped Mug. "Attacked by a man who appeared from nowhere and vanished in broad daylight. Your famous sticks of lumber didn't so much as say boo." The dandyleaf shot an accusatory vine toward the glass. "I thought you said we could expect a bit of help from that lot."

"Attacked? By whom?"

Meralda waved her hand at Mug for silence. "By someone posing as an Alon," she said. "Someone with magical assistance. I do not believe he simply slipped away on a busy street with half the guard out looking for him"

"Interesting. I, too, was the subject of an attack at approximately that time."

"You? Attacked?" Mug snorted. "With what, battering rams and pick-axes?"

"Someone attempted to latch a moderately complicated spellwork to my main structure. I deflected it, of course, but the construction of the spell was most unusual."

"Unusual how?"

"I have maintained an intimate familiarity with every arcane practice in all of the Realms," replied the Tower. "Vonat, Phendelit, Eryan, Alon. I am expert in them all."

"Your wooden friends do a lot of traveling, don't they?"

"Mug." Meralda rose and began to pace. "And this was something new?"

"It was."

"Do you know who sent it?"

"Not yet. I know the general area from which it originated. The spell caster was careful to maintain a considerable distance and employ a number of obfuscatory measures."

"Dorleigh and Ventham," said Mug. "Somewhere between those two streets, wasn't it?"

The Tower's tone took on a hint of bemusement. "Just so, construct," it said. "Just so."

Meralda frowned. Mug turned a trio of eyes toward her.

"I may be just a lowly construct, mistress, but I do read the *Post*. The Vonats rented out a couple of rooming houses in that neighborhood. They always do that, since they throw the kind of parties King Yvin won't stand for."

"I dispatched Nameless and Faceless to that area as soon as I detected the intrusion," said the Tower. "Their absence during your difficulty was thus my fault. I apologize."

"Well. Finally." Mug tossed his fronds. "Was that so hard?"

"The staves." Meralda thought for a moment. "Have they returned?"

"No. I can attempt to recall them now, if you wish. Though I cannot guarantee their timely obedience."

Meralda paused in her pacing. "No. Let them be. Though I would like to hear what they found, when they return."

"As you wish." The Tower fell silent for a moment. "Have you considered the matter of the curseworks, Mage Ovis?"

As if I've considered anything else, thought Meralda. "I have. Tower, a question. This unique new magic you encountered, could it be Hang magic?"

"I have considered that. I simply have no knowledge of the Hang or their arcane traditions. But given the presence of the Hang, it seems likely. You suspect collusion between Hang and Vonath?"

"I suspect a few rogue elements within the Hang may be involved. And all of Vonath, including the rats, the crows and the crickets."

The Tower hesitated.

"Humor."

Meralda chuckled. "An attempt. But if we face Hang magic, we need to know something about it. And who knows? There might be something in the Hang traditions that can help repair the spokes."

"A possibility."

There came a knock at the door. The image in the glass shook, and became nothing but a simple refection of Meralda and Mug.

Kervis stuck his head in the door.

"Ma'am," he called. "It's Mr. Donchen. He says he doesn't have an appointment, but he needs to see you." Kervis grinned.

"He's brought more food, too. They have two kinds of breakfast over there, and he's brought both."

Meralda pushed back her hair, wished she'd had time to comb it, and forced a smile.

"Well, show him right in," she called. "He's just the man I wanted to see."

"That was excellent," said Meralda, pushing away her empty plate.

Donchen smiled and made a little bow with his head. Meralda caught herself staring again, trying to guess his age. There were no wrinkles at the corners of his almond-shaped grey eyes. His short-cropped hair was a uniform inky black. His teeth were perfect, and a brilliant white.

He grinned back, and Meralda blushed.

"I am glad you enjoyed it," he said. "Though I must confess, I did not prepare any of this. Chef Inglee did all the work. I merely stole the serving cart."

"Well, I'm glad you did. I've had nothing but coffee in ages."

Donchen nodded. "You are a busy woman, Mage Ovis. Dining with possibly nefarious foreigners. Being attacked on the palace steps by vanishing Alons. It's a wonder you ever dine at all."

Mug bunched his eyes.

"You know about that."

"I was there."

"Didn't see you rushing to anyone's aid," muttered Mug.

"I was too far away," replied Donchen, nonplussed. "But not so far away that I couldn't confirm the use of a very familiar charm. I did in fact make an effort to track your assailant, Mage Ovis. I fear I failed in that effort, shortly after commencing it."

"Was he heading south, when last you saw him?"

Donchen nodded. "He was. This is significant?"

Meralda shrugged. "It's suggestive. The Vonats have rented a pair of boarding houses south of the palace."

"Hmm. I see." Meralda watched the man's face. He kept it blank, but she didn't need Sight to see his mind working behind his eyes.

"You said I could ask you anything, yesterday," she said. "Did you mean that?"

"I did."

Meralda leaned forward. "All right. Then I have a question. Who are you?"

"And none of that friendly cook business, either," added Mug. "You know what she means."

Donchen smiled. "I do. I will answer, though you may find it troubling at first. I am a ghost."

Mug snorted. "You eat a lot for a specter."

"That's not what he means," said Meralda. "Is it?"

"No. It is customary, you see, for persons of my position and background to spend a certain number of years as a *sohata*. A ghost. As a *sohata*, I may walk where I will, speak as I will, act as I will. No one of the House of Chentze sees or hears me. Thus, I am a ghost."

"But not the dead and buried sort? No rising from the grave or feasting on the blood of the living?" Mug stared hard at Donchen with all twenty-nine of his eyes. "Because we take a dim view of those sorts of goings-on here in Tirlin."

Donchen laughed. "I assure you, Mug, I neither rise from the grave nor feast on blood. I much prefer feather beds and vegetables."

"A ghost." Meralda searched his eyes for any hint of deceit. "So your Mighty Dragon has no idea you're speaking with me?"

"I am *sohata*, Mage Ovis. I walk unseen. My only voice the wind. The tradition is ancient and much venerated. Even private speculation concerning a ghost is believed to invite a bewildering variety of dooms."

That actually makes sense, thought Meralda. *No wonder he seems to do as he pleases. I could certainly use a year or two as a ghost myself.*

"You say you followed the Alon?"

"I did," said Donchen. "Though I suspect he was no more Alon than you or Mug or I. He was using a charm of concealment to alter his appearance. You suspected this too, did you not?"

Meralda nodded. She didn't glance toward Goboy's glass, but she knew the Tower was listening.

"I fear the charm employed the magic of my homeland," said Donchen, frowning. "For that, I apologize."

Meralda lifted an eyebrow. "Only a person with Sight could even detect magic," she said. "And only one with talent and training could identify it."

Donchen laughed and spread his hands. "I make no claims to any great prowess in the arts," he said. "But I do have some small knowledge. As a *sohata*, I have spent hours looking over Loman's shoulders. I may even have pocketed a trinket or two." He grinned and reached into his pockets with both hands.

"Why, look here," he said, placing two small objects on either side of his empty plate. "I can't imagine how these came to fall in my pockets."

Mug immediately aimed a cluster of eyes at each small device.

One appeared to be a small brass compass, the lid flipped open to reveal a needle, tipped in red, pointing steadily at the laboratory doors. But when Meralda looked closer, she saw that the face of the dial lacked any markings for directions. Instead, a pair of brass wheels, each worked with tiny Hang symbols, moved and spun according to workings she couldn't see.

The other device resembled a perfume bottle, complete with an elegant spray bulb. The glass was crystal, cut with ornate designs and gilded with delicate gold filigree.

"Hang ghosts have sticky fingers," observed Mug. "I'm beginning to like you after all."

"What are these?" asked Meralda, resisting the urge to pick them up and inspect them closer. "And why have you brought them to me?"

Donchen smiled. "This," he said, picking up the compass, "is a very simple device which will point out spellworks. Hang spellworks, I mean. Most of the arcane traditions of the Realms simply won't register, which is why the needle is ignoring the many wonders housed here and is instead pointing that way. South, isn't it? Well, our ships are docked south of here, and I'm sure that accounts for some of the indication. But see these dials? This one indicates distance. This one denotes intensity."

Donchen offered the device to Meralda, and she took it.

The needle pointed toward the door, and the tiny wheels spun and whirled.

"Those characters are numbers," said Donchen. "I'll scribble them and their Kingdom counterparts down for you before I go. We measure feet in nearly the same way. I'll leave figures for that too."

He picked up the bottle, and placed it carefully in Meralda's hand.

"This is a more, um, active magic," he said. "I hope you don't find a need for it. But, if you should find yourself facing hostile persons again, spray them with this. You'll find they cannot hide from you afterward, no matter where they run, no matter what spells they employ. If you see them again, you will know."

Meralda regarded the bottle carefully. It was nearly full of a clear liquid, and though the beveled edges of the cuts and the gold filigree made seeing inside it difficult, it seemed as though something moved deep within it.

"Don't suppose you've got a magic sword in a pocket somewhere, do you?" asked Mug. "Something a little more martial than a squirt of water to the nose?"

"Perhaps next time." Donchen rose and stretched. "I feel the need for a walk, Mage Ovis. I think I'll amble about your fair city for a bit. Perhaps I'll take in some new sights. What neighborhood would you suggest I visit, pray tell?"

Meralda rose and smiled. "I hear the area between Dorleigh and Ventham streets is interesting this time of year. You might even see a Vonat or two there, though I understand they try to keep out of sight."

Donchen nodded. "We'll just see how talented they are at that, won't we?" He bowed, tossed Mug a salute, and gathered up empty plates and dirty silverware.

"I'm sure we'll speak again soon, Mage Ovis," he said.

Meralda pulled his serving cart by her desk and helped him clear away the remains of the meal.

"I'm sure we will, Mr. Donchen," she said.

"Please. I am *sohata*. Call me Donchen. No one will hear."

"Only if you call me Meralda." Meralda blushed, for no reason she could determine.

Mug groaned and pretended to suffer a sudden attack of blight.

"You're going to trust him? Just like that?"

"Did I tell him about the Tower? Did I tell him anything he didn't already know?" Meralda stood, glared, and began to pace. "Perhaps you failed to notice he's been more than forthcoming, Mug. Far more than I."

"I think you're succumbing to his otherworldly charms," said Mug. "I think—"

"I found no evidence of dissembling on the part of the young man," said the Tower.

"Oh, what do you know? You yourself admitted you hadn't had a simple conversation in a thousand years. Now you're an expert at sizing up strangers?"

The Tower had no reply.

Meralda shook her head. *I wonder if Mug is right. I do like Donchen. There's something genuine under that self-deprecating humor.*

"Oh, he's a smooth talker, all right," muttered Mug. "But that doesn't change the fact that we know nothing about him other than what he tells us. Which he could be making up on the spot, for all we know."

"I don't think so, Mug. He's offered to help, which I need. So until he gives me a reason to distrust him, I'm not going to start."

"Fine. Just don't come crying to me when he turns out to be a Vonat in disguise."

Meralda glared. Mug tossed his leaves and glared back.

"Tower. Can you follow Donchen, watch what he does?"

"With ease." The scene in the mirror flashed, became a crow's eye view of the Hang as he pushed his serving cart back toward the kitchen.

Donchen smiled at the people he met in the halls, spoke to some, laughed with some. The image in the glass was silent, and Meralda found herself wishing she could hear what was said.

"Good thinking, mistress," said Mug. "I'll keep eyes on him while you work."

The image of Donchen shrank until it occupied only half the glass. In the other, a drawing appeared, depicting the Tower and the damaged curseworks which spun atop it.

Meralda sank back into her chair.

"All right," she said. "Let's start with the very first spell your master latched when he laid the curseworks. I need to know everything I can about the core of it, please."

The image in the glass shimmered. Some of it fell away, leaving only a whirling, tangled mass of fine lines spinning slowly against the dark.

"Observe," said the Tower. "There are four thousand, nine hundred, and fourteen elements. Each is independent of the other..."

The Tower droned on. Mug watched Donchen leave the palace. Meralda covered three pages of drawing paper with notes and sketches. Donchen ambled down crowded city streets, his hands in his pockets, his lips pursed in a carefree whistle.

Meralda called for coffee. Mug watched Donchen idle in front of stores, chat with strangers, wait and move with crowds as they were waved across streets by traffic masters.

"He's using magic of some sort," muttered Mug. "No one seems to notice he's Hang."

Meralda nodded, her pencil scratching across the page.

"It is a minor charm of concealment," said the Tower. "Phendelit in nature."

Mug imitated a derisive snort. "Stolen, then."

"Are you talking, Mug, or watching?"

"Both, mistress." Mug fell silent, his eyes intent on the glass.

Donchen stopped to speak with a skirted Eryan flower girl. He spoke. She laughed. He produced a coin, and she produced a yellow rose. Donchen took it and walked away smiling.

"Bet that's for you," whispered Mug.

And then Donchen rounded a corner. The image in the glass shifted, moving to keep the Hang centered in the glass.

As Donchen rounded the corner, he vanished.

Mug whistled and aimed a dozen suddenly rigid vines at the glass.

"Mistress!" he shouted. "He's gone!"

Meralda looked up, frowning.

The street scene in the glass turned back and forth, as though searching. Passers-by walked past, but Donchen was nowhere to be seen.

"Impressive," said the Tower.

"Impossible," sputtered Mug. "Mistress, he's made himself invisible!"

Meralda put her pencil down. "That's not possible, Mug."

"Then where is he?"

"He is precisely where he should be," said the Tower. "Observe."

The image shimmered. Meralda watched as pedestrians walked the sidewalk, and then she smiled.

"The people on the street can still see him, Mug," she said, pointing at the glass. "Watch. They're stepping aside. Slowing or speeding up to let him pass. It's just us who can't see him, because we're using a spell."

"Indeed. But see here." The Tower paused, and the glass flickered, and Donchen was once again walking down a crowded sidewalk. "I have adjusted for his spell."

Mug turned eyes toward Meralda. "That's no Phendelit spell he's using, is it, Tower?"

"It is not. I have not seen the like of it before. I surmise it is Hang."

"I'll bet a donut Mr. Fancy Pants knew you'd try to watch him, mistress," said Mug. "A bit out of character, wouldn't you say?"

"It's the Vonats he's hiding from, Mug, and you know it. He has no idea we're watching him too."

"I agree with the mage," said the Tower. "What a fascinating method of spell construction he employed."

"I'll want to see it too, when we're done here." Meralda rubbed her eyes. "If we're ever done here."

Mug groaned suddenly. "Oh, no," he said.

Meralda looked to the glass again.

Shingvere darted out of a shop, watched Donchen for a moment, and waved to someone inside. An instant later, Fromarch appeared and joined the other wizard before both began to march down the street behind Donchen.

Mug shook his leaves. "This will not end well," he said, as the two elderly wizards struggled to keep up with Donchen's leisurely pace. "A pair of trumpet sounding trolls would be less conspicuous."

The Tower spoke. "Another attempt is being made to latch a spell to my structure. I believe Donchen has detected its origin. He appears to be heading directly for it."

"Can you deflect this one too?"

"Easily. I believe it best if I allow it to latch, though. Doing so will prevent further, possibly more damaging, attempts."

A cab pulled to the curb beside Shingvere and Fromarch. A frail arm, clad in a loose white sleeve, beckoned to the wizards from the cab's suddenly opened door.

The image in the glass shifted, revealing a brief image of the side of the cab.

Loman, the Hang mage, grinned from inside. He spoke briefly, and Shingvere and Fromarch exchanged shrugs and then heaved themselves into the cab, which pulled back into traffic, pacing Donchen.

Meralda bit back an Angis word. The retired mages were known to most of Tirlin and all of Vonath. Donchen might be wearing a Tirlish face, but anyone looking for curious eyes on the street will certainly see the mages, and probably wonder about the man they seem to be following.

"Well, that does it," said Mug. "Nothing good ever came of that many wizards sneaking about."

"Tower," said Meralda. "Can you communicate with either Donchen or that bunch of meddlesome wizards?"

The Tower was silent for a moment.

"Doing so now will risk alerting any hostile practitioners in the area. Might I suggest an alternative?"

"Please."

"Finch's Movable Door."

Meralda shook her head. "We only have one of the pair. The other was burned in the palace fire."

"Mage Finch made three. He had a mistress on what is now

Hopping Way. The third door still stands, and the third key is hidden beneath Mitter's Hand of Letters."

"This is a very bad idea, mistress!"

Meralda rummaged through her desk. Pencils, pens, rulers. But there, in the top drawer, was a silver letter opener she'd received at commencement and hadn't touched since.

It wasn't as big as a dagger, but it would have to suffice.

"Oh, at least take the incinerator!"

"And ignite a dozen pedestrians, or burn down the entire block?" Meralda sighed. "Tower. What aisle, what shelf?"

"Aisle five, halfway down, fourth shelf from the bottom. I suggest you take a stool."

"Wisdom of the ages and the best he can suggest is a bloody stool," muttered Mug.

"The spell is latching to my structure now," said the Tower. "I will allow it. The spell caster is now at their most vulnerable. I suggest equal measures of haste and caution. I will be unable to communicate while I observe the latching. Fare thee well, Mage."

Meralda hiked up her skirts and ran.

Key in hand, Meralda faced Finch's Movable Door.

It leaned against the shelves. It was scuffed and dusty and the right side of it was charred nearly black. But the keyhole was intact, and the latch above it was whole.

"Mistress!" shouted Mug. "At least take a Bellringer!"

Oh, that won't attract any attention, thought Meralda. *No. This I do alone.*

She took a deep breath, pushed the old iron key into the worn old lock, and turned it.

The lock clicked. Meralda put her hand on the latch and pulled the door open. She saw only the shelves of artifacts through the open door.

She took the key from the lock, put it in her pocket, and stepped through the door and onto Hopping Way.

Blinking, Meralda stepped down the three worn stone steps that led from the weather-beaten door at her back. A tabby cat looked up at her with impassive green eyes and then padded away, tail flicking.

Pedestrians hurried past. None stared or drew back or even paused for a second glance. *Whatever spells Finch employed,* thought Meralda, *they were subtle.*

Meralda remained on the last step, looking for landmarks or any sign of Donchen or the three wizards. There, just four buildings down, she recognized the whipping flag of the Royal Post Office, and she realized she was perhaps a full city block ahead of Donchen and his erstwhile entourage.

Which puts me practically next door to the Vonats, she thought. The silver letter opener felt very small and dull in her hand. *What if Finch's Door revealed my presence?*

The Hang pointer in her pocket made a soft clicking sound. Meralda withdrew it, opened the case, and watched as the needle swung to face a point toward the Vonat compound.

The numbers in the dials whirled and finally settled. Meralda recalled Donchen's voice as he had counted aloud in Hang, pointing to each character as he spoke.

Five hundred and forty feet. The spell caster was only five hundred and forty feet from where she stood. Which meant Fromarch and Shingvere were only five hundred and forty feet from rushing headlong into the fringes of a Vonat spell.

Meralda darted off the step, nimbly fell in step behind a Phendelit flower girl, and headed toward Donchen.

As she walked, a pair of shadows fluttered past. Crows?

Meralda put her head down and hurried past the flower girl.

Donchen was indeed concealing his almond-shaped eyes and inky black hair behind a charm. The spell lent him the appearance of a weary Eryan dock worker, complete with battered felt cap and sooty, calloused hands from handling dirigible mooring ropes.

But the spell failed to extend to his soft-soled shoes. Meralda spotted them instantly, gliding down the sidewalk, and she put herself square in his path.

He stopped, his bearded Eryan face breaking into a wide grin.

"You're being followed," said Meralda, before he could speak. She caught his elbow and guided him off the sidewalk and into the doorway of a cigar shop.

"Really? What an amazing day I'm having. By whom?"

"Loman. And mages Shingvere and Fromarch. They're even sharing a cab."

Donchen sighed and rubbed his face. His hand passed through the specter of his beard. "Marvelous. Do you think our spell casting friend has spotted them yet? He's trying to transport a rather large spell, by the way. Where to, I have no idea."

"I know." Meralda wished Donchen was wearing his own face. "It's aimed at the Tower. I'll know more once it's latched. But for now, I need to keep Fromarch and Shingvere as far away from the Vonats as possible. They'll detect it, too, and there's no telling what they might do."

"Something involving a massive explosion, I surmise." Donchen put a finger to his chin. "I don't think anyone has seen me. Shall I go on ahead, see what I can see?"

Meralda nodded. "Go. I'll turn the mages around. But do be careful, won't you?"

"I am a ghost," said Donchen, with a smile. "As such, I have little to fear."

And he sauntered out of the doorway, and vanished into the crowd.

Meralda resisted an urge to watch him go. "Your shoes," she called, not knowing if he heard, or understood.

Then she whirled and made her way up the street in the opposite direction, darting to the edge of the sidewalk so she could see oncoming cabs well before they passed.

"We almost ran you over," growled Fromarch.

"What you almost did was ride headlong into a Vonat spell," said Meralda, forcing herself to keep her voice lowered to whisper. "And you waving the Infinite Latch around! What do you think might have happened if the Vonat had decided to hurl something your way?"

"We'd have ruined a room or two, what with all those stinking Vonat ashes," said Shingvere, waggling a finger at Meralda. "We're hardly first years, you know. I have done a bit of magic in my time."

Meralda hushed him with a furious gesture. All around them, bemused diners looked on, forks paused in mid-raise, ears turned and listening.

Loman, the elderly Hang wizard, laughed to himself as he tried to wrap Phendelit noodles around his fork.

"You still haven't told me what the three of you were out doing," said Meralda.

"We're just three old men, out enjoying a cab ride," said Fromarch. "Isn't that right?"

"Nonsense." Meralda glared. Loman met her gaze and winked. "Why were you following Donchen?"

"Who?"

"Never met the man."

"Donchen is dead," said Loman, in perfect New Kingdom. "How does one follow a ghost?"

"You're insufferable, the lot of you!" Meralda pushed back her chair and rose. "Do I have your words, as gentlemen and scholars, that you will take a cab back home and stay there? Please?"

Fromarch exchanged shrugs with Shingvere. "Fine. We've got a bit of beer to drink, as I recall."

"We certainly do."

Loman nodded owlishly. "I myself enjoy the occasional fermented beverage."

Meralda glared, turned, and stalked out of the diner.

Fromarch let the door slam shut before speaking.

"How did she know?"

"Search me," said Shingvere. "I was sure she was holed up in the laboratory."

"She is a very clever young woman," said Loman. "Do you often see crows inside your eateries?"

Fromarch frowned. "Never."

"My old eyes," replied Loman. "So, shall we do as your mage bids, and go home?"

"Eventually," said Shingvere. "Eventually."

Fromarch grinned and waved to the waiter for a check.

Chapter Fifteen

Meralda made her way back to the weather-beaten door on Hopping Way, put her key in the lock, and stepped through the door and into the dark narrow space between shelves in the back of the laboratory.

Traffic noise followed her until she closed the door.

"Mistress!" cried Mug. "Quick! Donchen is up to something."

Meralda darted out the aisle, dodging treasures as she ran.

Mug followed her progress with a single eye while he kept the other twenty-eight trained on the mirror. Inside the glass, Donchen sat on a bench at a trolley stop and read the *Times*.

Meralda leaned on her desk and tried to catch her breath.

"He's reading the paper," she said.

"Wait."

Donchen turned the page.

A bright yellow butterfly fluttered from the paper and flew quickly up and away, beyond the view of the mirror.

"That happens every time he turns the page." Mug waved his fronds. "Tower claims the butterflies are hidden by the same spell that made him invisible."

"The insects are massing around the building occupied by the spell caster," said the Tower. Its voice was muted and distant.

"Can you tell what they're meant to do?"

The Tower did not reply.

"Guess that's a no, mistress," said Mug. "That cab almost ran you down, by the way."

"So I'm told." Meralda pulled back her chair and sank wearily into it. "So our ghost is also a magician, if not a mage himself."

"Cook, mage, spy, ghost—when does the man sleep?"

Meralda picked up her pencil and idly began to doodle tiny Towers on a page of shadow latch calculations.

"The Vonats are up to something, Mug."

"Do tell." The dandyleaf plant turned a half dozen eyes toward Meralda. "Wait, did you see something, out there?"

Meralda shook her head no. *I didn't see a thing,* she thought. But an awful suspicion was blooming, and with it anger. "They're trying to latch something to the Tower." She added the tethers and the curseworks to her drawing. "Why do you think they'd pick the Tower, of all things? Why not the palace? Why not the Gold Room itself?"

Mug shrugged.

"Because they know about my shadow moving spell," said Meralda. "*My* spell. We know someone hid spells in the palace. Which means someone has been listening. In fact—Sir Ricard. I'd bet a purse of Vonat gold doubloons he's been waiting for weeks to give Yvin that ridiculous idea about moving the Tower's shadow."

Mug went still.

"Mistress."

"Yes. I think so. I think the spell they're latching to the Tower is intended to do something awful at the opening ceremony of the Accords. I think the Vonat are working with that small group of Hang Donchen mentioned. I think they want to wreck any chance of the Hang joining the Realms peacefully, and I think they plan to blame the whole thing on me."

"Make it appear as if your shadow moving spell goes wrong?"

Meralda nodded, her jaw clamped too tight to speak. *They mean to kill a great many people as Yvin gives his speech,* she thought. *The Hang delegation among them.* Ruin the Accords, infuriate the Hang, leave the Realms divided and weak. And all of it blamed squarely on her. On the female Tirlish mage, who had no business ever donning the robes in the first place.

Mug rolled a dozen eyes. "They don't know about the curseworks, though."

"No. Otherwise they'd simply have attacked them directly, and in secret."

Mug shivered. He looked toward the mirror, watched as Donchen released another yellow butterfly, and muttered an Angis word.

"Mistress, what are we going to do?"

Meralda's pencil lead broke. She rose.

"Nameless. Faceless. Right here, right now."

Mug went wide-eyed.

From the rear of the laboratory, amid the shadows and glittering and whirring and hissing, came the sound of fluttering wings. A pair of dark shapes darted down from the ceiling, and came to rest on either side of Meralda before assuming the forms of two rough hewn lengths of ironwood.

"I am not, nor will I ever be, your master, or his equal." Meralda swallowed, searching for her next words. *They're as likely to strike me down as they are to agree,* she thought. *But if I'm going up against the entire Vonat nation and who knows how much of the Hang, I need them.*

"Tower believes your master would not want this place laid waste by his hand," she said. "You either agree, or you do not. If you do, I ask for your help now. Not for me. Not even for Tirlin. But in deference to your master, who is fallen, but whose wishes nevertheless remain unfulfilled." She raised her hands, not quite touching the staves, but only a hand's breadth from them.

"What say you, Nameless, Faceless?"

"Mistress, I wouldn't..."

Meralda took each staff in her hand.

The laboratory fell silent, save for the gentle clicking of Phillitrep's Engine.

The staves were cool and unmoving in Meralda's grasp.

"Well, I'll be mowed and pruned," said Mug, after a while. "Congratulations, mistress. Tim the Horsehead just turned green with envy."

Meralda took a deep breath, and hoped the staves couldn't feel her shiver.

"Find the Vonat mage Humindorus Nam," she said. "I want one of you watching him at all times. See that you aren't observed yourselves. Can you project images into the mirror?"

The mirror flashed, showing a brief reflection of Meralda holding the staves.

"Good. I want to know where he is and what he's doing, starting right now. Show him when I ask. Show him even when I don't if he does anything interesting. Go."

The staves became blurs. With the sound of flapping wings, they vanished into the Mirror.

Meralda let out her breath in a long exhalation.

"That was brave," said the Tower. "Very brave indeed."

Meralda mopped sweat from her forehead and grinned. "Is the spell latched?"

"It is. I am now attempting to determine its nature. Part of the structure is Vonat in nature. Part is unknown to me."

"Hang."

"Most likely. I overheard your conversation with the construct. You believe this spell is offensive in nature."

"The construct's name is Mug," said the dandyleaf plant.

"I do," said Meralda. "Designed to release in tandem with my shadow spell."

"Ingenious."

"Is it doing further damage to the curseworks?"

"No. I was able to adjust the latching point. That, at least, is not a concern."

"Hurrah for small miracles," said Meralda. She sighed, glared at her empty coffee cup, and looked wearily toward the door.

"Mug, please watch the glass. Tower, I need a way to speak to you beyond this room. I assume there are other artifacts you have trifled with, over the years?"

"Fourteen, to be exact. All designed for observation, but two will suffice for communication. Tulip's Talking Jewel, and Montrop's Singing Flame."

"You're a nosy old barn, aren't you?" said Mug.

"The jewel, then. It should fit in my pocket. Aisle four, isn't it? Shelf, um, sixteen?"

"Just so."

Meralda marched off to fetch the jewel, and Mug turned his worried eyes back toward the glass.

"The sticks just sent word about Nam," said Mug, his voice squeaky and barely audible from the Jewel. "He's using some kind of fancy concealment spell. Tower thinks it might be Hang. The sticks think they can break it, but he'll probably notice if they do."

Meralda frowned and lifted the jewel close to her lips, covering it with her hand and pretending to stifle a sneeze.

"Tell them to wait," she said. "Tell them to stay close to the Vonat rooms. See if they can get a count of the people inside. But only if they can do so without being seen."

Meralda could hear Mug relaying the instructions to the Tower.

Her open topped cab pitched and bounced. Her cabman glanced back over his shoulder and smiled at her before quickly turning his attention back toward the busy street.

"Done," said Mug. "Donchen is gone, by the way. Heading back to the palace, on foot. If he shows up here, what do I tell the Bellringers to tell him?"

"Ask him to meet me for a late supper," said Meralda. "In the lab."

"Ooooo," replied Mug. "Shall I order flowers and violins?"

Meralda rolled her eyes and shoved the jewel deep into her pocket.

My feet ache, she thought. She'd used Finch's Door again to sneak out of the laboratory, hailing the first cab she saw after stepping onto Hopping Way. If the Vonats could sense the door opening, she knew she was undone. But old Finch's handiwork was nothing if not subtle. Even the Tower had marveled at its silence, in strictly magical terms.

And if the Vonats are watching me, it's best they see the Bellringers by my doors and think I'm still inside. Especially given where I'm heading, and what I'm about to do, she thought.

What I'm about to do. Is this the right thing? Am I saving Tirlin, or dooming it?

I wonder if Tim the Horsehead ever wondered that very thing.

Probably, Meralda decided. *After all, Tim's exploits were rather more desperate than mine. He was lucky, more often than not.*

I wonder if someday, some mage will say the same about me.

"We're here, ma'am," said the cabman, urging his ponies to a halt.

Meralda stepped out of the cab, placed a handful of coins into the man's palm, and hurried up the steps and into the shade of Fromarch's red brick house.

Fromarch himself met her at his door. "Took you long enough." He shoved a bottle of Nolbit's in her hand. "We're all here, Mage. I reckon you've got things to tell us."

Meralda took a long draught of the beer. "That I do, she said. "And you'd best lock the door."

"So the Tower is haunted after all," said Shingvere.

In the middle of the room, a single candle burned. Fromarch's tiny sitting room was midnight dark, and with all the windows shuttered and bolted the air was hot and stale. Meralda could barely make out the three wizards who faced her, and could read nothing in their faces.

Beside the candle sat a crude contrivance of wood and glass, which hummed and buzzed and sometimes spat tiny showers of bright blue sparks. Fromarch insisted it would render any attempt at arcane eavesdropping futile, and Meralda fervently hoped the elderly wizard was correct.

"She never said it was haunted, you daft old Eryan," muttered Fromarch. "She said it was alive. Bit of a difference."

"Gentlemen!" Meralda took a breath. "Please. Tirlin is in danger. It's up to us to save it."

"I was right about the Tower all along, but I see your point, Mage Ovis." Shingvere leaned forward, his face grim and unsmiling in the wash of flickering candle light. "So how do you intend to fight?"

Loman, the Hang wizard, raised his finger and smiled.

"Before you answer, young mage, it would perhaps be wise to dismiss me. I will take no offense. You do not know me. You are under no obligation to trust me."

"Shingvere. Fromarch. Do you trust this gentleman?"

"Aye."

"Without reservation."

"Then so do I. Please, sir, remain. This concerns you as well, since your people are being targeted."

Loman bowed his head briefly. "As you wish. Know that I am honored."

Meralda smiled, and the old man grinned back.

"I plan to allow the Vonats to believe they have latched a killing spell to the Tower," she said. "I plan to keep them believing that, right up until the hour Yvin takes the stage. Tower is studying the spell now. With any luck, I can render it harmless without alerting anyone that I've done so."

Fromarch nodded. "And the curseworks?"

"They will have to be stabilized or removed."

"Bit of a tall order, that."

"That's why she's Mage of Tirlin," said Shingvere. "Still, that's a lot for any one person to do, Meralda. Especially with who knows how many Vonats running around doing who knows what kind of mischief in the meantime."

"That's where you gentlemen can help. I need the Vonats, and any Hang helping them, kept busy for the next seven days. The Vonats want trouble at the Accords? Well, gentlemen, I say we give them trouble. Just not the kind they planned."

"What kind then?"

Meralda grinned. "Magical trouble. I don't care what kind. Just keep their mages busy chasing will-o-the-wisps. Make them think their Hang partners are spying on them. Make them think I am. Make them waste time. Make them waste effort." Meralda stood and smoothed her skirts. "The contents of the laboratory are at your disposal. I won't watch and I won't ask. Just don't burn down any historic landmarks. Can I trust you gentlemen? To make trouble?"

Fromarch slapped his knee and guffawed. "Oh, that you can, Mage. That you can, indeed."

"Anything for old Tirlin," said Shingvere, his eyes glinting in the candlelight. "Especially that."

Loman just smiled and sipped at his beer.

Meralda risked Hopping Way again and stepped through Finch's Door to return to the laboratory.

Mug greeted her with a mock salute. "All quiet," he reported. "Tower, any word from the sticks about Nam?"

"None."

"Are there any signs I was observed using the door?"

"Again, none. I believe the door's operation is unknown to anyone save us."

"I hope so." Meralda made for the doors and opened them just enough to speak through them. "I'd like some coffee and something to eat," she said.

"Yes, ma'am," chorused the Bellringers. Kervis frowned and tilted his head. "Ma'am, are you all right?"

"I'm fine, Guardsman," she said. "Just a bit hungry."

"Tervis spoke from beyond the door. "I smelled fried chicken earlier. Will that do?"

"Indeed it will. Thank you." Meralda closed the door.

"Mistress," called Mug. "Have a look."

Goboy's glass showed a door. A pair of black crows regarded the door with curious stares for a moment before taking flight. The glass did not follow.

"Nameless and Faceless." Meralda sat. The door opened, and a man stepped out into the sun.

"So this must be Humindorus Nam."

Meralda saw a tall man, dressed all in black, from the soles of his knee-high leather boots to the cowl of the robe that hid his eyes. He took a single step out into the sun, and then he produced a pair of dark lensed spectacles from a pocket and slipped them over his long beak of a nose.

That was the only time Meralda saw his face, though she never saw his eyes. She did see long shocks of greasy black hair, uncombed and wild, falling over a face dark with stubble. His mouth was a thin pale line set in a scowl.

And then the cowl fell over his face, leaving only a shadowed narrow chin.

"A bit melodramatic, wouldn't you say?" said Mug. "All he needs is a necklace made of skulls to complete the whole penny-novel villain look."

"The staves advise they will follow," said the Tower. "I discern no fewer than two dozen active spells latched to this man's person."

"Then he's suicidal," said Mug. "Latching spells to oneself is insane, isn't it, mistress?"

Meralda nodded assent.

So this is Humindorus Nam, she thought. *The most feared wizard in all of Vonath. The man who rose to his rank over the bodies of his rivals.*

The man who is determined to crush Tirlin and use me as his vise.

"Ask the staves to fan out," said Meralda. "I want to know if he's traveling with bodyguards."

Mug swiveled a dozen eyes toward Meralda. "The captain claimed he didn't have any, that using bodyguards would be considered a sign of weakness in Vonath."

"We're not in Vonath." Meralda watched Humindorus walk, watched as other pedestrians stepped out of his way and averted their gazes.

His strides were long and fast. His arms hung straight at his sides, his hands clenched into fists inside their black leather gloves.

"I don't see any butterflies," said Meralda, after a time. "Tower? Are they out of view?"

The image in the glass changed, as though the glass were snatched suddenly up into the air high above the street. No bright yellow butterflies fluttered below.

"No. Whatever their purpose, it appears they are not reacting to the wizard's departure."

The scene returned to street level, centered on the black-clad wizard's march through Tirlin.

"Thank you." Meralda pulled back her hair and yawned. "Mug, keep an eye on Ugly. Tower, ask the staves to keep their distance."

"Aye, Captain!"

"As you wish, Mage."

Meralda forced herself to look away from the image of Humindorus Nam's determined march through Tirlin. *No time for that now,* she thought. *As nasty as he looks, we have bigger problems.*

"Tower," she said, pulling a fresh piece of drawing paper from the stack at the corner of her desk. "I've had a thought. About the curseworks." She tested her pencil on the paper, and decided it was sharp enough to suffice. "Tell me about the composition of the outermost bindings."

The Tower began to speak. Meralda's pencil made tell-tale scratching noises on the paper.

Mug never took his eyes off the tall Vonat striding toward the palace in the glass.

"Mistress, pardon, but our Vonat friend is headed for the palace," said Mug.

"I expected as much. Never mind. Show me the Vonat boarding house, please."

The image shifted, becoming a crow's eye view of the buildings along Ventham Street.

"Are we looking for anything in particular, mistress?"

Meralda stabbed at the glass with her pencil. "That," she said. "Look."

A hundred yellow butterflies suddenly took silent flight.

"Our ghost friend has been busy," said Mug. "Look, they're splitting up."

The butterflies diverged, high in the air, flapping away in all directions. The image in the glass moved again, showing a view from on high.

All around the Vonat boarding house, doors opened, and furtive men came darting out. Each was accompanied by a tiny flock of yellow butterflies, flying so high Meralda knew they would be completely invisible from the street.

Once the last of the two dozen men had vanished from the glass, a stooped old man sweeping the sidewalk in front of a cigar shop straightened, put his broom against the wall, and sauntered away, stooped no more.

"He's good at this ghost business, I'll give him that," said Mug. "His butterflies follow the conspirators, and Donchen follows the butterflies."

"So it would seem."

Mug tapped the glass with a leaf. "And then what?"

What, indeed? Meralda rubbed her eyes and glared at the paper she'd covered with notes and diagrams. *What happens to the Vonats and their Hang conspirators will make little difference, if all of Tirlin is consumed by fire and pestilence a few days from now.*

Kervis knocked at the laboratory doors, and then shouted through them. "Pardon me, ma'am, but you might want to see this message," he said. "It's from the captain. Marked 'read me right now'."

Meralda stood and stretched. Her back hurt and her eyes watered and she wanted nothing more than a good hot soak in a bathtub and a good night's sleep on her soft, warm bed.

"Let me guess," she muttered, as she made for the laboratory doors. "I'm about to have visitors."

She threw the doors open. The Bellringers gazed inside, a nervous palace runner peeking into the laboratory from behind the brothers.

"Here it is, ma'am," said Kervis. Meralda took the envelope, tore it open, and read.

"Bad news, ma'am?"

"The captain will be here in a quarter of an hour," she said. "With half a dozen Vonat dignitaries."

"Including the wizard?" asked Kervis.

Meralda nodded, then put her hand gently on Kervis' hand when he reached for his sword.

"None of that. It's just a visit. They'll be excruciatingly polite, and so will I. And so will you two. Understood?"

The Bellringers nodded assent in reluctant unison.

"Knock when they arrive. Tervis, please keep your brother from skewering anyone. Tensions are high enough as it is."

"Yes, ma'am."

Meralda smiled at the brothers and closed the door.

She turned, took a deep breath, and marched back toward her desk.

"You're not going to let that creature in here, are you?"

"It's a tradition, Mug. But that doesn't mean I can't tidy up a bit first." She reached her desk and began filling its drawers with her notes and drawings, stuffing them hastily inside and shoving at them until they fit. "I need a plain reflection in the glass, please. Nothing more while our visitors are here."

The glass flashed, became nothing but a mirror, tarnished with age and neglect.

"The staves have opted to remain with you," said the Tower, as two dark shapes emerged from the glass and flitted toward the shadowed ranks of shelves. "I have warned them against any displays unless your life is in imminent peril."

Meralda frowned, but nodded. *I can hardly take them in hand and throw them out.*

Mug bunched his eyes together. Meralda caressed his topmost leaves and leaned down to meet his worried gaze. "He won't try anything here, Mug. You know that. So please, be civil, or be silent."

"Silent it is," he muttered. "Tower, can you still see through the glass, even now?"

"I can. They are approaching the door."

Meralda waggled her forefinger before Mug's eyes. "Hold the tongue you don't have, Mugglewort Ovis. Promise me."

"I promise."

"Good."

A knock sounded at the door. Meralda took a deep breath and made her way across the room to greet the Vonat wizard.

"Well, what a pleasant surprise," said Meralda, as she threw open both of the laboratory's ancient doors. "Welcome to the Royal Thaumaturgical Laboratory of Tirlin."

The captain did not return what Meralda hoped was her sweetest, most winning smile.

"May I present our honored guests from noble Vonath," said the captain, in a near growl. "Ambassador Moring."

A thin hawkish man, clad all in severe Vonat black, clicked his heels together as he executed the smallest of Vonat bows toward Meralda.

"Colonel Stranth."

Another heel click and bow, by another rangy Vonat. Meralda smiled at both men, who seemed intent on communicating their utter disdain for all things Tirlish with nothing but piercing, clench-jawed glares.

"Baron Stefan von Drake."

The aging baron met Meralda's smile with a leer and a brief whispered comment in Vonat to his fellows. The captain's face flushed the color of day old steak.

"The Mage to the Crown of Vonat, Humindorus Nam."

The Vonat mage came forward to stand before Meralda.

No, thought Meralda, as he approached. *He hasn't come to stand before me. He's come to stand over me. I hadn't realized how tall he is, from watching him in the glass.*

The Vonat sauntered between his companions, even forcing the baron to take a hasty step back lest he be bowled over by the wizard.

"So." He halted directly in front of Meralda, towering two feet over her. *Forcing me to crane my head to look up,* realized Meralda. *What a petty little man.* "The stories are true. Tirlin's mage is a woman."

"So I am told," replied Meralda. "Imagine my shock upon learning my gender from a newspaper article."

The Vonat's pale face flushed. Someone, Meralda suspected the captain, though she did not look away from Nam to see, stifled a snort of laughter.

Meralda kept her smile wide. The Vonat's bloodshot eyes bore into hers.

"So you've come for the traditional visit," said Meralda, brightly. "Well, I certainly don't want to keep you waiting. Won't you come in?"

The Vonat glared. Meralda kept her smile, stepped aside, and motioned toward the laboratory.

The Vonat stepped across the threshold. His companions moved to follow, but Meralda stepped in front of them, her hand uplifted.

"Tradition demands that the mage may visit," she said. "The rest of you may find ample seating on yonder stair."

The captain and three Vonats lifted their voices in protest.

Meralda slammed the door.

The Vonat turned at the sound. His face fell into a scowl.

"How dare you refuse my countrymen entry," he began.

Meralda shrugged. "Tradition demands that the Vonat mage be given a tour of the laboratory. It says nothing about ambassadors or barons."

Humindorus bristled. His left eyelid began to twitch.

"I am not accustomed to being spoken to in this fashion."

"How terrible. I suggest you lodge a formal complaint with your embassy. Now then." Meralda turned and pointed to the rear of the laboratory. "Back there, you see the Royal Repository of Arcane Artifacts. Over there is the Royal Water Closet. Yonder sits my desk. The rather attractive chair is mine as well." She put her hands on her hips and let her forced smile fall.

"I believe that concludes your tour, Mage. I'm sure you have many other duties to attend. Please feel free to drop by again when Tirlin next hosts the Accords, in twenty years or so. Good day."

I may have pushed too far just then, Meralda thought. Indeed, the Vonat's face was nearly purple with rage.

Would he dare lift a hand against me here?

"Insolent *woman,*" hissed the mage. "You know not who you abuse."

"Oh, I know perfectly well who I'm abusing," said Meralda. She found her smile again. "I'll not waste time pretending to be civil. Not on the likes of you. Show yourself out, won't you? I have work to do. Mage's work."

Meralda turned her back on the furious wizard, and marched toward her desk, counting the steps as she went.

One, two, three...

"We will meet again, girl. Oh yes. We will meet again."

Meralda waved briefly over her shoulder. She did not look back.

Four, five, six...

The laboratory doors were flung open with a bang. Booted feet stamped angrily from the room. Voices were raised outside, cut off as the doors slammed shut again.

Meralda reached her desk and sagged against it.

Mug's leaves whipped as if in a windstorm. "What was that, mistress? If he wasn't intent on murder before he certainly is now."

Meralda mopped sweat from her forehead and managed a grin. "Men who rage commit rash acts."

"Murder chief among them," said Mug. He emulated a heavy sigh. "Wait. I recognize the raging quote. Tim the Horsehead, isn't it?"

Meralda nodded, glad Mug couldn't hear the pounding of her heart.

"Mistress. I hope you know what you're doing. The man's name means life-taker, remember? No telling how many mages he killed just to print that on his stationary."

"What was I supposed to do? Serve him tea, polish those ridiculous boots?" Meralda yanked back her chair and sat. "As long as his attention is on me, it's not on the Tower. Heaven help us all if he finds the curseworks and realizes what they are."

"I am taking every effort to ensure that does not happen," said the Tower. The image in the glass shimmered and showed Humindorus Nam's thin back stamping down the stair, his cloak flapping behind him like a pair of furled wings. "You should note, however, that the wizard left behind a listening charm when you turned your back."

Mug squealed. The Tower continued. "Nameless rendered it useless. He has heard nothing."

"Thank you, Nameless," said Meralda. A shadow flitted across the ceiling.

A furious knock sounded at the door. "Mage!" cried the

captain. "Meralda! Are you all right?"

"Come in," cried Meralda. "I'm fine."

The captain and the Bellringers spilled through the door. Meralda turned in her chair to face them.

"What the devil...?" began the captain.

"I wanted a word with the mage, Captain. Alone."

The captain bit back his response. Tervis and Kervis exchanged glances, but took their hands off their sword hilts.

"He wasn't rude to you, was he, ma'am?" asked Kervis.

"No more than I expected." Meralda shook her head. "I am the mage to Tirlin," she said. "I appreciate your concern. I do, really. But I'm neither helpless nor foolish."

"No." The captain took in a great breath. "Forgive me, Mage Ovis. You know what you're doing."

Meralda smiled. "You need not apologize for being concerned, Captain. I'm concerned too. Which is why I'll ask you to assign as many keen eyed young men as you can spare to follow our Vonat friend about for the remainder of the Accords."

The captain tilted his head. "You know of course that we're already doing that."

"I suspected as much. Have these young men of yours been seen?"

"Not once. They're very good."

"Then assign a few with less skill. Encourage them to keep a safe distance. Just make sure the Vonat knows his movements are being watched."

The captain grinned. "Consider it done, Mage. Anything else?"

"Coffee. Lots of coffee." Meralda sighed. "And bring me a proper dagger. Not fancy or ornamental. One that fits in a boot."

The captain nodded, all humor gone. "At once. Tervis, fetch the mage her coffee. I'll stand watch in your place."

The captain winked, and the trio backed through the doors, closing them softly behind them.

The pot of coffee was empty when the Bellringers accompanied Fromarch through the laboratory doors.

The aging wizard bore a box of jelly filled pastries from Flayne's and a moth eaten burlap bag.

"Ho, Mage," he said, opening the box and offering the contents to Meralda. "Oh, go on, take one. You could use a bit of flesh on those skinny bones. Hello, houseplant. You're looking as leafy as ever."

Mug returned a mock salute. "Mage. Grey fur suits you."

Fromarch chuckled and bowed toward Goboy's glass. "Tower. I don't believe we've met, formally."

"Mage," said the Tower. "Greetings."

Fromarch nodded gravely. "After all these years. You could have said hello before, you know. I wouldn't have charged off telling the papers."

The Tower had no reply. Fromarch shrugged and grabbed a pastry. "Well, if you're not going to eat them I will, Meralda. Cost me a bloody five pence, you know."

Meralda rolled her eyes, but selected a cherry filled donut

and bit into it.

She closed her eyes, savoring the flavor. "I had forgotten how good these are."

"You've likely forgotten to eat at all today, I'll wager," muttered Fromarch. He wiped his lips on his sleeve. "But I'm not your mother. Came to fill this bag. Do you want to know what with?"

"Will knowing cause me to lose sleep?"

"Without a doubt. You said cause trouble. That's what our daft Eryan friend and the old Hang gentleman intend to do. We need a few things from the shelves. Bad things." The old wizard's face split into a rare grin. "Bad, bad things."

Meralda swallowed and raised her hands. "Take what you need. I don't want to know."

"Not even a hint?"

"Not even a hint."

Fromarch nodded. "Well, you might want to release the wards on aisle eight," he said. "Lots of bad things there."

Aisle eight. The relics from the second century. The Vonat War. Meralda forced a nod and rose, heading for the ward sigils hidden behind a false stone to the left of the doors.

"Oh. The red crate on the north wall. I'll want in that, too."

Meralda spoke the words that revealed the row of hidden sigils, and then traced the release pattern on the aisle eight ward.

"The red crate? The one every mage since the two hundreds has been warned never to open?"

"Always wanted to see what was in that bugger," said Fromarch. "If we don't know, the Vonats certainly don't. It feels like a night for surprises, don't you agree?"

Meralda bit her lip. "Are you sure about this?"

"'Fraid so, Mage. We're up against Hang magic we don't understand. We need something they aren't expecting."

Meralda spoke the word and traced a glowing pattern in the air.

"Done," she said. Another word hid the sigils. Meralda turned, but Fromarch was already disappearing among the shelves, humming a merry tune as he made for aisle eight.

"Good luck," said Meralda. Fromarch shouted something unintelligible back in reply.

The Tower spoke. "The contents of the red crate are known to me," it began.

"Will the contents wreak havoc on Tirlin and visit upon us widespread destruction this very night?"

"No. They are..."

Meralda made a motion for silence. "I don't want to know, Tower. Unless you think the mages can't control it."

"Their combined skills should prove sufficient."

"Then let's get back to work. I have an idea about the damaged tethers. I need to know how they maintain their spacing, as they rotate."

Meralda found her chair and sank back into it. The box of pastries sat on a corner of her desk, still open, the scent of fresh donuts wafting from it.

Meralda grabbed another and bit into it.

The Tower chuckled and began to speak, drawing symbols and equations in the glass as it did so.

Meralda counted chimes and stretched as four hundred and ninety-six timekeeping devices in the laboratory chimed out nine o'clock, all at once.

Nine o'clock. I must get a better chair, thought Meralda. *Something with a cushion.*

Above her came the faint sound of beating wings. Shadows flitted across the ceiling.

"One comes," said the Tower. "Donchen. The Hang."

"Is he perhaps pushing a silver cart?"

"Just so," said the Tower. "I shall conceal myself."

Meralda stood. "No. Not this time. He's either a friend and ally, or he's not. I believe he means no harm. Do you concur?"

Mug surprised Meralda by remaining quiet.

"As you wish, Mage Ovis."

There came a knock at the door. "Supper," called Kervis. "Smells good, ma'am."

Meralda rose and opened the doors. Donchen, clad in his purloined kitchen garb, greeted her with a wide smile.

"Hungry, Mage?"

"Famished," said Meralda. "Do come in."

Donchen handed bags to the Bellringers, and then pushed his cart inside.

"Fascinating," he said, peering into the glass as Tower caused a drawing of the tethers and the curseworks to spin and move. "And those have been there, deadly but unseen, for most of Tirlin's history?"

Meralda nodded. Donchen's meal, four courses, appetizers and a dessert, was making her eyes heavy. As if sensing her thoughts, Donchen rose nimbly to his feet, rummaged about in his serving cart, and finally withdrew a silver carafe and a pair of dainty white cups.

"Coffee?" asked Meralda.

"Coffee is sadly lacking compared to Hang beverages," replied Donchen. "But I hope you will find this equally invigorating. We call it chai-see. It's a tea, of sorts, made from the leaves of a plant with a variety of therapeutic properties." He sat the cups down amid the remains of the meal and poured both nearly full.

"To your health, Mage Ovis."

Meralda lifted her cup. The aroma from it was minty and sharp, reminding her of Shingvere's sweet sticks melted and mixed with cinnamon.

Donchen drank, and Meralda sipped at hers before smiling and drinking half the cup in a single delicious gulp.

"I knew you'd like it." Donchen's eyes twinkled. "I'll see that a tin or three makes its way to your door, Mage. I'll be violating a number of export acts by doing so, of course."

"I wouldn't have it any other way."

Mug stifled a small gagging sound. Donchen chuckled and lowered his cup.

"As long as I'm breaking my homeland's laws, Mage, I might as well give you this, as well." He reached into his shirt and withdrew a folded piece of paper. "Each of these persons had a butterfly relaxing on their doors or windows this afternoon," he added. "Some are Hang. Some are Vonat. Some, I fear, are Tirls."

Meralda took the paper.

"I would be most appreciative if that list found its way to both your king and my countryman, Loman," said Donchen. "Of course, you need not tell Loman where you got it. After all, ghosts can't make lists of traitors, can they?"

"How many names?"

"Thirty-seven. Nineteen are Vonats. Twelve, sadly, are my countrymen, arrived with me. Six are Tirlish, of various stations, mostly palace staff simply paid to look the other way so spells can be laid. Disturbing, is it not?"

"Deeply." Meralda put the list in her desk.

Donchen merely nodded and refilled her cup.

The Hang tea banished the heaviness from Meralda's limbs and left her feeling, if not fresh and alert, at least not weary and sluggish.

By the time Donchen's tea was gone, she and the Hang had covered three large pages of drawing paper with notes, and Meralda was finally beginning to see how the curseworks had remained in motion about the flat for so long without failing.

She caught herself chewing on the end of her pencil and blushed at Donchen's grin. "So each cursework is actually falling."

The Hang nodded. "But doing so sideways. That's the part I can't understand."

Meralda stabbed at a corner of the topmost paper with her pencil. "It's right here," she said. "He put a right angle on gravity. On *gravity*." She shook her head. "History just tells us the man was ruthless and powerful. But he was brilliant, more than anything else he might have been. The man turned gravity on its side just to make his spell more efficient."

"Thus keeping the entire structure turning without requiring a latched spell of any kind," said the Tower. "Well done, Mage Ovis. That single surmise escaped me for seven centuries."

Mug blew a fanfare of trumpets and bugles until Meralda silenced him with a glare.

"But we're no closer to repairing it than we were an hour ago. Tower, how long until the tethers fail?"

"Two hundred and eight hours, Mage. Give or take seven hours."

Donchen pointed to the image in the glass. "The damage to the tethers seems irreparable, at least to my untrained and ignorant eye."

"Hah," said Mug. "Untrained. Ignorant. Pull the other leg, won't you?"

Donchen pretended not to hear.

"It seems to me, though, that Mage Ovis has a certain detailed understanding of the structures involved."

Meralda shook her head. "I'm a long way from being able to

repair them," she said. "Certainly longer than two hundred hours."

Donchen nodded assent. "Repairing them seems an impossible task."

"I must concur," said the Tower. "Perhaps it is time to consider an evacuation of the city and surrounding countryside."

"If the tethers cannot be repaired, they must be replaced," said Donchen. He turned to face Meralda. "Do you agree, Mage Ovis?"

Shivers ran up and down Meralda's spine. "He laid gravity on its side," she said, quietly. "I am not Otrinvion. I could live to be five hundred and I still wouldn't be Otrinvion."

"No. But you are Meralda Ovis. You enchanted Mug to life when you were thirteen. You entered college that same year. You alone, of all Tirlin's mages, found the Tower's secret. We believe in you, Mage Ovis. Now you must only find a belief in yourself."

"What he said," piped Mug. "Who says you couldn't make right-side up go sideways? You figured out a way to bend sunlight just a few days ago." Mug sent his eyes toward Meralda. "You can do this, mistress. You've got to. I despise the country. Bloody bugs everywhere."

Meralda took a deep breath. *First thing I do,* she decided, *is put a picture of Tim the Horsehead in here. Right where I can see it. That way, if I have any more moments like this, I can look Tim right in his big brown horse eyes and think to myself 'Tim managed, and the man could only neigh.'*

"All right," she said loud. "Tower, how are the tethers attached to the curseworks?"

Night fell, and Meralda worked. Dawn found her asleep at her desk. The captain came with letters from the king, and departed with a copy of Donchen's list and an explanation that the Tirls listed should quietly be directed to duties far beyond the palace.

Meralda sent Donchen's original note to Fromarch, ordering Kervis to place it in Fromarch's hand and no one else's.

"He'll ask me where I got it," said Kervis. "What do I tell him?"

"Tell him a stranger slipped it under my door," said Meralda. "Tell him we caught sight of a fat man dressed all in a white-trimmed red coat running down the stair, and that moments later we heard reindeer on the roof."

Kervis ogled. "Father Yule?"

Meralda nodded gravely. "That's as good as any, Guardsman. Say that and nothing more."

I wonder what will happen to the Hang on the list, Meralda wondered, *when Loman learns of this. Which he surely will.* She considered asking Donchen, but then rejected the idea. *It's really no concern of mine.*

Or is it, said a little voice deep in her mind, *that you don't want to risk angering Donchen by asking him?*

Meralda felt herself blushing. "Nonsense," she muttered, stabbing at the paper with her pencil. "Nonsense."

"Mistress?"

"Nothing, Mug. I'm just tired."

"No surprise there. Shall I send for more coffee?"

Meralda sighed. How many pots, in the last few days?

"Why not," she said. "Send for two."

Chapter Sixteen

Meralda began to measure the passage of her days by the arrival and departure of Donchen and his silver serving cart.

The mysteries of the cursework tethers fell away, inch by inch. By midnight of the second day of her self-imposed exile inside the laboratory, Meralda began to understand how the tether spells were integrated into the much larger array of the Tower's structural spells.

By two in the morning, Meralda found a way to use the twelve original latching points to tether new spells.

By four, she could see a way to overlay new spells onto the old, and activate them when Otrinvion's tethers began to fail in earnest.

Mug slept. The spark lamps in the laboratory were too dim to keep him alert. Meralda poured the dregs of her last cup of coffee into Mug's pot, smiled when he muttered something about beetles, and then fell asleep herself with her head down on her desk.

Donchen knocked softly at the laboratory doors. A moment

later, he opened them and looked inside.

Meralda did not awaken. Donchen and Tervis crept past the door, Donchen as silent as snow, Tervis rattling and scraping with every step. Still, they managed to reach Meralda's desk without disturbing her slumber.

"Should we wake her?" whispered Tervis.

Donchen shook his head. "I think not."

Tervis wriggled out of his red guardsman's coat and draped it gently over Meralda. She shifted, but did not wake.

Donchen motioned toward the door. Tervis followed, attempting without success to tip-toe in his steel toed boots.

Outside, Donchen pushed the doors closed, and then put his back to them.

"I'll be glad to stay, if one of you gentlemen would care to nap," he said. "Tomorrow is likely to be another very long day."

The Bellringers exchanged glances.

"Pardon, sir, but we'll remain at our posts," said Kervis.

Donchen smiled and shrugged. "As you wish. I'll stay too. Have I ever told you gentlemen the story of Murdering Hosang and the Five Wandering Grooms?"

The Bellringers shook their heads.

Donchen took in a deep breath, and began to speak.

"Good morning, Thaumaturge!"

Meralda regarded the captain with bleary, half-open eyes.

"You needn't be so cheerful about it, you know."

The captain grinned. "Sorry. Here's coffee. And a biscuit with ham. I know it's not quite so fancy as you're used to, these days, but I left my silver serving cart in my other pants."

Meralda groaned and rubbed her eyes. The captain chuckled.

"Forgive me, Meralda. It is a bit early for humor, now that you mention it. Nearly ten of the clock."

Meralda's eyes flew open, and she shot to her feet. "Ten? Ten in the morning? Mug! Why didn't you wake me?"

Mug kept all of his eyes aimed at the ceiling. "Oh my, deary me, how did I forget? Observe how contrite I am. Some days I have the brains of a cucumber, isn't that right?"

Meralda glared. The captain put the biscuit in her hand. "The houseplant did you a boon, Mage. You've been running yourself ragged, these last few days. We need you alert. Especially now."

Meralda paused, hot biscuit halfway to her lips. "Now? Why now?"

The captain grinned. "There's been quite a lot of trouble, Mage. Started small, a couple of days ago. I didn't bother you with talk of it. But last night—my, oh, my—last night was quite a busy one, for our friends the Vonats. Eat. I'll talk. You look half-starved."

Meralda bit and swallowed.

The captain pulled back the rickety old chair Fromarch favored on his visits and sat. "Looks like we've got a war of wizards on our hands, Meralda. Spells flying all over the place. Bangs and thumps and lights at all hours, that's how it started. Vonats complaining that their quarters were either haunted or cursed.

Yvin even moved the lot of them, twice. Didn't make much of a difference."

Meralda nodded and fought to keep her face blank. *Fromarch and Shingvere,* she thought. *Armed with heaven knows what.*

"Saw some of it myself. Two wagonloads of Vonat laundry marched right out of the palace, they did. Marched all the way across town, all the way up the park wall, all the way around it." The captain slapped his knee. "You should see the dancing gargoyles, Mage. All dressed up in Vonat underclothes. They claim the Vonats nearly declared war, right here in the palace."

Meralda nearly choked on her biscuit.

"You wouldn't know anything about that, would you now, Mage?"

Meralda shook her head. "I haven't left this room for two days, Captain. I certainly haven't had time to animate anyone's unmentionables."

"It's been three days, Mage, and it's a good thing, too. The Vonats can't accuse you of making off with their socks when everyone in Tirlin knows you're holed up in here trying to move the Tower's shadow." The captain's grin didn't falter. "That is what you're doing, isn't it, Mage Ovis?"

Her mouth full, Meralda just nodded. The captain snorted.

"Well, Meralda, I hope you know you can call on me anytime, for anything. I don't have to know why, and I won't ask any questions. You do know that, don't you?"

"I know. And I thank you."

The captain shrugged. "Well, I've said my piece. I'd better be off now, in case that pair of daft old codgers manages to start a war right here in our kitchens." He rose, reached into his jacket, and withdrew a short, black bladed dagger in a black felt sheath.

"I didn't forget, by the way. Had this special made for you. Double edged. I had old man Kinnon put the edge on it. It'll cut daylight. Blade is black so it won't shine in the dark. Hilt is soft leather for a good grip. The felt will keep it from nicking your ankle. Will it do?"

Meralda took the dagger. It was heavy in her hand, and cold.

"Perfectly," she said.

"I hope you never do more than put it away in a drawer when all this is over with," said the captain. "But if you use it, strike underhanded, with the blade level. It's good sharp steel. Go right through leather." His face darkened. "I've got a granddaughter your age. You be careful, you hear? Don't go breaking any old men's hearts."

Meralda put the dagger on her desk and caught the captain up in a sudden fierce hug.

"Just a few more days, Captain. A few more days, and we can all go back to pilfering the royal kitchens and idling on the royal stairs."

The captain didn't reply. He patted Meralda awkwardly on her back, and when Meralda released him he turned and stomped out the doors.

"Sounds like the daft codgers have been busy," said Mug, once the doors were firmly shut. "The bit about the marching clothes? Shingvere's, or I'm a petunia."

Meralda made for the laboratory's tiny water closet. Mug watched her go, then turned his eyes to the notes she'd left the night before.

His eyes all went wide at once.

"Tower," he said, in a whisper. "Does this mean she's found a way to save Tirlin?"

"It is possible," said the Tower, matching Mug's whisper. "Your mage is possessed of a formidable intellect."

Mug's eyes hovered over the page, darting back and forth across it in a wild tangle of motion.

"You're an ancient construct possessed of a formidable intellect yourself," said Mug. "Do you think this will actually work?"

The Tower was silent for a moment.

"It seems plausible. If a number of assumptions and estimates are correct."

Mug emulated a sigh as the sound of running water issued from the back of the lab.

"Don't overwhelm me with your confidence."

"We have no time to pursue further research," it said. "This is Tirlin's only hope."

Mug tossed his leaves. "Sunlight," he said, to the glass.

Warm, bright morning sun flooded the desk, bathing Mug's leaves in light and warmth.

"Well." Mug spread his leaves and closed his eyes. "I suppose it will have to do."

Meralda emerged from the water closet at the same time the Bellringers knocked at the door and announced coffee and pancakes.

"No sign of Mr. Donchen this morning, ma'am," said Tervis. "Shame, too. I was looking forward to some more of those Hang vittles."

Meralda beckoned the Bellringers inside with a frown.

"Did either of you sleep last night?"

"Yes, ma'am."

"No, ma'am."

Meralda sighed. Kervis kicked his brother in the shin, causing Tervis to yelp and amend his reply.

"Mr. Donchen stayed with us until a couple of hours ago," said Kervis. "Said he had some bird watching to do." Kervis frowned. "I told him most Tirlish birds don't fly till after sunup, but he left anyway."

Bird watching, mused Meralda, as she cleared a place on her desk for her breakfast. *What are you up to, Donchen?*

"Thank you for breakfast," said Meralda. "Now then. I'm heading for the Tower at three bells. Both of you will now go get a few hours sleep." She raised her hands at their protests. "Have the captain send up a pair of guards. That's an order. I'll lock the doors and set the wards. A dozen Vonats couldn't get past both. Go." She stabbed a bite of pancakes with her fork. "I'd better not see either of you until three of the clock."

"Are you sure, Thaumaturge?"

Meralda glared. Kervis caught his brother's elbow and led him out.

"Back to the Tower, is it?" said Mug.

"I've got enough of the shadow moving spellwork finished to latch it. It'll give me an excuse to have a look at the Vonat spell, too."

"It'll also expose you to anyone out there with mischief on their mind," said Mug.

Meralda swallowed and shrugged. *I won't even mention that I'm going home to change and have a proper bath,* she thought. Mug would lose leaves.

"It has to be done."

"So you're nearly done with the shadow spell?"

"I'm taking quite a few shortcuts," said Meralda. "I've halved the number of refractors. It won't be as bright as day, but the king won't be in deep shadow, either."

"Ooo, Yvin will have a fit."

"If he wishes." Meralda put down her fork and found her coffee. "He can always ask for my robe back. Another night in this chair and I may give it to him anyway."

"Now you sound like Fromarch."

"Hush, Mug."

"Now you really sound like Fromarch."

Meralda shrugged and sipped coffee until her mind was clear again.

"You put a ribbon in your hair," said Mug.

Meralda regarded the park from atop the nearly completed spectator's bleachers which now lay full in the Tower's long shadow.

The park was full. Two dozen dirt smeared Alons charged and bellowed and ran, and a crowd of several hundred spectators gathered about them, all hooting or jeering or shoving each other for a better look at the running mob of Alons. Food sellers wandered, hawking their wares in strident tones. Minstrels played and sang, often so close to one another their songs were little more than shouting matches.

"It's a red ribbon," added Mug. "In case anyone asks."

"I know perfectly well what color it is. I did, after all, put it there. It's just a ribbon. I often wear hair ribbons."

"Seen Donchen yet?"

"I have no idea where he might be."

"Well, keep looking, he's bound to turn up."

"I'm not looking!"

"No, of course not, you were just pointing your eyes toward the crowd, my mistake."

Kervis came charging up the wooden stair. "Ma'am," he began, breathless. "I told—the foreman—he'll blow a whistle—when everyone is clear."

Meralda smiled. "Thank you, Kervis. Please make sure no one ascends the stair after the whistle is blown."

Kervis nodded. "Yes, ma'am."

"I didn't see Mr. Donchen, by the way."

Mug snickered.

Meralda turned, and Kervis stamped away down the stairs.

"Mistress," said Mug, all humor gone. "Look west. By the ice cream vendor. Tall man in a black hood."

Meralda didn't look. "Is it him?"

Mug's eyes swiveled and bunched.

"Yes. Just standing there. Arms folded. Can't see either of his hands."

"He wouldn't dare attack me openly here."

"No, that would be rash." Mug shook his leaves. "Sorry. No, I don't think so either. But let's get this done, mistress. I'd feel safer with a few feet of solid stone between me and Ugly, if you don't mind."

Meralda reached into her right pocket and withdrew the Hang magic detector. She opened it, and watched as the needle swung around to point south, toward the Hang ships still moored at the harbor.

She laid the device down. The needle never moved, and the rings never spun.

"Keep one eye on that, if you please."

Mug aimed a bright blue eye at the dial.

From the base of the Tower, a whistle blew. Meralda could see a ring of curious workmen gather in the shade, mopping their brows and watching her. One waved.

"It's time," said Meralda. She found her long copper latch, broke the silver thread she'd strung through its open ends earlier, and spoke a long, soft word.

"Sight," she whispered.

The Tower flared to life, now glowing with a flickering corona that clung to it like sheets of pale, bluish flames.

The copper tube grew warm in her hands. Meralda spoke the word that released the new latch, and the tube leaped in her hands as the first part of the shadow spell flew toward the Tower.

Even with her Sight, even knowing where to look and what to look for, Meralda couldn't see any hint of the Tower's subtle actions as it accepted the new spell and gently latched it in place.

If Humindorus Nam is watching, thought Meralda, *let him spend the rest of his life wondering just how I managed to latch that.*

The copper tube in her hand grew cool. The ends began to rime, and Meralda laid it down next to her notes.

"Ugly is leaving," said Mug. "He try anything, mistress?"

"Not that I could tell." Satisfied that the latch was firmly in place, Meralda let her sight fall. "Still, he walked all the way out here for some reason."

"Probably just curious about the Tower," said Mug. "I'd bet a pound of good mulch Shingvere and Fromarch aren't far. Might have ruined his plans, if he had any."

"Possibly." Meralda began packing her bag with her various implements and her wind whipped notebook.

"Back to the flat?" asked Mug. His voice fell to a whisper. "Won't you at least take the captain and a dozen guards, this time?"

Meralda shook her head. "Why? Tower means me no harm. There's no ghost."

"It's not Tower I'm worried about. What if Ugly sneaks in, somehow? What if that's his plan, to catch you on the stair alone?"

Meralda hefted her bag. "I won't be alone."

"Mistress, the lads mean well, and I'm sure they'd be handy in a fight against irate middle-schoolers, but this could turn deadly."

"And if I summon the captain and a platoon of pikemen, what does that say about the Mage of Tirlin, Mug?"

"It says she's surrounded by large men with sharp pointy things."

"It tells the world I'm afraid. It tells the world I can't go about without relying on soldiers. No, Mug. I'll take the Bellringers, but no more."

Mug flung his vines. "Can you at least tell if you-know-who and you-know-what are nearby?"

Meralda shrugged. "I have no idea. And I can't wait until I do. Please, Mug, don't worry." Meralda grinned and patted her bag. "I've taken extra precautions."

Mug grunted. "Well. I'll just stay here and keep watch."

Meralda patted his topmost leaves. "Thank you, Mug. I'll be back soon. You'll see."

Meralda turned and mounted the stairs. The Bellringers looked up, squinting into the sun.

"To the Tower, ma'am?"

"To the Tower. Please make sure someone watches the stairs. I don't want Mug disturbed."

Kervis darted off, grabbing a pair of idling palace guards by their bright red shirts and ushering them toward the stairs.

Meralda waited until the bewildered guards were in place, and then she led the Bellringers on the short walk to the Tower.

The Tower was as dark as ever, as silent as ever, and as empty as ever.

Meralda felt none of the dread she'd come to associate with her previous trips up the winding stair, though. *Yes, I know I am being watched. Yes, I know the shadows hide an ancient and powerful being.*

But Tower now has a name, of sorts, and I can't feel threatened by him, even if he is the handiwork of Otrinvion the Black, himself.

Meralda smiled up at Kervis, whose wide-eyed gaze and sweaty face belied anything but calm. Tervis, too, was pale and wary, his hand continually darting to touch the hilt of his sword.

Meralda watched the shadows at the edge of her magelamp for any tell-tale sign of Nameless or Faceless. She listened between the scrape of boots on stone for any hint of wings. But she saw only darkness, and heard only echoes and silence.

Perhaps the staves are being discreet because of the Bellringers, she thought.

Or perhaps they simply aren't here at all.

The stair wound up and up and up, vanishing in the dark above and swallowed by the dark below. Meralda counted steps until she reached nine hundred and forty, and then she called the Bellringers to rest.

Both put their backs to the wall and eyed the shadows warily. Meralda fumbled with her bag and then withdrew a glass sphere held at the end of a long brass funnel by a net of faintly luminous gold wires.

She handed the magelamp to Tervis. "Hold this please," she

said. "This will only take a moment."

Tervis played the light over Meralda and nodded wordlessly.

Meralda turned away from the Bellringers and forced herself to stare out into the chasm just beyond the tips of her boots.

The Vonat spell should have latched here, she thought. *It should still be here, even though Tower has pulled its teeth.*

Time to see just what Humindorus Nam had planned for the Accords.

"Sight," said Meralda, closing her eyes. The emptiness before her seemed to pull at her, urging her closer to the edge, urging her to bend, to lean, to take that one simple step...

Meralda held the glass sphere aloft, and spoke another long word.

The Tower was flooded with a brief, sudden light.

In that light, Meralda's Sight showed her a tangle of dark, harsh magic. Great parts of it still lay coiled, still under a strange tension, still ready to snap and lunge and strike, if only the right word was spoken aloud.

Meralda traced the comings and goings of the glowing structure before her. *Yes,* she thought, *I can see how Tower moved this, shifted that, forced this other to bend and come loose. But what of that helical component? Why does the whole thing wrap not just around itself, but inside itself, twice over?*

"Mage?" asked Kervis, his words faint and hollow, as though spoken through a thick fog or a fresh snow.

Meralda raised her free hand for silence, and pushed her Sight deeper inside the Vonat spellwork.

But it isn't all Vonat, is it, she thought. *Certainly, some of it. But half is something new.*

Something foreign.

Meralda didn't dare close her Sight long enough to consult Donchen's magical pointer, but she knew the needle would still point to the ships.

Still, this is Hang. But what does it do?

Meralda urged the sphere to reveal more. The glass began to sag, and a drop of it fell to the stair, smoking and hissing.

Meralda pushed deeper. The formations inside the spellwork danced and spun, rolling and straightening, flashing suddenly from the Tower's floor to the flat, like cold, bright lightning.

Lightning.

"Oh, my."

"Ma'am?"

"Nothing."

Lightning. Plain and simple. The word is spoken. The structure unfolds. The coils are released.

And then a ring of deadly, concentrated lightning springs from the Tower and falls into the park. Bolt after bolt, until the latch fails.

The hand holding the melting glass began to shake. How many would die? Dozens? Hundreds?

And I'd be blamed, she realized. *He'd wait until I invoked the shadow moving spell. Make it appear as if a clumsy Tirlish mage–a woman, at that–accidentally called down death on the royal houses of all the Five Realms, and the Hang.*

Wrecking the Accords. Sending the Hang home, perhaps forever. Leaving the realms distrustful and perhaps even vengeful against a devastated, kingless Tirlin.

All of that laid at my doorstep.

Meralda felt her teeth grinding, and forced her jaw to relax. *It's not going to happen*, she said to herself. *The spell has been disabled. Oh, it looks formidable enough. But when the word is spoken, if it is spoken, the whole wretched mess will simply spin and thrash and fall apart.*

Meralda took a deep breath, and dropped her Sight.

The glass globe sputtered and dripped. The heat of it warmed her hand, even from the end of the handle.

Kervis and Tervis regarded her with something like terror.

"Ma'am," said Kervis. "Is everything...all right?"

"It is now. Forgive me, gentlemen. I assure you, all is well."

The Bellringers nodded, their eyes still wide.

Meralda spoke another word. The globe ceased its glowing, and began to pop and crack as it suddenly cooled.

Meralda propped it carefully against the wall. The glass was so soft it flattened and deformed against the stone.

"I'll just leave this here and pick it up on the way down. Remember where it is, and don't trip over it later."

The Bellringers chorused agreement. Meralda hefted her bag, and resumed her careful march back toward the flat, scowling at the dark all the way.

Sunlight spilled into the flat. Meralda and the Bellringers put their backs to the walls and sat, catching their breath.

"I'm not going to miss doing this one bit," said Tervis, after a time.

"Oh, I don't know, it's fun after the first few thousand steps," added Kervis with a sweaty grin.

Meralda laughed and rose. *One last thing to do,* she thought. *And the shadow spell will be in place at last.*

I just hope there's still a Tirlin in which to use it.

Meralda fumbled in her bag, found the pair of holdstones and the intricate device of brass and silver that would shape the refractors upon their release. She put the device in the center of the floor, spoke half the word that bound it to the latch, and watched as the cogged gears located at each of the compass points rotated precisely half a revolution each.

Then she let out her breath in a sigh.

"That's that," she said. "Hurrah. Another victory for applied magic."

The Bellringers stood.

"We knew you could do it," said Kervis, blushing. "You're the smartest person we've ever met, and that's a fact."

Meralda found a weary smile. "And you are the bravest. Thank you. Let's get back to the park, shall we? I could use something to eat."

"Me, too," said Tervis. "We should have brought some apples."

"I'd rather eat with my feet on the ground," said Kervis, opening the door to the flat. "Ready, Mage?"

"Ready." Meralda pushed back her hair and brushed her magelamp to life. "Mind your step."

Kervis grinned and stepped out of the light. Meralda followed, and Tervis locked the door behind.

A dozen steps down the stair, Meralda saw something black flit and dart just beyond the reach of her magelamp's white glow.

A dozen steps later, she was sure she heard, fainter than a cricket's footfall, the sound of crow's wings beating.

Neither Kervis nor Tervis gave any sign of seeing shadows or hearing fluttering in the dark.

Meralda kept one hand in her bag and hurried down as fast as she dared.

"I do love the feel of the sun on my face," said Kervis, as he stepped out into the light.

Meralda nodded, too out of breath to comment. Tervis brought up the rear, armor clinking and clanking as he hurried to catch up.

Meralda could see Mug waving his fronds from high atop the stands. She waved back. If Mug was shouting the din in the park made it impossible to hear.

Meralda searched the crowd ahead for any sign of Humindorus Nam, but saw only idling Tirlish and grinning, bruised Alons and a group of assorted carpenters all hurrying about their tasks. Hammers rose and fell. Saws cut and glinted in the sun.

Fromarch peeked from behind a stack of lumber, flashed Meralda a rare wide grin, and vanished.

Meralda let out her breath all at once. "Let's fetch Mug and be off," she said. The Bellringers hurried to her side. "I'll get us some lunch on the way to the palace."

"Don't have to tell me twice," said Kervis, who hurried for the stands. "I'll fetch Mr. Mug. Won't be a moment!"

"Don't forget his sheet," called Meralda.

"I'm sure Mr. Mug will remind him, ma'am," said Tervis. He peered out at Meralda from behind his too-large helm. "Ma'am, it's none of my concern, but you looked to be a mite angry back there. Did we say something wrong? Kervis didn't mean anything about that Alon football he likes to watch."

"No, nothing of the sort," said Meralda, quickly. "I saw some...difficulties with the spell. That's all. Extra work. I'm just grumpy these days."

Tervis smiled. "Well, as long as it weren't nothing we did."

Kervis came charging back, a swaying, sheet-covered birdcage muttering in his hand.

"I'm going to be thoroughly sick," said Mug, from within.

"Oh, let me have him," said Meralda. Kervis handed the cage to her. "Here, we'll be sitting still very soon."

"Not soon enough. Oh. Donchen stopped by, mistress. Said to tell you something. Please slow down! I'm not a swinging vine, you know."

Meralda glared, but slowed her walk.

"Yes? What was it?"

"His message?"

"Yes, his bloody message!"

"He said your bag is very heavy, and any carpenter in Tirlin would be proud to carry it for you some day. Are we walking up and down hills, mistress? Because it feels that way."

Meralda frowned. "My bag isn't that heavy..."

Meralda paused to let a trio of carpenters pass. One smiled at her and winked, and for an instant his face was Donchen's.

"Actually, I could use some help," she said aloud.

"I'd be honored," said the man. His face was now Tirlish, his clothes stained and sweaty, his brown hair filled with sawdust. "Where are you heading, milady?"

"Just down the walk," said Meralda. "Thank you for helping."

Donchen hefted the bag across his shoulder. "Think nothing of it," he said. His fingers flew in a series of small gestures. "We can speak, for a bit. You were followed here, Mage. I believe he meant you harm."

Meralda smiled, as though discussing the sunshine. "What stopped him, then?"

"Three very determined wizards with a bagful of horrors. Your friends have been quite effective, Mage. The Vonats are beginning to distrust their co-conspirators. And each other. Remind me to avoid playing your card games with any of them."

Meralda nodded. "And you? What have you been up to, sir?"

"Oh, idling in beer halls, gambling at dice, napping."

"I doubt that."

Donchen grinned. "We're nearly there. You're bound for your laboratory?"

"Yes. More work to do."

"I'll bring supper. Until then, be wary. I fear Nam's mischief was merely delayed."

"I have a bit of horror in my bag as well," said Meralda. "But I thank you for your concern."

Donchen smiled and nodded. "I'll be close all the way to the palace," he said. The Wizard's Walk ended, leaving Meralda and Donchen to weave their way through the crowd to the curb, where Angis waited atop his buggy.

"Mug was right," said Donchen, as he handed the sheet-covered bird cage to Meralda. "It is a nice red ribbon."

And then he was gone, lost in the noisy crowd.

Mug feigned snores until the park was well behind them.

Tervis dozed in his seat. Angis and Kervis sang atop the cab, laughing at each other's missed notes. Meralda pulled the ribbon from her hair and shoved it down in her bag and fumed as the carriage made its way slowly toward the palace.

Mug remained silent, though Meralda did catch a glimpse of a small brown eye peeking up at her from beneath the bed sheet's edge.

The carriage rolled to a halt. Meralda leaned out of her window and saw that traffic up and down the street was at a standstill. In the distance, she heard whistles blow.

"Looks like a pair of fools have gotten their harnesses tangled up ahead, ma'am," shouted Angis. "We might be here for a bit."

Tervis stirred, rubbed his eyes, and reached suddenly for his sword.

Meralda's door was flung open. Sunlight rushed in.

Time slowed to a crawl.

Tervis shouted. Whether a warning or his brother's name or hers, Meralda couldn't say.

Someone tossed a bundle of dirty rope through the open door. Meralda kicked at it, slid away from it, and tried to open the cab's other door.

The handle wouldn't budge. As Meralda struggled to open it, something struck the door hard from the outside. A length of thick dirty rope fell through the open cab window and looped itself over Meralda's right shoulder.

The rope stank of oil and soot. A remote, perfectly calm corner of Meralda's mind noted that the oil must have come from the dirigible docks, and that the stains would never come out of her blouse.

Tervis grabbed the rope with one hand and tried to draw his sword with the other. The cab was too confined to let his blade clear the scabbard. Tervis twisted and pulled, but before he could draw he was yanked whole by his ankles from the cab and dragged out the open door.

More stinking rope fell through the cab window. Meralda tried to slide away, but the ropes moved about her, pinning her right arm, wrapping themselves tight about her ankles, coiling and climbing up both her legs.

Mug screamed. A loop of rope coiled and struck like a serpent, smashing Mug's cage nearly flat.

The ropes holding Meralda flexed and stood, knotting themselves suddenly into a crude simulacrum of a person, with loops of rope for arms, for legs, for trunk, for head.

Meralda managed to get her left hand in her bag before a turn of rope closed about that wrist, too.

Outside the carriage, Tervis screamed and Kervis swore and Angis flailed away at something with his stick. Meralda could see blades rising, men running, and impossible lengths of rope standing and moving and fighting.

Her hand closed about a warm, smooth metal cube as the rope man before her leaned down and slid his open noose of a face over Meralda's head.

As the rope around her neck began to tighten, Meralda pulled the metal box from her bag and spat out the short harsh word that loosed the spell inside.

There was a flash, the smell of fresh air after a summer thunderstorm, a crack of infant thunder.

The rope man gripping Meralda sagged and dropped to the cab's floor. The ropes about her arms and legs fell away.

She pulled the rope around her neck over her head, flung it down, and leaped from the cab, Mug's crumpled, sheet covered birdcage in her hand.

Kervis and Tervis rose from the cobblestones, each covered in tangled ropes, each red-faced and winded. Angis leaped down from his cab, his nose bloody and his eyes wild.

Mug moaned softly beneath his bed sheet. Meralda grabbed Tervis and dragged him toward the sidewalk, where a frightened crowd gathered.

"Move away!" shouted Meralda. "They'll be getting back up any moment now. Move! Run!" She lifted the icy cold cube and held it high. "Magic! Run!"

The crowd scattered. Meralda dragged Tervis as far as she could, then waved to Angis and Kervis to follow.

"Go!" she shouted. "Indoors! Hurry!"

Angis mopped blood with a handkerchief and spat. "Not without you, Mage." He'd lost his stick, but he bent and pulled a short plain knife from his right boot. "I'm too old to run, anyway."

"Ma'am, they're moving," said Kervis, lifting his sword. "What do we do?"

Run like I told you, thought Meralda.

But they won't. They'll stand here and try to fight a hundred feet of mooring ropes with swords and kitchen knives.

She put Mug's cage behind her, searched Milhop's Irresistible Void for any hint of remaining capacity, and then let it fall to the street.

Filled. Impossibly so, but filled nonetheless. Useless.

The ropes stirred, coiling and shifting, animated again by some dark, foreign spell.

Whistles blew, down the way, and horns answered. *The guard will be here in moments,* Meralda thought.

A rope man rose. And another.

But the guard will be too late.

Tervis and Kervis moved to stand on either side of Meralda, blades level and ready, faces frozen in identical masks of grim determination. Angis cussed and bled and spat, shifting from boot to boot as if deciding on a dance.

The rope men stood. There were five, then six, then seven.

"It's you they want, Mage," said Angis. "Take to your heels. We'll hold them here."

Meralda dropped her bag. She held her arms out beside her, hands open and empty, and as the rope men advanced she called upon her Sight.

Instantly, a pair of flitting shadows descended, darting and swooping, just out of her reach.

"What oath would you speak to us, imperiled mage?"

"No oaths," said Meralda, aloud. The steady scratch-slide of ropes dragged across cobblestones grew louder. "No vows. You help me, or you don't. The choice is yours."

"No oath?" said one.

"No vow?" said another.

"Many would pledge their lives."

"Many would offer their souls."

Kervis took a step forward. Tervis did the same.

"One cannot deny she is brave."

"One cannot deny she is wise."

"I do not love these things of rope."

"Nor I. Are we agreed?"

Meralda's hands closed about two plain ironwood staves.

"Behold, Mage," said one. *"This is how."*

Meralda's mind filled with wonders.

As one, the rope men charged, arms flailing like whips, legs looping up and out, ready to catch, ready to coil, ready to wrap and knot and choke.

Meralda's Sight expanded, clarified, became an all-encompassing panorama that showed not just the ropes that bore down on her, but the spells that gave them shape and lent them motion.

Meralda laughed. Pure, wild, unfettered magic blazed suddenly through her veins, her heart, her mind. She marveled at the simplicity of it, at the ease with which she could form it, shape it, bend it to her will.

No equations. No diagrams. No symbols.

Just magic. Just will.

Just...*this.*

Meralda lifted Nameless and Faceless, crossing them above her head. Without even a word she loosed a wave of raw power that lifted the rope men like so many dry leaves, spinning them into a flailing tangle before incinerating rope and spells alike into a short-lived puff of golden incandescent air.

Every window for two blocks shattered. Horses bolted, dragging cabs and carriages up onto the sidewalks and sending them careening into storefronts and lamp posts. Two water mains burst, flooding streets and sending panicked crowds fleeing.

"Now the true test," said one.

"Let us see," said the other.

Meralda's Sight raced. Everywhere, wonders lay hidden, coiled in impossibly small spaces she had never dreamed existed. Magic infused every stone, every brick, every breath of air, always in easy reach for anyone who dared seize it.

So easy, thought Meralda. *So easy*...

She heard voices. Distant, yes, and faint, but familiar, somehow. Friends, perhaps.

Voices full of concern.

Still, such power, so close, so simple to take.

"Ma'am, he's hurt! Please! We need you right now!"

Someone tugged at Meralda's sleeve.

Kervis. Kervis was speaking.

"Mr. Mug! Say something! Mr. Mug!"

Mug.

Meralda let go of the staves. They leaped into the sky, vanishing instantly, something very like approval hanging briefly in their wake.

Meralda's head spun. She forced her Sight away, fell to her knees, blinked and squinted until she saw nothing but dirty cobblestones and the wild fearful eyes of Kervis and Tervis.

Kervis held Mug's cage. He was carefully prying away the tangled bed sheet. Meralda gasped, her stomach knotting when she saw Mug's bird cage was crushed nearly flat in the center.

Angis caught her by her shoulder, keeping her from toppling over.

"I think you got rid of the buggers, Mage," he said. "You tend to your friend. I'll watch your back."

Tears welled up in Meralda's eyes and she saw Mug's motionless leaves caught in the bent bars of the bird cage.

One of his eyes stuck through the bars. It was crushed, and leaking sap.

"Oh Mug," she said. "No, no, no."

Kervis bent down, his dagger in his hand.

"I can pry the cage apart, ma'am," he said. "Then we can get him out of there. Will you let me do that?"

Meralda managed to nod. She laid her hand on Mug's crushed leaves, but he did not stir.

"Mug."

Kervis gently pushed her hand aside, put the tip of his knife through the crushed cage's frame, and then slowly pried up.

"Hold the other side," he said, to Tervis.

The cage slowly expanded. After moving the knife, Kervis was able to pull it out far enough to remove the cage's bottom, and free the motionless dandyleaf plant.

"Water!" bellowed Angis, at the circle of confused faces Meralda could just barely see through her tears. "A pitcher of water, man! Crown's business!"

In a moment, a pitcher of water was thrust in Meralda's hand.

She poured it onto the clump of dirt that had survived the blow. Mug's roots trailed from it, limp and still.

Angis gripped her shoulder.

"A wee bit more, lass."

Crying, Meralda emptied the pitcher.

Mug's stalk twitched. His roots underwent a spasm, and then clutched hard at the clump of soil.

A single green eye opened, swiveled up to hang close to Meralda's nose, and blinked.

"Please tell me you did bad things to whatever hit me," he said, in a tiny, weak voice.

Meralda cried, unable to speak. She stroked Mug's wilted leaves and nodded.

"I'll need a new pot," said Mug. His open eye began to wobble. "And some of that fancy Eryan peat."

Booted feet charged up, and shouts to make way sounded.

"The guard is here," said Kervis. "Keep an eye on them, little brother." He sheathed his sword and turned to meet them.

"I'll be going to bed now," muttered Mug. "Don't mind the dishes."

Then his eye closed, slumped, and fell.

Meralda hugged him to her chest, wet roots and all.

"We're here," said Kervis, gently. "May I take him? The wards..."

Meralda managed a nod, and carefully handed a wilted, drooped Mug over to Kervis.

Forty special palace guards surrounded Meralda and the Bellringers, ringing them in steel. The captain himself stood at Meralda's back while she opened the laboratory doors and spoke the word that soothed her wards.

"You lads go first," said the captain. Meralda didn't argue.

Mug groaned softly as she took his cage.

The guards closest to the stairs tensed and called for someone to halt. Meralda turned, watched Donchen slowly take the last pair of steps, his arms raised, his face grim and smeared with something dark.

Oil, thought Meralda. *He's got oil on his face.*

"Let him through," she said. The words caught in her throat the first time, and she had to lick her lips and take a breath and try again.

"I said let him through."

The ring of guardsmen parted, and Donchen made his way to Meralda.

Donchen was filthy. His clothes were torn and streaked with filth. He stank of the gutters, and something even worse.

"I was there," he said. "They were waiting in the sewer beneath the street. I tried to stop them." He dipped his head in a tiny bow. "I failed."

"Come inside."

Kervis and Tervis sidled past Meralda and entered the laboratory, hands on hilts.

"It's empty," said Kervis, after a moment.

Meralda took Donchen's hand. He looked up at her, eyes wide in surprise, and then smiled.

His hand is warm, thought Meralda. *What a silly thing to notice. Of course his hand is warm. It's a hand.*

"We'll be right here," growled the captain. "If anything wants in it can see how it likes being cut to pieces first."

"Thank you, Captain," said Meralda, feeling her face flush crimson at the stares of so many guards.

She pulled Donchen inside, and quickly shut the door.

Donchen mopped at his face with a clean washcloth as he perched in her rickety spare chair.

"So you think he'll heal?"

Meralda gently pushed Mug's new soil down. Mug remained upright, his leaves twitching now and then. All his eyes were closed, and he muttered now and then, but never quite formed words.

"He will." Meralda frowned and cleared her throat. "Of course he will. His roots are intact. His stems are bruised but not broken. He'll be fine."

Goboy's mirror streamed bright, warm sun onto Mug. Meralda gave him another half-turn so all his leaves could take in some light.

Donchen nodded. His lower lip was split. His right eye was going puffy and dark. Meralda could tell from his stiff posture and barely hidden grimaces he had bruised, if not broken, ribs beneath his soiled white shirt.

I've never seen a more handsome man in all my life, she thought.

"I smell like an outhouse," he said, grinning. "I do hope you'll forgive me for that. It is not a practice in which I habitually engage."

"Nonsense. Tirlish sewers smell of roses and perfume," said Meralda. "You still haven't told me what led you to enter one in the first place."

"I carry a device similar to the one I gave you. It showed the presence of Hang magic along your route. I happened to be traveling ahead of you, so I took a bit of a detour and found a group of singularly unusual ropes gathering below the street."

"And you tried to fight them all, at once?"

Donchen shrugged and grimaced at the effort. "I did first attempt to reason with them, Mage. But they were determined to do you harm. I decided to slow them down by entangling myself in all of their various lengths. Oh, how they struggled to escape my implacable grasp!"

Meralda smiled. "I see that. I imagine they were close to surrender when my carriage arrived."

"Very nearly. Another moment and I'd have made bell pulls of them all."

"Grapefruit," muttered Mug. "Prancing hornbill."

Donchen laughed, wincing.

"The truth is, Mage, they overwhelmed me from the first. My own magical defenses failed. Almost as if they were anticipated. Troubling, that."

"I thought your butterflies revealed all the Hang conspirators. Have they not been...?"

Meralda hesitated, searching for words.

"Tried? Executed? Boiled in oil?" Donchen shrugged. "Truly, Mage, I don't know what, if any, actions have been taken against them. The machinations of the House of Chezin are often well beyond my understanding."

I find that troubling, thought Meralda.

Donchen's slate-grey eyes met Meralda's. "I am pleased to see that your own arcane defenses proved more than adequate."

Meralda remembered the thrill of power she felt while holding Nameless and Faceless.

"Many of the older artifacts here are quite powerful," she said. The lie lay bitter on her lips. "The king will be livid when he gets the bill for the water mains."

"A small price to pay, I think."

Is that pain in his eyes?

"Thank you for coming to my rescue," said Meralda.

"Quite the contrary. You came to mine. I was being throttled right below your feet, when you turned my assailant into a rather showy cloud of ash." Donchen stood. "I *do* smell of an outhouse. Might I borrow yonder water closet, before Mug wakes and decides I am a compost heap?"

"I'll have fresh clothes sent up," said Meralda, wrinkling her nose. "I can send for some of your own, if you like."

Donchen rose slowly from his chair, holding his ribs as he moved. "Actually, I'd prefer a guard uniform, if that's not too much a slap in the face to Tirlish military tradition. Mail shirt, helmet, sword. Can that be done?"

Puzzled, Meralda shouted for Tervis, who came at a trot.

"Yes, ma'am?"

"I need a uniform," said Meralda. "In Donchen's size. With arms. Can you do that, quietly, without telling anyone why?"

Tervis grinned and straightened. "Right away! Straight sword or Argen curved?"

"Straight, please," said Donchen. "And sharp. Very sharp."

Chapter Seventeen

Donchen's plain straight sword flashed as it fell. He stepped back with his right foot, pivoted, and when he stopped the tip of his sword was a finger's breadth from Kervis' throat.

"You simply draw your opponent's blade to his right, and then you step, turn, stab," said Donchen. He flicked his sword away and fell back into a defensive crouch. "Now you try."

Kervis nodded and charged.

Tervis sat beside Meralda and mopped sweat, fresh from his own bout with the Hang. "He's so fast," he whispered. "Faster than Sergeant Smithy, that's for sure."

Meralda looked away from Donchen and Kervis and leaned back in her chair. *He looks Tirlish, in that guardsman's garb,* she thought. *Dashing, in fact, even with a black eye and a split lip.*

"I'm sure he is," she said.

Tervis nodded at Mug. "He looks better, ma'am. Not so wilted. Has he said anything yet?"

"Nothing that made sense. But he's dreaming. Watch."

Mug's leaves shivered, and his eye stalks moved as if in a sudden puff of wind.

"That's a good sign, isn't it, ma'am?"

"I'd be far more worried if he was perfectly still."

Tervis nodded.

"I like him. I'm going to miss seeing him, when the Accords are done." The Bellringer's face reddened. "We'll miss seeing you too, ma'am, if you don't mind me saying so."

"Of course I don't mind. I didn't want bodyguards, you know. But I've quite enjoyed your company. Who knows? I might ask for a permanent deployment."

Tervis lit up with a wide sudden smile.

"We'd like that, ma'am!"

"I'll see to it, then. If your brother agrees, of course."

"He will. We've, um, talked about it. Please don't tell him I told you that."

"I won't."

"Well, I'd better get back to practice," said Tervis. "Thank you, Mage."

"Thank you, Guardsman."

"I didn't order shoes," said Mug. "Oblate spheroid."

Meralda patted the dandyleaf's tossing leaves until they were still.

"As I was saying," said the Tower, in a near whisper. "The only point of contact between the tethers and the curseworks appears to be this juncture, here..."

A diagram appeared in the corner of the sunlit glass. Meralda copied it onto her paper, and then set about finding its secrets.

Donchen, clad now in the waistcoat and leggings and shiny buckled shoes of a nobleman of old, raised Kervis' hand and smiled.

"Right foot, left foot, turn, pirouette," he said.

Kervis stumbled, trying to stand tip-toe in his guardsman's boots. He frowned and looked down at his long, flowing ball gown.

"I don't think I like this dream," he said.

Meralda lifted her head from her desk and shook it, trying to wake.

Mug turned his eyes toward her, whole again. "None of that, mistress," he chided, waggling vines at her. "Someone went to considerable trouble to bring this dream about. Please sleep just a few moments longer. It's important."

"Indeed," said Tower, from inside the glass. "A fanfare, if you please."

Mug sounded a fanfare, complete with trumpets and drums.

Footfalls sounded from the shelves. There came the sound of a door slamming shut.

Meralda rose and whirled to face the shelves. My back aches, she thought. *My arm is numb where I slept on it. I can't be dreaming.*

Tim the Horsehead stepped into the light.

"You are, indeed, dreaming," he said. He turned his equine head so he gazed at Meralda through his right eye. "Though it is a singular sort of dream."

"Tim the Horsehead couldn't speak." Meralda sagged. "It is just a dream."

"I can speak perfectly well in dreams," replied Tim. "May I come closer?"

Meralda shrugged. "Please do."

Tim approached.

Meralda watched. He's wearing the robes of office, she noted. *The very same clothes depicted in his portrait in the Gold Room.*

"Well, I'm working with your memories, after all," said Tim. He moved to stand two short steps from Meralda. "We've been very impressed with you, you know," he said. "All of us. We look in from time to time." He raised a gloved hand and pointed at Mug. "He'll be fine, by the way. You needn't worry."

Meralda pinched her side.

It hurt.

Tim remained, perfectly solid, not the least bit dreamlike.

He smelled of cologne Meralda couldn't name. His muzzle was whiskery and going grey.

Beneath the cologne, Meralda realized he smelled very faintly of...a stable?

Meralda's heart began to race. What if this is really Tim, somehow?

"We? We who?"

Tim curled back his lips in a horse's toothy grin. "We former thaumaturges. All this time, thinking the Tower was haunted, when it is this laboratory that is full of ghosts." He made a sound somewhere between a whinny and a laugh. "The very walls in this place are infused with old, old magic. We mages leave a part of us behind."

More figures stepped from the shadows between the shelves. Some solid, some faded and ghostlike, some little more than shadows themselves.

None moved far from the dark.

"We know of the threat to Tirlin, and your efforts to stop it. We salute you, Mage Meralda Ovis. As not just one of us, but the best of us."

"I am no such thing."

Tim whinnied again in laughter. "We shall soon see. Tirlin's darkest hour is nearly upon us, Mage. Know that we who wore the robes before you stand at your side."

"Can you render the curseworks harmless?"

Tim shook his long head side to side.

"We are but ghosts now," he said. "That task is yours, and yours alone."

Meralda sighed. "I don't know if I can do it," she said. Her voice shook. "I just don't know."

"I would be troubled if you said otherwise," said Tim. "I, on the other hoof, have the utmost confidence in you, Mage."

"Everyone keeps saying that," said Meralda. "This is pre-kingdom magic. It doesn't make sense, half the time. It's like trying to untie knots in the dark. I could fail as easily as not." Meralda felt her face flush hot, and a sudden anger ran through her. "And you know what they'll say? They'll say I failed because I'm a woman. That will be my legend. Fool scrap of a girl let the kingdom burn."

Tim nodded. "I felt much the same burden, so many times. The stuff of legends is nothing but trouble to the persons unfortunate enough to make them. On the whole, I'd rather have been off fishing."

Meralda surprised herself by laughing.

"I've always wanted to meet you. You're the reason I'm here, really."

Tim bowed. "My apologies, then. It was never my intention to be a bad influence on the youth of Tirlin."

"You're exactly as I imagined."

Tim stepped forward, his horse head swaying to and fro as though seeing who was close by.

"May I tell you a secret, Mage Meralda Ovis?"

"Please."

Tim's whiskery horse mouth tickled Meralda's right ear.

"You're not the first woman to wear the robes."

"What?"

Tim's horse head flashed, and when the light died, he–she–looked back at Meralda from a woman's smiling face.

"I knew I'd never be named Mage as a woman, back in the bad old days of 1517," she said. She looked down at her bosom ruefully and shrugged. "But it occurred to me that the robes would hide everything but my head and neck."

"You're not Tim?"

"Tam, actually. I even developed a taste for hay. Imagine that." She ran fingers through her long brown hair. "Tam couldn't even read for the college. Tim took the robes and saved the kingdom, more than once. What a difference a single letter makes. And a bit of magic."

Meralda remembered to close her mouth.

"I'm not the only one, either. Brontus. Caplea. Sebrinal."

Shapes stirred, stepped forward, waved.

"I'm the fifth woman to wear the robes?"

"We're not sure about Abelt, and he or she won't say. Fifth or sixth. But you're the first who hasn't hidden who you are."

"I had no idea."

"That's rather the point. But see here, Mage. This business with the curseworks. Have you given any thought to how you might use them, to Tirlin's advantage?"

"Use them? The only sane thing to do with them is keep them where

they are. Isn't it?"

"Indeed. They're monstrous. Each an abomination. Combined? We're not sure any of the Realms would survive their release."

"Making them useless."

"Not exactly," said Tam. Her face was long and plain, but her eyes were merry and bright. "Often, I found that the perception of a thing was far more useful than the thing itself, if you get my meaning. Remember Covair?"

"You held off fifty thousand Vonats with a pair of silver wands."

Tam's eyes twinkled.

"Ten thousand, perhaps. The wands weren't even silver. I painted a pair of sticks. I'd run right out of spells, Mage. I had a biscuit in my pocket and a knife in my boot. And not a single Vonat pikeman dared cross a line I scratched in the sand with my boot, just because I grinned at them and invited them to try."

Meralda stared.

"That's history for you, Mage. Half of it is misquotes and the other half is flummery. I enjoyed the flummery most of all. In fact, I highly recommend it. Am I being too mysterious?"

"You want me to use the curseworks to scare the Vonats into behaving themselves?"

"It's just a suggestion. You'd have thought of it yourself, sooner or later. We just wanted to save you the time. Mage to mage, you know."

Meralda's mind raced.

"The curseworks? Weapons?"

Tam beamed. "Just so." She took a step back, and her horse head reappeared.

"We wish you well, Mage Meralda Ovis," said Tim, shaking his mane back into place. "Know that we are all very proud to call you sister."

"Don't go. Please, I have so many questions."

"My time here is nearly spent, Mage. You face a dark hour. You will soon be forced to choose between power and stealth. Between might and wisdom. Between the easy way, and the hard. I do not envy you that."

Tam raised a hand in salute. "Oh, aisle ten, shelf twenty-two, slot fifteen. A little something not in the Inventory. Better range than the speaking jewel you're using now. And get yourself a new chair. That one will ruin your back."

Before Meralda could speak again, she awoke, face down on her desk.

She bolted upright, found her arm asleep, her back aching.

Mug stirred restlessly on her desk, his eyes still closed and drooping. The Bellringers were gone, as was Donchen. Goboy's glass was focused on the palace spire, which glowed in the first faint rays of dawn.

It was a dream, she thought. *But was it just a dream?*

Meralda rose, stiff and sore. Her pencil lay on her topmost page of notes, just where she'd dropped it. The paper was filled with diagrams and calculations and scribbled questions for which there were no good answers.

Something in the top right corner caught Meralda's weary gaze.

A calculation had been crossed out and rewritten.

The hand wasn't hers.

Below the revised equation was a note, penned in a tiny precise hand.

You dropped the Esrat variable there, Mage. I did the same thing when I was sleepy.

Below that was a T.

Meralda shivered.

"Thank you, Mage," she said, aloud. "Thank you."

"Crawling up the windowpanes, I don't know," mumbled Mug.

Meralda stroked his topmost leaves and shuffled toward the water closet.

At noon, Mug awoke.

"You see what trouble all this moving about brings, mistress," he said, spreading his leaves to the sunlight pouring from Goboy's glass. "Bruised stems, eyes gone missing."

Meralda came running from the shelves, her hands full of holdstones and long silver wands.

"Mug!"

"Mistress!" Mug turned half a dozen eyes toward Meralda as she dumped the contents of her arms down on her desk and leaned over Mug's bedraggled fronds. "How long have I been resting?"

"Two days." Meralda stroked his leaves. "I was afraid you weren't going to wake up at all."

Mug gently wrapped Meralda's wrist in a vine and squeezed. "You seem to have all your limbs. What of the lads? And Angis?"

"All fine. Donchen got the worst of us all, fighting those things in the sewer beneath us."

"So I take it we won the day."

Meralda nodded. "Nameless and Faceless appeared. I took them up. No more magical rope men."

Mug turned more eyes toward Meralda. "They just swatted the nasties in a show of selfless goodwill, did they?"

"Something like that."

Mug imitated a snort. "You'll tell me when you're ready, I suppose. The work on the tethers. Making progress?"

Meralda pulled back her chair and sat. "I think so." She pushed wands and holdstones aside to reveal her latest set of notes and diagrams. "If you feel up to it, this is where I'm stuck."

Mug sent eyes hovering over the paper, and was silent for a moment.

"Mistress. This is impressive. Tower thinks it will work?"

"Tower is cautiously optimistic," said Tower from the glass. "Although it must be noted that the basic underpinnings of the mage's theory are untested and, in fact, untestable."

"Cheery as always," said Mug. "Good to hear your voice again, though."

"You were missed as well, Mug." The Tower shifted the image in the mirror to avoid a shadow cast by an approaching dirigible.

Mug sighed happily in the fresh wash of sunlight.

"The Bellringers will want to say hello," said Meralda. "They've been bringing you rainwater from a wooden cask out back, because they were convinced plants couldn't possibly enjoy the taste of water from the tap."

Mug chuckled. "I'll be sure and thank them." His eyes halted over Meralda's notes. "T? Who is T? And what is he doing correcting your math?"

Meralda smiled. "Someone I dreamed up," she said. "But never mind that now. We've got so much more to do."

Back to the Tower, thought Meralda. *This time, though, I won't be caught unawares.*

The army cleared the streets ahead and sealed them off behind, keeping Meralda's armored pay master's wagon well away from any other traffic. Two dozen mounted guards rode about her, swords drawn and gleaming, while an Army dirigible soared low overhead, ready to dispatch its soldiers via dropped lines at the first sight of trouble.

"Hello, mistress," said Mug. "Can you hear me? Is this thing working?"

The trio of stern-faced palace guards seated across from Meralda looked warily about at the sound.

"What's that?" asked one.

"It's nothing," replied Kervis. "It's certainly not a voice."

"What?" said Mug. "Speak up!"

"It's not a voice you need to hear," said Kervis. "None of us hear it, do we, Mage?"

Meralda rolled her eyes in exasperation. "Oh, we all hear it, but I'd appreciate it if you gentlemen would pretend you didn't."

The guards smiled and nodded.

Meralda raised an intricate glass and brass device to her lips. "I told you to wait until I called you," she said. "Unless you saw something threatening. Have you seen something threatening, Mug?"

"Um, no. I just wanted to be sure this thing works."

"Satisfied?"

"Being quiet now."

Meralda lowered the device and sighed.

The box quietly gathering dust on aisle ten, shelf twenty-two, slot fifteen had been marked simply 'Vars. Notes.' It had contained a stack of old parchment pages from which the ink had long since fled.

But the box had a false bottom, and wrapped in silk Meralda found a pair of identical glass devices. Pushing a copper switch on the side of either one while speaking caused the other to sound with the speaker's voice, and no method Meralda tried was able to eavesdrop on the conversation. Even the jewel was detectable, if one knew what to look for. But Tam's device might as well be made of ghosts and shadows.

Which made these either handiwork of Tam herself, or something even older she purloined and kept hidden.

Meralda grinned.

One day, I'll hide them again myself, and thus snub my nose at the

Official Inventory.

"We heard the king will be there," said Kervis, in a whisper.

Meralda nodded. The king's note had been terse, but at least informative. *Inspect the stands and the Tower,* it read. *Discuss final instructions for loosing the shadow moving spell,* etc. etc.

And all done under heavy guard. Meralda wasn't sure what message Yvin was trying to send by going through with such a risky meeting in the first place, or to whom the message was meant. *I have quite enough to worry about without involving politics,* she thought. *That's the king's problem.*

I just have to see that Tirlin doesn't erupt into flames and doom before Yvin delivers the first word of his speech.

The pay master's wagon rattled and lurched, its iron wheels raising sparks on both sides as the driver urged his eight horse team faster and faster. Built to carry gold, the pay master's wagon was armored, sturdy, and nearly unstoppable, although its ride was anything but smooth. The thundering hooves of the guards weaving expertly about the wagon added to the din, leaving Meralda thoroughly bruised and nearly deaf by the time the wagon reached the last street before the park and began to slow.

The Bellringers kept their eyes on the windows, wary of every passing shadow. The guards seated across from Meralda did the same.

The wagon rolled to a halt. The hoof beats surrounding it slowed and finally stopped as well.

Orders were shouted. More guards, this time on foot, rushed to the wagon. After a moment, Meralda's door was opened and the captain, himself, peeked in.

"We're here," he said. "Looks safe enough, at the moment. Yvin is waiting."

Meralda clambered down from the tall, iron-clad wagon. A breeze ran through her hair.

The Bellringers followed and took up positions on either side of her. The guards formed two lines about them, and with a nod from Meralda the party started down the walk.

The guardsman immediately to Meralda's right smiled at her and winked.

Meralda grinned and blushed and nearly stumbled.

Donchen kept in perfect step with his fellows.

"Been a lot more trouble for the Vonats," said the captain, as he ambled beside Meralda. "We had to break up a fight between them and some of the Hang five-master crew last night, in fact. Of course I couldn't understand what was being said, but it seems some bad blood has sprung up between them. I wonder why that is?"

"I'm sure I have no idea," said Meralda.

"No, of course not, you wouldn't. Still. Someone sent a spell their way that filled their sheets with bed bugs and their shoes with centipedes. They lodged a formal complaint with the Accords Hospitality Commission, did you know that? Threatening to sue Tirlin."

Meralda kept her face carefully blank. "I'm sure the king will launch a formal investigation," she said. "Such mischief cannot be tolerated."

The captain nodded. "Student pranks, I'm thinking."

"Precisely."

The Tower still loomed, dark and brooding against the clear blue sky, but the park, itself, was transformed.

The stands that Meralda had last seen as skeletons of lumber were complete, making a half-circle around the Tower that rose up and up and up, nearly as tall as the Old Oaks themselves. Fresh white paint gleamed in the sun, and atop the tallest ranks of seats a hundred pennants waved and snapped in the cool midday breeze.

The King's Rise faced the stands, engulfed in the shadow of the Tower. Painters still worked furiously about it, hanging from ropes and racing across scaffolds as they hurried to complete the rise's red, blue, and gold color scheme in time for the Accords.

Standing, hands on hips, at the base of the rise was King Yvin himself. Even from a distance, Meralda could make out the tapping of the royal foot and the glower of the royal face.

"I'm not late," she said.

"Pardon?" asked the captain.

"Nothing." Meralda forced a smile. "Let's not keep him waiting."

"So that's clear, then," said the king. He leaned on an unpainted stretch of the rise's upmost rail and stared at the Tower's black bulk. "You accompany me up here. I sit. You move the shadows. I thank you, you take to the stairs, the band strikes up, and I stand up and start when they finish. That about it?"

Meralda nodded. Something in the king's weary tone and wary eyes troubled her far more than usual.

I suppose I'm not the only member of the court with a burden, these days.

"And you've taken steps to solve our other little problem."

Meralda realized she'd been wondering all day just how she'd reply to that very question.

"I have, Your Majesty."

The king grunted. "Finally. Brevity. The rest of the court could take lessons from you, Mage." He stared for a moment longer. "You don't like me very much, do you, Mage Ovis?"

"Sire?"

"You heard me."

Meralda's mind raced. "I hardly even know you, Sire. As a person."

The king nodded. "That's true enough." He flicked a scrap of wood off the rail. "Did you know old Fromarch threatened to renounce the robes if I didn't approve your appointment?"

"He did what?"

The king chuckled. "I've never seen the man so angry. He was ready to throw away a lifetime of hard work for you." The king shrugged. "I had an epiphany, right there in the Gold Room. I don't think anyone ever felt that passionate about His Majesty King Yvin the Sixth."

"I don't know what to say, Your Majesty. Except that I'm glad you're wearing the crown right now. I can't think of a better head to go beneath it."

"Same thing my wife said. Must be a bit of truth to it, then?" He managed a weary grin. "I want you to know, Mage, that however the Accords go, I'm glad Fromarch fought so hard to put you in those robes. He was right. For once."

Meralda put her hand on the king's where he gripped the railing.

"I want you and the queen to come down to the laboratory, after the Accords," she said. "Mug can play us some music. I can show you the relics."

"The queen plays a mean hand of whist," said the king.

"So does Mug. But I warn you, he cheats."

The king laughed. Meralda moved her hand.

Yvin marched away, bellowing at his personal guard, who quickly surrounded him as he tramped down the steps.

Meralda watched him go, then she reached into her bag for her implements and pretended to inspect her shadow moving spell while her own guards idled far below.

I need to enter the Tower and work from the flat to install the new tether spells, she thought.

But how can I possibly make half a dozen trips to the flat when my every trip to the park will be accompanied by half the army and at least one dirigible?

The Vonat wizards will know I'm not doing anything to the shadow spell. They'll suspect I'm meddling with theirs, which I'm not even supposed to know about.

Donchen had suggested removing Finch's Door from the house on Hopping Way and sneaking it under cover of night directly into the flat. Mug had even grudgingly agreed this was the best possible solution, although sneaking anything the size of a door into the Tower was going to prove difficult.

A shadow flitted across Meralda, and with it came the faint fluttering of wings.

Of course there is another way, she thought. *I'd hoped I wouldn't be forced to try it.* But standing there on the rise and seeing the crowds gathered about the Tower, Meralda knew with a sinking in her heart there was only one way to enter the Tower in secret.

Two shadows flew past, as if hearing her thoughts. *Which they might well do, since I dared to take them in hand.*

My life is filled with dares these days.

"Tower reports that the Vonats are watching their spell carefully, mistress," said Mug's tiny voice from Meralda's pocket. "He's impressed they can do that at a distance."

Meralda reached into her own pocket and pressed the copper stud while covering her mouth as if from a cough.

"I'm all done here," she said. "Coming home."

"Glad to hear it." Mug paused. "Mind you don't trip on any Vonats."

"Mistress," said Mug. "Respectfully, that's the single least appealing idea you've ever espoused." Mug waved his leaves at Donchen, who stood frowning by Meralda's desk. "Mr. Ghost. Help me here. Tell the mage why holding ancient evil staves while they fly through Goboy's brittle old mirror is a monumentally bad idea."

"I find nothing fundamentally at fault with the supposition," said the Tower. "They move their own masses easily across the spectral threshold with no observable discontinuity."

"Was I asking you? Was I?" Mug swiveled his eyes back to Donchen. "Well?"

Donchen's frown deepened. "I cannot lay claim to understanding the process by which the staves use the mirror as a portal," he began.

Mug groaned. "I retract the question."

Donchen shrugged. "I see no reason why a person would suffer, if the staves do not. Even so, I volunteer to try a crossing first. Tirlin can do without a moderately skilled chef, Mage Ovis. But it cannot do without you."

He means that, thought Meralda. *He'd take up the staves and step into the glass and not show an inkling of fear.*

She smiled, but shook her head no. "Thank you, Donchen. From the bottom of my heart. But taking the staves is very much up to the staves, and in any case I don't believe they'll let me come to any harm."

Yet, thought Meralda. *No harm just yet.*

"Still, we could perhaps test passing an inanimate object back and forth through the glass," said Donchen, eyeing Meralda speculatively. "Something of your approximate mass and composition?"

"Careful," grumbled Mug.

Meralda rose and brushed back her hair. "No. I'm sorry, Donchen, but the staves can either be trusted, or they cannot, and without them, we are already undone." She held out her hands and took a deep breath. "Nameless, Faceless. To me, please."

The air about Meralda snapped, as if a solid door was slammed shut, and the staves appeared in her hands.

"Mistress!" cried Mug.

"Your mistress is a brave woman," said Donchen. "Know that if she comes to harm I will set about finding a very sharp axe and a very hot fire."

Meralda smiled.

"Did you hear?"

"*One heard,*" came a voice Meralda knew only she could hear.

"*As did this one,*" said the other. "*Neither mages nor mirrors will suffer harm.*"

"To the Wizard's Flat," she said.

The staves leaped in her hand. The laboratory simply vanished. She felt the slightest, most subtle sensation of being lifted, and then–

Then, the Wizard's Flat.

Bright sun streamed through the windows. Silence gripped the air. With the door still shut, not a single sound penetrated the Tower's thick walls.

Meralda let go of the staves. They flew to their indentations in the floor and stood there, still and quiet in the sunlight.

"Thank you," said Meralda.

"Mistress! Mistress, we can see you," cried Mug's voice, from Meralda's pocket. "Are you all right? Are you all there? Donchen is pacing, mistress. Muttering about kindling wood."

Meralda raised Tam's speaking device to her lips and smiled. "I'm perfectly intact, Mug," she said. "It wasn't even unpleasant."

She heard Mug sigh in relief.

"Well, what now, mistress?"

"I'm here, Mug. I might as well get to work. I'll be busy for a bit. Watch, but please don't speak."

Meralda dropped the speaking device back in her pocket, closed her eyes, and raised her Sight.

"I may need some assistance here," she said. She felt the staves place themselves in her hands, felt the first rush of power flow from them and toward her.

"Sight," she said aloud.

The hidden spaces that filled the flat revealed themselves, one by one, wonder by wonder.

Chapter Eighteen

"The *Times* is predicting rain for the commencement ceremony, mistress," said Mug, shuffling quickly through the newspapers scattered on a workbench with quick motions of his vines. "The *Post* is promising sun."

Meralda shrugged, her attention focused on the delicate mesh of steel she struggled to solder in place between two curved lengths of springy copper. Smoke rose up and tickled her nose, and she bit back a sneeze as she secured the last bit of steel and held it fast to let the molten solder cool.

The Accords begin tomorrow, she thought. *And if I am unable to restore the tethers, rain will be the least of anyone's problems.*

"Done," she said, frowning at her handiwork. "That should speed things up in the flat."

Mug swiveled half his eyes toward her latest creation.

"You're getting very good at metal-working, you know."

"Thank you, Mug."

A soft knock, one-two-three, one-two-three, one, sounded at the door.

"That would be supper," observed Mug. "He's certainly punctual, your Donchen. That's a fine quality in a man, you know."

Meralda turned so Mug wouldn't see her blush. "He's hardly my Donchen," she said, before walking for the door.

Mug chuckled at her back.

Donchen and his cart trundled into the room, filling the laboratory with the smell of the Hang dishes Meralda was coming to love. Donchen smiled above his cart and greeted Meralda with a sweeping bow.

"Your dinner is served," he said, in a perfect rendition of a refined Eryan accent. "I took the liberty of providing the Bellringers with egg rolls and fried rice."

Meralda laughed and executed a curtsey. "Why thank you, kind sir. I do hope you'll join me?"

Donchen smiled. "After I see us served, of course," he said. "Pray be seated, while I prepare the table."

Mug groaned from across the room. "I'm still trying to heal over here, you two," he cried. "This isn't helping."

Donchen pushed the cart to Meralda's desk, covered it with a stark white linen tablecloth, and began dispensing the meal. "I brought you a decanter of spring water, all the way from my homeland," he said, to Mug. "This particular spring is said to both heal the wounded and grant them one wish."

"I wish my new eye to be yellow, then," said Mug. He waved a small, but growing eye bud toward Donchen. "See? The one I lost is budding back out."

Donchen leaned down and inspected the bloom critically. "You heal quickly, Mr. Mug. I am glad to see that."

Meralda found chopsticks and glasses and poured cold tea from a silver pitcher.

"He's doing remarkably well." Donchen reached into the cart and produced a crystal flask capped by a delicate filigree of silver worked into the shape of a grinning dragon's head.

"The spring water," he said.

Meralda took the flask and watched it glitter in the light as it turned. "Do all the springs in Hang grant wishes?"

Donchen grinned. "According to some. I am of a more skeptical bent. But the healing qualities of this spring are at least supported by some evidence."

"You are certainly free with the treasures of the House of Chentze," said Meralda.

Donchen shrugged. "The waters of healing are best drunk by the wounded."

"That has the sound of a proverb."

Donchen straightened the napkins, nudged an errant piece of rice back into its bowl, and brought his hands together.

"It is just that. Part of a legend, actually. Would you care to hear the rest?"

Meralda pulled back his chair and motioned him to sit. He laughed and sat.

Meralda pulled her own chair close to his.

"I'm starved. You talk. I'll eat."

Donchen handed her an egg roll, and began his story.

"He's twenty-two, by the way."

"Who?"

Mug rolled his remaining twenty-eight eyes. "Your friendly Hang ghost. Donchen. He's twenty-two years old. Not really so much older than you."

Meralda frowned. "And just how do you suddenly know his age?"

"I said 'Tell me how old you are.' He said 'twenty-two'. I asked him if those were the same as Tirlish years, and he went into a wholly unnecessary explanation of planetary rotation, but the upshot is that yes, Hang years and Realm years are the same thing. So he's twenty-two and now you know and you are very welcome."

Meralda felt her cheeks flushing. "I didn't ask you to ask the man his age!"

"No, and that would have been another very simple question." Mug brought a wobbling cluster of blue eyes toward Meralda. "Mistress, I may be a bit vegetative, but I've lived with you mobile folk long enough to know a few things. About gentlemen and ladies..."

"Mugglewort Ovis. That is quite enough." Meralda rose and stalked away. "The very existence of Tirlin hangs by a thread. The Vonats are aiming spells who knows where this very moment. The Accords may see an epic disaster born. Do you really think I have time to behave like some..." she fought for words "...moon-eyed schoolgirl?"

"I understand the situation, mistress. I do. But to reply to a question with a question, what better time than now to, um, explore exciting new friendships, shall we say?"

"Any time would be better than now, if I wanted such a thing."

"Which you clearly don't."

"Of course I don't. He is a Hang noble of some sort. Or a spy. Or both."

"When he isn't cooking you elaborate meals, that is."

"I haven't asked for a single scrap, Mug, and you know that!"

A knock sounded at the door. Kervis stuck his head inside and peeked about.

"I've got a fresh pot of coffee," he said. "And some pastries."

"Bring them in," said Meralda, with a final glare at Mug. "I'll be working all night."

"Yes, ma'am," said the Bellringer. He brought a carafe of coffee and a plate full of donuts inside and placed them carefully on a workbench.

"Anything else, ma'am?"

"No," said Meralda, suddenly weary. "Thank you. That was very thoughtful."

Kervis nodded and darted back through the doors.

Mug turned his eyes back toward the glass and began to hum. Meralda poured a cup of coffee and returned to her calculations, pretending she didn't recognize the old Phendelit wedding march Mug sang.

Twenty-two. He looks a bit older, mused Meralda, instantly chiding herself for doing so. *What difference does it make to me, whether Donchen is twenty-two or sixty-two? If we survive the Accords he'll soon be boarding that monstrous ship of his and sailing away forever, anyway. Even the Hang can't cross the Great Sea on a whim.*

"Seven times five is most certainly not sixty," said Mug. He pointed with a vine toward Meralda's latest scribble. "Someone's mind is wandering."

Meralda crossed out the error and resumed her calculations without a word. Mug regarded her with a pair of sad blue eyes for a moment, before turning his attention back to the mirror, and its slow deliberate sweeps of the halls and corridors near the laboratory.

"Are you sure this is necessary? It's nearly midnight, mistress."

Meralda shook her head. "I know the time, Mug. What of it?"

"The Tower. At midnight. Hello? Haunted tower, dead of night? You don't see a potential for mischief anywhere in that description?"

"I can assure you my volume is free of any phantasmal presences," said Tower. Meralda thought she heard a hint of amusement in Tower's careful tone. "At midnight, or any other hour."

"Well, you wouldn't bloody know if you were haunted, now would you? That's how ghosts work. Showing up where you know they can't possibly be."

"So the presence of a ghost is confirmed by the absence of a ghost?"

Meralda raised her hand for silence. "I'm going, Mug. Tower will be with me. So will Nameless and Faceless. I can't save the kingdom on banker's hours."

"I still don't trust you-know-who and you-know-what," whispered Mug.

"I know." Meralda rose, picked up her equipment bag, and moved to her workbench, where she began sorting the instruments strewn atop it and filling her bag. *Holdstones, wire mesh field director, spare latching wands, a dagger in my boot. I might as well wear a helm and carry a sword, too. Maybe then Mug would stop tossing his leaves at me.*

Midnight, in the Tower. Meralda shivered and pushed the thought aside. *Tower is hardly an ancient spectre of evil. And I am hardly a fainting penny-novel maiden, ready to swoon at the first sight of an errant shadow or sound of far-off laughter.*

"That should suffice." Meralda looped the bag strap over her shoulder and faced Mug and the mirror. "Nameless, Faceless. To me, if you please."

The staves appeared in her hands.

"Be careful, mistress."

Before Meralda could reply, she was whisked away into the flat.

Mug watched as Meralda's form blurred for an instant before simply vanishing. Even with his fastest eyes, he could see nothing of her actual passage through Goboy's fragile old glass.

"I'm never going to get used to that," he muttered.

Then he sought out Meralda's shadowy form in the darkness of the flat.

Meralda worked in the dark, using only her Sight and her touch to carefully weave her own tether spells among the turnings of the damaged originals.

Tower murmured to her, now and then, his soft words relayed by Mug through the speaking device.

The first new tether took root in Tower's central shaft, and then spiraled out, wrapping the old tether as it went, and stopping just short of attaching itself to the cursework whirling through the night.

"Done," said Meralda.

"I shall count," said Tower, through Mug. "One. Two. Three..."

Thirty seconds passed.

The tether held.

Meralda let out her breath.

"Mistress," said Mug, his tone hushed. "It worked."

Meralda sank to her knees for a moment. Her heart pounded, and her head felt light, and for an instant she nearly lost her Sight.

This may work after all, she thought. *I didn't truly believe it would.*

Tower spoke. "I am prepared to proceed with the remaining structures when you are ready, Mage. Well done."

Meralda rose. "My feet are killing me," she said.

Mug laughed. "Words for the ages, mistress. You take all the time you need."

Meralda stretched, yawned, and straightened. "Let's get this done." Then she extended her Sight, and began latching the second tether to Tower's central spellwork.

One by one, the tethers latched, coiled, and spun. Tower reported no wobbling or changes in speed. Meralda sent Nameless and Faceless out into the night, pushing her Sight through them, watching the circling curseworks for any sign of trouble, and seeing none.

The new tethers glowed bright amid Tower's ancient spells. Meralda loosed the final portion of her spell upon them, concealing them from any Sight other than her own, and one by one they dimmed and appeared to vanish.

From far down the Tower, there came the sound of tramping boots upon the stair.

Meralda froze. The sound stopped.

Perhaps I'm imagining things, she thought. *I'm exhausted.*

A cough echoed up through the dark.

Meralda closed her hand tight about the speaking device and brought her finger to her lips.

"Mistress, what is it?" whispered Mug.

Meralda pointed down, and then she released the brass shaft that activated the speaking device.

The unmistakable sound of boots scraping on the stair resumed.

I can't have Mug shouting about ghosts when he hears that, she thought.

"Staves," she mouthed, silently. "To me."

Nameless and Faceless fell silently into her hands.

Meralda moved to the open door, keeping to the edge of it. The night was moonless and dark, but stray city lights through the windows in the flat might still show her outline to anyone on the stair, if they were looking up.

Meralda listened.

Someone was in the Tower. Someone was on the stair, still far below, but climbing.

Meralda knew the park was under full night guard, and the Tower doors were locked and warded and ringed with a dozen hawk-eyed Special Duty soldiers who were, themselves, being watched by another two dozen palace regulars. And probably Fromarch and Shingvere and whatever odd magics they had aimed at the place.

But the boots scraped and the man coughed again and Meralda even saw a faint blob of yellow-gold light begin to bob on the stair, far below.

"*One comes,*" said Nameless from her right hand.

"*He is hidden by strange magics,*" said Faceless from her left.

"Is he known to you?"

"*Humindorus Nam.*"

"*Shall we strike him down?*"

Images formed in Meralda's mind's eye.

She saw the staves swooping down, saw them striking at the Vonat like hawks. Saw him scream and flail and fall, shrieking, shrieking, gone.

She saw how she could remove his spells even as he fell. Saw how she could take them into her, make them hers, make them far more powerful than the Vonat ever imagined they could become.

"You could defeat him that easily?"

"Who can say?"

"Shall we try?"

The single word 'yes' formed on Meralda's lips. Such an easy word to say. And why not say it? The man sought out the destruction of Tirlin. *He is obviously here to ready his deadly electrical spell, so the commencement speech will see the death of hundreds.*

And he tried to kill me, just days ago.

Why not say yes?

So easy to say yes.

She felt a peculiar expectant silence from the staves.

What would Tam have done?

"You know your master's likeness," mouthed Meralda, to the staves.

"Indeed," they chorused.

"Clothe me in it. His likeness. His voice. The aspect of his magics. Can you do that?"

"It is done," said Nameless. *"Behold."*

The air before Meralda became a brief mirror, and in it stood Otrinvion the Black.

He was indeed tall, as the legends said. Tall and scarred and black-haired and dark-eyed. His beard covered many of the scars on his face, but not all. The hands that gripped the staves were huge, strong, covered in sigils and runes which moved and changed shape.

Meralda looked away, lest those eyes peer right into the secret places in her soul.

"It has been long since we beheld him," said Nameless.

"May he rest in peace," said Faceless.

The mirror vanished.

"Maintain this appearance," said Meralda. She took a deep breath. "His voice, too."

Meralda took to the stair, stepping quietly until Nameless showed her a way to silence her own movements. After that, she walked quickly, watching the Vonat's tiny light weave and wobble its way up toward her.

Meralda stopped.

Humindorus Nam stopped as well. His light flared suddenly brighter. The sound of harsh Vonat words, spoken in a chant, echoed up the Tower's empty expanse.

"Now?" asked Nameless.

"Now," said Meralda.

Her awareness merged with that of the staves.

Light, she thought, and light there was, blazing from both staves, flooding the midnight dark of the Tower with the sudden harsh light of day.

A hundred feet down the stair, the Vonat whirled, dropping his tools, gasping at the sudden blaze of light.

Meralda caught a single brief glimpse of the man's wild eyes and open mouth before he lifted his own staff and hurled a gout of fire directly at her.

Nameless showed Meralda a hidden space, and time slowed about it. The rushing gout of wild flame stopped, beautiful, a blooming crimson flower made of fire and heat and light.

Meralda flicked it into oblivion with ease.

The Vonat waved his staff, and the air was filled with knives. They flashed toward Meralda, a school of shiny razors, until she sent them hurtling back toward the Vonat with the merest flick of her hand.

The Vonat's staff, a thing of moaning wet bones wrapped in iron, shielded its master with a cloak of ice. The ice broke when the knives struck, filling the Tower with the sound of tinkling and shattering, far below.

Meralda spoke through Otrinvion's throat, her voice loud and strong and harsh.

"How dare you disturb my rest?" she said. Echoes rolled like thunder. "How dare you invade my home?"

The Vonat rose and shouted a word and surrounded Meralda with a clinging, choking cloud of thick, deadly smoke.

Meralda dispelled it with a glance. The Vonat sent a wave of serpents slithering up the stair, each hooded and hissing and dripping with venom. Meralda burned them to ash before any could strike.

A rain of acid hail, a burst of killing wind, a screaming voice that cried madness into the mind and despair into the heart. A second wave of fire. A mass of flying whips. A sudden rain of spears.

All came hurtling toward Meralda, and all fell before her newfound power.

So easy, she thought, as each attack failed, as the staves showed her hidden things filled with power.

Why not strike him down?

Why not strike them all down?

The Vonat sent a final burst of hungry shadows at Meralda, and then sank to his knees, breathless and spent.

"Who are you, to trouble me?"

Meralda felt the words leave her throat, but was unsure for an instant who spoke them.

"Who are you, to dare my wrath?"

Who are you, to use my voice?

"Is this not what you wanted?" asked a stave.

"Is it not power you sought?" asked the other.

I could have it all, thought Meralda. *Power in every shadow. No more struggling. No more doubt.*

No more Meralda.

What was it Tam had said?

"There will come a time when you must choose," Meralda remembered. "Choose between power and stealth. Between might and wisdom. Between the easy way, and the hard."

Meralda took a deep breath.

"Behold, son of Vonath," she said, in Otrinvion's booming voice. "You would dare intrude, dare seek to ensorcel my home? Then see the price of thy impertinence. Look up, and see!"

Meralda reached forth and gripped Nam's chin and forced his head up before imposing her Sight full upon his.

She showed him the curseworks, showed him the tethers. Showed him the moving, living mass of spells and magics that coursed through the Tower.

"Fire, Vonat."

She showed him the curse of fire, how it would devour stone and iron, such was the ferocity of its burning.

"Wind."

She showed him dark funnels of black wind that fell from a boiling sky before marching across the lands, ravaging everything in their path.

"Pestilence."

She forced the Vonat to see each of the dozen curses.

She reached out, and gave her tethers a subtle twist, and when it was done the curseworks were aimed right at the heart of Vonath. She showed that to the wizard, forcing him to watch as doom after doom engulfed his homeland before spreading like a rush of fire across the Realms.

By the time the last curse landed, he shook in her grasp.

"Each of these shall be loosed upon your lands, should you trouble me once more. When they are done, Vonath shall be a wasteland, a place of bones and ghosts. Do you doubt this, magician? Do you need further proof of my powers?"

Meralda relaxed her grip. The Vonat sagged, coughing and sputtering, before managing the single word 'no'.

"You will depart," said Meralda, to the sputtering Vonat. "You will depart my home at once. You will trouble me no more. Be gone, meddling magician. Be gone, or taste my wrath."

Meralda looked into the secret places one last time. She saw the Vonat's travel spell, how he had transported himself directly into the Tower from his own makeshift laboratory in his room at the palace. She saw the killing spell he sought to prepare, making ready to wreak havoc on the Accords.

And she saw the fear in the man's eyes. Fear of her.

"Enough." Meralda reached out and moved her will just so, and the Vonat was cast screaming out of the Tower, and his killing spell evaporated like so much morning dew.

The sudden silence in the Tower rang almost like a bell.

Meralda sank on the stair, herself again, shaking and sweating and tired.

"Master would approve," said a stave.

"Indeed," said the other.

"Let's go home," said Meralda.

"As you wish, Mage Meralda," said one.

The dark of the Tower vanished, became the warm soft glow of the laboratory.

Fromarch was there, his face lined with worry. Shingvere, too, not smiling, no twinkle in his eyes.

Donchen moved to meet Meralda, his hand extended. She took it, and leaned against him as they walked to her desk and her battered old chair.

"We saw," said Mug. "I think you may have done it, mistress. Fixed the Vonats as well as the tethers. I don't think Nam will ever come nosing about the Tower, again."

"We'd rather have seen you throw him off the stair, Mage, but you're the one in the robes now, not us." Fromarch and Shingvere gathered at Meralda's desk as she sat.

Donchen looked down at her and smiled.

"Well done, Mage," he said. "I am glad to have you back."

Weariness settled on Meralda like a robe made of lead. She felt herself slipping out of wakefulness, felt her head settle down onto her desk despite her efforts to remain upright and alert.

Donchen's words sang her to sleep. "I am glad to have you back." He'd put just a bit of emphasis on 'you'.

He understands, she thought. *Somehow. He alone understands.*

And then Meralda slipped away into a deep sleep, where she dreamed of eating hay with Tam and flying kites with Tower while Donchen served everyone eggrolls and ghosts.

Chapter Nineteen

"Special Accord Early Edition," read the banner on the *Post.* "Historic Accords Commence Today! Midnight Light Show in Tower—Portends or Pranksters? Crown Denies Rumors of Vonat Pullout! Are Eryans Taking Our Jobs?"

"What?"

"I'm just reading the headlines, mistress," cried Mug. "I don't write them, you know."

Meralda stuck her head out of the water closet door. Her red hair hung in a wet bunch as she toweled it dry. "Which story would you like me to read first?" asked Mug.

Meralda bent over, letting her hair fall down straight before trying to comb the worst of the tangles out. "Let's hear what Yvin is denying about a Vonat pullout."

Mug scanned the page. "Our rotund monarch denies categorically that only an intense series of wee hours meetings kept the Vonats in the Accords," he said.

"Which means that's exactly what happened," said Meralda.

"He also denied that only the combined pressure from all the other Realms, including threats of united military embargoes, kept them here. Interesting. I wonder what spooked them so badly? See what I did there? Spooked."

Meralda groaned.

"Humindorus Nam must be ready to run all the way back to Vonath about now," mused Mug. "He can't know his fancy lightning spell is gone. Bet he's worried that if it fires off the dread shade of the Black will loose a barge load of doom all over his homeland." Mug chuckled. "Mistress, that was sheer genius."

Meralda shook her head, remembering the fear in the Vonat's wizard's eyes. "I did what I did for the good of Tirlin, Mug. I wish there had been another way."

"There was another way, mistress. The long way down. But that isn't your way, and all things told I suppose I'm glad of it."

"Thank you, Mug. I think." Meralda darted barefoot back into the water closet, where she combed her hair and decided to send for her clothes, since it seemed obvious she'd not be returning home before Yvin's commencement speech in the morning.

"Do you think the Vonats will really be scared into behaving themselves, mistress?"

Meralda shrugged at her reflection.

"I suppose that all depends on how much sway Nam has with his superiors," she said. "And how willing they are to believe in ghosts."

"You showed him the curseworks, though. Think he can work out a way to see them for himself, maybe show his regents they're really there?"

"Tower believes he can make them visible, if he sees that they're trying."

"Well that ought to buy us fifty years or so of good behavior.

Oh, look. Your boyfriend is heading this way. Looks like he has breakfast."

Meralda pretended she hadn't heard. In a moment, though, Kervis knocked at the door before announcing Donchen.

Meralda turned out the water closet light and hurried out, wishing her hair was dry. Donchen rolled his cart into its customary spot and smiled at Meralda.

"Good morning, Mage," he said. "I trust you are rested?"

"As much as one can be, sleeping at one's desk. That smells wonderful!"

"Thank you. It's a special meal, based on an old family recipe. I had to raid the ship's stores for some of the ingredients. I do hope you find it palatable."

Meralda cleared her desk and scooted her chairs into their places. "I'm sure I'll find it delicious," she said. She watched Donchen open the cart and begin to dispense the contents, and saw him wince when he reached for a silver bowl of steaming rice.

"Are you all right?"

Donchen ginned ruefully. "I assure you, Mage, I am in perfect health."

"Ha," said Mug. "You limped the whole way down the hall, and you were favoring your right arm, too."

Meralda put her hands on her hips.

"Tell me. No more obfuscations."

Donchen nodded, and sagged, resting his left hand suddenly on the serving cart.

"There were those who were displeased with the contents of the list I gave you, Mage." He winced. "They made the unfortunate decision to fly in the face of tradition and attack a *sohata*. I'm afraid they nearly spoiled our breakfast, in doing so. But I believe the Chongit sauce will prove acceptable, despite this..."

Meralda pointed to Donchen's chair. "Sit," she said. "At once. You were assaulted? By the ones you named?"

"Not all. Only nine. They nearly caught me by surprise. I do tend to become distracted when I'm in the kitchen."

Meralda moved to stand beside him. He looked up at her, his customary half-smile growing. "They are no longer a threat, Mage. Not to me, nor to the Accords. You asked once what the House of Chentze intended to do with them. I believe they intended to do nothing. Better that the traitors be slain by a *sohata*, you see. Better for Chentze. Better for the families of the conspirators. Not so good for me, perhaps, but as you can see, I have survived."

The man just fought and possibly just killed nine people, thought Meralda. She remembered her own moment, on the stair.

And then he finished making breakfast.

Meralda put her hand on his.

"The sauce will not retain its subtlety, if it gets cold," said Donchen. "And we both have a very long day ahead."

Meralda squeezed his hand, and finished setting her makeshift table.

Donchen dozed in his chair.

Meralda pretended to fuss over her nearly empty plate and

watched him sleep.

"The captain is heading up the stairs, mistress," whispered Mug.

Meralda sighed and rose. "Coming to see me, I imagine."

"Doubtlessly." A knock sounded at the doors.

Meralda moved quickly to them. "Come in, Captain," she said.

The captain tramped inside. "I suppose you've heard," he said. "Something scared the whole Vonat wing nearly back to Vonath last night. Lights in the Tower, too. I don't suppose you know anything about that?"

Meralda feigned an innocent smile. "Not a thing, Captain."

"Good for you, Mage. Oh, the king sends his regards. And a message. 'Well done.' He asked me to tell you that in person. But of course you don't know what it means."

"I certainly don't."

The captain nodded. "Of course not. By the way. The Vonats have locked their best wizard in a closet. He keeps ranting about phantoms and curses and swatting at thin air. Claims two wingless black crows are following him. Wingless crows, ha." The captain's weary face split into a grin. "Never liked that man."

"I only met him once," said Meralda. "He seemed a bit unstable."

The captain slapped his knee. "Well. I've delivered my message. I'm off. Probably won't see you again before commencement, Mage." He stuck out his hand. "But I want you to know this, Meralda Ovis. All those things you haven't done, and don't know anything about? Good work. Damned good work."

Meralda took his hand and shook it.

"Mage."

"Captain."

He let go of her hand, and marched out, still grinning.

Kervis stuck his head in the door. "Mage?"

"Yes, Kervis?"

"This might not be a good time, but—well, Tervis and I—we got you something. For being so nice, and all."

The Bellringer's face flushed suddenly crimson.

Meralda laughed. "Well, come in and let me see it! You too, Tervis. I see your shadow."

The Bellringers marched in, their eyes on the floor.

Kervis held a small box wrapped in white paper in his hand.

"It's not much," said Tervis.

"But we hope you like it," finished Kervis.

Meralda took the box, and unwrapped it carefully. Inside was a silver necklace, and on it was a single silver leaf, that shone in the light.

"We thought it would remind you of Mr. Mug, and the time we fought the rope men," said Kervis. "You saved us all that day, Mage. This is our way of saying we'll never forget."

Tears welled up in Meralda's eyes. She blinked them back and fastened the necklace around her neck.

"Thank you. Thank you both," she said. "I'll treasure it always."

The Bellringers smiled and Kervis grabbed his brother's sleeve and they hurried back out the door.

"Mistress!" cried Mug. "Mistress, come quick!"

Donchen stirred, suddenly alert, and leapt to his feet.

Meralda hurried to his side. "Mug, what is it?" She searched the glass for any signs of Vonats in the Tower, or on the stair.

"My eye! My new eye!" Mug waved an eye bud in front of the glass. "It's opened! And it's yellow!"

Meralda laughed. Donchen relaxed, and leaned against her, his arm going around her waist.

"I wished for a yellow eye and I got one," said Mug. "I'd say your spring has some magic left after all, Donchen."

"Perhaps it does," he said. "I once drank from it myself."

"What did you wish for?" asked Mug.

Donchen hugged Meralda tight. "Only those things I seem to have found."

"Mistress," said Mug, gazing at her with his new yellow eye. "You look...mage-like."

Meralda frowned. Her deep blue robes hung shapeless about her. The wool was hot and she was sure it was making her neck turn red and itchy. The sleeves were too long, despite her instructions to the royal seamstress that they be shortened and tradition be hanged.

I'm almost glad Donchen isn't here to see me in this wretched thing, she thought. *Especially if I break out in hives because of it.*

He'd simply said he had to go, and that he'd be close by for the Accords. Meralda wondered where he'd gone, and why. But something sad and wistful in his voice left her unwilling to question him further.

"I wish I could go with you," Mug said. "I feel as if I should be there. Your big day and all."

"I need you here, Mug. Keeping an eye on the Tower."

Mug tossed his leaves. "True. Still. I'll be glad when this is done, mistress. I miss the kitchen windowsill."

Fromarch stuck his head in the door. "Well?" he asked. "Are you decent?"

"I might as well be wearing a tent," said Meralda. "Do come in."

Fromarch darted inside, accompanied by Shingvere.

Fromarch was clad in a simple, but poorly fitted, black robe. Scuffed black work boots peeked out from beneath, and the wrinkled collar of a white Phendelit dress shirt showed at the neck.

Shingvere, though, was dressed in a flowing red and black Eryan mage's robe, complete with billowing sleeves and a blood-red sash. His hood was thrown back, his beard was trimmed and combed, and his eyes twinkled above his broad smile.

"Mage Meralda, you look wonderful," he said. "Shame that robe doesn't fit a bit better, you'd have half of Erya proposing marriage right there in the stands."

"What the devil would she want with a lot of half-wit Eryans," grumbled Fromarch.

Meralda raised her hands. "I'm glad to see you both. I

haven't had a chance to thank you for keeping the Vonats busy, these last few days."

Both mages guffawed and exchanged grins. "Haven't had that much fun in years," said Fromarch.

"We put a basilisk in their swimming pool," said Shingvere. "'Tis a crying shame that didn't make the papers."

"I do not want to know," said Meralda. "At least not yet."

"We'll have a beer soon," said Fromarch. He shot a look at Shingvere. "Think she knows yet?"

"Knows what?"

"She doesn't know. He didn't tell her. That rascal."

Meralda frowned. "Who? Tell me what? What rascal?"

A trumpet blew. A knock sounded at the laboratory door. "They're telling us we need to go," said Kervis, through the door. "If you please, I mean, ma'am."

Before Meralda could speak, Fromarch and Shingvere whirled and hurried out, chattering idly in tones that clearly conveyed their amusement with themselves.

Meralda glared at their backs and hurried to collect her things.

The trip to the park took nearly three hours.

Traffic was choked to a near standstill. Soldiers, some Eryan, some Phendelit, most Tirlish, lined every street and stood on every corner.

Every carriage, even Meralda's, was stopped and inspected and then stopped and inspected again. The guards were polite and efficient and Meralda was sure nothing escaped their watchful eyes.

If the Vonats intend to start trouble today, she mused, *they'll need to be very clever indeed.*

The Bellringers stared out their windows on either side of Meralda, their faces alert and wary. Meralda scanned the streets for Donchen, but if he was there, he was concealed.

The Tower loomed up finally, rising above every other rooftop. The park wall hove into view, its dancing gargoyles still clad in various scraps of Vonat underwear.

It's nearly all over, thought Meralda. *I should be happy.*

She thought of watching the Hang five-master sail away, and her heart sank like lead in her chest.

He'll be leaving soon. I've avoided facing that. But once the Accords are done, once the Hang go home, will I ever see him again?

I don't even know his full name.

"Mistress," said Mug, his voice tiny and distant over the din of traffic and the rumble of the carriage. "Mistress, I found Donchen. Thought you might be wondering where he is."

Meralda lifted the speaking device to her lips.

"Thank you, Mug. Where is he?"

"He's with the Hang. Just milling about, all dressed up in fancy robes of some kind. He doesn't look happy. Also, he keeps looking about, watching for someone. Wonder who that could be?"

"Thank you, Mug." Meralda put the device back into her bag.

She thought of the Hang ships leaving again, and pushed all

thoughts of Donchen away until her carriage finally reached the park.

From the park down the walk to the stands took another full hour. Meralda spent most of that time resisting a growing urge to scratch at all the places the robes made her itch.

At last, though, she reached the stands, and was ushered to the lofty seats reserved for the king and his retinue.

She climbed past the Phendelit contingent, who nodded and waved. She passed through the glowering ranks of the Alons, who muttered and stared, although Red Mawb did at least nod to her in greeting. The Eryans were friendlier, with several calling out her name and doffing their hats to her as Meralda climbed past. The Vonats, who insisted on occupying seats higher than the Eryans, met Meralda with glares and exchanges of whispers.

Finally, she passed within a shout of Donchen. He waved to her, smiling, and she waved back before the press of the crowd behind her forced her to move on.

The Bellringers were seated at the bottommost rank of the king's seats. Meralda continued on alone for another half-dozen rows, until she was seated a single rank below the king and queen themselves.

She looked out across the park and struggled to catch her breath.

Not a single patch of green grass showed anywhere. It was as if all five kingdoms of the Realms had somehow dispatched their entire citizenry to take up positions standing in the park.

Hats. A sea of hats. Half bore feathers, half showed flags. All shaded eager faces upturned toward the king.

The noise was deafening, as each of the spectators shouted above the others, until the whole of the park was filled with a growing, thunderous din.

Slowly, the stands filled, as the delegations from each of the Realms took their places. The Vonats stalked in last, their glowers and glares obvious.

Absent from their ranks was Humindorus Nam.

All the while, the shadow of the Tower swung slowly and inexorably over the stands. Mug read off the time at fifteen minute intervals, and Meralda felt her stomach tighten into knots as she realized her shadow moving spell, which was untested and hurried, would be seen by all the Realms in just a few moments.

The king began to leaf through the pages of his speech as the edge of the shadow fell across the podium.

"Mistress," said Mug, his tone edged with fear. "Mistress. Oh no. mistress, Tower says someone is meddling with the tethers."

Meralda's heart froze as she fumbled for the speaking device.

"Tower. The old tethers or the new?"

Mug spoke in the background before answering. "The old ones, mistress. They're doing the same thing you did. Trying to latch something to the flat."

"From where? Inside?"

"Tower can't tell. But no, not inside. From a distance, somehow."

"Nam."

"Probably. mistress. Tower says unless he's stopped, you'll need to attach your tethers in the next few minutes."

Meralda stood. She saw the king eye her quizzically, saw a

dozen guards tense and look her way.

"Nameless," she whispered. "Faceless. To me."

The staves fell into her hands. People about her gasped and stared.

"I'm off to move the shadow," she shouted, with a smile. "Pray continue, Your Majesty."

Yvin didn't blink. "Tend to it, Mage," he said. "Just as planned."

Meralda nodded, and the staves lifted her up and whisked her away.

Wind howled in her ears. The robe of office flapped so hard it stung. The air grew cold and then damp and then dry again.

"I need to know where he is," she said, to the staves. "Show me."

Tirlin wheeled below her. Meralda extended her Sight, using secret spaces to enhance it, make it more subtle and sensitive than she'd ever dreamed possible.

The city shone below her, laced with magics, old and new. Most were simple household magics. Water was heated. Milk was cooled. Fires were kept from creeping out of hearths. Toys danced and moved.

Others were larger, more complex. Some filtered out the lifting gas for dirigibles. Some pumped water. Some kept lamp gas from leaking and burning.

But that one. That one, blazing a peculiar shade of green, sending tendrils of influence from a tiny basement room in east Tirlin toward the Tower. What was that?

Meralda flew toward the light, watching it solidify around the flat.

Saw it begin to bite into the tethers, one by one.

Meralda willed the staves down, and down they soared, hawk-quick, owl-silent. She saw a single face as she passed, mouth open in shock behind an apartment window, and then she was back on her feet, standing outside a weather-beaten door.

She extended a hint of power, and the door exploded, sending splinters flying in every direction.

Meralda stepped through the ruined doorframe.

Humindorus Nam glared back at her, his staff of bone glowing and hissing in his hands.

A mound of skulls sat atop a table before him. The skulls chanted, issuing dry whispers from between grinning, clacking jaws. Atop the heap of skulls a bright light played, and from that light led the strands of power that ravaged the tethers.

"Why?" asked Meralda. "What would drive you to do this, knowing the consequences?"

Nam spat. "They speak of peace," he said. "Reconciliation. A joining with the Realms." He shoved his staff of bone down deep into the light, where it smoked and screamed. "They would surrender. Surrender, to the likes of you."

"We're not asking for surrender. We're not at war."

Nam's staff howled in agony. Meralda smelled the sudden stench of burnt hair and watched as blisters rose up on the man's arms from the heat pouring off the light.

"We'll be at war in a moment," said Nam. "Let your shade's curseworks fall. Let them burn away the weakness that chokes the heart of Vonath. Let them make us strong again, so we might ride forth and strike you all down!"

The man's arms turned black and began to sizzle, and he shoved them harder against the light and laughed.

Meralda raised Nameless and Faceless. "Don't make me do this," she said. "I don't want to kill you."

Nam coughed blood, gripped a muttering skull, and raised it toward Meralda.

"I, on the other hand, don't mind killing you at all," said Fromarch.

The old wizard raised the Infinite Latch and shouted a word.

Meralda found the hidden place that slowed time. Even slowed, she was barely able to enclose Fromarch and herself in a sphere of safety, before the combined forces of what Fromarch would later claim were nine hundred and seventy industrial grade thermal spells reduced the tiny boarding house, the mound of skulls, and Humindorus Nam to a fine snow of ash that fell until the next rain finally washed it from the sky.

Meralda bore Fromarch and herself away from the lingering heat before returning to normal space.

The aging wizard blinked. "Still alive. Imagine that."

Meralda glared. "What were you thinking?"

Fromarch shrugged. "I was thinking my hands are too old to care if they've got blood on them," he said. "My gift to you, Mage Meralda. Now I'm well and truly retired. I see a pub." He took a step away. "Don't you have a shadow to move? A kingdom to save?"

"You are incorrigible."

Fromarch waved, dropped the latch, and ambled away.

Meralda snatched up the latch. "Back to the stands," she said, as Fromarch vanished inside a tavern. "Quickly."

The staves caught her up, and the street and the tavern and the blossoming cloud of ash fell away below her.

The king didn't blink as Meralda settled back into her seat. He merely nodded her way, as though flying mages were as commonplace as sparrows or rain in modern metropolitan Tirlin.

As her neighbors in the stands gaped and stared, Meralda smiled and brought the speaking device to her mouth.

"Tower isn't sure what you did, mistress, but the interference has stopped."

"The tethers?"

"Failing as we speak, mistress." Mug paused. "Yours will have to replace them any moment now."

"I understand. Tell Tower I am ready."

"Good luck, mistress."

The shadow of the Tower engulfed the last column of seats, and the podium moved into its center.

The king nodded.

Meralda rose.

She raised her Sight. Her shadow moving spells hung ready,

shimmering in the dark, gossamer tangles of cobwebs moving in a gentle wind. Meralda could see the black masses of Nameless and Faceless flitting to and fro amid them.

Meralda spoke the word of unbinding, and the tangle of spells stretched and pulled and took shape.

The crowd gasped. Applause broke out, grew, became a thunder that drowned out the voices from the park.

Meralda opened her eyes.

The Tower's shadow was gone, pierced through its heart with the bright light of day.

Donchen's eyes met hers. His smile was warm and wide.

"You did it," he mouthed. *"Mage Meralda."*

Meralda smiled back, and the crowd stood and kept applauding.

"The tethers," shouted Mug. "Beginning to tear. It's now or never, Meralda." He said something else, but his words were lost in the roar of applause. "...I love you, you know that."

"I love you too, Mug," said Meralda.

As the king took the podium, Meralda called the staves to her, and spoke the words that woke her tethers.

"Welcome to Tirlin," shouted the king.

Meralda watched the curseworks whirl.

One by one, she watched the ancient tethers fail.

The new spells took hold. The curseworks wobbled.

Wobbled, but did not fall. Before the king was done speaking, they stabilized, soaring above an unknowing Tirlin as smooth and sure as kites on a string.

"Mistress," piped Mug, from her bag. "Mistress. Tower says the you-know-whats are showing no significant signs of instability. I think that's his way of saying you've saved the Realms." Meralda heard Tower speak in the background. "You've done it, mistress. The tethers are holding. Better than the old ones, according to Tower. Throw yourself a parade. It's done."

Meralda let go her staves. They took to the air, darting and wheeling and chasing and gone.

"Welcome to Tirlin," said the king again, in closing. "We look forward to a bright future together."

Meralda put her face in her hands and cried.

The stands emptied slowly. Meralda waved her guards away, though the Bellringers remained close by her side until she ordered them to go and eat supper and then go home.

The park, too, slowly disgorged its crowds, leaving nothing but handbills and sandwich wrappers and bright bits of trampled ribbons behind, being scattered by the wind. A small army of trash-men, burlap bags hanging empty at their waists, set about spearing litter with pointed sticks and placing it in their bags.

A child with a familiar kite ran among them, and this time his kite soared skyward with no hint of hesitation.

I can't even stand up, thought Meralda. *I've never been so exhausted in all my life.*

A shadow fell upon her, and she looked up to find Donchen at her side.

He sat, his hands in his lap, his eyes on the darkening sky

behind the Tower.

"Quite a long day," he said. "Especially for you, I gather. Trouble at the last moment?"

Meralda nodded. "Nam. Went after the tethers. Nearly killed us all."

Donchen nodded. "But here we are. Thanks to you, I assume."

Meralda remembered that awful moment when Fromarch loosed the latch. "I'd rather not speak of it."

"Then we shall not. Ever, if you wish it."

The child's bat-winged kite darted and swooped Donchen waved to the child, who waved back and shouted a greeting lost in the breeze and the distance.

"There is still much unresolved," said Donchen. "I regret I have been unable to learn the identity of the man who used hidden spells to gain entrance to your king."

Meralda shrugged. *That seems so long ago*, she thought.

"What was the point of all this, anyway?" she asked, after a long moment watching the Tower's shadow reform.

"The Accords?"

"No. The Vonats. Those among your people who worked with them. The spells in the Gold Room. All of it. Why?"

Donchen sighed. "Politics, for the most part, I suppose. My people are staunch traditionalists. This new partnership with the Realms is upsetting to some of those in power."

"I've noticed something, Donchen."

Donchen smiled. "And what is that, Meralda?"

"You're very careful with your words. You said 'for the most part.' Which implies there's something more."

"Does it really?"

"It does. Is now the time you stop being forthcoming?"

Donchen shook his head. "All I have are suspicions. Suspicions, rumor, and scraps of legend. None of it makes sense, even to me. But I tell you the truth, Mage Meralda. When we're both rested, we'll have a nice meal of sweet and sour pork and then we'll find a comfortable couch and I'll tell you all of it, rumor and legend alike."

"Fair enough." Meralda brushed back her hair. "You'll be leaving soon, won't you? Going home, I mean. Back across the Sea."

Donchen shrugged. "One day. But not soon. Perhaps not ever. Politics are involved, I'm afraid. One of the reasons I've spent so much time here in the Realms."

"Fromarch and Shingvere hinted at some dark secret concerning you," said Meralda. "Please don't tell me you're heir to the throne."

Donchen laughed. "Hardly. Well, only in the most oblique manner possible."

Meralda turned to face him. "What?"

"I am the second son of the second son of a House that once rivaled Chentze," he said. "Que-long is childless. The shuffle for power has already begun." He shrugged. "I want no part of it."

"Your status as ghost?"

"All of us in line for the throne share it," he said. "It is meant to protect us from assassination. And perhaps to teach us self-reliance. In any case, my ghosthood expires next year. If I am in Hang when it expires, my own very personal expiration is likely close behind."

"So you're a prince?"

"In a manner of speaking. But a most reluctant one. I prefer the kitchen to the throne room. Would you be able to keep company with a humble chef, I wonder?"

Some last vestige of the shadow moving spell careened past and engulfed Meralda and Donchen in a brief, warm burst of light.

Meralda moved closer, turned Donchen's face toward hers, and drew him into a kiss.

He took her hands in his.

The light failed. The Bellringers grinned and elbowed each other and turned suddenly away.

"Welcome to Tirlin," said Meralda. "Let's stay and watch the sunset."

Frank Tuttle

Frank Tuttle first began writing under the woefully mistaken impression doing so would release him from the burden of ever doing honest work. "It turns out writing is hard," said Frank as he pulled out great handfuls of hair. "That was never mentioned in Strunk and White's *Elements of Style*."

Frank's first published works appeared in print magazines such as *Weird Tales* and Marion Zimmer Bradley's *Fantasy* Magazine in the late 1990s. Since then, Frank has published six Markhat novels and a variety of shorter works.

Frank rarely resorts to hair-pulling these days, preferring to weep inconsolably while affixing his toupee.

Frank invites you to visit his website www.franktuttle.com, or email him at franktuttle@franktuttle.com.

Other Titles by Frank Tuttle

The Mister Trophy

The Cadaver Client

Dead Man's Rain

The Markhat Files

Hold the Dark

The Banshee's Walk

The Broken Bell

Brown River Queen

Wistril Compleat

Coming Soon

All the Turns of Light

CPSIA information can be obtained at www.ICGtesting.com
Printed in the USA
LVOW04s0007070315

429562LV00012B/241/P